...large family filled with secrets and idiosyncrasies,
yet you still love those family members throughout it all,
then *A Regency Invitation* is a book you'll love....
Regency at its best."
—*Romance Junkies*

and for
Nicola Cornick

THE RAKE'S BRIDE
"…vivid detail…rollicking tug-of-war…subtle humor…"
—*Publishers Weekly*

Joanna Maitland

MY LADY ANGEL
"…a Regency Romp tinged with poignancy…"
—*Romantic Times*

Elizabeth Rolls

THE UNRULY CHAPERON
"…seductively sensual…pure bliss to read."
—*Romance Junkies*

NICOLA CORNICK

became fascinated by history when she was a child, and spent hours poring over historical novels and watching costume drama. She still does! She has worked in a variety of jobs, from serving refreshments on a steam train to arranging university graduation ceremonies. When she is not writing she enjoys walking in the English countryside, taking her husband, dog and even her cats with her. Nicola loves to hear from readers and can be contacted by e-mail at ncornick@madasafish.com and via her Web site at www.nicolacornick.co.uk.

JOANNA MAITLAND

was born and educated in Scotland, though she has spent most of her adult life in England or abroad. She has been a systems analyst, an accountant, a civil servant and director of a charity. Now that her two children have left home, she and her husband have moved from Hampshire to the Welsh Marches, where she is reveling in the more rugged country and the wealth of medieval locations. When she is not writing or climbing through ruined castles, she devotes her time to trying to tame her new house and garden, both of which are determined to resist any suggestion of order. Readers are invited to visit Joanna's Web site at www.joannamaitland.com.

ELIZABETH ROLLS

was born in Kent, but moved to Melbourne, Australia, at the age of fifteen months. As a child, she spent several years in Papua New Guinea, where her father was in charge of the defence forces. After teaching music for several years she moved to Sydney to do a master's in musicology at the University of New South Wales. Upon completing her thesis, Elizabeth realized that writing was so much fun she wanted to do more. She currently lives in a chaotic household with her husband, two small sons, two dogs and two cats. You can contact the author at the following e-mail address: www.elizabethrolls@alphalink.com.au.

NICOLA CORNICK
JOANNA MAITLAND
ELIZABETH ROLLS

A Regency Invitation to the House Party of the Season

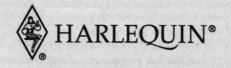

HARLEQUIN®

TORONTO • NEW YORK • LONDON
AMSTERDAM • PARIS • SYDNEY • HAMBURG
STOCKHOLM • ATHENS • TOKYO • MILAN • MADRID
PRAGUE • WARSAW • BUDAPEST • AUCKLAND

ISBN 0-373-29375-5

A REGENCY INVITATION
Copyright © 2004 by Harlequin Books S.A.

First North American Publication 2005

The publisher acknowledges the copyright holders of the individual works as follows:

THE FORTUNE HUNTER
Copyright © 2004 by Nicola Cornick

AN UNCOMMON ABIGAIL
Copyright © 2004 by Joanna Maitland

THE PRODIGAL BRIDE
Copyright © 2004 by Elizabeth Rolls

CONTENTS

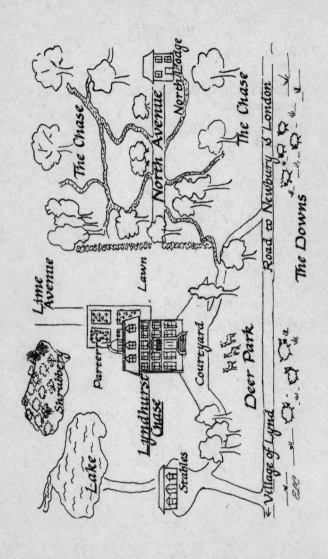

THE FORTUNE HUNTER

Nicola Cornick

Please address questions and book requests to:
Harlequin Reader Service
U.S.: 3010 Walden Ave., P.O. Box 1325, Buffalo, NY 14269
Canadian: P.O. Box 609, Fort Erie, Ont. L2A 5X3

Prologue

Major Anthony Lyndhurst
requests the pleasure
of your company
at a House Party
at Lyndhurst Chase
from 27th August 1819.

RSVP

July 1819

'I need you to do something for me, Peter,' the Marquis of Quinlan said to his eldest son. 'Damned nuisance, but there it is. Someone has to do it. Can't do the job myself. Drink, you know.' He waved a bottle of Canary wine towards his nether regions in a vague gesture of disgust.

'Shocking for the performance. Makes me droop in my vitals.'

Peter Quinlan replaced the stiff white invitation card on the drawing-room mantelpiece, where it nestled amongst the other invitations to the final *ton* routs and ridottos of the Season. The Marquis of Quinlan was still welcome in some drawing rooms despite his propensity to drink the house dry. He never accepted the invitations, however. These days he seldom left the house at all.

Peter turned to face his father. The Marquis was slumped in a *fauteuil* beside the white marble fireplace. One of his hands grasped a battered walking stick; the other grasped the neck of the bottle of wine. He appeared to have dispensed with a wine glass and would tilt the bottle to his lips every few minutes. He was wearing a dressing robe printed with dashing hunting scenes and his tousled grey hair had not recently seen the ministrations of a comb.

The Marquis's attire clashed frighteningly with the ornate painted cherubs and shepherdesses rioting over the drawing-room walls in decadent display. Neither Quinlan House nor its owner was noted for the refined nature of their decoration.

In contrast, Peter Quinlan was all that was restrained and elegant, as though he were unconsciously rebelling against his father's excesses. Austere in a coat of dark blue superfine and buff pantaloons, he looked quite out of place amidst all the baroque splendour.

'You have my commiserations on your affliction, sir,' Peter said politely, 'but I am not quite clear how I can be of help.'

'I need you to marry an heiress,' the Marquis said,

wiping his mouth on the sleeve of his robe. 'Wedded, bedded, consummated all right and tight—'

'I understand, sir,' Peter said, before his father's language became even more descriptive. 'You have made such a request before.'

'This time I'm ordering you,' the Marquis said testily. 'Never knew such a fellow for shilly-shallying! Need the matter tied up by the end of September.'

Peter's eyes narrowed thoughtfully. His father was determinedly avoiding his gaze and making a fuss of smoothing the lapels of his robe with a hand that was slightly unsteady. Peter felt the customary mix of helpless exasperation and deep pity. The Marquis of Quinlan had been drinking himself and his estate into the grave for years.

Peter had not realised the extent of the problem until he had returned from the wars four years previously. He had been shocked by the degeneration in his father's health. In vain had he attempted to wean the Marquis from the bottle, even engaging the support of various physicians in the process. The Marquis had given them all short shrift, telling them brusquely that since the death of Peter's mother his closest relationship had been with his wine cellar, and he intended to keep it that way.

Peter spoke with deceptive softness. 'Why the indecent haste, sir?'

The Marquis shifted as though he was sitting on hot coals. He picked up the bottle, realised that it was empty and allowed his chin to sink onto his chest.

'Bank…mortgage…foreclosing…no further credit…' were the only words that Peter could distinguish from his father's muttered reply, but they were sufficient to allow no misunderstandings. The Marquis of Quinlan was bankrupt.

'How much?' Peter said gently.

The Marquis fidgeted, but he gave a straight answer. 'Thirty thousand.'

Peter mentally doubled the figure. His mouth set in a hard line. As heir to the impoverished Marquisate he had known that one day the promise of his title would be sold in exchange for a lady's fortune. He had simply not imagined the experience would ambush him with such ruthless haste. There seemed very little to say. His father had sold his inheritance down the river and if he wanted to keep any of it he would have to marry at once.

The Marquis triumphantly drew another bottle from beneath the walnut table at his side and raised it in a drunken salute. 'No need to worry, my boy. Made a splendid match for you! Bagged you a plump pigeon, don't you know, flushed a hind from cover...'

'Please spare me the sporting metaphors and come to the point, sir,' Peter said. His voice took on a hint of self-mockery. 'Who is the fortunate lady you have already secured for me?'

'It is Anthony Lyndhurst's cousin,' the Marquis said. 'Take a special licence with you, there's a good chap, then all will be settled post haste.'

Peter glanced towards the mantel again, where the stark black-and-white invitation to the house party seemed to spell out his inevitable fate. Lyndhurst's cousin. He frowned, trying to remember the Lyndhurst ancestry.

'I was not aware that Anthony Lyndhurst had any close female relatives,' he said slowly. 'I thought the Earl of Mardon and his brother, that fellow William Lyndhurst-Flint, were his nearest relations?'

'Cousin, second cousin, what does it matter?' The

Marquis shrugged his shoulders beneath the riotous dressing robe. 'The girl's as rich as a nabob. That is the point at issue.'

'And does she have a name, sir?' Peter enquired, the very slightest edge to his voice.

The Marquis paused, looking slightly taken aback. 'Name? I imagine she must since it is customary. Damned if I know what it is, though.' He took a swig of his wine. 'Bad blood in the Lyndhurst family, of course, but it cannot be helped. For a fortune of one hundred thousand pounds you could marry the devil himself with my blessing.'

'Generous of you, sir,' Peter murmured. He ran a hand through his thick, dark hair. One hundred thousand pounds. It was a huge sum.

Seductive visions flitted before his eyes. With one hundred thousand pounds he could rejuvenate the Quinlan estates and develop all those new-fangled agricultural ideas that so fascinated him. His father had once been a good landlord before he had bled his land dry in order to stock his cellar. After that he had pretended he had not cared for the country or his estates.

'Gentry pursuits,' the Marquis had said, gruffly, on the occasions that Peter had tried to tackle him about the neglect of Quinlan Court. 'All very well for some country baronet, but hardly the thing for a Viscount. Leave it be.'

After that, Peter had done what little he could to alleviate the tenants' difficulties. He knew his father disapproved of his interference. It seemed to him that the Marquis would infinitely prefer for him to lounge about town seducing women, reading the *Gentleman's Magazine* and achieving absolutely nothing at all rather than attempt to rescue an estate that had degenerated through poor management and old-fashioned profligacy. Evidently that was the role of an impecunious Viscount.

Peter's vision of rural bliss faded. He could never buy such a dream on his wife's money. Perhaps he was too damned proud, but it went against the grain with him. If he married an heiress he would touch only the smallest amount of her fortune to pay off the most immediate debts and make improvements to the Quinlan estates, and even that would offend his sense of honour.

'I am uncertain what your objection could be to the Lyndhurst family,' he said, recalling his father's equivocal remark. 'I thought Anthony Lyndhurst was highly regarded.'

The Marquis snorted. 'The man murdered his wife! Very bad *ton*.'

Peter scowled, driving his hands forcefully into his jacket pockets. 'That is arrant nonsense, sir,' he said. He had been a young lieutenant serving under Major Lyndhurst at Waterloo and had seen his courage under fire. It was ridiculous to suggest that the Major was a murderer just because his wife had disappeared in mysterious circumstances.

The Marquis waved one hand, splashing wine on to the Turkish carpet. 'No need to call me out, boy! I know the man is a damned war hero. I was merely repeating the gossip.'

'Then pray do not, sir,' Peter said moodily. 'Not if you wish me to stay and finish your brandy.'

A half-drunk, half-mocking smile twisted the Marquis's mouth. He nodded towards Peter's untouched glass. 'Fortify yourself, then. You will need it.'

Peter's lips twitched. 'How so, sir? What new shock could you possibly have in store for me?'

'The bride,' the Marquis elaborated.

Peter raised his brows. 'Please go on.'

'The chit can be no blushing débutante,' the Marquis said bluntly. 'All that generation are in their thirties. And it seems most unlikely that she is still a virgin.'

Peter took a mouthful of brandy. It tasted good. He resisted the impulse to take another immediately after. His father's situation had always made him wary of drinking too much.

'On what basis do you make that astounding remark, sir?' he enquired mildly.

The Marquis shot his son a look. 'The girl's reputation was ruined years ago when she was caught at a radical meeting smoking a clay pipe. Dreadful outcry, as I recall. They blamed it all on her governess, but the chit was headstrong even then.'

Peter smothered a grin. He had to admit that both pipe smoking and radical politics were singular interests for a lady, but he could not see the immediate connection with sexual impropriety.

'I beg your pardon, sir,' he murmured, 'but you will need to be more plain. In what way does the pipe smoking affect the lady's chastity—or lack of it?'

The Marquis looked irritated. 'Damned radicals! Illiterate, ignorant and immoral! They're all depraved. Hiding behind hedges and plotting revolution! Damned unBritish!'

Peter's blue eyes lit with a flicker of humour. His father's politics had always been of a traditional persuasion, though he felt it was unfair to impugn his future wife's honour on the basis of such flimsy evidence.

'I think you may malign my bride, sir,' he murmured, 'yet even if it were so, surely she would still be preferable to the devil himself.' He sighed. 'Ah well, at least with her fortune we shall have the money to afford to improve the ventilation to let the pipe smoke out.'

The Marquis stared. 'You're a damned cold fish, Peter,' he grumbled. 'Have you nothing else to say?'

Peter shrugged. 'We have no money, I am obliged to marry and you have found me an heiress,' he said. 'What else is there to be said? I will take the special licence with me to Lyndhurst Chase once I have ascertained the lady's name.' He drained his brandy glass. 'I suppose I should count myself lucky,' he added. 'I hear that Lyndhurst has the best hunting, shooting and fishing in Berkshire. His house party may be quite enjoyable. But for now I am off to White's. May I call Sumner to assist you to bed?'

The Marquis slumped back in his chair. 'No, you may not. You may call him to fetch another bottle from the cellar for me.'

Peter called the butler and went down the steps of Quinlan House and out into Grosvenor Square. The London night was warm, with a fading violet sky made hazy by smoke. The dusty smell of summer was in the air. Peter looked about him and ached to be away from the city in the fresh, crisp air of the countryside. Failing that, he wished to be reunited with a brandy bottle, and quickly. Be damned to his abstemiousness. He could drink a toast to his future wife. His lips twisted. It was rich that his father thought him heartless when it was the Marquis who had parcelled up his heir and sold him off like a piece of merchandise. But then, the Quinlans were descended from fifteenth-century merchants. Trade was in their blood. If he had to go hunting fortune, then so be it.

He turned his steps towards St James's. It did not occur to Peter that neither he nor his father had spared

a single thought for the feelings of the Lyndhurst bride
and still less did he imagine that perhaps she had even
less desire to marry an impoverished Viscount than he
had to marry a radical old maid.

Chapter One

Miss Cassandra Ward, distant cousin to Anthony Lyndhurst of Lyndhurst Chase, heiress to one hundred thousand pounds and radical sympathiser, clung to the damp branches of the oak tree as she tried to wrestle an ungainly, home-made banner into place and tie it with string. She had never been very good at tying knots.

'Bread to feed the hungry' proclaimed the banner in huge, uneven letters. It was a garish green and red, with the letters sewn haphazardly upon it in white cloth. Like the tying of knots, needlework was not one of Cassie's strong points.

Several of the letters were already flapping in the breeze, having been wrenched loose by sharp twigs as Cassie climbed the tree. It was starting to rain and the drizzle made both the banner and Cassie's clothes hang limply, but she was determined—absolutely determined—to give Viscount Quinlan such a disgust of her that he would turn his carriage about immediately and drive back to London. She could take no risks that Anthony and John and this high-handed nobleman would determine her fate between them. It was her intention to remain unwed until she was twenty-five and the mistress of her own fortune. And that was that, as far as marriage and Cassie Ward were concerned.

Of course, Anthony had presented the matter in terms of a choice: Viscount Quinlan had been invited to the house party to meet Cassie and to see whether the two of them would suit. He was a former soldier like Anthony, and therefore no doubt deemed a suitable match. There was no duress involved. Yet Cassie felt her situation keenly. With no close family of her own, she knew that she was a burden on her cousins and that they would be happy to see her safely wed and settled. And sometimes, in her most private moments, Cassie would admit to herself that she felt a certain yearning for a home and family of her own. But she had always been courted for her money and Lord Quinlan was no different. He was a fortune hunter and Cassie detested men of that stamp.

Cassie peered out of the tree to see whether the Viscount's carriage was approaching. She had heard on the best authority that he was due to arrive at the house party that very afternoon, but the precise timings were vague. She might be stuck up the tree for a number of hours and already her limbs were chilled and aching. It was late summer now and the leaves were starting to turn copper and gold. The wind was increasing as a thunderstorm rolled in from the Downs and the grasses were bending along the track that led from the hamlet of Lynd to the estate of Lyndhurst Chase. Cassie shivered in the breeze.

A single horseman was approaching along the track now. Cassie shrank back against the trunk of the tree as she tried to judge whether or not this was her quarry. The indications were contradictory. It was easy to see that the horse was a prime piece of bloodstock. They had bred horses at Lyndhurst Chase for centuries and Cassie had an eye for these things. On the other hand, the gentleman had no groom accompanying him and no luggage. Perhaps this was the Viscount and he had chosen to ride whilst his carriage followed behind. Cassie held on to a stout branch with one hand and leaned forward, the better to see the gentleman's face.

The horseman reined in a mere twenty yards from where she sat, removed his hat and shook the rainwater from the brim. Cassie stared hard. She could see that he was young—much younger than she had anticipated her suitor to be—with dark hair and broad shoulders, and he sat the horse with innate skill and ease, his hands light on the reins. There was something about the contained strength and elegance of him that made her insides quiver unexpectedly. Her hands quivered too. Her fingers slipped against the rough bark and she made a convulsive grasp for the branch, scoring her fingers. The leaves rustled. The gentleman looked up and directly at her.

Now that she could see him properly Cassie was obliged to admit that he was rather handsome. She had not been able to gather much reliable intelligence about Viscount Quinlan, but the meagre reports suggested that he was at least thirty if he was a day, dissolute and prone to wearing vests, although Cassie thought that these two must surely be mutually exclusive, for what woman in her right mind would wish to be seduced by a man in a vest? This gentleman logically could not be the Viscount, for he was far too young and good-looking to be a degenerate.

She looked at him thoughtfully. He had slanting, watchful eyes, but there was a hint of humour in the hard lines of his face, as though he smiled often. He was not smiling now, however. His gaze was narrowed on her with acute assessment. Cassie found it so disconcerting to be the focus of his interest that her throat dried and a ripple of heat washed right through her, despite the inclement weather.

Abruptly she remembered why she was there and decided that she could not take the risk on this *not* being Viscount Quinlan. She brandished the banner. 'Truth and Liberty!' The words came out as a croak rather than the radical rallying cry she had intended. She was not even sure that the gentleman had heard her. He was looking at the banner now with his head tilted to one side.

'Bead to feed the hungry?' he queried.

Cassie glanced at the wilting banner and rubbed the rain out of her eyes. 'Bread!' she said crossly. '*Bread* to feed the hungry!'

'Ah.' The gentleman nodded. 'That makes more sense. I confess I was a little puzzled by the missing letter.'

Cassie frowned. She was feeling quite confused herself. It did not seem right that this gentleman should be calmly sitting discussing spelling with her when she had intended to frighten him with her outrageous radical politics. She had been told for so long that radical politics *were* outrageous that it had never occurred to her that not everyone would react in the same way. She tried again.

'Justice to punish crimes!' she shouted.

The gentleman smiled. His eyes held a wicked glint now and Cassie gulped to see it. He seemed in no way discomposed by her behaviour. In fact, he seemed positively fascinated by her. There was a very particular light in his eyes as they rested on her and it made her stomach patter and her toes curl just to see it.

'A very laudable sentiment,' the gentleman approved. 'I am entirely in favour of justice to punish crimes.'

'Are you Viscount Quinlan?' Cassie demanded, abandoning her limited attempts at finesse and getting straight to the point.

'Are you going to come down from that tree?' the gentleman countered, the glint in his blue eyes now looking remarkably like a challenge.

Cassie trembled slightly. She had the oddest feeling that were she to climb down she would end fair and square in his arms and that somehow, that was the appropriate place to be. She looked at him for a long, loaded moment.

So this is the one…

A shiver of sensual awareness crept along her skin, turning her hot and cold at the same time and scattering her senses to all points of the compass. She was too flustered to move or even speak.

'Well?' the gentleman prompted, his smile deepening.

Cassie trembled again. The banner flapped in a sudden gust of wind. The tree creaked, its branches shifting, and Cassie's hand slipped against the trunk. She made a grab for something firm to hang on to, but her fingers raked the air. She tumbled down on to the track, the banner wrapped wetly about her in a flurry of green and red. Her last memory was of the gentleman's highly bred mount snorting in panic and its flailing hooves coming down towards her as she hit her head hard and slipped inexorably away into darkness.

Peter Quinlan was accustomed to women throwing themselves at his feet. His lack of fortune had never been much of a deterrent to those bored ladies of the *ton* who had taken a fancy to him. After all, they had not wanted to marry him, only to amuse themselves. There had been the occasional young lady who had fancied herself a Viscountess, but Peter had never entertained the idea of marriage with any of them.

On this occasion, however, he was obliged to acquit the young lady of any ulterior motive. He instinctively started forward as she fell out of the tree and Hector, taking fright, turned so sharply that he pirouetted as though he were in a circus.

'Hell and the devil!' Peter wrenched on the reins and the horse's hooves thudded into the soft clay mud of the track a mere two inches from the girl's head.

Peter leaped from the saddle, soothed Hector with a few soft words and a stroke of the nose and abandoned him in somewhat cavalier fashion to go down on his knees on the track beside the girl's unmoving figure.

She was lying on her side in the mud, the gaudy banner tangled in the skirts of her green-velvet riding habit. Her hat had come off and her thick, dark hair was escaping its somewhat inexpertly applied pins and half-covered her face. The riding habit, soaked by the rain, clung to her figure like a second skin.

Peter stripped off his gloves and brushed back the strands of hair from her face. It was thick, silky and a dark copper brown, and it curled confidingly about his fingers. Her skin was soft, coloured the pink and russet of an apple. She looked to be no more than one and twenty and she was extremely pretty. He suspected that this was none other than Miss Cassandra Ward, whose name appeared on the special licence even now in his wallet. Miss Ward, the radical old maid whom his father had warned him might be no better than a fashionable impure. To Peter's relatively experienced eyes she looked extremely virginal. He felt astonished. He felt awed. And then—fatally for his financial ambitions—he felt guilty.

Cassie was breathing gently but regularly. Peter sent up a silent prayer of thanks. He unwrapped the radical banner from about her and, after a moment's thought, stuffed it down a rabbit hole in the bank by the side of the road. He lifted her gently in his arms. For a small woman she felt surprisingly resilient. She was not heavy, but she was no lightweight either. He hoped it was a sign of sturdy good health.

The hamlet of Lynd was a mere hundred yards back down the road. Looping Hector's reins over his arm, Peter strode along the track, mud streaking his riding breeches and the rain running in rivulets down his face. Cassie turned her head against his shoulder and snuggled closer to him with a pleasurable little murmur. Peter looked down at her. Her eyes were closed, the lashes wet and spiky against her cheek. Her generous mouth was tilted up in a faint smile. Whatever she was dreaming of must be very enjoyable indeed.

Peter's imaginings were also extremely enjoyable but highly improper. The soft pressure of her body in his arms was impossible to ignore. Her skirts had ridden up to reveal a pair of very slender ankles. Her petticoats foamed over his arm as he carried her. Peter bent his head so that his lips brushed the softness of her cheek. A fierce desire twisted within him. Her mouth was so lush and full, and so close to his own. He ought not to be thinking about kissing a lady when she had sustained a blow to the head and was unconscious in his arms, but…

Hector snorted wetly in his ear.

'Thank you, Hector,' Peter said, his ardour abruptly dampened. 'I needed that.'

The village of Lynd looked deserted and the inn, appropriately named the Angel's Arms, was closed and shuttered. Peter freed one hand to bang energetically on the door and a few moments later was relieved to hear the shuffling approach of one of the inn servants. As the door swung open he realised that this stocky individual with forearms like corded barrels was in fact the landlord himself. The man took one look at the recumbent figure of the girl and started forward.

'Miss Cassandra! What have you done to her, sir?'

Peter was not remotely surprised to receive the confirmation that the young lady in his arms was his intended bride. He was an intelligent man and the radical banner had rather given the game away. He was more offended to be unjustly accused.

'I have rescued Miss Ward from an accident on the road,' he snapped. 'Be so good as to stable my horse and then fetch a doctor to attend to the lady. And pray send to Lyndhurst Chase and call the landlady and show me to the parlour.'

The innkeeper appeared confused at this barrage of orders. 'Beg pardon, but what do you wish me to do first, your honour? I am on my own here, for my wife is visiting her sister over Barrington way and the groom is on an errand to Watchstone and—'

Peter cut short the explanations. 'Then pray stable my horse. I will find the parlour on my own. And when the horse is safely stowed, fetch the doctor.'

'Aye, my lord,' the landlord said, having expertly sized up Peter's horse, appearance and attitude and adjusted his mode of address accordingly.

The inn was small and Peter had no difficulty in finding his way to the one tiny parlour. A fire was lit against the dampness of the day and the room was almost overpoweringly warm. He laid Cassie down on an ancient lumpy red sofa, which was clearly somewhat of a luxury for a country inn, placed a cushion under her head and eased his cramped arms with a sigh of relief. He would need to open a window or both of them would start to steam as their clothes dried out.

The landlord came in as he was pushing against the window frame, which stubbornly refused to move.

'It's stuck, my lord,' the landlord said helpfully. 'The rain blows off the Downs this time of year and the wood swells.'

'So I see,' Peter said. He went swiftly back to Cassie's side, taking her hand in his. She was breathing regularly and her face was regaining its pink colour, but she did not stir. Her fingers slid between his and she tightened her grip on his hand. Peter felt a disconcerting tug of concern and tenderness deep inside.

'The doctor?' he asked abruptly, over his shoulder.

'Yes, my lord.' The landlord rubbed the palms of his hands nervously against his trousers. 'I sent one of the village lads, my lord. He goes direct to the Chase once he has found Dr Nightingale.' He looked dubiously at Cassie's prone body. 'You'll be wanting hot water, my lord, and something restorative for the young lady. Took a tumble, did she?'

Peter glanced at him. 'She fell from a tree,' he said.

'Ah.' The landlord looked unsurprised, as though Miss Ward falling out of trees was a common occurrence in the vicinity of Lynd. Peter suspected that it probably was. The landlord was still weighing him up, his shrewd blue eyes fixed upon him, clearly uncomfortable about something.

'I'm thinking you'll be staying at the Chase for Major Lyndhurst's house party, my lord?' he said.

'That is correct,' Peter agreed.

The landlord blew out his lips. 'Ah. But you'll not be Viscount Quinlan?'

Peter frowned. 'Why not?'

The landlord looked him over. 'They said he was an older man.'

'I see,' Peter said. 'The hot water and brandy for Miss Ward?'

'Dangerous, these London folk.' The landlord looked disapproving. 'Not sure about these house parties, neither. Opportunity for dancing and gambling and hunting, and not always of the sporting variety neither… Heard Quinlan was an ageing roué who drinks like a fish and suffers the gout. Couldn't leave you alone with Miss Ward if you were the Viscount. Quite unsuitable.'

Peter briefly considered attempting to defend his reputation and that of all other denizens of the capital, and then decided that the landlord would never leave him alone with Cassie if he did.

'You may see that I do not fit that description at all,' he said. 'You may safely leave Miss Ward with me. I assure you she will come to no harm.'

The landlord looked suitably grateful. 'Very good, my lord.'

He went out and Peter straightened up, sitting on the edge of the sofa beside Cassie. He was concerned that she should discard her damp riding habit, for there was a grave danger of her developing a chill if she lay there in wet clothes. It was damnably awkward that the landlady was absent. He could hardly start to undress a lady himself. Even he had some sense of decency.

His fingers strayed to the tiny mother-of-pearl buttons at Cassie's throat. Her collar was high and tight and Peter thought that she would breathe more easily if it

were undone. He slid the first four or five buttons from
their fastenings, turned back her collar and exposed the
slender whiteness of her throat. Her skin smelled faintly
and sweetly of lime blossom and cool, fresh air. Peter
stared at the impossibly fragile line of her jaw and the
curve of her neck.

His gaze dropped lower. The material of the riding
habit strained over Cassie's breasts, covering her like a
lover's touch. Peter wanted to peel away the layers of
damp material that clung to her and explore the naked-
ness beneath. The idea was so cool and tempting, yet so
heated and exciting that it transfixed him.

One copper-coloured curl nestled in the curve of her
throat. Peter's gaze slid down the line of shining mother-
of-pearl buttons to the hollow between her breasts. There
was a delicate gold chain about her neck that disappeared beneath the neckline of her chemise, slender links
of filigree against the paleness of her skin. Peter's fingers
idly traced the line of it to where it vanished beneath the
crisp white of her petticoat. The chain felt warm. So did
Cassie. So did Peter, who was also aware that his riding
breeches were becoming very tight and it was not from
the shrinking effects of the rain on the leather.

Cassie turned her head and rubbed her cheek gently
against his sleeve. Molten desire pierced Peter at the
trusting touch. He got to his feet with a muffled curse.
What was he doing, taking advantage of an unconscious
woman in an isolated inn? Not just any woman, either,
but his promised wife to whom he had not even been
formally introduced. Did that make it better or worse
that he wanted to ravish her? He was not sure. What was
certain, though, was that he was a scoundrel to be thinking in this way. Far from being an experienced woman
of the world, Miss Ward was a complete innocent, and

he was harbouring thoughts of her that were impure in the extreme.

Peter strode across to the window and stared blindly out of the steamy panes. He had not counted on feeling an immediate, strong attraction to his bride. He had thought to make a rich match out of necessity, not desire. This made matters decidedly complicated.

The door opened to admit the landlord with a creaking wooden trolley. A bowl of water balanced on the top of it lurched with each step. On the lower shelf was a bottle of repellent black liquid, a glass, a clean white cloth and, Peter was glad to see, a brimming tankard of ale.

'Blackberry cordial, my lord,' the landlord said, happily oblivious to Peter's evident discomfort. 'My wife swears by it—says it is sovereign against the chill.'

Peter dampened the cloth in the warm water and gently wiped the smears of mud from Cassie's face, then, taking the glass of cordial, he raised Cassie's head from the cushions and tilted it to her lips. After a few seconds her lashes fluttered, she opened her eyes and she looked directly at him. Peter's heart contracted with an unfamiliar emotion. She had brown eyes lightened with flecks of gold and green like the sun on autumn leaves and they were so wide and honest they seemed to see into his soul.

'Thank you, sir,' she whispered. Then she smiled. 'My name is Cassandra Ward.'

'How do you do?' Peter said. 'I am Peter—'

But Cassie's eyes had closed again and her head drooped against his shoulder. There was no indication that she had even heard him. With a sigh Peter laid her back against the cushions.

The landlord was peering over his shoulder. 'Reckon doctor will be along soon enough,' he said, scratching his head. 'Excuse me, my lord. I shall go and see what keeps him.'

Peter picked up the tankard and took a long and grateful draught. The whole situation was damnably difficult. On the one hand he wanted to ride to the Chase and warn Anthony Lyndhurst of his cousin's accident. It was the courteous thing to do. Besides, he would feel better—safer—away from the heated confines of the inn parlour and his own heated fantasies, which were, he was sure, a product of the roaring fire. On the other hand it would be difficult to explain to Lyndhurst why he had abandoned his cousin in the inn without so much as a landlady in attendance. Such behaviour seemed unchivalrous at best and no way to make a good impression on his future cousin-in-law.

He glanced dubiously at Cassie's sleeping form, then opened the door and stuck his head out into the passage to see what was going on. There was the sound of voices from the taproom and the rumble of barrels on the stone floor. Evidently the landlord was taking receipt of a new consignment of ale. The doctor had not yet arrived.

Out in the yard the rain had set in, sweeping down from the hills and shrouding the countryside in a threatening grey blanket. There was no sound but for the distant rumble of thunder. The village seemed deserted. Hector stuck his head over the top of one of the loose boxes and snorted with bad temper. Peter turned the collar of his coat up against the rain and beat a hasty retreat back into the inn.

To his surprise, he found the landlord had returned to the parlour and was in the act of refilling Cassie's glass of cordial. She was sitting propped against the sofa cushions and there was colour in her cheeks and a sparkle in her eyes. With her bright gaze, tumbling hair and tantalisingly unbuttoned jacket, she looked like a wanton angel, but when she saw Peter she broke off whatever she was saying and her gaze narrowed on him thoughtfully. Peter squared his shoulders. This, then, was the moment in which she remembered that he was the dissolute Viscount Quinlan, come chasing her fortune, and gave him the rightabout.

'I am glad to see you so much recovered, Miss Ward,' he said.

Cassie gazed at him for a moment longer and then her face broke into a mischievous smile. Under Peter's incredulous gaze, she drained the glass of cordial and put it down, curled her legs under her and patted the sofa beside her in a most confiding gesture. Peter stared. This was incomprehensible. Respectable ladies—and *surely* Miss Ward was respectable—simply did not behave in so open a manner to chance-met strange gentlemen.

Peter allowed his gaze to travel over her thoughtfully. She was looking very flushed now and it could not be attributed entirely to the heat of the room. She was also blinking in a sleepy manner. One of her elbows slid off the arm of the chair and she gave a peal of laughter.

There was no getting away from it. Miss Ward was not entirely sober. In fact, Miss Ward was *drunk*.

Cassie was beckoning to him. She put one small white hand on his arm and leaned closer. She did not smell of alcohol fumes. She smelled of blackberries and honey, and Peter found that he was already leaning forward to kiss her before he realised and drew back hastily. She might be foxed, but he was bewitched. He would do better to remember that he was a gentleman and she was a lady alone and unprotected.

Cassie evidently had not realised his difficulty. She

was looking at him earnestly and blinking with the short-sighted determination of the very drunk.

'I have something I wanted to tell you because I like you,' she whispered, her breath tickling his ear. 'Can you keep a secret?' She did not wait for his confirmation. 'I am much richer than everyone thinks, you know. I have a fortune of two hundred thousand pounds. I never usually tell anyone because they try to marry me when they find out. Everyone comes hunting fortune.'

Peter stared deep into her eyes. He knew all about fortune hunters. Two hundred thousand pounds... His father had only known the half of it. He could almost see the special licence smoking in his wallet, giving off fumes of greed and guilt.

He got to his feet and vented his guilt and bad temper on the landlord, who was stoking up the fire to an even greater blaze. 'What the devil was in that cordial?'

The landlord jumped. 'Why, nothing, my lord. Merely some brandy and my wife's special blackberry potion.'

'I am not supposed to drink alcoholic beverages,' Cassie said merrily, from her position on the sofa. 'I discovered it when I became foxed on a sherry trifle as a child. The smallest amount makes me *very* intoxicated. Excuse me,' she added, yawning widely, 'I feel a little sleepy.' Without paying further attention to either of them she lay back against the cushions and closed her eyes. A second later, she emitted a tiny snore, followed by one a little louder.

Both men looked at her disbelievingly and then the landlord's shoulders slumped. 'Beg pardon, my lord,' he muttered, 'I had no notion Miss Ward was so susceptible. There's barely a nip of brandy in the cordial and no one else suffers any ill effects.' He shot Cassie's recumbent figure a gloomy look. 'Reckon she'll just have to sleep it off.'

'If the doctor takes much longer she will have plenty of time,' Peter said caustically. 'Have you sent to Lyndhurst Chase yet?'

'Aye, my lord.' The landlord scooped up the offending bottle of cordial and looked as though he wanted to scurry for cover. 'Physician's at a lying-in over at Watchstone, but the boy's gone to the manor to let them know of Miss Ward's accident and my wife will be back soon.'

'If her other remedies are as effective as the cordial we may do better without them,' Peter said.

'Aye, my lord.' The landlord hovered in the doorway, clearly anxious to be gone. 'I will leave you to it, then?'

'I do not believe either of us have much choice,' Peter said. He was already resigned to a spell of nursemaiding until a carriage from the Chase reached them. It was not how he would normally have chosen to spend time alone with the enticingly pretty Miss Ward, but it behoved him to remember that he hàd *some* principles.

'Pray bring me a bottle of claret,' he added. 'It will help pass the time.' He paused, his conscience pricking him. 'And thank you. You were not to know that Miss Ward should not touch alcohol.'

'Thank you, my lord,' the landlord said, looking relieved.

There was silence in the parlour but for Cassie's gentle breathing, the crackle of the fire and the soft sigh of the rain against the windows. Peter had found a twelve-month-old copy of the *Quarterly Review* and settled down to read. He perused an article about the sentimental poets and then an obituary of a worthy Member of Parliament of whom he had never heard. He had just begun skipping through a piece of very bad verse when he realised that Cassie was awake and watching him with those glorious, golden brown eyes. This time on seeing him, Miss Ward's gaze narrowed to an angry gleam. Peter knew at once that both her sobriety and her memory had returned. She sat up straight as a ramrod.

'You *are* Viscount Quinlan, aren't you?' she said, in an accusatory tone. 'Do not pretend to me. I know you are the fortune hunter!'

Chapter Two

I know you are the fortune hunter…

Cassie watched as Peter Quinlan folded his magazine and put it aside before getting to his feet and coming across the room towards her. She had not intended her words to be quite so abrupt, and as he drew closer she felt a definite shiver of apprehension. The man's physical presence was almost tangible: powerful, authoritative and devastatingly male. She had sensed the same sureness and confidence in other men that she admired—her cousins John, Anthony and Marcus—but they had always treated her as a little sister and she had seen them very much in a fraternal role. Now she discovered it was an entirely different experience to be the sole focus of the attention of a man like this. It made her feel quite dizzy. She shifted back against the sofa cushions.

'Yes,' Peter Quinlan said, holding her gaze, 'I am the fortune hunter.'

Their eyes locked. Cassie bit her lip. She had not expected him to be so honest. She had thought that he would be like every other man who had ever paid court to her fortune whilst pretending that he would love and honour her forever. She was not sure whether his frankness made her feel better—or more alone.

Peter smiled at her. The smile softened the uncompromising lines of his face and reached those dark blue eyes, making them warm. Cassie felt that heat sweep through her from her toes to her suddenly pink cheeks. She prayed that it was the effect of the brandy and not the effect of the Viscount's proximity. She was prey to various contradictory feelings, but most noticeable was a curious excitement that was sending her blood tingling through her veins and giving the flutter of butterfly wings in her stomach. It was not like her to feel so giddy.

She remembered how she had felt in that moment on the track, when instinct had told her that this was the man she had been waiting for, and not merely to frighten him away with her wayward behaviour. Instinct was sweet and persuasive, but it was notoriously unreliable in Cassie's experience. It was instinct that had told her to accompany Miss Crabbe to the radical meeting when she was seventeen because she had thought it would be interesting. It was instinct that had led her astray before.

'So, you admit you are a fortune hunter,' she said slowly. 'I thought that you would dissemble. Most men do.'

Peter sat down beside her on the sofa and took one of her hands in his. It did not seem like an impertinence. On the contrary, it seemed warm and intimate and entirely the right thing to do. Cassie blinked, wondering if the brandy had seriously impaired her judgement.

'I would never be dishonest with you, Cassandra,' Peter said, and Cassie's heart did an odd little flip, both at his use of her name and the intimacy of his tone. 'I cannot deny that I came to Lyndhurst Chase seeking a wealthy bride, but—' he smiled again and Cassie's blood fizzed '—I am very glad that I have found it in you.'

His hand was stroking her fingers gently now and the touch was soothing and yet so distracting that Cassie's head spun. She tried to remember the Viscount's reputation. These must be the practised compliments of an experienced seducer. She should not lower her guard. She put one hand to her head. It ached slightly from the effects of the cordial and the heat of the room.

'It is most unfortunate that we should meet when I am not feeling quite the thing,' she complained, 'for I am certain to be a great deal less civil to you than had we met under other circumstances, sir.'

Peter smiled again. 'I think it important that we are both honest,' he said, 'so please do not be concerned for my sensibilities. What is it that you wish to say to me, Cassie?'

Again he said her name like a caress. It had never sounded like that on anyone else's lips. Cassie took a deep breath as she tried to remember just what it was she *had* intended to say. She felt a little shaky.

'I have resolved not to marry, my lord,' she said, 'so I fear that your journey is in vain. I become mistress of my own fortune when I am five and twenty and that seems far preferable to me than giving it away to someone else.'

To her surprise, Peter did not try to persuade her otherwise. He merely sat looking at her with that cool, assessing blue gaze until Cassie felt quite light-headed.

'I respect your point of view,' he said at last. 'However, if you *were* to consider marriage, would there be any circumstances under which you might view me as a suitable candidate?'

Yes, oh, yes. Cassie just managed not to say the words

aloud. There was something all too suitable about Peter Quinlan in so many ways, and it flustered Cassie to think about it.

'That is a theoretical question, my lord,' she pointed out, managing to hold on to her common sense.

'Granted. But on a theoretical basis—am I acceptable?'

Peter's fingers tightened very slightly on her own. Cassie repressed a shiver of awareness.

'I am not sure that you *are* acceptable, my lord,' she said severely, trying and failing to remove her hand from his grasp. 'There are grave concerns about your character, for instance. I overheard Cousin John and Cousin Anthony talking about you. John said that you had rakish tendencies and he had doubts on that score about promoting a match between us. What do you say to that?'

'I think that it is encouraging to think that your cousins are so concerned for your welfare,' Peter said.

'You have not answered my question.'

Peter smiled. 'You noticed.'

'I did. So?'

There was a look of resignation on Peter's face. 'Very well, I confess it. You have me on the rack already, Miss Ward.'

'This,' Cassie said severely, 'is not a very good start, Lord Quinlan. So you are a fortune hunter and a rake. Do you have any redeeming features?'

'Many. I am very honest, as you perceive.'

Cassie found herself smiling against her will. There was something oddly disarming about such a blatant admission of fault.

'It is surprising that Anthony and John thought you were the most suitable candidate to court me,' she said.

'Perhaps,' Peter said, 'they recognise my excellent qualities and hope that you will come to see them too.'

Cassie snorted. 'I think it very annoying that they are so anxious to marry me off at all. Marriage brought no happiness to Cousin Anthony. He never speaks of it, of course, but I know that he has been miserable ever since Georgiana disappeared and he is forever saying that he has no wish ever to marry again.' She flung out one hand in a gesture of disgust. 'Then there is Cousin John. He and his first wife rubbed along together tolerably well in public, but everyone in the family knew that she detested him.' She turned away from him suddenly, a lump in her throat. 'Yet they seek to marry me off because they are not quite sure what to do with me!' She looked at Peter a little defiantly. It seemed odd to be confiding in a man who was to all intents and purposes a stranger, and yet there was something about him that drew her confidence.

'I could not bear to find that I was tied to a man I could neither love nor respect,' she finished, a little sadly. 'He would take all my money and care nothing for me, and it would be intolerable.'

'Cassie,' Peter said again. 'It need not be like that.'

He shifted a little closer to her until Cassie's thigh was pressed against his. She could feel the sensuous rub of her velvet skirts against his leg. Her skin prickled with new and tempting sensations.

'I…'

Peter smiled. 'Yes?'

Cassie wrinkled up her nose as she tried to concentrate. 'I am sure it would be exactly like that if I were to marry someone like Cousin William,' she said. 'He is forever pressing me to wed him.' She saw a shadow of expression touch Peter Quinlan's eyes, but it was gone before she could interpret it.

'William Lyndhurst-Flint?' he asked.

'Yes. He is Cousin John's brother. He has been trying to marry my money for years. My chaperon favours him as a suitor for me, but I do not care for him at all.' A flush came into her cheeks. 'He is a disgusting lecher. He pesters the maidservants. His valet is no better. Master and man have that much in common.' She caught her breath as Peter put a hand beneath her chin and tilted her face up so that she met his eyes.

'Has your cousin ever tried to touch you?' he demanded. His fingers were gentle against her cheek, but his tone required an answer and this time there was no misreading the anger in his eyes.

'Yes,' Cassie said. She smiled a little. 'He tried to kiss me once when he was drunk. I slapped his face. We never mentioned the incident again, but he knows not to try his tricks on me.'

She expected Peter to let her go then, but instead she saw a flash of amusement in his eyes.

'I might have guessed,' he said softly. 'You are a remarkable woman, Miss Cassandra Ward.'

Cassie blushed and dropped her gaze. Peter's fingers traced the line of her jaw with a featherlight stroke; it seemed extraordinary to her, but it felt as though there was wonderment in his touch. It felt as though he was *discovering* her and could not quite believe what he had found. She was not a fanciful girl, but Peter Quinlan's touch wove dangerous enchantment.

'And would you slap any gentleman who touched you?' he asked. His tone was quiet, but there was something beneath it that made Cassie tremble.

'I would do if I did not like him,' she said, meeting

look for look, 'and I have yet to meet a gentleman that I *did* like.'

Peter smiled. 'So the real question,' he said gently, 'is whether or not you like *me…*'

He touched the corner of her mouth lightly, then slid one finger along her lower lip. There was an expression in his eyes that made Cassie feel weak inside. She swallowed hard. She could feel herself leaning towards him, her eyes already closing as though in anticipation of the kiss…

Her eyes snapped open and she sat back swiftly. 'I know what you are doing and you won't succeed!'

Peter burst out laughing. 'What am I doing, sweetheart?'

'You are trying to seduce me,' Cassie said, struggling to ignore the skip of her heart that his endearment provoked. 'It is too bad of you, my lord. You said that you would be honest with me.'

Peter raised his eyebrows. 'I assure you there is no pretence, Cassie.'

'You want to kiss me!'

The amusement deepened in Peter's eyes. 'I cannot deny it. Do you want to kiss me?'

Cassie looked at him. The answer was yes, and it was written clearly on her face, but inside her there was a flutter of apprehension as well as a quiver of excitement. She bit her lip. Suddenly she looked—and felt—very young.

'I…I do not know.' She strove to be truthful. 'That is—yes, I do…' She went hot at the admission, looking at him from under her lashes.

'You do want to kiss me?'

'Yes! But…'

'But?' Peter shifted slightly. She sensed that he was

holding himself under tight control and the thought heated her blood. He would not force himself on her. Of that she was certain. She felt a rush of relief and pleasure that he was not that sort of man. Experienced, perhaps. Persuasive and powerful, certainly, but he was still no ravisher of innocents. She could feel him easing back from her and she met his gaze very openly.

'Your wooing is very swift, my lord. I am not certain I can keep up with you.'

The dark desire in his eyes contrasted with the restraint in his touch. He leaned forward and brushed his lips to hers. 'Do you want to try? It is a simple matter...'

If he had pounced on her or crushed her in his arms, Cassie would probably have pulled away from him, but the gentleness of the caress stole her heart and destroyed her resistance.

She had known him for such a short time. Her head was fuzzy with brandy and desire and yet this instinctively felt right. There was the echo of tenderness and the promise of strength in his hands as he held her. It felt wicked and delicious and yet somehow safe—in a completely dangerous way. She had lived for one and twenty years and yet had never experienced anything like this in her life before. With a flash of transforming feeling she knew that she wanted Peter's hands on her body. All of her body. With no clothes between them. And she wanted to touch him in return. The knowledge rocked her, made her breathing shallow.

If I marry Peter, I will be able to feel like this every single day, she told herself, and almost fainted at the thought. It seemed outrageous, exciting and deeply satisfying. She put up a hand to the nape of his neck, tangling it in the thick dark hair there, stroking him and pulling him closer. She kissed him—shyly and inexpertly, her lips bumping against his—and she heard him groan, and then he deepened the kiss, his tongue sliding between her lips and invading her mouth, and Cassie's mind spun.

Their breath entwined. The kiss seared her with its intensity and passion and yet she was not afraid. When he freed her mouth she turned it against the roughness of his cheek, raining kisses along the hard line of his jaw until he captured her lips again, gently covering her mouth with his and tasting its softness. Cassie lay back against the cushions and felt the hard weight of Peter's body follow her down, his hands about her waist. His lips trailed along the curve of her throat, barely touching, a moist, velvet stroke of pure pleasure. Delicious warmth surged through Cassie's veins and she arched against him, unable to repress a little whimper of satisfaction as his hand came up to brush against the curve of her breast.

And then, when denial was a mere shadow at the back of Cassie's mind, Peter wrenched himself away from her. She lay still for a moment, winded with shock and blank passion, and then she opened her eyes to see Peter was standing across the parlour, both hands resting against the cold panels of the wainscot, and breathing as hard as though he had been running.

She half-sat, and he turned his head to look at her. There was a heated glitter in his eyes that scalded her. He looked as though he was in pain.

'I am going out,' he said.

Cassie stared at him bemusedly. 'Out? But—'

She saw his gaze drop to the neckline of her riding dress, where several more buttons had come adrift. Enlightenment came to her in a flash. She was inexperienced, but she was not stupid. A deep blush spread across her cheeks. 'Oh! I... What have I done?'

'It isn't your fault.'

Peter came across the room towards her, but stopped when he was still several feet away. 'Cassie, it is not your fault,' he repeated. Their eyes met. Peter put out a hand and touched her cheek, a tender touch. 'I swear—' he began, and then the door opened violently and Major Anthony Lyndhurst and the Earl of Mardon burst into the room.

'Perhaps you did not understand my original invitation, Quinlan,' Anthony Lyndhurst said coldly. His eyes were almost black with anger. 'When I invited you to the house party, it was not in the nature of suggesting a debauch. I scarce know whether to call for the vicar or to hit you across the room.'

Peter rubbed his forehead. Nothing but abject apology would do now and even that was barely adequate when explaining to a man how one had almost come to seduce his ward in an inn parlour.

It was several hours later. As befitted gentlemen, neither Anthony Lyndhurst nor John, Earl of Mardon, had expressed their views of his execrable behaviour on the way back to Lyndhurst Chase. They had bundled Cassie up into the carriage, curtly bid him to follow on behind, and given him the distinct impression that if he were cowardly enough to turn tail and flee, one of them would call him out, and if that one failed to maim him, the other would be in reserve to finish the job. Thus it was that Cassie had been handed over to her chaperon without the chance of another word between them and Peter was now enduring a painful interview in the library. He had not been offered the opportunity to change his wet clothes and he certainly had not been offered a drink.

The wet ride to Lyndhurst Chase had given Peter ample opportunity to reflect on the disaster that was his whirlwind courtship of Miss Cassandra Ward. He could recall with excruciating clarity the moment at which the parlour door had opened. Cassie's state of enchanting disarray was plain for all to see. Her hair was loose about her face, her buttons were undone to reveal the tender curves of her upper breasts and her gown had slipped from one shoulder. Her appearance could hardly be expected to provoke the same appreciation in her male relatives as it had in him. Worse still, his own state of arousal was difficult to disguise and, judging by the look of searing contempt bent on him by his host, he had no need to waste time in trying. It was obvious to all what had been going on.

'I can only beg your pardon,' Peter said now. 'I meant no disrespect to Miss Ward. We had been talking, and—' He made a slight gesture. He and Cassie *had* been talking, but even now he was uncertain how they had moved from that relatively innocuous occupation to one that was rather less chaste. And Anthony Lyndhurst seemed quite unimpressed, as was only to be expected.

'Talking!'

Peter caught his look of undisguised disgust, an expression that seemed to be echoed in the baleful stare given him by the old setter dog curled up in front of the fire. It seemed that no one at Lyndhurst Chase was particularly pleased with him. Peter shook his head.

'My apologies, Lyndhurst. I appreciate that I have broken every law of proper conduct. There is nothing that I can say to excuse my behaviour.'

Surprisingly, Lyndhurst's face eased slightly. Peter

kept quiet. There *was* no justification for his behaviour and he was not going to insult either of them by pretending otherwise.

Lyndhurst turned away and strolled towards the window. 'Can I infer from your behaviour, Quinlan, that you are not indifferent to my cousin?'

Peter looked up. Lyndhurst was gazing out across the gardens towards the lake. His stance was relaxed enough, but the line of his shoulders was tense.

'I can safely say that indifference is the last emotion I feel for your cousin,' he agreed. 'Miss Ward has my greatest respect and admiration.'

Lyndhurst almost smiled. He gave him a searching look and Peter could see that he had read in his face all the things he had carefully left unsaid. Naturally it was out of the question to say: *'I am helplessly attracted to your cousin, Lyndhurst. I want to ravish her and I almost did so and I am afraid that with the slightest encouragement I shall probably fall madly in love with her…'* Out of the question, the sort of statement a sane gentleman would never make, yet blindingly, hopelessly true for all that.

'I see,' Anthony Lyndhurst said. 'Then will you accede to an immediate betrothal? Under the circumstances I think it would be for the best. There were a number of witnesses…'

Peter winced at the thought. He could not permit Cassie's reputation to be tarnished. He eased his breath out in a long sigh. He had come to Berkshire intending to marry a fortune. He had come with ruthless intent and he had not expected to experience more than a polite respect for his intended bride. Why, then, did the fact that he was so strongly attracted to Cassie seem to make matters more complicated? Suddenly he felt responsible for her feelings as well as his own. He did not want her to feel forced into a match because of what had happened between them.

He looked up to see that Lyndhurst was watching him. 'I would like to have the opportunity to court Miss Ward formally before I make my declaration,' he began. 'We have had little time to get to know one another.'

Lyndhurst gave him a mocking smile. 'You had time enough to compromise her, it seems,' he said. 'You may woo my cousin in form after the betrothal, Quinlan.'

There was a moment of silence and then Peter nodded slowly. 'Very well. I should be honoured to marry Miss Ward,' he said.

Lyndhurst held out a hand and Peter shook it. Lyndhurst poured him a glass of brandy. Peter accepted it. The atmosphere warmed into something approaching friendliness and the conversation turned easily to mutual friends, shared history and the plans that Lyndhurst had for the entertainment of his house party guests. Neither of them gave another thought to the fact that Cassie might also have an opinion on the subject of her proposed marriage and that it might not be quite what they anticipated.

Chapter Three

'Come out, Miss Cassandra. I know you're under there.' The tones of Eliza, Cassie's maid, penetrated the two fat, feather pillows that Cassie had pulled over her head in an unsuccessful effort to blot out the day.

'Miss Cassandra!' Eliza's tone became stronger. 'Come out before I pull all the bedclothes off you!'

With a groan, Cassie flung the pillows away and emerged blinking into the light of day. It was a lovely morning. Eliza had thrown back the curtains and the room was flooded with sunlight. Cassie lay on her back and stared at the shadows moving across the ceiling. She remembered that all the house party guests were supposed to be lunching by the lake that day, then having an impromptu dance after dinner in the evening. When it had been planned she had thought that it sounded rather fun. Now she did not even wish to get out of bed.

When she had returned from Lynd the previous afternoon, Eliza had bundled her into bed, force-fed her a hot posset to ward off a chill, and had stood guard over her like a lion, so that no one else, least of all Cassie's chaperon, had had the chance to come near her. Worn out with strong drink, sweet passion and exhaustion,

Cassie had fallen into a dreamless sleep. It was only when she had woken in the morning, her head clear and her mind all too active, that all the unwelcome aspects of the situation had occurred to her.

She had behaved in an utterly abandoned manner. Anthony and John would be furious and disgusted at her shocking behaviour. Lady Margaret, her chaperon, would be icily disapproving. Even Eliza, notoriously indulgent, would censure her. Like as not, everyone in Lynd and at the Chase would have heard what had happened at the inn, because everyone *always* knew everybody else's business.

She would have to face Peter Quinlan over the breakfast table. She blushed to think of it and to remember what had happened between them. For she did remember it. She remembered every last kiss and caress.

She thought about how she had felt when she had first seen Peter Quinlan on the road, the warm and breathless grip about her heart as her eyes had met his. She was one and twenty; she had experienced—or rather, endured—three London Seasons. She had met any number of personable men and for obvious reasons they had made themselves extremely pleasant to her.

Not a single one of them had affected her the way that Peter had done.

For a moment she had allowed herself to think on the sweet sensuality of their embraces. Even now the recollection made her shiver with remembered passion. But there was no doubt that she had made a fool of herself. For amongst all the other mortifying things that she remembered, she also recollected that she had told Peter Quinlan that she had two hundred thousand pounds, and what had followed surely could not have been a coincidence.

With a groan, Cassie had pulled the pillows over her head and prayed devoutly for deliverance.

Now she rolled over on to her stomach and regarded Eliza's small, upright figure with wariness. The maid had been her closest friend and ally since she was a child, a woman whose sound common sense had guided Cassie more than all the governesses and chaperons in the world could do. From her teachers Cassie had gained book learning and, in one notable case, an understanding of radical politics. From Eliza she had learned good principles and received great affection.

'I know what you are going to say,' she began.

Eliza extracted a clean chemise from the chest of drawers beside the window and held it up critically to the light. She tutted.

'This petticoat is creased. It's not what I am saying that counts, Miss Cassandra,' she added. 'Mrs Bell saw you through the window of that inn parlour and she told Mrs Deedes, who told her sister who works in the laundry, who told the upper housemaid who was overheard whispering about it by your chaperon.' Eliza put the chemise down and shook her head slowly. 'You're in a proper state, Miss Cassandra, and no mistake. Your cousins are furious that you've compromised yourself fair and square. You will have to get married and no messing.'

Cassie rolled over and watched Elizabeth as she went to the wardrobe and started to search through the dresses hanging there. The word 'compromised' seemed to have a cold and very final ring to it.

'Compromised?' She paused. 'Oh, not the blue striped gown, please, Eliza! It makes me look like a lumpy schoolgirl.' She sat up, clasping her knees and resting her chin on them. 'That sounds rather harsh. I had not thought of it in those terms. Besides, it is very contrary of John and Anthony to be annoyed when they were the ones who wanted me to marry in the first place!'

'There's ways and ways of doing these things,' Eliza said, and there was both exasperation and affection in her tone. 'You never think about the consequences of your actions, Miss Cassandra.'

Cassie opened her mouth to dispute this, then fell silent as she realised that there was some truth in Eliza's assertion. There was the sound of a step outside the door and her maid shot her a warning glance. A second later there was a brief knock at the bedroom door. Cassie sighed heavily as Lady Margaret Burnside came into the room without waiting to be invited.

Cassie's chaperon was as immaculately polished as a burnished mirror. Her blonde hair had never been known to permit an unruly curl. Her perfectly plucked eyebrows were like twin crescent moons and her skin was white and smooth. As one of Cassie's closest relatives on her mother's side, she was considered by the Lyndhurst cousins to be the ideal person to have charge of Cassie. Unfortunately, Cassie detested her.

'Good morning, my dear.' Lady Margaret approximated a kiss a half-inch from Cassie's cheek. She smelled strongly of violets. 'I hear I am to congratulate you on your betrothal.' She smiled patronisingly. 'That was quick work! The Viscount is indeed an ardent lover. One might even say a *professional* seducer!'

Eliza, who was folding Cassie's stockings neatly into piles, muttered something that sounded suspiciously like, *'You're a fine one to talk.'*

Lady Margaret turned her head and gave her a sharp glance. 'What was that you said, Ebdon?'

'Beg your pardon, m'lady,' Eliza said stolidly. 'I was thinking that Miss Cassandra needed you to give her a fine talking-to on the subject.'

'You are right, of course,' Lady Margaret said, with a chilly smile, 'though it is scarce your place to say so.' She turned back to Cassie and touched her hand in a gesture of sympathy.

'Do not reproach yourself, however, my dear little Cassie. I was speaking to Lord Quinlan after dinner last night. He is an absolute charmer and easily experienced enough to sweep an innocent like you off her feet. You should not feel ashamed over falling for such practised seduction.'

Cassie felt the chill inside her increase. Lady Margaret's words, calculated and spiteful as they were, nevertheless struck a chord. She could not get away from the fact that she had told Peter Quinlan that she was heiress to a vast sum, greater than anyone had ever suspected and after that he had worked swiftly and efficiently to engage her interest, to seduce her, to compromise her into a position where society's rules obliged her to wed him... She just managed to repress another groan.

She had allowed Peter Quinlan liberties that she had never previously dreamed of permitting any man who was not her husband. It was lowering to admit it, but she had enjoyed his kisses to the point of abandonment. She had participated enthusiastically in her own downfall.

Even worse, Peter had told her honestly that he had come a-courting her for her money and not for herself alone. Yet she, like a naïve little idiot, had fallen for his charm and straight into his arms. Damn Peter Quinlan for being so attractive and damn the blackberry cordial and double damn her own weakness and *triple* damn Lady Margaret, who was sitting on the edge of her bed now, picking idly at the coverlet with her immaculate fingernails and smiling at Cassie in that condescending manner, which told her just what a silly little girl she really was.

'I am not intending to marry Lord Quinlan, ma'am,' Cassie said, bristling with a mixture of shame and anger. She cleared her throat. 'This is all a misunderstanding.'

Lady Margaret laughed like a hollow tinkle of bells. 'I do not think so, my love. Not after your performance in that inn. Your cousin is anxious to hush the scandal and has agreed to an immediate engagement. There is nothing for you to consent to. It is all agreed.' She got to her feet in an elegant swish of silk skirts, but when she reached the door she paused, one hand on the frame.

'By the way, my love, I should take Lord Quinlan and be thankful if I were you. A young lady in your position cannot afford to be too particular and you will get no better offer.' Her gaze fell on the blue striped gown that Eliza was stoically folding to replace in the wardrobe. 'Sweetly pretty, my love, and very youthful. Just right for you.'

There was a painful silence after she had left the room.

'Betrothal,' Cassie said furiously. 'How dare they! They take a great deal for granted!'

'Spiteful old harpy,' Eliza said, shutting the blue gown away in the cupboard and shooting the closed panels of the bedroom door a malevolent look. 'Always stirring up trouble, she is! No better than Haymarket ware neither.'

'You go too far, Eliza,' Cassie said hastily.

'Some of us,' Eliza said with an ominous sniff, 'see things that others do not.'

Cassie sighed sharply. For all that she disliked her chaperon, she had never seen any evidence of the alleged impropriety that Eliza alluded to. It seemed most unlikely, given her cousins' concern for her reputation, that they would appoint a scandalous chaperon. Eliza's suspicions must surely be baseless.

'Mr Timms and I,' Eliza said, with finality, 'think that madam is no better than she ought to be.'

Cassie sighed again.

'No doubt that was what you and Timms were discussing the other day on the stairs,' she said. 'I saw you looking very cosy together.'

To Cassie's surprise her normally forthright maid looked almost coy. She closed her lips tightly and a slight flush came into her cheeks.

'Mr Timms and I were discussing the merits of Holland starch, Miss Cassandra. I'll have you know that we have been acquainted for many years and nothing more than a few kind words have ever passed between us.'

Cassie could tell that Eliza was ruffled. She jumped from the bed and gave her an impulsive hug. 'I am sorry, Eliza. I meant no harm. It is merely that I had observed that you value Mr Timms's good opinion.'

Eliza's stiff figure softened and she half-smiled. 'I know you did not mean anything by it, my pet.' She sighed. 'Mr Timms and I…well… Sometimes I wish…'

'Yes?' Cassie prompted.

'I wish we had had our own chance of happiness,' Eliza said, in a rush. Cassie noticed that her hands were busy folding and refolding a petticoat with little jerky gestures. 'We have known each other nigh on twenty years, but being in different households with our own responsibilities… Well, it was not to be. And now I think it is too late. No point in talking about it. There it is.'

'Oh, Eliza!' Cassie's brow puckered. She felt a pang of acute sympathy for the maid's plight. She had had no notion that Eliza's feelings ran so deep and could tell that the brisk tone she had adopted hid much more painful emotions.

'Now…' The maid turned her face away, clearly not wishing to pursue the subject any further. She pushed Cassie gently towards the armada chest, where she had laid out a walking dress in cherry pink.

'I thought the pink today, to match your pretty face.' She held Cassie at arm's length for a moment and smiled. 'You're as bonny as a May morning, so don't let that sour old puss tell you otherwise. She's only jealous.'

'Eliza—'

'And,' the maid continued inexorably, 'don't believe a word she says about your Viscount neither. It's you he's come to wed, Miss Cassie, not some old trollop!'

Cassie sat down heavily on the chest, almost squashing the gown, which Eliza whisked out from under her.

'If he had indeed come to woo me, then that would be a different matter, Eliza, but in truth it is my money he wishes to wed.' She sighed. 'Show me a gentleman who does not! Even Great-aunt Harriet once said that it was indecent for a young girl to have so much money as I.'

Eliza put her hands on her sturdy hips and viewed Cassie shrewdly. 'You are an heiress and you are never going to be able to get past that, my pet, until you can see a man for what he is and judge whether he cares for you alone. Yon Viscount seems a likely fellow to me. I would give him a chance.'

Cassie looked up. 'It seems Anthony has already given him his chance by consenting to a betrothal! Of all the mob-handed, arrogant, masculine things to do.'

'Stop feeling sorry for yourself, do,' Eliza said sharply. She gave Cassie a little push. 'And go and put your clothes on. Don't expect me to wait on you!'

Cassie slid off the chest and obediently reached for her underclothes. 'I am minded to wait until I am five and twenty and may have control of my own fortune,' she said, her voice muffled as she pulled her petticoats over her head. 'John and Anthony cannot *make* me marry even if I have ruined my reputation. Why should I care? They can all go hang.'

Eliza snorted. 'There are some as are cut out to be wizened old maids, Miss Cassie, and others like you are not. Besides, you don't want to be stuck with that Lady Margaret for another four years. You'd run mad.' She held out the pink gown for Cassie to put on. 'Don't you want a home and family of your own?'

Cassie put her hands up to her cheeks suddenly. 'I don't know, Eliza. What I do know is that I grow tired of everyone telling me what to do. Live here, marry there…' She let her hands fall. 'No one asks me what I want, so…' Cassie said with determination, 'I shall simply have to show them. I will show Anthony and John and Viscount Quinlan—' she invested the name with dislike '—that they do not take my consent for granted!'

'Then the good lord help them!' Eliza said devoutly. 'You will be careful, though, won't you, Miss Cassie? Think matters through sensibly now…'

'Of course,' Cassie said, her eyes bright. 'You know that I always do.'

* * *

Peter had been lingering at the breakfast table far longer than was his usual wont. He would have preferred to be taking a ride about the estate than sitting indoors on so glorious a morning, but he was determined to wait until Cassie had put in an appearance. He wanted to speak with her. He was surprised to find that he felt a little nervous.

He was not certain that the adorable Miss Cassie Ward would accept his proposal of marriage. He had never put his fate to the touch before and he was discovering that it mattered to him a great deal that she should agree to be his bride. A night's lack of sleep had not caused him to have second thoughts about the marriage. On the contrary, he was anxious to secure Miss Ward as his wife. However, he did want the chance to court her properly. He did not wish her to be forced into a betrothal as a result of their encounter at the inn. He wanted her to want *him*.

The beds at Lyndhurst Chase were supremely comfortable, but Peter had tossed and turned, alternately pricked by conscience and tormented by erotic images of the delectable Miss Ward. Never before had he been struck down by so powerful and instant an attraction. He was not entirely sure what had happened to him. All he knew was that he wanted Cassie Ward herself far more than he wanted her fortune, and if this was his final come-uppance as a rake and a fortune hunter, then he would embrace his fate with gratitude.

Conversation around the table had languished a little while ago. In the absence of a hostess at Lyndhurst Chase, Sarah, Countess of Mardon, was at the head of the table and was conversing in low tones with her husband, the Earl, who sat on her right. At the other end of the table, with the ancient setter dozing contentedly at his feet, Anthony Lyndhurst appeared engrossed in the *Morning Post* and every so often exchanged a few words with his Cousin William beside him. Lyndhurst-Flint in turn was chatting desultorily with Lady Margaret Burnside. Peter had known William Lyndhurst-Flint vaguely at Eton, although Lyndhurst-Flint had been a few years older. He had never liked him. Lyndhurst-Flint had had a reputation as a bully who forced younger boys to lick his boots and used the Eton Wall Game as an excuse to beat up the smaller pupils.

It was an oddly restricted group for a house party and Peter thought it bore out the rumour he had heard that, along with finding Cassandra a husband, Anthony Lyndhurst was taking the opportunity to appoint his heir. The field was small and it seemed to Peter that William Lyndhurst-Flint must be in with a good chance. However, perhaps the man was not certain of inheriting and that was why he persisted in pushing his suit with Cassie.

The door opened and Cassie came in, pausing on the threshold, her hand on the doorknob. Peter's heart contracted. She looked outwardly collected and calm, but there was a flicker of apprehension in her eyes.

There was a little ripple around the breakfast table. Peter saw Lady Margaret watching Cassie with a bright, speculative look. She exchanged a glance with William Lyndhurst-Flint and made absolutely no effort to ease her charge's situation. In that moment Peter saw exactly how Cassie stood with the rest of the family; Mardon and Lyndhurst's brotherly indulgence, Lyndhurst-Flint's speculative amusement, Lady Margaret's malice… Peter started to feel angry.

'Cassie!' Sarah Mardon said, smiling sweetly. 'Come and join me down here. We can talk about our plans for the picnic.' She patted the seat beside her.

William Lyndhurst-Flint got to his feet with studied charm. 'Surely you should sit here, little cousin, beside your betrothed.' He shot Peter a look. 'I beg your pardon, the engagement is not yet formal, is it?'

Peter saw Cassie blush at the reminder, though whether with temper or embarrassment he was not sure. His anger hardened as he saw the way the other man was so casually trying to queer his pitch. He put his napkin down and stood up. He was taller than Lyndhurst-Flint and for a moment Lyndhurst-Flint looked intimidated.

'Allow me, Miss Ward,' Peter said with immaculate courtesy. He held the chair beside the Countess for Cassie and she slid into it with a slight, unreadable look at him over her shoulder.

'Thank you, my lord,' was all that she said.

Once again, conversation languished around the table. Lady Margaret was twitting the Countess over the curious behaviour of her personal maid.

'I found that odd creature Dent polishing my doorknob this morning! Strange behaviour for an upper servant!'

The atmosphere in the breakfast room felt odd and tense with no one quite at ease. Peter watched Cassie as she sipped a cup of chocolate and ate a piece of toast. This morning her glorious copper brown hair had been subdued into a neat braid and no curls allowed to escape. She was dressed in a gown of pink that became her very well. Peter, an observant man, saw Lady Margaret flick the gown a comprehensive look and her mouth thin with displeasure. He hid a smile. Evidently the chaperon disliked competition from her charge.

Anthony Lyndhurst put down his paper and rose to his feet.

'I thought to show you about the estate and the stud farm this morning, Quinlan, if you would care for a ride,' he said. 'The ladies are planning a picnic luncheon by the lake with boating afterwards, but we have time for a ride out before we join them. I would like to show you my horses. I imagine you are a connoisseur of bloodlines.'

Peter opened his mouth to accept the invitation, but was forestalled. Cassie Ward had also risen to her feet and was facing him, her determined little chin set firm, her golden brown eyes sparking.

'I must plead a prior claim on my *betrothed*, Anthony,' she said, stressing the word. There was a thread of steel in her voice. 'Surely you are not to whisk him away when we are barely acquainted?' She turned to Peter. 'Lord Quinlan, I would like to speak to you in the library. Now, if you please.'

'Lord Quinlan,' Cassie said, with arctic chill, once the door was closed behind the two of them, 'allow me to clarify a couple of matters. We are not compromised, we are not betrothed and we are certainly not getting married.'

Peter looked at her. Her eyes were flashing with indignation, but she was standing very stiff and tense. Her voluptuous, vulnerable mouth was quivering, betraying her feelings. Peter felt a stab of compassion for her. She was very young and inexperienced to be plunged into such a situation.

He wanted to talk to her, but the library was not the place. It felt oppressive and enclosed. He could not reach her here, where duty and convention would squash her spontaneous spirit. She would dismiss him and he would never get a chance to convince her that he wanted her more for herself than for all the fortune in the world.

'Well?' Cassie demanded, fizzing with indignation, clearly unable to wait any longer for a response. 'Are you not going to say anything?'

'Yes,' Peter said. 'Will you come riding with me?'

Cassie looked startled and—he would have sworn—tempted. Then she put her hands on her hips and faced him squarely.

'What has that to do with the price of fish? Did you not understand me, my lord? I would prefer not to go anywhere with you. I would prefer that you leave Lyndhurst Chase directly. Now. At once! Is that clear?'

Peter could not repress a smile. 'As crystal, Miss Ward. Indeed it would be difficult to misunderstand you.'

Cassie looked aggravated. 'Then why are you still here?'

'Because I would like to speak with you and I find this room unsuited to my purpose,' Peter said. 'Hence I wondered whether you would like to come riding with me. It is a very beautiful day and I feel that our acquaintance would prosper out of doors.' He strode over to the window, then turned back to look at her. He noted that Cassie could not help one quick, betraying glance outside, as though the beautiful morning beckoned to her too.

'The climate is not the point at issue here, my lord,' she said.

Peter smiled. 'I beg your pardon, Miss Ward. What is the point?'

'The point,' Cassie said, her chin tilting dangerously, an angry sparkle in her eyes, 'is that you deliberately set out to compromise me yesterday, Lord Quinlan.'

Peter had been expecting this. He suspected that Cassie had come to breakfast with her feelings already ruffled by someone—her chaperon, perhaps—who had intentionally set out to paint him as a ruthless seducer. He remembered that Cassie had told him the previous day that Lady Margaret supported William Lyndhurst-Flint's suit. And then there had been Lyndhurst-Flint's calculatedly provocative comment at breakfast. Both of them would take any opportunity they could to ruin his chances, and they had already started.

'It is rather unfair to accuse me of setting out to compromise you,' he said mildly.

'Is it?' Cassie's gaze narrowed. 'I thought it was quite plain. I told you that I had two hundred thousand pounds and from that moment you determined to seduce me.'

Peter drove his hands into his jacket pockets. 'Now that is *definitely* unfair.'

Cassie looked nonplussed. 'Indeed? Do you deny it, then?'

'Of course,' Peter said. 'I wanted to seduce you long before you told me about the money. I wanted you from the first moment I saw you up the tree with that ridiculous banner.' He took a step closer to her. It brought them a mere two feet apart. He could see the puzzlement and the reluctant curiosity in her eyes. 'You are utterly seducible, Miss Ward,' he finished gently.

Cassie glared. 'And you are outrageous, Lord Quinlan!'

'I am sorry if I offend you,' Peter said. 'I promised yesterday always to tell you the truth and I have been scrupulously careful to do so.'

Cassie drew a deep breath. 'There are times—surely there are times!—when it is better to prevaricate, or at the very least moderate your opinions!'

Peter laughed. 'It surprises me to hear you say so, Miss Ward. I would have thought that you of all people are always transparently honest.'

'I am! I did not expect you to be, however.' Cassie was looking at him, frowning, as though she was not quite sure what to make of him. 'Upon my word, Lord Quinlan!' she burst out. 'I do not know whether you are the most skilled trickster that I have ever met or…' She paused.

'Or someone who wishes to forget all about the damnable money and simply take you to bed?' Peter suggested.

'Lord Quinlan!' Cassie sounded as appalled as an octogenarian dowager.

Peter saw the shock in her face and underneath it, intriguingly, the faintest hint of fascination as she considered his statement. He traced her thought processes with interest. She was remembering the way that reckless desire had ambushed them at the inn; she was thinking of the persuasive seduction of their kisses, she was wanting much, much more…

Then the colour rushed into her face as she realised just how inappropriate her thoughts were. She turned away abruptly. Peter could tell that she was completely flustered that the interview had not gone the way she had planned, but that she did not wish to give him the advantage of knowing it. He went across to her and put a hand on her arm.

'Miss Ward.'

There was a flare of nervousness in Cassie's eyes as though she almost expected him to make good his shocking declaration and sweep her up the wide oak stair to bed there and then.

'My lord?' She moistened her lips.

Peter took her hand in his. 'All I ask is that you give me a chance to court you,' he said. 'You knew that I was a fortune hunter. I made no secret of it. You can trust me to be honest with you.'

Cassie's head was bent. The sun shone through the dusty windows and picked out the strands of copper and gold in the richness of her hair. Peter ached to touch it. She looked up at him suddenly and his senses leapt. Her fingers trembled slightly within his grasp and he tightened his hold.

'Tell me the truth, then,' she said urgently. 'What happened yesterday in the inn… *Did* you plan that, my lord?'

Peter winced. He was pinned in the honesty of her gaze. There was something about such vulnerable candour that stripped away any pretence. He had never met anyone like Miss Cassandra Ward and her very openness brought out all his protective instincts. He wanted to shield her from all the disillusion and disappointment that life could bring on one who had no defences. He wanted to guard her against all comers. A marriage of convenience was not good enough for her. No fortune hunter on earth could be worthy of her. Devil take it, he wanted to save her from *himself*.

'I did not plan it,' he said slowly. 'I promise you that.' It was difficult for a man of his experience to admit that manners to restrict yourself to one lady when you have not yet secured her hand in marriage.'

'Hmm.' Peter moved in closer still. 'You would not say, then, that you were prey to a certain jealousy?'

Cassie jumped. 'Of course not!'

'Miss Ward, you are a liar.' Peter turned her face up towards his. 'I can read it in your eyes,' he said.

'You are certainly close enough to read anything you choose there,' Cassie snapped. She tried to wriggle away from him. The silky material of the peignoir slid across his chest to devastatingly arousing effect.

'So I am,' Peter said. 'What else can my proximity to you tell me?'

His hand slid down her silken sleeve and came to rest on the curve of her waist. Cassie could feel the warmth of his touch. It was a shocking reminder of how sheer were her nightdress and peignoir and that she was naked beneath the flimsy layers.

Peter's hand spanned her waist, his fingers spread against her ribcage. He leaned forward until his breath stirred Cassie's curls.

'I can feel the beat of your heart,' he murmured. 'You seem a little agitated, Miss Ward.'

Cassie pushed half-heartedly and pointlessly against his chest. 'Of course I am agitated,' she said. 'You are standing a deal too close to me for comfort, Lord Quinlan.'

'Is it comfort that you want from me?' Peter asked. His breath feathered across her cheek. 'Admit the truth, Cassie. Admit that you were jealous. Admit that you want me. Not for comfort, but for something quite different…'

His lips were tracing the curve of her throat now, pausing above the line of her collarbone, brushing aside he had lost his head, but it was essential to make her understand the truth. 'I have told you that I find you all too attractive, Miss Ward,' he said ruefully, 'and what happened yesterday was the proof. I lost control.'

Cassie was looking at him shyly from under her lashes. 'I see,' she said, and, searching her face, he saw that there was pride and amusement under that diffident surface. Damn it, the minx was *pleased* that she could have such an effect on him, and here was he helplessly dangling like a fish on her line...

He reached out to pull her into his arms, but she read his intention and drew away, fending him off.

'Oh, no, you do not, Lord Quinlan! You have asked for the opportunity to court me and you have it. But—' she flicked him a challenging glance '—that courtship does not involve kissing.'

The air between them was suddenly alive with sensual tension. Peter caught her arm and drew her closer to him. 'I have conditions too,' he said softly, his mouth an inch from hers. 'I am happy to abide by your terms for a little while, Miss Ward, but I will take something on account.'

And he kissed her, swift and hard, letting her go before the urge to pull her closer still and ravish her became too strong. When he released her she was breathing quickly and there was a heat and turbulence in her eyes that almost overset all his good resolutions.

'You are certain that you will persuade me to marry you, then,' Cassie whispered. She pressed her fingers to her lips in an unconscious gesture.

'I am.'

'How very arrogant you are.' She raised a haughty brow.

Peter smiled, that wicked, glinting smile that brought the colour into her cheeks. 'I would wager on it,' he said.

'Why?'

'Because you are not indifferent to me,' Peter said. 'If you were, I would have left Lyndhurst Chase by now. I will not force my suit on a reluctant lady. But you, Miss Ward…' his smile deepened '…you will be my willing bride soon. Of that I am convinced.'

Cassie turned her shoulder to him and swept out of the room then, but Peter followed with a whimsical smile. He knew that she was intrigued against her will and that her curiosity would eventually lead her straight back into his arms—if only he had the patience to wait that long.

Chapter Four

Peter gave Cassie ten days of the most perfect, irre-proachably respectable courtship. Anthony Lyndhurst had arranged a number of entertainments to keep his guests amused. There was hunting, shooting and fishing for the gentlemen; games of croquet and cricket on the lawns, an outing to the Assembly at Newbury and in-vitations to dine with various country neighbours and acquaintances. Throughout it all, Peter wooed Cassie with absolute decorum, dancing with her in the evening, escorting her into dinner, riding about the estate with her and rarely touching her other than to hand her into a carriage. They were in each other's company almost all the time. Cassie kept expecting him to press his suit or to kiss her. He did neither.

When he failed to meet this expectation, Cassie told herself that he needed her money and no doubt he would be prepared to be patient to get it, but such thoughts seemed to demean Peter's evident regard for her. She could not deny that he was sincere in his respect and his attention to her, and under that scrupulous courtesy the feelings ran hot between them. She could feel it in his touch and see it in his eyes, and it was all the more exciting for the fact that it was banked down and held under such strong control.

She found herself starting to reflect on what it would be like to marry him. It would be an escape from Lady Margaret's domestic tyranny and her cousins' benevolent rule. She would have her own establishment in which to exercise all those managing tendencies, which had so far been thwarted. And she would have Peter and those kisses and caresses that had been denied her these ten days past and for which she secretly ached. No doubt it was wanton of her to feel that way, but Cassie had never been one to pretend about her feelings.

It troubled Cassie more than she liked to admit to think of Peter sleeping but one floor below her. Sometimes she would lie awake in her bed, all her senses seeming alive and alert, waiting for something, anticipating something… There would be a pitter-pat of excitement in her stomach and a feverish buzz in her blood, and she would toss and turn restlessly for what seemed like hours. Peter was disturbing her sleep and in Cassie's book that was a problem that required a solution.

'Better the devil you know,' Eliza said one night, when Cassie was preparing for bed and had confided in her maid that she had thought of accepting Peter's proposal as a means of achieving some independence.

'That would be the worst reason to marry Lord Quinlan,' the maid continued. 'A chaperon's tyranny is nothing to that of a husband. Marriage is a very serious matter, not to be entered into lightly.'

'I suppose so,' Cassie said. Eliza's words only seemed to echo her own uncertainty.

'It is not a privilege given to all of us,' the maid continued with a slight edge to her voice. 'Use your chances wisely, Miss Cassandra.'

Cassie looked at her, remembering Eliza's words a few days before about her feelings for Timms. She had always thought of the maid as such a practical homebody that it was a shock to realise that Eliza must have had her hopes and dreams of a family and home of her own. Hopes that she now thought were lost.

'Now if you want Lord Quinlan because he's a handsome gentleman, then that's a different matter, of course,' Eliza was saying. She cast Cassie a shrewd look. 'Couldn't blame you, neither.'

'Eliza!'

'Well, now,' the maid said imperturbably, 'no need to pretend that you do not think him a good-looking man.'

'I admit that he is,' Cassie said, 'and I doubt that I am the first lady to think so.'

Eliza sat down on the end of the bed, her hands full of the silk stockings that she was sorting. 'That is another matter entirely, my pet. Are you afraid that you could not hold him?'

'Yes,' Cassie said, baldly. She fidgeted with the brightly coloured bedspread, then looked up to meet Eliza's thoughtful gaze. 'I am not indifferent to Lord Quinlan, but I am uncertain that I could bear to risk all for him only to find I had lost him after marriage.' She stopped, staring into the shadows. 'I have a pile of money and very little else,' she said with a faint smile. 'I do not wish to give the money away and find I am left with nothing.'

'A very practical attitude, my pet,' Eliza said, patting her hand.

'Is it so wrong of me to want a man who wants me alone?' Cassie asked. Her shoulders drooped. 'Sometimes I do not feel wanted, Eliza. My mother—' She broke off, feeling it disloyal to criticise Mrs Ward, who had been an invalid for many years.

'Your mother wanted you right enough,' Eliza said comfortably. 'Your cousins love you too, Miss Cassie. That is why they want you to be happy. Go about it the wrong way sometimes—' she sniffed '—but their hearts are in the right place. Except for that William, of course. He's not worth the cost of his jacket and nor is that fancy valet of his neither.'

Cassie smiled and squeezed Eliza's hand. 'Thank you, Eliza.'

Her maid smiled fondly. 'Seems to me that you have two matters to resolve, pet—how Lord Quinlan feels about you, and how you truly feel about him. Then all will be right and tight.'

'Is that all?' Cassie said, laughing.

'That's right.' Eliza got to her feet. 'Think you can manage that, Miss Cassandra?'

'Oh, yes,' Cassie said. 'And if I can persuade him to kiss me into the bargain, then so much the better.' She reached for her peignoir. 'I think that I shall go up on to the roof and sit quietly in the cupola for a little. It always helps me to think when I am up there.'

'You'll do no such thing,' Eliza said, stopping her hand before she could scoop up the negligee. 'If Lord Quinlan sees you in that get-up, it'll be more than kisses you'll be getting, Miss Cassie, and no mistaking! If you really must think, then sit by the window. It's the same view as you get on the roof and a fair sight more comfortable.'

After Eliza had gone, Cassie slipped behind the curtains and curled up on the window seat. She opened the sash so that she could feel the cool night air. The shadows of the trees tossed in the ragged moonlight tonight.

Yet, despite the wildness of the evening, it seemed that Cassie was not the only one suffering from insomnia that night. The inhabitants of Lyndhurst Chase seemed to be out and about. Cassie saw one of the maids—she thought it was Sarah's maid, Dent—come out of shadows and creep across the courtyard in a very furtive manner. She heard the cheerful tones of Eliza upraised on the night air, answered by the gruff voice of Timms, Anthony's valet. And as she was about to retreat to the warmth of her bed, she saw a gentleman's figure detach itself from the darkness at the corner of the house and slide like a ghost behind the yew hedge. Cassie sat up straighter. Something about the set of his shoulders and the way he moved made her think it might be Peter, and she found she was smiling to think that she might be the cause of *his* insomnia. Perhaps he ached for her too and had gone out to take the air before trying to sleep.

Then the shadow of a lady slipped by from a different direction and hurried behind the yews after the man. There was a faint scuffle of gravel; a laugh, cut off quickly, and Cassie found herself subject to a wave of searing jealousy that started at her toes and swept up to her throat, bringing the heat into her cheeks and a sick anger with it. How *dare* Peter Quinlan come to Lyndhurst Chase to court her, then take his pleasure with one of the maids? How dare he! It might be the way that rakish London gentlemen felt they could behave, but it was certainly not acceptable to Cassie.

Without further ado, she stormed out of her bedchamber and down the broad oak stairs, her slippers pattering on its wooden treads. She raced down the corridor and knocked on the door of Peter's room. She was fully expecting there to be no reply; when a low masculine voice bade her enter, she was stunned.

The voice spoke again, a hint of impatience in the tone this time. 'Come in!'

Then the door was flung open from within and Cassie found herself face to face with Peter. He was dressed— or rather undressed—in nothing but his pantaloons and shirt, which was open at his throat, the neckcloth discarded. That in itself was enough to hold her silent. There was a mixture of amusement and unqualified surprise on his face as he saw her. Behind him, Cassie could see a candle lit on the table beside the bed, the bedcovers rumpled as though Peter had been lying on top of them and a book lying face down on the bedspread.

Peter was alone. He had been reading. He was not out in the garden dallying with the maids. The discoveries jostled for space in Cassie's head whilst Peter waited and she groped for words to explain herself.

'It's you!' Cassie took a step back. As an opening gambit she was aware that it was not very satisfactory.

'Yes,' Peter said cordially, his interested gaze missing no detail of Cassie's unorthodox attire. 'Was there something that I can do for you, Miss Ward?'

'Yes! That is, no!'

Cassie was so confused to find him there when she was expecting him to be absent *in flagrante* that she knew she was making no sense. Then, while she gaped, a door opened stealthily down the corridor and Peter caught her arm and pulled her into his room in one quick movement, closing the door behind them.

'What on earth are you doing?' Cassie demanded, recovering her senses.

'I am avoiding scandal. What are *you* doing,' Peter countered, 'knocking on the doors of gentlemen's bedchambers in the middle of the night?'

'It is not the middle of the night,' Cassie argued, 'and it was only the one bedchamber. Yours!'

'The question still remains,' Peter said. He folded his arms. He looked unyielding and Cassie had the sudden conviction that she had got herself rather deep into difficulties entirely through her own impulsiveness.

'You never think about the consequences,' Eliza had said to her, and once again her maid had been proved right.

Cassie gulped. 'I was not expecting to find you here,' she said.

Peter raised one black brow. 'Then why come looking for me in the first place?'

It seemed a logical question. Cassie fidgeted with the ribbons on her peignoir as she tried out and rejected various replies.

'Because I wanted to know—' She stopped and started again. 'Oh dear…I thought I saw you out in the gardens, you see.'

'I am sorry, but I do not see.'

Cassie was torn between embarrassment at her predicament and irritation at his obtuseness. The one thing that did not occur to her was to prevaricate. Though it was humiliating to admit it, she had to tell him the truth. 'I thought you were with someone,' she said crossly. 'Out in the gardens.'

Comprehension and amusement leapt into Peter's face. 'I see now.'

'This,' Cassie said, 'is quite mortifying.' She surreptitiously backed towards the door. 'I think I should leave.'

Peter came towards her with a very deliberate tread. He stopped when he was a mere couple of feet away and allowed his gaze to travel over her. Cassie suddenly became acutely aware of her tumbled hair, the transparent filminess of her nightdress and peignoir and the very particular way in which Peter was regarding her.

'Mortifying is not the word to describe my feelings at this moment,' he murmured.

Cassie gave a little wail as she remembered Eliza's comment about the peignoir. She retreated further. Peter followed.

'So,' he said thoughtfully, 'you thought that I was involved in dalliance in the garden with another lady?'

'No!' Cassie said, blushing to the roots of her hair.

'Yes, you did. So you came rushing in here to see if your supposition was correct, not expecting to find me.'

'But you are here,' Cassie said, her back coming up against the door panels, 'so evidently I made a mistake.'

'Yes, you did.' Peter was still talking in the same soft tones, but Cassie found them far from soothing. There was something rather dangerous about such quiet absorption, and when Peter leaned one hand against the door, trapping her between the panels and his body, she tried unsuccessfully to flatten herself. Her breath came in quick gasps. She was aware that the tips of her breasts were just brushing Peter's shirt and the friction—and the knowledge of her body's reaction to it—was far too stimulating to be comfortable.

'What I would like to know,' Peter said, 'is why it mattered to you whether or not I was with another lady?'

Cassie forgot her embarrassment briefly in sheer indignation. 'What a ridiculous question!' she said. 'You are here to woo me, Lord Quinlan, not to dally with someone else. Such behaviour is quite unacceptable.'

'So you feel possessive towards me,' Peter pursued.

Cassie frowned. 'Not in the least. It is merely good

the soft material of her peignoir so that he could touch his tongue to the slope of her shoulder. Cassie's insides dissolved. Her legs trembled. She felt her nipples harden still further against the gossamer lightness of the night-dress. Then Peter's hand came up to cup her breast and she slumped against the door in utter weakness.

'I admit it,' she whispered. 'I admit anything that you like…'

She felt Peter smile against her skin as he bent his head to kiss her bare shoulder. 'You are, as always, very honest, Miss Ward,' he said. He moved away from her a little, keeping one arm about her to support her. 'A pity you could not have waited a while longer before you capitulated,' he said, a smile in his voice, 'but there will be time enough for that.'

He raised her hand to his lips and pressed a kiss on the palm. 'Goodnight, Miss Ward.'

Cassie shot out of the bedroom door with a mixture of relief and deep disappointment, and dashed up the stairs to regain the peace of her own bedchamber. Her body was humming. She rained down curses on her own head for the impetuosity that had delivered her to Peter Quinlan's door and on Peter's head for being able to arouse her with the slightest touch. Once again, sleep eluded her. As the clock struck one, and two and three, Cassie thumped her pillows and vowed that tomorrow she would sort the matter out for good. In that moment she promised herself that she would make Peter Quinlan ache for her as she ached for him. She would bring him to his knees.

By the time that morning arrived, Cassie's resolution was strong, but she had not yet devised a plan to put it into action. Peter remained—not aloof, precisely, but maddeningly imperturbable. It seemed that he considered himself quite in control of their courtship. Cassie resolved to throw him off his stride.

The morning was fine and it had become their practice to go riding together immediately after breakfast before joining the other guests for whatever activity was the order of the day. This morning they rode down the North Avenue and turned back to look at the house floating serenely amidst the wood with the golden ball on its cupola catching the sun. A herd of deer crossed their line of sight, paused, and disappeared into the woods.

'Is Quinlan like this?' Cassie asked as they slowed their horses to a dreamy walk and wandered through the woodland glades. The air was thick with sunlight and the smell of late, wild honeysuckle.

'No,' Peter said. She watched his reminiscent smile and realised how fond he was of his inheritance. 'Quinlan is in Yorkshire. The countryside is much bleaker and more rugged than here, but it has a beauty all its own.'

'Yorkshire!' Cassie was startled. 'I had not realised that your estates were in the north.'

'I am afraid so.' Peter smiled at her. 'The first Lord Quinlan was a merchant who loaned a great deal of money to King Charles I. The King felt obliged to ennoble him, but did not want such a parvenu anywhere near his court so he gave him lands in Yorkshire instead.'

Cassie laughed. 'But you have other estates elsewhere, do you not?'

'In Devon and Kent, but Quinlan Court is our main seat.' Peter glanced at her. 'Attending to Quinlan requires a great deal of time away from London, I fear.'

'What a pity,' Cassie said, with a wicked sideways

smile at him. 'That would not suit me at all. I am so *very* attached to the events of the Season, you know.' She could tell from the look he gave her that he was not sure if she meant it.

'Is that so?' he said easily, after a moment. 'Then I am wondering why have I never met you at any of those events…'

'My chaperon only permits me to attend the most respectable of balls and parties,' Cassie said. 'It is unlikely that I should meet you there.'

'How so?'

'Because, as I mentioned to you at our very first meeting, you have something of a rake's reputation, my lord. Although…' Cassie put her head on one side and viewed him thoughtfully '…your attire is so modest that many ladies might mistakenly consider you quite harmless. Is that deliberate?'

'It is the deliberate effect of poverty,' Peter said, smiling, 'nothing more.'

They had reached a small meadow encircled by trees, where the grass grew high and the bees buzzed in the clover. Peter swung down from the saddle and held his arms out to lift Cassie down. For one long, dizzying moment her body was held tight against his and then she was set on her feet.

'So do *you* think me a rake?' he continued. 'You might have cause to believe it.'

'Only if you think me a wanton,' Cassie said thoughtfully. 'You might have cause to believe that too.'

'I would never believe that, Cassie.' The ring of truth in Peter's voice put sincerity past question. 'In the inn you had sustained a fall and a blow to the head, not to mention the intoxicating effects of the landlady's cordial.'

'Next you will be telling me that I was not responsible for my own actions,' Cassie said, smiling.

'I suppose that you were not,' Peter said. 'That was why I did not want you to be constrained into marriage with me.'

'Peter,' Cassie said, putting a hand out to him. 'I knew what I did.' She paused. 'I knew very well,' she repeated softly.

They were both very still. The drone of the bees seemed loud in the silence. The rich, abundant smells of late summer filled the air and made Cassie feel quite light-headed. The sun was warm against her face. All her senses seemed to quicken. She wanted Peter to catch her to him and tumble her down in the long grasses. The blood beat swift and light in her veins.

Peter tore his gaze from hers and took a step away from her, and the moment was broken. 'Perhaps we should return to the house, Miss Ward.'

'In a little while,' Cassie said. 'There is something I wanted to ask you first, if I may.'

She seated herself on a broad oak log, spread her skirts demurely about her and looked up at him.

'What would you do with my money if you had possession of it?' she asked.

Peter's face darkened. He made an involuntary gesture. 'Another of your frank questions,' he said ruefully.

'You don't like it, do you?' Cassie said perceptively. She was watching his face. 'You do not like the thought that you would be taking my money.'

'No,' Peter admitted, 'I do not like it.'

He sat down beside her, plucked a blade of grass and turned it over thoughtfully between his fingers. The wind was light today, blowing from the west, warm on their faces. Peter sat forward, rested his elbows on his knees and let his gaze linger on the hazy distant hills.

'I would have to use some of your money to pay off my father's debts,' he said, his voice tight with feeling. 'Papa's health has deteriorated a great deal in the past few years and he has sometimes turned to drink for consolation.' He broke off, the set of his mouth grim.

Cassie touched his sleeve in a quick compassionate gesture. 'I am sorry. I did not know. Has it been difficult for you?' She held her breath as she waited to see if they had achieved sufficient intimacy for him to give her an honest reply or whether he would turn her away with light words. When he answered her seriously, her heart leapt.

'I do not know how to help him,' Peter admitted, gripping her hand. 'It is the most damnably frustrating thing. The servants do their best, of course. They are devoted to him, but...' He shrugged. 'All I seem able to do is watch and wait for matters to take their inevitable course.'

Cassie shifted closer to him along the seat and for a moment rested her head against his shoulder. It felt broad and comforting, but this time she was the one wanting to comfort him. 'You must have been lonely, watching, trying to help...'

Peter turned his head and pressed a kiss against her hair. 'I was. I am. It frustrates me past bearing.'

'If you bring Quinlan back to prosperity, you will have done much to save your father's legacy,' Cassie said. 'I know it is not the same, but it is something good that could come out of this.'

'Yes,' Peter said, 'I would like to introduce some improvements to the Quinlan estates. They are in a shocking state of neglect. They need new farm buildings and new agricultural methods, new crops, new herds... Once the farms are bringing in an income again I could reinvest the profits.' He turned his head and gave Cassie a self-deprecating smile. 'Have I spent all your fortune yet?'

'Twice over,' Cassie said cheerfully. She wanted to kiss him, but she felt too shy to instigate the embrace. It was not a kiss prompted by desire but the need to offer comfort. Instead she gave his arm a squeeze and got to her feet, shaking out her skirts. 'It sounds like a whole life's work to me, Peter Quinlan.'

A life's work to share...

She saw that he had read her thoughts. Their eyes met and the moment seemed to stretch out between them. The late summer sunshine spun a web of light between them. Peter got slowly to his feet.

Cassie went across to him and put one hand on his chest.

'I do not ask for your undying love, Peter,' she said softly, 'only for your respect and regard. If you can prove to me that you care for me, then I will accept your proposal of marriage and we may rebuild Quinlan together.'

She looked at him for a long moment and saw all the conflict and doubt in his eyes, and beneath it a longing that took her breath away. She was not sure what that meant. Perhaps he did not really wish to marry her, but needed her money, and as an honourable man found this difficult to accept and act upon. She hoped not. She prayed that his doubts sprung from another cause and wished that she had the courage to ask him directly. She hesitated on the brink of it, but in the end realised that for once she did not wish to hear an honest answer, in case it was not to her liking.

Cassie frowned a little, feeling a sudden urge to cry. It had been a monumental decision for her to offer this to him and she was still not wholly certain why she had felt it right to do so now. She did not even know if she had done the right thing. She was acting purely on instinct again; an instinct that told her that there was something between herself and Peter that was strong enough to build a life upon.

Prove to me that you care for me...

Peter felt a rueful laugh break from him. He covered Cassie's gloved hand with his. 'Oh, Cassie... As usual you take my breath away.'

Cassie's expression was earnest. She raised her fingers to his lips in a fleeting gesture, then turned and walked quickly back to where the horses were tethered.

Peter followed more slowly. He already cared deeply for Cassie, but suddenly that did not seem enough. He wanted her; in some deep, hidden part of him he could admit that he needed her desperately. But Miss Cassandra Ward, with her openness and devastating honesty, did not deserve the second-best of a man who merely cared for her. She deserved to be loved wholeheartedly, without artifice and to the exclusion of all else. And, unless he could give her that, then he should not be thinking of making her a declaration. If he wanted Cassie, he was going to have to prove he loved her and prove it to both of them.

Peter stopped. He watched Cassie as she gently stroked the nose of her grey mare and fed her carrots from a secret cache in her pocket. She talked softly to the horse as she did so. The sun was on her face and in her glorious golden-brown eyes.

She looked exactly what she was: warm, generous,

full of life and eminently lovable. Peter's heart, which had been cold for a very long time, lifted just to look upon her. The tantalising prospect of a life lit by Cassie's flame drew him on. If only he could show her that he loved her.

But how did one *prove* that love? It was not a matter of gifts or expensive baubles, particularly when one was an impoverished fortune hunter courting a woman who could buy you up seventeen times over. He could not merely tell her. Words were cheap and easily disbelieved. Somehow he had to find a way to demonstrate his feelings; prove to Cassie Ward that her price was above rubies. Only then could he make her a declaration from the heart.

Chapter Five

Peter was no closer to a solution by dinner that night. Throughout the long meal he sat and watched Cassie as though he could not take his eyes from her. If anyone had asked him what he had eaten, he could not have told them. He could not even explain how his happiness had come to be so bound up with Miss Cassandra Ward and in so short a time. All he knew was that in her company he felt complete and that, now she was found, he could not bear to lose her.

It was after dinner that night, when the rest of the party were taking tea and playing *vingt-et-un*, that Cassie and Peter took a stroll through the parterre and out on to the lawns. The suggestion, made by Cassie, had at first received a firm refusal from Lady Margaret. Looking at Cassie's indignant little form and Lady Margaret's self-satisfied smile, Peter knew that the chaperon was being deliberately obstructive and that Cassie felt frustrated by her obduracy. As Peter had Anthony Lyndhurst's permission to woo Cassie, some kind of latitude might be permitted, but it seemed that Lady Margaret intended to allow none.

'I think,' Sarah Mardon intervened gently, 'that dear

Cassie and Lord Quinlan might be permitted to take a small walk within the parterre, Margaret. I am sure we may trust to Lord Quinlan's honour to behave as a gentleman should.'

Peter thought that Lady Margaret looked fleetingly bored at the concept of men behaving in gentlemanly fashion. 'Just as you wish, Sarah,' she conceded gracefully. 'I am only Miss Ward's chaperon, after all.'

There was a slightly awkward silence. Sarah Mardon looked irritated but determined and Cassie even more so. She grabbed Peter's hand and pulled him out into the corridor that led to the garden door. The sun had set and the last pink streaks lit the western sky as they went down the garden steps.

'I was meaning to ask you,' Cassie said hesitantly, after they had gone a little way in silence. 'You never drink very much, do you, Peter? I was watching you at dinner. You are very abstemious. Is that because of your experience with your father?'

Once again her perception silenced him. For years he had been prey to the dread that one day he would find his drinking slipping beyond his control, that one glass of brandy would imperceptibly become a bottle, two bottles, three... That the Quinlan estates, whose very survival depended on him dragging them out of neglect before it was too late, might be lost forever.

'I suppose that it is something that is always in my mind,' he admitted.

Cassie did not say anything, but she drew closer to him so that their bodies touched, and her presence was comforting and conveyed all the things she did not put into words.

They walked on beneath the huge harvest moon. They reached the end of the parterre and wandered beneath the elm trees down the western avenue. Neither of them spoke, but the silence was happy. The moonlight fell on the leaves and dappled the grass beneath their feet.

'I sometimes wish that I had a brother or sister, you know,' Cassie said, tucking her arm companionably through Peter's as they wove their way between the trees. 'Then I see the way that William and John strike sparks off each other and think that it might not be comfortable at all.'

'The atmosphere at dinner was certainly very strained,' Peter agreed. He had felt awkward as an outsider in such an unhappy family gathering. 'Have they quarrelled?'

'Over money, I expect,' Cassie said, sighing. 'William racks up the most tremendous debts and John is so upright and reliable it is enough to give him apoplexy!'

'There were seldom two brothers more dissimilar,' Peter commented. He had huge respect for the Earl of Mardon and significantly less for William Lyndhurst-Flint.

'It is doubly unfortunate since Anthony is considering whether to make William his heir,' Cassie said, brow wrinkling. 'He does not expect to remarry or have children of his own and I think he has a kindness for William since they were both younger sons without prospects.'

'Yet surely he must see his weaknesses?' Peter asked.

'I think he is not blind to them. But Anthony sees that William needs the money more than John does, or I do, or Marcus…'

'Marcus Sinclair?'

'Yes, do you know him? He is another of my cousins.'

'We have met,' Peter said. He smiled. 'Sinclair is a good man.'

'I thought that he would be here for the house party,' Cassie said thoughtfully. 'I cannot think what has happened to him.'

'Did Lyndhurst invite no other guests?' Peter asked.

'Only Ned Devereaux,' Cassie said, laughing. 'He is a very rude young man. He does nothing but drink and gamble. He disappeared without even saying goodbye.'

'Not a candidate for your hand in marriage, then,' Peter said. He was resigned by now to the intense possessiveness that such a thought aroused in him.

Cassie shot him a look. 'Would that concern you, Peter? I dare say he wishes for a rich wife, but I fear that I am not she.'

Peter smiled, drawing her gently around to face him. 'I am glad to hear it. I am jealous of any man who comes within ten yards of you, Cassandra Ward. They had better keep their distance.'

Cassie's smile was serene in the moonlight. 'How fierce you sound! And what would happen if they did come near me? After all, Lord Anstey danced with me after dinner at Watchstone Hall two nights past.'

Peter's hands tightened on her shoulders. 'He will not do so again.'

Cassie paused. There was a small silence between them. 'Are you making me a declaration, Lord Quinlan?' she enquired.

'No,' Peter said. 'Not until I can *prove* to you that I care for you, Miss Ward.'

And then she was in his arms and he was kissing her as he had dreamed of kissing her all week. Cassie pressed closer to him, tousling his hair with her fingers and pressing little kisses over his face until he turned his head and claimed her mouth with his own again, hungrily, demanding satisfaction. She felt deliciously soft

and yielding against his hardness. A picture came into
his mind of her, wanton and ruffled as she had been in
the inn at Lynd, her buttons undone, her gown sliding
off one shoulder. He could not help himself. He coaxed
the bodice of her dress down and raised one hand to cup
her breast.

Cassie caught his shoulders, arching against him. He
pushed her gently backward until she came up against
the broad trunk of one of the lime trees. Her head fell
back and he tangled one fist in her thick chestnut hair
to draw it aside and expose the slender line of her throat.
He doubted that she understood the effect that she had
on him, but the truth was that she made him burn with
her smooth skin and her silky hair and those sweet,
sweet breasts…

Peter bent his head and took one nipple in his mouth,
flicking it lightly with his tongue, sucking and biting
gently. Cassie trembled. She put her hands back, feeling
the rough bark of the tree trunk against her palms, her
nails scoring the wood as the sensations uncoiled within
her. For a long, dizzying interval she gave herself up to
the pleasure of intimacies she had never even imagined,
and then the cool evening breeze ruffled along her naked
skin and she shivered convulsively until Peter drew her
close against the hardness of his body and she shivered
again with latent desire and turned her face to his again
for another kiss.

They clung together with the discovered passion of
two people who had once thought that they might be
making a marriage of convenience, but found that they
had a deep need for one another.

'You bring me to my knees, Cassie,' Peter said, when
finally he paused for long enough to draw breath.

To his surprise Cassie laughed, a delighted and spontaneous giggle. 'Oh, good,' she said. 'That was exactly what I had planned.'

Peter stayed outside for a little after Cassie had gone back into the house. Leaving aside the impropriety of them both appearing together, looking as though they had been exploring each other rather than the gardens, there were purely practical reasons why he needed some time to recover before anyone saw him.

The wind was rising in the woods now and there was the threat of thunder in the air. Peter walked slowly through the parterre and made his way back on to the terrace, pausing for one final look out across the moonlit gardens.

A voice spoke close by. '…saw them together in the gardens just now. I may as well kiss that fortune goodbye…'

It was a man's voice, but Peter was not sure which member of the house party was speaking, nor where he was. At first he thought that he was not alone on the terrace, but then realised that the conversation was taking place above his head, in a first-floor bedroom whose window was open and whose occupants no doubt did not realise how their voices carried on the night air.

'I have a plan.' This was a woman now. 'If it does not serve, then I fear that you are on your own, my dear, but until then do not repine. The money may yet be yours.'

Peter felt a cold shiver trickle down his spine like a shard of ice. Those light, cool tones surely belonged to Lady Margaret Burnside. Peter had never felt that Lady Margaret had Cassie's interests close to her heart and now he was certain that it was Cassie's fortune that she was referring to.

He missed the next few words but then there was a peal of laughter from above and Lady Margaret's voice again.

'My dear William, I think not! I explored all your secrets years ago and I have other interests now. Someone a deal more exciting than you, my dear…'

Peter turned on his heel and strode back indoors. He had no wish to eavesdrop of Lady Margaret's amorous secrets. He was not surprised to discover that she and William Lyndhurst-Flint were old lovers. They seemed to have a great deal in common.

He could hear Mardon and Lyndhurst chatting over a glass of brandy behind the closed doors of the library, but he had no inclination to join them, preferring the solitude of his room and time to think about Cassie. He went slowly up the broad oak stairs. On the first-floor landing he saw Cassie's maid deep in conversation with Timms, Anthony's valet. Timms had been the Major's batman during the wars and Peter knew him from that time. He raised a hand in greeting and went into his bedroom.

As soon as he was over the threshold he stopped dead. Something was wrong. His soldier's instinct for danger, dormant for several years, sprang to life. He closed the door quietly behind him and stood listening. Someone was waiting for him in the room.

'Good evening, my lord.'

There was the rustle of silk from the bed and he turned to see Lady Margaret Burnside uncoil herself with sinuous elegance and slither off the bed to stand before him. She was wearing a clinging gown of jade gauze that seemed to outline and accentuate every last curve of her figure. She must have come directly from William Lyndhurst-Flint's room.

Peter looked at her. There was a triumphant knowledge in her eyes as she confronted him, the knowledge of a woman who was completely confident of her own attractions. Her tongue came out and licked slowly over her lower lip.

'I am finding this house party confoundedly boring,' she drawled, drawing close to Peter, 'and I thought that if you were also finding the entertainment tame, my lord, we might amuse one another...'

She moved so close that her breasts were brushing against his chest. Peter could smell the overpowering scent of violets emanating from her body. It did not mask the feral scent beneath. Even less appealing was the smell of alcohol on her breath. He took a step back. He was not shocked or even particularly surprised to find her here. He had met plenty of women like Lady Margaret Burnside, women who were lascivious and amoral, but seldom had he met one who could conceal that corruption beneath so faultlessly respectable a façade. The only emotion that he felt as he looked at her was a species of anger that Lyndhurst and Mardon had not realised the truth and thought that this woman was good enough to chaperon their cousin.

'I doubt that we share the same taste in entertainment, madam,' he said coldly. 'And whatever you are looking for, I assure you, you will not find it here.'

He saw her eyes narrow with calculation and a shade of resentment. It appeared that she was not accustomed to rejection. She trailed her fingers down his shirtfront. Peter's skin crawled. He raised his hand and brushed her questing fingers aside.

'Are you certain you cannot help me?' Lady Margaret's voice had sunk to a throaty purr. 'You will find me a deal more exciting than your innocent little bride.' She paused. 'And she need never know. It could be our secret.'

Peter moved away. The memory of Cassie's touch, the sweet taste of her and the scent of her hair still filled his senses. Her warmth and generosity filled his heart. He felt nothing but repulsion for her chaperon.

'You mistake, madam,' he said. 'I find Miss Ward entirely delightful and I have no desire to have any secrets from her.'

'I am sure you find the prospect of her money delightful,' Lady Margaret agreed drily. 'However, a man with a rake's reputation surely needs more than a milksop maid to keep him satisfied.'

Peter's lips thinned. 'I am not sure how much plainer I may be without giving offence, madam. You must forgive me if I am too blunt. I am not interested in your offer. Kindly leave my room.'

Lady Margaret paused a moment. Her eyes had narrowed like those of an angry cat. If she had had a tail, she would have been swishing it.

'Very well, my lord,' she said, 'but a word about secrets…' She placed a hand on his arm and it was all Peter could do not to shake her off violently. 'There are some matters that are best kept from your future wife. If you were to tell her about this evening, for example, then I would feel obliged to claim that it was *you* who attempted to seduce *me*. Your situation with Miss Ward is all too fragile, is it not, and I am certain you would not wish to see all that delicious fortune disappear over the horizon…'

She gave him another razor-sharp smile and slipped out of the room.

Peter sat down on the edge of his bed. He was taken aback to find his blood buzzing with anger. That such a cold-hearted, amoral woman was Cassie's closest female companion seemed outrageous to him. Lady Margaret's utter lack of loyalty and scruple appalled him and her cold, calculated attempts at seduction disgusted him.

He remembered the conversation that he had overheard between Lady Margaret and William Lyndhurst-Flint. Had this been Lady Margaret's plan—to seduce him and then denounce him before everyone? If so, she had taken a grave gamble and one that had failed to pay off. Peter rubbed one hand across his brow. He had the disquieting feeling that Lady Margaret Burnside had not finished with him yet.

His gaze fell on his portmanteaux. The bags did not look to be in quite the same position as when he was last in the room. A chill tiptoed down his spine. Suddenly urgent, he crossed the room and dragged the cases out of their corner, reaching inside the smaller one for the pocket book that held the special licence. He took it out and flicked it open.

It was empty.

It was not difficult to achieve an interview with Lady Margaret Burnside the following morning. Indeed, Peter suspected that she was waiting for him to approach her. It had taken a great deal of self-control not to go after her the previous night and demand that she return his property. But that would have been playing into her hands and he was determined not to give her any advantages.

That morning the house party guests were to go riding on the Downs and take a light picnic luncheon to eat at an ancient historical site called Cuthbert's Castle. Peter was first down into the hall after breakfast, and, though

Lady Margaret was not one of the riding party, she was waiting for him.

It was not private, but he took his chance. 'Good morning, madam.'

Lady Margaret gave him a melting smile. 'Good morning, my lord. But perhaps you do not find it a very pleasant morning? You look as though you did not sleep well. Perhaps there are matters on your mind?'

Peter looked at her. This morning she looked like the cat with the cream. 'I am certainly concerned that an item in my possession appears to have gone missing last night,' he said grimly. 'I wondered whether you had any idea of its whereabouts, madam?'

Lady Margaret cast her eyes down with false modesty. 'Indeed, I have no notion to what you refer, Lord Quinlan. How should I?'

Her deliberate evasions infuriated Peter. 'I fear that I do not believe you, madam. I think you know precisely to what I refer. I believe you found it last night when—'

'When I was in your bedchamber?' Lady Margaret finished sweetly. 'Let us not speak of that in public, my lord. I am happy to reassure you that you have nothing to fear from me. I shall be discreet! I have no desire to upset your marriage plans.'

Some element of triumph in her face or voice caused the hairs to stand up on the back of Peter's neck. He spun around. Cassie was standing on the bottom stair. Her eyes were wide in an ashen face. It was horribly clear that she had overheard Lady Margaret's last words. Peter's heart gave a lurch. He cursed himself for the lack of patience that had given Lady Margaret this opportunity.

He started forward. 'Cassie...'

Lady Margaret gave Peter a knowing smile and drifted away. The rest of the party were clattering down the staircase, chatting loudly.

'Cassie…' Peter said again, reaching out to her desperately. Her face was blank with shock. It was as though she did not even see him. All her hopes and fears were there for him to see in that instant, and he knew Lady Margaret had shattered them all with her deliberate spite.

The others milled around them. There was no opportunity to talk or get Cassie on her own. Peter felt desperation rise in him. Lyndhurst started to engage him in conversation and he responded automatically, watching Cassie all the while. The horses had already been brought to the door. Sarah Mardon swept Cassie down the steps with her and out into the courtyard. As though to make matters worse, William Lyndhurst-Flint fell in beside Peter and tried him sorely with his light attempts at man-to-man conversation. Peter could see Cassie riding up ahead, her back very firmly turned to him.

He finally caught up with her when they reached the racecourse on the top of the Downs and dismounted to consider the view. Peter spared the rolling scenery a half-second glance, then caught Cassie's arm and drew her into the shelter of the rubbing house.

'I must speak with you,' he said.

Cassie was still pale, but at least she was seeing him now. His heart lifted a little with hope that she might at least listen to him.

'Not here,' she said, her mouth setting obstinately.

'Yes, here,' Peter said. He was as tense as a coiled spring. 'I am not prepared to wait for some convenient moment.' He could feel the stiffness in her. Her body was poised for flight. He held her tightly.

'It is true that Lady Margaret came to my chamber last night,' he said rapidly, knowing that nothing but the absolute truth would do now. He felt shock rip through Cassie like a flood tide; felt her tremble. So she had not quite believed it of him until now. It seemed cold comfort when she would think that he had just confirmed her worst fears.

'I see,' she said dully.

'I doubt that you do,' Peter said. 'I sent her away. Nothing happened between us. I swear it.'

Cassie's eyes were smoky with doubt. 'I see,' she said again.

'It is you that I want—' Peter started to say, then stopped as he saw the cynicism in her eyes.

'Of course,' she said.

He shook her slightly. 'No! Not for the money. Damn it, Cassie, I would marry you without a penny! I love you! I just do not know how to prove it to you—'

There was the crunch of gravel underfoot and William Lyndhurst-Flint came around the side of the building. Never had a man been more unwelcome.

'Sorry to interrupt, old chap,' Lyndhurst-Flint said with patent insincerity, 'but there is a storm blowing up. We thought it better to return to the house and arrange some alternative entertainment for today. Didn't want you to get left behind, you know.'

Cassie freed herself from Peter's grasp. She gave him a long, thoughtful look. 'We may talk later, Lord Quinlan.'

'Hope there's nothing wrong, old fellow,' Lyndhurst-Flint said, smirking slightly as he watched Cassie walk away. 'Terrible shame for you if it were all to go awry—'

Peter gave him such a hard stare that he stopped abruptly.

'Your commiserations are received in the same spirit that they were given,' he snapped, and followed Cassie back to where the horses were tethered.

By the time that they were halfway back to the house, the thunderstorm was rolling across the hills at their back. The wind was rising and the first fat drops of rain were starting to fall from the edge of the cloud. Cassie urged her horse to a reckless speed as it plunged down the combe. She wanted to outrace her demons.

Had Peter been telling her the truth? She wanted to believe him, but her wretched money kept getting in the way. She had known him for so short a time and had taken such a great step in deciding to trust herself to him. Now her steps were faltering.

She thought of Lady Margaret, elegant, polished, and not so much older than Peter himself. Cassie had always felt that her chaperon effortlessly achieved all the town bronze that she so significantly lacked. And Peter was used to a more sophisticated society, one in which no doubt there was nothing odd in courting an heiress and bedding a mistress at the same time. Cassie knew that it went on. Just because Peter could set her feelings alight with the slightest touch, she was not naïve enough to think that she was the only one.

She smothered a tiny sob. For a little while she had allowed herself to think that Peter's interest was focused solely on her. She had believed that he loved her. She wrinkled her brow as she wondered why it had always felt such a struggle to gain affection. First she had had to compete with her mother's illness to gain attention, then with all of her cousins' other interests, then with

Lady Margaret's elegance and always, always with her own huge pile of money.

Cassie squared her shoulders. As Eliza had pointed out a little while ago, no good came from feeling sorry for oneself. There were plenty of people who would be glad to suffer the kind of misery that her wealth brought her. Cassie smiled slightly, feeling a little better. The rest of the party were mere specks on the hill behind her. She had outrun them all. She had had some time alone to think and plan. So she would talk to Peter Quinlan and judge for herself whether he was telling the truth. Then she would make her decision. It was all very ordered and decisive. Cassie felt pleased with herself that for once she was approaching matters in entirely the right way. No losing her head and compromising herself, no marching impulsively into a gentleman's bedchamber. A measured, sensible discussion was all that was required.

Chapter Six

The rest of the group caught up with Cassie as she was dismounting on the gravel of the courtyard. It was raining in earnest now and there was no time for chat as they handed the horses over to the grooms and hurried inside.

The house was dark and quiet. Ufton, the butler, was crossing the hall from the library and looked slightly taken aback to see them returned so soon.

'We will take a light luncheon in the dining room in half an hour, if you please, Ufton,' Sarah said. 'It was too inclement for our picnic, I fear. We shall have to go out another day.'

Cassie put a hand out and touched Peter's arm. It was now—before her nerve deserted her—or never.

'I need to speak with you,' she whispered, and saw the flash of relief that crossed his face at her words. He looked tired and strained and her heart twisted with emotion. She gestured across the hall. 'In the library. Please.'

The rest of the party was milling around. Anthony made some mention of a game of billiards. Sarah started towards the staircase to change her clothes before luncheon. Cassie and Peter set off towards the library.

And then there was one of those strange moments that happen even in the most ordered of households when everything appeared to stop.

One of the younger housemaids was coming down the main staircase, carrying her cleaning brushes and fire-box. She looked nervous upon seeing the family, but rather than scuttle towards the backstairs, as Cassie expected her to do, she hesitated, clearly anxious. There was a long silence when everyone seemed to stand waiting and Ufton glared at the girl, evidently shocked and angry that a maid had dared to use the main stairs and had not effaced herself against the wall when her betters had returned.

'What are you doing here, girl?' he snapped. 'Get down the backstairs! At once!'

To Cassie's shock, the maid dropped the brushes, put her hands up to her red cheeks and started to wail. 'I can't, Mr Ufton! I can't! They're occupied!'

The butler strode forward and shook her impatiently by the arm. 'Explain yourself! What are you talking about, child?'

The housemaid had started to cry. 'I can't take the backstairs, sir. They're already in use. I saw the two of them together earlier and no ways am I going down there! Don't make me!' She broke off in a welter of tears.

Ufton looked almost apoplectic as the household discipline fell apart around him—and all in front of his employer. He gave the maid a hard stare that promised retribution, and marched towards the backstairs, throwing the door open so that it bounced on its hinges. The crash reverberated through the house and brought some of the other servants out into the hall to see what was going on.

'Mr Ufton's on the warpath again,' Cassie heard one of the footmen whisper gleefully.

There was a scuffle, a feminine squeak, and then Ufton gave an exclamation of wrath and dragged a figure out through the doorway by the scruff of its neck. Cassie heard William give an exclamation.

'Grant!' William's face stiffened as he saw his valet in Ufton's iron grip. 'What in God's name were you doing down there?'

One of the footmen stifled a guffaw. Cecil Grant smoothed back his hair and ostentatiously adjusted his breeches. There was a very self-satisfied smirk on his face. In that moment it was clear to everyone exactly what he had been doing on the backstairs.

The maid was snivelling and Sarah Mardon had put a comforting arm about her. 'That Mr Grant is a devil with the servants—' the maid gulped '—but since he took up with her ladyship he's been even worse! Like a ravening dog, he is.'

Anthony Lyndhurst put his cousin to one side and strode forward. His voice cracked like a whip. 'Kindly explain yourself, Grant.'

Cecil Grant remained insolently silent. From the staircase below came another feminine shriek and voices upraised in a sudden babble of sound.

'I do believe,' Anthony said grimly, 'that your latest paramour has been caught fair and square down in the kitchens, Grant. I can scarce believe such profligate behaviour with the female servants. *Disgraceful*—'

He broke off abruptly as Timms and Eliza appeared through the door, dragging between them the dishevelled figure of Lady Margaret Burnside. Her hair was falling down, her skirts were crumpled and, most shockingly of all, her bodice was askew and unbuttoned.

'Mr Grant's paramour, Major,' Timms said expressionlessly. 'Found *in flagrante*, so to speak.'

Everyone looked at Lady Margaret, who was trying vainly to force her ample bosom back into her bodice.

'*Lady Margaret!*' Sarah Mardon said in horrified tones.

'I cannot believe it!' Cassie said, shocked to the core. She stared in fascinated disbelief at the once-immaculate figure of her chaperon.

'Trollop!' Eliza had been waiting a long time to have her opinion of Lady Margaret confirmed. 'Hugging and kissing on the backstairs like a common strumpet! Carrying on for days, they have been, but too clever to be caught out 'til now.'

Cassie looked from Lady Margaret to Cecil Grant. 'Oh!' she exclaimed. 'It was Grant I saw you with in the gardens two nights ago, Lady Margaret, not—' She glanced up at Peter and fell silent abruptly.

Anthony's face was like thunder. He turned on the pair. 'You are both dismissed. You will leave this house *at once.*'

William Lyndhurst-Flint started to protest. 'Dash it all, old fellow, what am I supposed to do without a valet?'

'You may use Timms's services if the matter concerns you so much,' Anthony snapped.

William reddened as he glanced at Timms's impassive face. 'No, no—there's no need for that. One of the footmen will do.'

Anthony made a brusque gesture. 'Whatever you wish, just not *now*, William!'

His cousin fell silent, biting his lip.

Lady Margaret was smoothing the disordered skirts of her gown. She looked angry and disdainful. There was a slash of colour high on her cheekbones and her lips were a line of compressed fury as she confronted Anthony. 'You dare to dismiss me like a servant, Major Lyndhurst? I am the Lady Margaret Burnside!'

'You may be the Queen Dowager for all I care, madam,' Anthony said, furiously. 'You will not behave thus in my house!'

Lady Margaret's eyes narrowed. Her gaze swept around the group, travelling from face to face. Cassie's gaze followed. Sarah was looking horrified, with the sobbing maid wilting against her; John Mardon had an expression of absolute distaste on his face as he regarded the chaperon; William was failing to meet her eyes. Cassie took Peter's hand in hers and gripped it hard.

'Very well,' Lady Margaret said slowly. She fumbled in the pocket of her skirt and extracted a crumpled piece of paper, brandishing it in one shaking hand. She turned to Cassie and there was a bright, malicious gleam in her eyes that made Cassie recoil.

'Since I am to be dismissed, it seems that I may do you one favour before I go, Cassandra.' She flashed Peter a look. 'You foolish chit, you have been finely taken in. Lord Quinlan needs to rush you to the altar before the bank forecloses and the family is ruined! He planned it all from the beginning. See...' She held the piece of paper under Cassie's nose.

There was a shocked, deadly silence. Cassie snatched the special licence from Lady Margaret's hand and read it quickly. Her chaperon had been correct; it gave permission for the marriage of Peter Alexander James Quinlan to Miss Cassandra Eleanory Ward and it was dated the week before Peter had come to Lyndhurst Chase. There was no denying it: he had brought the special licence with him. He had been determined to force the marriage through. For all his fine words, it appeared that he had never intended to give her a choice.

She tried to keep her face blank, but she could feel her expression disintegrating slowly. The special licence wilted in her hand. She thought of the night before and the sweetness of Peter's kisses in the moonlight. With all her heart she wanted to believe him sincere, but she had known him so short a time to trust him so absolutely, and she could not bear to have this happen here, now, with all these people watching her.

'I am sorry that your cousin is nothing but a silly little girl,' Lady Margaret was saying stridently to Anthony. 'She is heedless and ungovernable. I suppose it is only to be expected with a mother who cared for nothing but her own ailments and a fortune that came from trade originally and no doubt brought with it some of the other qualities of the ill bred.'

Cassie made a small choking sound. She saw Anthony draw breath to intervene, but he never got the chance to open his mouth, for Peter was before him.

'I beg your pardon,' he said, 'but I believe such remarks on breeding and behaviour fall ill from your lips, madam.'

Cassie gasped. 'I—' she began, but Peter put her gently to one side. There was a look in his eyes that stole her breath with its protectiveness and its fury.

'Just this once,' he said, 'I want to speak for you. I promise I will never do it again.' He moved until he was standing directly between Cassie and Lady Margaret.

'Pretending that she is such a lady,' Lady Margaret was continuing furiously. 'Why, the Ward family is insignificant and nothing distinguishes her but that ridiculous fortune!'

'Miss Ward is your superior in every way, madam,'

Peter said cuttingly, 'and I think that you are well aware of that fact. It takes more than a title and a pretence of morality to make a lady. Lest you forget, we have all seen your behaviour this morning.'

The hall was so quiet that a pin could have been heard to drop as Peter continued in the same measured tones, 'Miss Ward has the goodness and generosity of spirit that you so singularly lack, madam. If ever she has behaved in a manner that you have considered unruly, I suspect it is from sheer frustration at the strictures placed on her.' He widened his gaze to include the rest of the family, who were standing dumbstruck now. His gaze seemed to linger on William Lyndhurst-Flint, who withered a little beneath its coldness.

'I appreciate that most of you care deeply for Cassie and have always acted in what you have regarded to be in her best interests,' Peter said. 'I beg you now to allow her to choose her own future. She has the strength of character to make the right decisions, if you will only permit her the opportunity to do so. Do not force on her a chaperon whom she dislikes. Do not make her marry if she has no wish to do so. If she wants to wait until she is mistress of her own fortune, then please…' he paused and looked around at them '…permit her to make that choice. And as for you, Lady Margaret…' he paused '…I think it best that you go now.'

Unbelievably there was a smattering of ragged applause from the group of servants gathered by the backstairs door. It died swiftly as Anthony's head snapped around to look at them.

Cassie blinked, as though she had stepped into a bright light. Something shifted in her mind then, in the dark corners where all her fears and frustrations had been penned in: the neglected child of the invalid mother, the little girl who wanted to be loved but had secretly considered herself a burden to her relatives, the ungovernable débutante who had done outrageous things for attention and the woman who had only ever been courted for her money... She looked at Peter and saw him neither as a man seeking her fortune nor as a means of escape from a circumscribed existence. He was the man who would stand up for her and speak for her against the whole world because he cared for her alone. The enormity of it all overwhelmed her and there were prickly tears in her eyes and a lump in her throat that prevented her from speaking, but through the tears she looked at Peter and felt her love for him burst free.

Lady Margaret was leaving. Angry, vitriolic to the last, she was edging away from the group and running the gauntlet of the assembled servants.

Peter's face was tense and hard. He looked at Cassie and then shook his head slightly as though there was nothing more that he could say. He went across to Anthony Lyndhurst and held out his hand.

'I beg your pardon, Lyndhurst,' he said. 'I know that I have offended your hospitality. I think it would be better were I to leave.'

And he turned on his heel, brushed past the rest of the group without a word and set off up the stairs.

Everyone looked at Cassie. There was a short silence, and then Anthony, smiling slightly, said, 'What would you like to do, Cassie?'

And Cassie gathered her skirts up in one hand and ran up the staircase after Peter without another word.

She found him in his dressing room, throwing various items randomly into his portmanteaux. She closed the door behind her and stood leaning against it. When he saw her he straightened up and looked at her. There was a hard expression in his eyes.

'I think that you had better leave me to complete my packing,' he said.

Cassie took a deep breath. Her heart was hammering hard and she felt almost light-headed with apprehension, but she was not going to give ground now. She took out the special licence. 'I want to talk to you,' she said.

She saw his face fall at the sight of the incriminating piece of paper, but he said nothing.

'It is true, isn't it,' she said. 'You did bring this marriage licence with you with the intention of sweeping me off my feet.'

'It is true.' Peter threw a pair of shoes in the rough direction of the bag. 'That was my intention.'

'And when we met at the inn,' Cassie pursued. 'You said that you had not planned what happened, but was that a lie?'

'There was never any lie nor any pretence,' Peter said. 'I was bewitched by you, Cassie. I fell in love with you and not your money. The only thing I could not do was prove it to you.'

Cassie's heart leaped at his words, but she kept her tone steady. 'And now?'

'Now I am leaving.'

Cassie came a little closer. 'You will have to find another heiress to court.'

Peter's smile was tired. There were lines on his face that she wanted to reach up and smooth away. She kept quite still. If she touched him she would be lost and never finish what she wanted to say.

'I do not think that would be a very good idea,' Peter said.

'Then you will lose Quinlan Court.'

'Very probably.'

Cassie took a step towards him. She could feel her heart beating. 'If I wanted you to stay…' she began.

His gaze came up to hers. There was an expression in his eyes that made her throat ache. He waited.

'You said that you had not been able to prove to me that you loved me,' she said, and now her voice was not quite steady. 'That is not true. You have proved it to me today.' She looked at him, her gaze pleading with him to understand.

'I should have let you speak for yourself,' Peter said, with the ghost of a smile. 'That, after all, was what I was trying to say.'

Cassie nodded. 'Just this once,' she said, her smile mirroring his, 'I will forgive you. For who else would have spoken up for me and defended me and *understood* me so well as the man who loves me?'

She saw the vivid flash of expression in his face. The boots fell from his hand to crash on the floor and then he was across the room and was kissing her violently. He picked her up and practically threw her on to the bed, following her down into its embracing folds, tangling his hands in her hair, holding her head still so that he could ravish her mouth with feverish need.

Their clothes came off in a storm of ripping material and flying buttons. Peter's hands were on her everywhere and her whole body lifted to meet his touch. The excitement and the urgency slammed through her and she pressed closer to him, a little shudder going through her as she felt the ruthless efficiency with which he removed the last layers of material between them. He pinned her down with his hands on her hips and his mouth was hot on her breast and when he slid inside her, her mind and body splintered simultaneously into tiny fragments and she would have screamed aloud in ecstasy had Peter not covered her mouth with his own. It was over in a few, blinding, desperate, exquisite minutes.

They fell apart, panting, damp with exertion, and Peter tumbled her into his arms and buried his face in her hair.

'I'm sorry,' he said, muffled.

Cassie struggled to free herself sufficiently to see his expression. Her mind was still spinning and her blood pounding, but she was in no doubt that it had been the most blissful experience of her entire life.

'Sorry?' she said. A cold breath of doubt touched her heart. 'Was it not meant to be like that?' she enquired politely.

She saw his rueful smile. He looked heartbreakingly dishevelled and worried and so utterly delicious that she felt her insides melt to look on him.

'No, my darling, it was not,' he said. 'The first time with one's innocent bride is supposed to be slow and gentle and considerate—' He broke off as Cassie gave an unladylike snort of laughter and rolled over, entangling the twisted sheet about her naked body.

'Gentle!'

'I know. I wanted you too much. I've always wanted you—from the very first.'

Cassie's laughter stilled and she put a hand out and touched his lips. The expression in his face changed. He slid a hand around the nape of her neck and swiftly, inexorably drew her face down for his kiss.

'Like this,' he said, in the second before his lips touched hers.

Cassie held him to her as he kissed her, rubbing her hands over the smooth skin of his back, distracted by

the satiny feel of him under her palms. When he broke
the kiss she pulled away a little.

'Peter, should we not talk now?'

'No,' Peter said, and he took her mouth again before
she could argue with him, kissing her until she was
breathless. The hard, lean length of him was pressed
against her and Cassie wriggled closer still, a gasp escaping from her as he pinned her down beneath his
weight.

'Peter…'

'My love?' He bent his head to her breast. The heat
flooded through her, intense, pleasurable. Cassie gave a
little moan.

'Peter…'

His fingers slid up the soft skin of her thigh, slyly
stroking, then slickly inside her. Cassie arched and
squirmed as the sensation pulsed deep within her. She
was tantalised, ravished, silenced. She turned her face to
his in mute appeal, shifting her body eagerly to accom-
modate his until he answered the unspoken plea and
eased himself inside her again, this time slowly and with
utter tenderness. But then Cassie caught him to her and
raked her fingernails down the hard muscles of his back
and the whole thing became most ungentle and his gasp
of urgent pleasure turned her feelings inside out. The
sheer excitement and power of it sent her tumbling over
the edge into absolute delight, pulling Peter with her as
she fell.

And after that they slept for a long time.

Cassie awoke to find the sheets tangled about her in
wanton disarray, her clothes scattered across the floor
and Peter's arm lying across her in careless possession.
She felt so happy that she held her breath for a long

moment, afraid to burst the bubble. Then Peter turned his head on the pillow and opened his eyes and smiled at her.

'Cassie? Sweetheart…'

'We must get up!' Cassie shot up in bed as she realised how late it was. 'We have done this all the wrong way round. I never get things right!'

'It felt very right to me,' Peter murmured, holding her still. He pressed his lips to the damp skin in the hollow above her collarbone.

'But we were supposed to get married first and now everyone will know what has been going on and we have missed luncheon and probably dinner as well.' Cassie covered her face with her hands. In her mind was a vision of the entire population of Lyndhurst Chase lined up outside the bedroom door like a disapproving reception committee.

Peter took her hands gently away from her face.

'My darling, you may have forgotten, but I have a special licence that has been hidden away in my pocket for two weeks—apart from the time it has spent in Lady Margaret's possession, of course.'

'Hmm…' Cassie said. She started to feel a little easier. 'I suppose that it would be a pity to waste it when you went to so much trouble to bring it in the first place.'

Peter leaned on one elbow and looked down into her face, smoothing the unruly hair away gently.

'Indeed it would. And since I have just taken you without benefit of clergy, my love, I intend to remedy that as soon as possible.' He kissed the side of her breast. 'If you still want to marry me, that is.'

Cassie smiled radiantly into his eyes. 'I think that would be rather splendid,' she said. She pushed him gently away as his caresses threatened to distract her.

'Let us make haste to find the vicar,' she said, 'and then perhaps we may think about doing this again—more slowly this time.'

'We can certainly try,' Peter said.

The wedding was a very private affair in the church at Lynd with Anthony and Eliza as witnesses, John and Sarah representing the rest of the family and Timms attending on behalf of the servants. As the solemn words of the marriage service were exchanged, Cassie saw Eliza give Timms one speaking look, then turn aside surreptitiously to wipe a tear from her cheek on the pretext of sniffing the bouquet of late summer roses that she was holding. Timms's face was even more impassive than ever, his bearing stiff and soldierly, but beneath it Cassie thought that she sensed a certain emotion. She wondered whether Eliza would ever achieve that home and family for which she longed.

The wedding breakfast back at the Chase was a triumph of culinary expertise whipped up at a moment's notice and later they all retired to the ladies' sitting room to sit and chat contentedly about the day.

'I am planning on holding a fireworks party up on the roof as part of our celebrations,' Anthony said later, smiling at Cassie. 'I thought it most apt, and a fine culmination to our house party.'

'Great-aunt Harriet will be sick as a cushion to have missed the wedding and all your entertainments here,' Cassie said mischievously. 'You had best break the news to her gently, Anthony, or you will never hear the end of it.'

Anthony groaned. 'She will hear of it soon enough, Cass. I had this letter from her only this morning.'

He passed a sheet of stiff paper across to Cassie. She immediately recognised the sharp, black writing:

'I am astounded that you did not see fit to invite me to Lyndhurst Chase for your house party, Anthony. Such a breach of manners would never have occurred in my younger days, but I fear that your generation are sadly lacking in courtesy... I can only be charitable and assume that my invitation was sent and failed to reach me. On that understanding I am setting out for Berkshire immediately...'

Cassie giggled. 'Oh, no! Great-aunt Harriet will be with us any day! How diverting. If one is looking for fireworks, look no further!'

'Diverting is one word for it,' Anthony said morosely. For a moment he seemed sunk in gloom, then roused himself a little. 'Are we to enjoy your company for at least a short while before you take your wedding trip, Quinlan?'

'A few weeks, perhaps,' Peter said, 'to give me the opportunity to organise something appropriate.' He smiled at Cassie. 'If you do not mind, Lyndhurst?'

'Delighted, old fellow,' Anthony said. He saw the way that Cassie was pulling on Peter's arm, practically trying to drag him from the room. 'Do not let me hold you up now, though,' he said with a resigned look. 'I imagine that the two of you will be wanting to...ah...spend some time alone. Better go before my cousin quite wrenches your arm from the socket, old chap, in her desperation to have you all to herself.'

'Poor Anthony,' Cassie said, as they went up the oaken stairs to bed. 'I do believe today has been very hard for him. Did you see the look on his face when we were in church? I swear he must have been thinking of Georgiana, for he could not quite disguise his unhappi-

ness. I wish—' She broke off, shaking her head. 'I want
him to be happy too!'

'I know,' Peter said, stopping to kiss her. 'You want
everyone to be as happy as you are.'

'Yes! For then there is poor Eliza as well.'

Peter put a finger to her lips. 'You cannot manage
everyone's life for them, Cassie, no matter how you wish
it! You can only let matters take their course. And who
knows what might happen?'

'I suppose so.' Cassie snuggled closer. 'And for tonight I am very content to concentrate on my own af-
fairs.'

They had reached the door of their room and Peter
carried Cassie across the threshold before putting her
down gently. She turned up her face for his kiss, but for
a moment he stood gazing down at her before he took
a step back in an oddly formal manner.

'Cassie,' he said, 'there is something that I must give
you. I should have done it sooner but then, as you so
rightly pointed out, we have done things the wrong way
round.' From the pocket of his jacket he took a battered
little box and held it out to her. Cassie took it and opened
it slowly, her eyes widening in wonder as she saw the
sapphire ring that nestled in the velvet bed within.

'It was my mother's betrothal ring,' Peter said, adding
apologetically, 'it is the only item of family jewellery
that my father has not sold or pawned.'

Cassie slipped it on to her finger and smiled mistily
at him. 'It is very beautiful, Peter. It means a very great
deal to me.'

'I brought it with me,' Peter said, 'along with the special licence.' He cleared his throat. 'There is something
else,' he said.

Cassie's eyes widened as she searched his face.

'You may remember that you said a little while ago that you did not ask for my undying love, only my respect and regard?'

'I remember,' Cassie whispered.

'Well, I fear that you have it anyway,' Peter said. 'My undying love is yours to do with as you will.' He watched as the delicious smile lit her eyes and curved her lips and he felt a huge surge of love swell within him and almost crush him with its pure intensity.

Cassie saw it, too, reflected in his eyes. Her own were brimming with happy tears. She took a step forward and touched his cheek. 'Oh, Peter, you idiot!' she said. 'I love you too.'

'So romantic,' Peter murmured, and then he picked her up in his arms and carried her to the bed and demonstrated his undying love for her in the most blissful and thoroughly satisfactory way imaginable.

AN UNCOMMON ABIGAIL

Joanna Maitland

Chapter One

Amy Devereaux paused outside the door to the master bedchamber and listened. Nothing. Nor should there be. The master of the house was at dinner with all his guests. Amy herself had seen his valet below stairs not five minutes before, comfortably settled with a decanter of port. And since poor Major Lyndhurst had no wife to warm his bed, there was no one else who had reason to be in his bedchamber.

Still, Amy hesitated.

She put her hands to her huge, ugly cap to ensure it was still straight. A tiny wisp of hair had escaped just above her right ear. Ruthlessly, she tucked it away. No one must see her hair. Its silver-blonde colour was much too memorable. As were her violet-blue eyes, even hidden behind thick spectacles. Either might lead some of those above stairs to look *at* her, instead of *through* her, as they normally did. And that could be a disaster for her role as Amelia Dent, high-class dresser to the noble Countess of Mardon.

Amy's heart was racing. She reached for the door handle and turned. It slipped under her damp palm. Goodness, she was nervous. She rapidly wiped her hand on the skirt of her plain, loose-fitting gown.

Deep breath. Turn the handle. Walk into the chamber as if you had every right to be there. And if anyone should be there to challenge you, you have only to say that you are on an errand for your mistress and must have mistaken the room. Do it now!

In a trice, Amy was inside and had closed the door at her back. She let out a long breath. Although it was still light outside, the curtains were tightly closed. With no candles burning, there was only the light of the fire to see by. Amy stood for a moment, waiting for her eyes to adjust to the gloom, then scanned the huge empty chamber. Everything was in immaculate order. Except that a tall screen stood between the door and the fireplace, no doubt to keep the draught from the Major while he took his bath.

Oh, heavens! What if the maids had yet to come to empty it?

With pounding heart, Amy moved swiftly towards the fireplace. She dared not search the room until she had checked the bath.

'Good evening.'

Amy let out a gasp and stopped dead. There, standing in the bath tub in front of the fire, was a totally naked man.

'Hand me that towel, will you?'

Amy could not move. Her throat was suddenly so tight that she could barely breathe. Her skin seemed to be on fire.

Every last inch of it.

'Are you deaf, woman? The towel, if you please.'

For a long, dangerous moment, Amy could not tear her gaze from his naked body. Eventually, she forced herself to bow her head and close her eyes against the sight. But the image was still there, engraven on her mind. The first naked man she had ever seen. Leashed power under smooth skin, shimmering with the last drops of moisture from his bath.

He had grown tired of waiting. With an oath, he stepped out of the bath and reached for the huge towel hanging in front of the fire.

But he made no move to wrap it round his naked body. Instead, he turned back to Amy, the towel dangling from his fingers. He looked at her searchingly, studying her scarlet face for a long moment and then allowing his gaze to roam slowly over her body. Even in the half-light, he was stripping her with his eyes. As if she were as naked as he!

At last, his eyes came back to her slightly bowed head. They were hard eyes. Assessing eyes. 'Who are you?' he snapped. 'What are you doing here?'

Amy swallowed nervously, not daring to look directly at him. Her brain was refusing to function. She could not think. And she certainly could not speak.

He cursed again. More vehemently this time. Then, with a single supple movement, he put his hands to Amy's shoulders and drew her towards him. She could feel the soft warmth of the towel against the skin of her neck. And the strength of his long fingers biting into the flesh of her shoulders through her coarse gown.

'Perhaps this will restore your voice,' he murmured softly.

And then he lowered his mouth towards hers.

Amy was too shocked to pull away. She felt, for a second, as if she were dreaming. A misty dream filled with the subtle scents of soap and clean skin. Then the dream burst into life. With vivid colour. And the warmth of his mouth hovering just above her own. Amy's parched lips seemed to open of their own accord, and she ran her tongue over her bottom lip.

'No,' he said softly against her mouth. 'Tempting…but no.' He put her brusquely away from him and busied himself with the towel.

Amy found herself staring at the floor with wide, unseeing eyes. What on earth had happened to her? Why had she done nothing to stop him?

The man now had his back to her. He was bent towards the fire, towelling his legs. She must have made a sound of some kind, for he turned his head to look up at her. His expression was a mixture of boredom and distaste. 'For such a knowing piece,' he said harshly, 'you are remarkably tongue-tied. Do you make a habit of offering yourself to your betters? We are not all so easily taken in, you know.' He straightened. Then he wrapped the towel around the lower half of his body.

At last!

'I did not—' Amy's voice cracked. She took a deep breath and swallowed hard. 'You are mistaken, sir. And your words are insulting.' She risked one quick glance at his face.

He raised his eyebrows. 'Indeed?'

Stupid, stupid! No servant would ever say such a thing to a gentleman. Even when it was true! 'I beg your pardon, sir, but you…you have done me an injustice. I did not do…what you suggested. My mistress is a visitor in this house and I…I mistook the room. I must go. My mistress will be wondering what has become of me.' Amy turned for the door.

'One moment.'

The urge to flee was strong, but Amy curbed it. She

did not turn back to him, however. She was afraid to meet those penetrating eyes.

'We both know that your employer does not need you at present. She will have gone down to the dining room long since. Just who is this mistress of yours?'

'The Countess of Mardon. I am her ladyship's personal maid.' Amy put as much pride into her voice as she could.

'Are you, indeed? Well, well. And what is your name, pray?'

'Dent, sir.' Amy turned back to face him then. She must focus on the part she played. A high-class servant would not cower, even in the face of such an intimidating man. She straightened her shoulders, but kept her eyes demurely lowered.

His head was cocked slightly to one side as he assessed her. His long fingers were stroking his jaw absently. Even in the gloom, Amy could tell that he had not shaved for at least a week, perhaps longer. His wet hair hung almost to his shoulders. Who on earth was he? What was he doing in Major Lyndhurst's chamber? And bathing, of all things?

'I was not aware that another guest had arrived,' Amy said politely. She was pleased at how calm she sounded. 'Do you expect to make a long stay, sir?'

She had surprised him into a sharp laugh. 'Why, if I did not know better, Dent, I should almost have thought you were a lady born. Many a débutante could do no better. I congratulate you.'

Amy felt herself blushing with embarrassment all over again. Or was it anger at her own hasty tongue? She could not afford to be unmasked. She had risked too much to come this far.

She dropped him a servant's curtsy. 'If you will excuse me, sir, I have errands to fulfil for my lady. I apologise for having disturbed you. I hope you will…not feel it necessary to complain of me. I…I cannot afford to lose her ladyship's good opinion.' She tried to assume an anxious expression, suitable for a servant who feared to lose her place. It was just possible that even this man had a hint of chivalry in his nature. Somewhere.

He was surveying her with narrowed eyes. No sign of chivalry. None at all. 'I shall not speak of this encounter to your mistress,' he said slowly. 'But I require something from you in return.'

Amy's heart plummeted to her heavy-soled boots. So he was no different from the rest of the lechers in this house.

'I require you to say nothing about my presence here. To anyone. Not even to Major Lyndhurst himself. Do you understand?'

'I— Yes.'

'And we have a bargain, Dent?'

Amy took another deep breath and raised her chin. She could feel his direct gaze on her face. She gave him a sharp nod. 'Yes, sir. We do.'

In that moment, he smiled at her. Suddenly all the harshness in his face had disappeared. He seemed much younger, dashing even, in spite of that unshaven chin. 'Then I suggest, Dent, that you return to your duties. Unless you would prefer to remain to help me dress?'

Amy gasped. And fled from the room.

It was only when Amy reached the safety of the Countess's chamber that she saw the state of her cap. There were wisps of blonde hair everywhere! Amy muttered a very unladylike curse and set about putting her

appearance to rights, consoling herself with the thought
that no one else had seen her.

He had seen her.

He knew who she was. Or who she was pretending to
be. He could betray her secret.

But he would not. For she, equally, could betray his.
For some unfathomable reason, the gentleman so nonchalantly taking a late-evening bath in the host's bedchamber did not wish his presence in the house to be
known. Why on earth could that be?

Amy racked her brains, in vain. It seemed a total nonsense. In fact, it was just one more unanswered question
in a house that was full of them, a house that appeared
to have swallowed her brother, Ned, without leaving any
trace at all.

Carefully holding the breakfast tray level, Amy closed
the bedchamber door with her shoulder and leant back
gratefully against the panelling. 'I must be all about in
my head,' she muttered, closing her eyes for a moment.

'Dent?'

Careful! Someone else must be here! 'Yes, m'lady.'
Amy straightened once more and moved across the room
to the curtained bed. 'I have brought your breakfast
early, as you ordered, m'lady.'

Lady Mardon, looking deliciously flushed, was reclin-
ing against a heap of lace-trimmed pillows.

Her husband was talking quietly, standing by the head
of the bed, dressed in only a thin silk dressing gown,
and looking as if his almost naked presence were the
most normal thing in the world. 'And Anthony has
planned a shooting party for today, so I shan't be back
till late afternoon, I suspect.'

'Oh,' responded his wife, sounding disappointed.

He smiled warmly down at her. 'If you should feel a need to check up on us, you could always go up on to the roof. One can see for miles from there.'

The Countess looked up at him through her lashes. 'Perhaps. If I have nothing more interesting to do…'

He grinned and ran a hand across the greying hair at his temple. 'I should not dream of interfering with your plans, my dear. And now I will leave you to have your breakfast in peace.' He bent to drop a chaste kiss on his wife's cheek. 'Enjoy your day.' Totally ignoring the abigail, he strode round the bed and disappeared through the connecting door to his dressing room.

Amy swallowed hard. This was yet another unforeseen aspect of her position. For all his apparent nonchalance, it was clear that the Earl had just left his wife's bed. Under his fine silk dressing gown, his legs and feet were bare. She dared not think about the rest of his body. Naked male bodies were…dangerous.

Lady Mardon craned her neck round the side of the bed to ensure the door was firmly closed behind her husband. Then she grinned nervously at her so-called abigail. 'Lord, Amy! That was much too close for comfort. If I had thought for a moment how much deception I should need to practise…'

'I know. You would never have agreed to do it.' She placed the tray carefully across the Countess's lap. Then, with a deep sigh, she perched on the edge of the bed and impudently stole a piece of toast. 'Believe me, Sarah, if I had had the least idea of how difficult it would be, I should never have asked you to help me.' She bit into the toast and chewed thoughtfully. 'But you are not really *deceiving* your husband, you know. He doesn't notice servants at all, unless they displease him. I swear

I could appear as myself tomorrow and he would not recognise me.'

The Countess gave a short laugh. 'Yes, I think you're right, Amy. But he's not…not unfeeling, you know.'

Amy noticed that the Countess was suddenly blushing. Not surprising, perhaps. When Amy had first entered the room, Sarah had had the air of the cat who had stolen the cream. Sarah and her Earl clearly enjoyed the pleasures of their marriage bed. Whatever those might be.

The Countess's gaze was now fixed on the tray. 'It's just that he…he has always been surrounded by willing servants. He takes them for granted.'

Amy reached for a second piece of toast. 'So do most of the gentlemen in this house. But they have different ways of showing it. I prefer to be ignored, I think. Both above *and* below stairs.'

'Oh, dear. You haven't given yourself away, have you?'

'No. Thank God.' Amy knew that she, too, was now flushing. Guilt, of course. If Sarah only knew what had happened in Major Lyndhurst's bedchamber… That unknown man was possibly the one gentleman in the house who might recognise Amy without her disguise. She swallowed at the vivid memory, at the way he had stared at her. He had been stark naked, but it was she who had been embarrassed. He was proud. Arrogant, even. It had been a shock to see him, of course, and yet… She had not thought a man's body could be so beautiful. Her own body seemed still to carry the imprint of his touch. It was as if the warmth of his fingers was—

'Amy?'

Forcing her thoughts back to the present, Amy said, 'You would not believe the lengths I have had to go to in order to avoid the wandering hands in this house, Sarah. Not always successfully. First, there was that loathsome man, Grant. He has gone, thank God, but his erstwhile employer is cut from the same cloth. I have just had another encounter with William Lyndhurst-Flint. When he saw that I was carrying your breakfast tray, he came up behind me and put his hand—' She shuddered. 'I would willingly have tipped your chocolate over his head. He is disgusting.'

'Maybe he has noticed how pretty you are behind those horrid spectacles.'

'Sarah! Would you defend him? Why, he has not the least idea what I look like. His eyes have never once risen as high as my face.' Ignoring Sarah's embarrassed giggle, Amy went on, warming to her subject, 'And he is just as bad with the other female servants. Always touching, *accidentally* brushing up against them. He had his hand under the skirt of one of the housemaids yesterday. If I hadn't come upon them—'

'Amy! You must take care!'

'Don't worry, Sarah. I behaved precisely as a high-class lady's maid should. I exclaimed in disgust and looked down my nose at them both. You would have been proud of me. And the maid will take pains to avoid him in future, I dare say.' She paused. 'Shall you tell your husband?'

Sarah hesitated. 'No,' she said finally. 'I don't think I can. John and William are not on good terms. Even if John believed it, he would not wish to take William to task. There have been so many quarrels, you see, and John knows how much it upsets me to see brothers at outs. Especially as it is my fault.'

Amy's brows rose.

'John always said he would never marry again. That

William would be his heir. And William became used to the notion, I'm afraid. When John and I married, and then the boys were born... Well, you must see that William was bound to feel much aggrieved. John feels guilty about it still.'

'And so he makes allowances for his brother's womanising?'

'Oh, not that, surely?'

Amy shook her head. 'Actually, I think it's an automatic reaction with him. He sees a female form—*any* female form—and he just has to touch it.'

'Not with ladies, Amy.'

'No? Well, perhaps his urges are limited to servants. He sees no need to restrain himself with them. With us.' She grimaced at the thought of where she now belonged. Even temporarily.

The Countess was sipping her chocolate appreciatively. 'It would have been better if you had pretended to be a governess or a companion, you know. Then William would have treated you properly. As a lady.'

'He might have. But you know that it would not have served. How would I ever have discovered anything about Ned's disappearance? As your abigail, I am able to go below stairs without questions being asked. And I have to have a ready excuse if I am found where I should not be. To search a bedchamber, I have to walk in boldly, as if I had every right to be there. So far...' She crossed her fingers, hidden in the folds of her skirts, and fixed her gaze on the floor, remembering. 'So far the rooms have all been empty. But if I were to encounter someone, I should simply say that I was on an errand for you and had mistaken the chamber. What could a governess say if she were caught? Or a companion? No one would believe such a tale from either of them.'

'Yes, I suppose. Oh, you are such a talented actress that it seemed the perfect solution when you first suggested it. But that was before you actually had to play the part! I should never have dreamed it would be so difficult. And so dangerous. Your reputation will be in shreds if you are caught.'

'Yes, I know. And life below stairs is…not quite what I expected. They have even more rules there than we do! If it were not for you, Sarah, I should have been unmasked almost as soon as we arrived. Luckily, since you are the highest-ranking lady here, I take precedence over all the other female servants. If I don't understand what is going on, I simply behave as though it is all beneath my exalted notice.' Amy laughed a little nervously. 'I have to tell you, my dear, that on one or two occasions I had no idea what on earth they were talking about. So I put my nose in the air and just mentioned to the housekeeper that we do things very differently at Mardon Park. It was as well that your husband's valet was not around to hear me tell such a Banbury tale.'

'Amy Devereaux, you will come to a bad end!'

'No doubt I will,' replied Amy with a conspiratorial grin, 'especially if anyone hears you calling me by that name. I am Dent, the abigail, if you please, my lady. Amelia Dent.' She fetched Sarah's wrapper. 'And now, if your ladyship has finished your breakfast, may I ring for the maid to remove your tray? And which gown would your ladyship have me lay out for this morning?'

The sound of a carriage on the drive came clearly through the open window. 'Goodness,' Sarah exclaimed. 'Who can that be? Surely not Great-aunt Harriet already?'

Amy handed the wrapper to Sarah and crossed to the

window. 'I can't see anything from here, I'm afraid. Shall I go downstairs and find out who it is?'

'Yes, do. If it is Great-aunt Harriet, she will not have brought a maid, so, if anyone should question you, you may say that…that I sent you down to offer assistance to Miss Lyndhurst after her long and tiring journey.'

Amy grinned. 'You, too, are fast becoming an accomplished liar, Sarah. But thank you. The more excuses I have to loiter near the guests, the more chance I have of finding out what it was that Ned discovered. I'm absolutely sure it was something here, in this house. Something important. And dangerous.'

'Be careful, Amy. If Ned was right… Just think. If Ned really has been kidnapped, as you fear, then you could be at risk as well. Would it not be better to confide in John? I'm sure he would help you.'

'If he did not have an apoplexy first, on finding his wife's old friend in the guise of a servant.' At Sarah's pained look, Amy went on, in a rather more reasonable tone, 'You must see that I cannot confide in your husband, Sarah. I have nothing to confide. I could say only that Ned wrote to say that he had discovered something smoky at Lyndhurst Chase. That he said he would tell me all about it when he arrived home. And that he never arrived. Although *I* feel sure that something has happened to him, that is because I know Ned. Anyone else would assume he had simply gone off somewhere— gambling with his friends, perhaps—and had failed to tell me of his change of plans. And it might be true, too. Except that I feel certain that it is not.'

'But you have discovered nothing.'

'Nothing about Ned's whereabouts, I admit. However, I did hear Lady Quinlan complaining about Ned. She was saying that he had left the Chase without taking his

leave of her and the other guests. She thought he was
unpardonably rude. Now, Ned can be reckless and selfish, I admit, but even *Ned*'s manners are not as bad as
that. He would have taken his leave in the proper form.
Unless something, or someone, prevented him.'

'Yes, I see. What do you think it means?'

'It means that something has happened to Ned. And
that it happened here, at Lyndhurst Chase, when he was
about to leave. Whatever he discovered must be…
important enough for someone to risk a kidnapping to
protect it. At least, I hope it was a kidnapping.'

'Amy? You don't think—?'

'I don't know what to think, Sarah. I just pray that,
wherever he is, Ned has not come to any real harm.'
Amy swallowed hard in an attempt to quell the nerves
that were churning in her belly at the thought of what
might have happened to her brother. No one would have
harmed him. Would they? He was little more than a
thoughtless boy, after all.

Amy rubbed her damp palms on her skirt. She must
stop worrying and start doing something. 'I had better
go down to meet the new arrivals, if I am to be seen to
be of service. I do not relish the thought of a trimming
from Miss Lyndhurst for my tardiness. I have not forgotten that she is renowned for her very sharp tongue.'

At that, Sarah smiled again. Amy was glad to see that
the worried frown had left her friend's face. It was
enough that Amy herself should fret over Ned. There
was no need to infect Sarah as well.

'Amy!'

Amy was already halfway to the door.

'Remember, Amy dear, that if Miss Lyndhurst should
test her venom on you, you must behave like a servant,
not a lady.'

Amy dropped a demure curtsy. 'Yes, your ladyship. Of course, your ladyship. Having learnt my skills at your ladyship's side, how could my behaviour be anything but that of a perfect lady's maid?' She curtsied again, making no effort at all to hide her broad grin.

Sarah shook her head in mock despair. 'I knew I should never have permitted a mere servant to share my breakfast.'

Chapter Two

'Certainly not! At my age, I am due a little more consideration. I shall have a bedchamber on the first floor.'

'As you wish, Aunt Harriet.' Major Lyndhurst's face was grim. His mouth was drawn into a tight line as he looked down at the bird-like old woman.

'I should think so, indeed!' Miss Lyndhurst glanced round towards her companion. The woman almost seemed to be trying to melt into the background. She was staring down at the ground, her face totally hidden by the poke of her dark blue bonnet. Amy could not tell whether she was young or old, though she was certainly rather thin, like her mistress. Amy felt a sudden pang of sympathy. It must be a nightmare to work for an old harridan like Miss Lyndhurst. No doubt the companion was poor and had nowhere else to go.

Amy swallowed hard at that thought. If something had really happened to Ned, she, too, might be forced to earn her own living. In any way she could.

Major Lyndhurst did not appear to have noticed Amy's arrival. All his attention seemed to be focused on the empty space between his great-aunt and the companion. He had begun to frown heavily.

Miss Lyndhurst poked him in the chest with her brass ear trumpet. 'Are you going to leave me standing here all day, Anthony? I thought your mother would have taught you better manners than that.'

Major Lyndhurst glanced sideways at the old lady. There was a question in that look, Amy decided. And something else, too. Not malice exactly, but…something dark.

'I had instructed my housekeeper to give you a chamber on the second floor, ma'am, so that you would not be disturbed by the comings and goings below. At present, all the suitable rooms on the first floor are taken, and—'

Miss Lyndhurst waved her ear trumpet perilously close to her host's face. 'Balderdash! Don't give me your lame excuses, lad. Just move 'em elsewhere!'

'As you wish, Aunt,' he said again. 'I shall move William. But I cannot evict anyone else from the first floor in order to provide a suitable room for your companion. She may have to be accommodated on one of the upper floors.'

'Nothing of the kind,' snapped the old lady. 'Miss Saunders will sleep in my dressing room. I take it you *are* able to offer me a chamber with a dressing room?'

The Major threw her a baleful look. For a space, he said nothing at all. Then, at last, he said, in a harsh voice, 'In your *dressing* room, Aunt? How very…singular. If you had warned me that your lady companion had such…er…unusual needs, I should certainly have made special arrangements to deal with her, I can assure you.'

Miss Lyndhurst narrowed her eyes, but said nothing. She began to tap her foot instead.

Catching sight of Amy at last, the Major said curtly, 'Did Lady Mardon send you? Good. You may escort

Miss Lyndhurst and her companion up to the ladies'
sitting room. And then tell the housekeeper to move Mr
Lyndhurst-Flint's belongings and to make his room
ready for Miss Lyndhurst and her companion.' He
glanced yet again at the lady in the blue bonnet. Amy
could have sworn that he was suddenly absolutely furious. But why?

Amy curtsied obediently and took a pace forward.
'Will you come this way, please, madam? The ladies'
sitting room is on the first floor, overlooking the garden.'

Miss Lyndhurst showed no intention of moving a step.
She looked Amy up and down with dark, beady eyes.
Amy felt the skin of her back suddenly becoming quite
clammy. Miss Lyndhurst was a downy one, and no mistake. Amy must be very, very careful now.

'Who the devil are you?' the old lady asked rudely.

'Dent, madam. Lady Mardon's abigail.'

Miss Lyndhurst's brows rose. 'Don't look much like
a proper lady's maid to me.' She pulled off a glove and
reached out to rub the stuff of Amy's skirt between
finger and thumb. 'What kind of a lady's maid wears
something like *that*? Wouldn't give it to a scullery maid.
I know that Lady Mardon has something of a reputation—'

'Aunt Harriet—' There was a clear note of warning
in the Major's voice.

'Hmph! Even Sarah Mardon should know better. I
shall speak to her about it. Immediately. Where is she?'

'Her ladyship is taking breakfast in her bedchamber,
madam. Knowing that you would not have brought your
own maid, she sent me down to offer my services.'

'Don't need any services,' snapped the old lady. 'Miss
Saunders here will look to all my needs. That's what a
companion is for.' She began to walk briskly towards

the front door. Then, throwing a quick glance over her shoulder towards her great-nephew, she added, 'Ain't that right, Anthony?' She did not wait to see how he responded, but merely beckoned impatiently to her companion to follow.

Amy was astonished. The Major was positively glowering at Miss Lyndhurst's departing back. She was certainly very trying, but until now, the Major had behaved as the perfect host to all his guests, even when they were at their most provoking. Now, confronted with one acid-tongued old lady, he seemed to be on the point of exploding.

'This way, madam,' Amy said blandly.

Miss Lyndhurst nodded once. And then, with a fleeting smile in the direction of the ear trumpet she carried, she followed Amy into the entrance hall and began to climb the stairs. Her silent companion, head still bowed, followed in her wake.

'Miss Lyndhurst has arrived, Sarah.'

Lady Mardon took one look at Amy's face and said, with a grimace, 'I can see that she has already made her mark. You are as white as a sheet.'

'Your husband's great-aunt has a tongue that could melt ice at twenty paces.'

'Yes, I know. And I'm not sure she altogether approves of me, either. She retired to her house in Cornwall after our wedding, but she made it clear that— Oh, perhaps it will be different now. After all, I've given John two sons. His first wife didn't do that, in spite of her grand pedigree.'

'Er...that's not exactly the problem. I should warn you, I think, that she is about to take you to task for your taste in abigails. She does not think I am suitably dressed for the part.'

'Is that all?' Sarah smiled. 'Now that I *can* deal with. I shall tell her that, while your skills are of the highest order, your unfortunate addiction to piety does not allow you to dress as befits your station. Just make sure you trot out the right biblical quotations when she twits you about it. For she will, I promise you.'

'You sound very confident, Sarah. What if—?'

'I can give as good as I get, my dear, on any subject except my suitability as a wife for a belted earl. If Aunt Harriet should say anything about that—'

Amy put a gentle hand on her friend's shoulder. 'I am sure she will not. Why should she, after all? You have made John so very happy, besides presenting him with two sturdy sons. Miss Lyndhurst has only to see the two of you together to know that you are ideally suited.'

'Perhaps. I don't think she actually believes in marriage. I don't know the full story, but I think she was jilted in favour of a richer catch when she was quite young. She swore then that she'd never let any man have dominion over her. Apparently she didn't shed a single tear when her former lover was killed in action in the American wars. She couldn't have really loved him.'

'If he did marry someone else, I'd say it was more the case that *he* never really loved *her*, Sarah.'

'It's not always possible to marry for love, even nowadays, Amy. Everyone needs to eat. Look at you. If Ned—'

'I'd rather not discuss my gloomy prospects just at present, if you don't mind, Sarah. I need to concentrate on finding out what's happened to Ned.' She laughed a little bitterly. 'With luck, my dowry—small though it is—may still be intact. I do hope so, since I may need it to buy Ned's freedom.'

'But you cannot! Without a dowry, you—'

Amy shrugged her shoulders eloquently. 'I know my chances of making a good marriage are diminishing by the day. After all, it's seven years since I had my Season, such as it was. Perhaps I need this practise as an abigail. Who knows? I may end up doing it for real one of these days.'

'Nonsense. I shouldn't allow it. Nor would John. You could always make your home with us. The boys would love it.'

'Your sons already have a splendid governess looking after them. They do not need another.'

Sarah ignored her. 'And *I* should love it, too.'

'A companion, then,' Amy said flatly. 'I shall obviously have to watch Miss Saunders, to see how a lady's companion should behave. Shall you be as much of a harridan as Miss Lyndhurst, do you think?'

'Of course. How could you think otherwise?' Sarah tried to keep her face straight, but failed.

And Dent, the pious lady's maid, soon joined in the laughter.

Amy had barely left the Mardons' bedchamber when she almost collided with a small black-clad figure coming out of the door to the backstairs.

'What—? Oh, it's you again, Miss Dent. Thank goodness.' The housekeeper was puffing hard from the exertion of rushing upstairs. She shot a searching glance down the hall towards the main staircase. There was no one in sight.

'Is everything quite well, Mrs Waller?' Amy said politely. 'You look a little put out, if I may say so.'

'Aye, and so would you be if—' She stopped short, glancing round impatiently. Still no one. 'I've been trying to find that highty-tighty footman who's supposed to valet Mr William. Heavens knows where the man's got to. Got ideas above his station, I dare say, since Grant was turned off. It should be the valet's job to move Mr William's things up here, not mine. Nothing is done yet, and Miss Lyndhurst will be getting more testy by the second.'

Amy smiled and nodded at the older woman. She hoped it struck the right note of confidence, and sympathy. 'Yes, indeed she will.' Amy was glad to see that the housekeeper was relaxing a little now. It was an opportunity not to be missed. 'I left Miss Lyndhurst and her companion in the ladies' sitting room, as you know, ma'am, and Miss Lyndhurst... Well, to be frank, ma'am, she looked fit to explode if her room wasn't made ready in two shakes. It's an impossible task for you, on your own, without Mr William's valet. Might I offer some assistance? At least until the new valet turns up?'

'You are very kind, Miss Dent. You, of all people, know that I can't trust the maids with Mr William's fine things. If you would help me with the folding and so on, we could be done in a trice. I just have to give the maids their instructions first, about making up the bed and airing the new room. And then we can make a start on packing up for Mr William.'

'Of course, Mrs Waller. I should be glad to help. Indeed, I'll go and make a start now, shall I? While you're dealing with the maids? I've had the sharp edge of Miss Lyndhurst's tongue once already this morning. The sooner we can make her room ready, the more chance we shall all have of avoiding her censure in future.'

The housekeeper beamed. 'You are a treasure, Miss

Dent. Thank you. I shouldn't be but a moment or two…provided those girls are where they ought to be. Flighty pieces, most of 'em, I may tell you. If I didn't keep my eye on everything, there would be dust and dirt everywhere. 'Tweren't like that when I started out in service.'

'Nor when I started,' Amy said, nodding vigorously. 'We were taught the value of hard work. And standards. Cleanliness is next to godliness.'

'Quite so,' agreed Mrs Waller. 'I— But I must go. I will join you in Mr William's room shortly.'

'Er…which is Mr William's room, Mrs Waller?' It would not do for the housekeeper to think that Amy already knew exactly where all the guests were housed.

'I beg your pardon, Miss Dent. I had forgotten for a moment. Of course, there's no reason for you to know. Mr William is in the yellow bedchamber, next to the ladies' sitting room. He is to move up here, to the room above the Major's.'

'Excellent. I shall go and get started.' Amy led the way back across the hall to the door to the backstairs. At the last moment, she stood aside. 'After you, Mrs Waller,' she said. It was a clear acknowledgement of the housekeeper's status below stairs. Mrs Waller flushed with pleasure and then, with a murmur of thanks, stomped off down to the basement.

Amy followed her down as far as the first floor. She had five minutes, ten at most, to start searching Mr Lyndhurst-Flint's room. On this occasion, at least, she had a cast-iron excuse if she was caught. And the redoubtable housekeeper to be her witness.

Amy quickly laid aside the first pile of shirts and took up another. Mr Lyndhurst-Flint certainly did not stint

himself on the quality of his linen. She paused for a
second to smooth her palm over the beautiful fabric. Her
brother, Ned, had nothing half so fine. They could not
afford such luxury. Indeed, Amy could begin to play the
part of an abigail only because the Devereaux household
lived in straitened circumstances. She knew how to do
menial tasks because she had had to learn to do many
of them at home.

Carrying the pile of shirts, Amy moved to the little
writing table by the connecting door. It was an untidy
mass of papers. Grant might have tidied them, knowing
his master's habits. But the young footman who had
temporarily taken the dismissed valet's place probably
would not dare.

Amy glanced quickly towards the door. It was safely
closed. And with the shirts in her hand, she would appear
to be busy with the packing, if Mrs Waller should appear.

Amy pushed the papers about, trying to see what they
were without disturbing them too much. Bills, mostly,
and large ones at that. A letter or two, containing nothing
of note. An invitation. And under them all, a part-
finished letter from Mr Lyndhurst-Flint himself! Amy
drew it out and began to scan it. It was—

Voices came from the corridor just outside! Men's
voices. Hastily Amy returned the sheet to its place and
crossed to the door, catching up yet more of the linen
as she did so.

The voices were clearer now. With her ear placed
shamelessly against the heavy wood, she could make out
every word.

Mr Lyndhurst-Flint's voice came from just beyond his
own door. 'It was not a happy occasion, Anthony,
though I am glad I was present. Had I not been, they

might have called for the pistols there and then. Think of the scandal it would have caused! Frobisher was as drunk as a wheelbarrow. He could barely stand. And Marcus was little better.'

'We have scandal enough as it is, William,' replied Major Lyndhurst acidly. 'What the hell did Marcus think he was doing?'

'I have no way of knowing, I'm afraid. He was in a very strange mood that night. That I will say. Never heard him say such things before. Perhaps it was the drink. Marcus has always been so very insistent on the importance of duty, and loyalty—especially to you—that I was shocked to hear him refer to you as he did. And then, to couple it with such remarks about Georgiana—'

'*What?* What did Marcus say about my wife?'

'I…I can't remember precisely, Anthony. Pray do not glower at me like that. It was not I who spoke slightingly of your wife, I assure you.'

'Are you telling me that this quarrel between Marcus and Frobisher was over *my* wife?' The Major's voice had sunk to a venomous whisper.

'I— Well, yes. I can't remember exactly what was said. I had had quite a few glasses myself. I seem to recall that Frobisher took Marcus to task for what he had said. Can't remember the way of it, exactly. But I do remember Marcus's threat. No one could forget that. He stood there with his lips drawn back, like a dog baring its teeth, and his eyes blazing. He looked like some kind of fiend. And he said that, if he ever laid eyes on Frobisher again, he would kill him. He meant it, too. If I'd been in Frobisher's shoes, even drunk as he was, I'd have taken myself off and kept my head down.

Obviously, he didn't, though. Or he wouldn't be at death's door now.'

'Damn Frobisher!'

'Anthony! The man may be dying! And if Marcus really is responsible, we should—'

'Enough, William! I have no desire to hear anything more on this subject. I do not permit anyone—*anyone*—to speak of my wife.'

'But what are we going to do about Marcus? He will surely be found sooner or later. And, if Frobisher dies, Marcus could hang.'

There was no reply. Amy could hear retreating footsteps. It sounded as if Major Lyndhurst had stalked off without another word. Mr Lyndhurst-Flint was alone.

Amy went quickly back to the clothes press, offering up a silent prayer that Mrs Waller would arrive soon. For, if Mr Lyndhurst-Flint chose to enter the room, Amy would have no defence against his vile advances.

Recognising the housekeeper's voice in the corridor outside, Amy let herself relax once more. She was safe from Mr Lyndhurst-Flint. For now.

Marcus was thoroughly bored. And frustrated. It had been weeks now, and still there was no news. Why could it not have been resolved by now? It had seemed so simple at the time.

It was not simple. Not simple at all. And the delay was threatening Marcus's relationship with Anthony. If only Anthony knew the whole story of what had happened…but no one would dare to tell him. It was impossible to repeat such fearful insults to any man of honour. If Anthony learned what Frobisher had said of him, Anthony would certainly demand satisfaction. There would be even more bloodshed.

Marcus cursed silently. It was his own fault. He should have been better prepared. He should have given Anthony a plausible version of the quarrel, one that Anthony would accept without question. As it was, Anthony had listened to Marcus's hastily concocted account and had claimed to be convinced. But as the days passed, Anthony's doubts about Marcus's assurances had clearly begun to grow. Marcus could not blame him. In Anthony's place, he would have thought the same, no matter how close their friendship.

Marcus resumed his pacing up and down the dressing room. It was not much, but at least it was exercise of a kind. What he would not give for a good gallop in the fresh air!

At the mere thought of the joys of fresh air, Marcus sneezed loudly. Good grief! He couldn't be sickening, could he? That would be the last straw. He felt in his pocket for his handkerchief. He had none. Yet another consequence of his hasty flight from London. He was already subsisting mostly on linen borrowed from Anthony so that the lower servants would not suspect his presence in the house. Since he was already wearing one of Anthony's shirts, he might as well borrow his cousin's handkerchieves as well.

He pulled open the top drawer of the chest and pushed aside the pile of carefully laundered handkerchieves, looking for the most worn.

But Anthony had no old or worn ones at the bottom of the pile. Instead, he had a tiny miniature of a pretty dark-haired lady, with a very fair complexion.

Intrigued, Marcus lifted the portrait out of the drawer to have a closer look. She was quite lovely. And also very young indeed, probably just out of the schoolroom. It was only then that Marcus realised, with something of a shock, that this must be Anthony's mysterious wife, the woman who had deserted him while he was fighting for his country on the field at Waterloo.

Why on earth had Anthony kept it? Surely he could not love a woman who had treated him so foully? Not a word had been heard from her in four long years. She had done nothing to scotch the vile rumours that had become common currency among the *ton*. Frobisher, deep in his cups in that gaming hell, had parroted them without a qualm. That Anthony Lyndhurst had murdered his wife after catching her with her lover. That Anthony Lyndhurst had ensured that his wife's lover fell on the field at Waterloo. That Anthony Lyndhurst, for all his wealth, was not a man whom a gentleman would wish to know.

Lies! Every word of it! There was no more upright and honourable man in England than Anthony Lyndhurst, as Marcus well knew. But the *ton* much preferred a juicy rumour to respectable truth. Those lies had acquired a status by virtue of constant repetition.

And because the woman had refused to appear to prove them wrong!

Marcus turned a little towards the window in order to look more closely at a woman who was clearly a stranger to duty and loyalty. He tried to find signs of duplicity or vice in her features. But he could not. It was a sweet face, with hazel eyes gazing candidly towards the portraitist. There was no sign of the woman she had become. Perhaps she had been corrupted by—

The door slammed with incredible violence. 'Marcus!' Anthony thundered.

Marcus looked up with a start. Anthony was clearly furious. His whole body was stiff with anger. He threw Marcus a look filled with hatred and, it seemed, disgust.

Then he strode forward and snatched the portrait from Marcus's frozen fingers, before pointedly turning his back.

Marcus was shaken. He had rarely seen Anthony so affected by anything. Anthony was always in control. Yet there had seemed to be a tremor in his fingers when he seized the portrait. And now, there was a rigid set to his shoulders that suggested he was struggling to master some powerful emotion.

'Anthony, forgive me,' Marcus began, taking a step towards his cousin and touching him lightly on the arm. 'I had not intended to pry. I found it when I was looking for—'

Anthony shook off Marcus's hand. He did not turn. 'I have no wish to discuss what you were doing or what you intended, Marcus. You have betrayed my trust. Think yourself lucky that I, at least, have enough family loyalty not to betray *you.*'

Marcus was so shocked he could not speak. This was Anthony, his cousin, and his closest friend. He must not allow a rift to develop between them, especially over a traitorous woman. He took a deep breath, preparing to make an abject apology.

It was too late. Anthony pushed the miniature deep into his pocket and marched out of the room without a word.

And without once looking back.

Chapter Three

Amy rested her elbows on her bent knees and her chin on her hand. She had to come to a decision. So far, she had achieved nothing worthwhile. There had been that half-finished letter in Mr Lyndhurst-Flint's chamber, to be sure. But that held no clue to Ned's whereabouts.

The only place left to search was the Major's bed-chamber. She had already checked all the others. And the office and the library downstairs.

She shifted uncomfortably on the thin mattress, but she knew she had no right to complain about her accommodation. She had a room to herself. Quite a spacious room, too, with a view of the lawn and, beyond it, the mile-long grassy ride leading to the North Lodge. Could Ned be somewhere in the woods flanking the ride? Injured? Perhaps even—? Amy shuddered. She could never begin to search all those woods. There were acres and acres of them.

She had to concentrate on the house. She would have to return to Major Lyndhurst's bedchamber. And its mysterious occupant.

Amy felt her skin growing hot at the memory. It was embarrassment, of course. It must be. She had been such a fool to stand there, rooted, and let him put his hands on her...

Oh, dear. No. This was not the way to save Ned.

She swung her feet round on to the floor and stood up, automatically reaching for her spectacles and smoothing her skirt. She searched her mind for a few appropriate biblical sayings, preferably from the Old Testament. Amelia Dent was the kind of person who would delight in fire and brimstone, and the mortification of the flesh. Flesh... Amy swallowed hard at the vivid picture conjured up by that word, a picture of that naked man... If only he had been fat, or old, or ugly. But he was none of those things.

And he might still be there, waiting, ready to pounce on her the moment she entered the room. She could not go back there.

She must. She had no choice.

Not for the first time, Amy wondered why she had not confided in Sarah. Surely Sarah would have been able to tell her about the dark stranger? But, then again, perhaps not. For if Sarah knew about him, she would have said something, would she not? Sarah did not keep secrets from Amy. And she would be hurt to learn that Amy had kept a secret from her.

The truth was that Amy felt bound by that stupid promise. And, if she were honest with herself, she was intrigued, too. Why had he forbidden her to say anything to Major Lyndhurst? The Major, of all people, must have known there was a stranger in his chamber. And the Major's valet, too. He must have—

Amy paused in the act of straightening her cap. Yes, Timms must know. Amy had heard him telling one of the young housemaids not to go into the Major's bed-chamber to clean unless Timms himself was there. It had seemed very strange at the time. Amy had assumed that Timms wanted to keep a protective eye on the Major's belongings, that he was concerned that the maid might break things. But what if it were more than that? Smoky. Yes. It was smoky. And Ned had used that very same word in his letter.

The answer must be in Major Lyndhurst's bedchamber.

And, as soon as the guests were safely downstairs, Amy was going to find it. No matter what the risk.

By the time Amy stood once more outside the Major's bedchamber, she had persuaded herself that the dark stranger would certainly be gone. It was days since her encounter with him. It was impossible to believe that the Major was concealing the stranger on a long-term basis. The man might have been there for a day or two, no doubt for perfectly good reasons. Whoever he was, he must be gone by now. There was no risk of encountering him while she searched the Major's room. It was absurd to think otherwise. Nevertheless, Amy had to take several deep breaths before she could force herself to turn the handle and enter the room.

She found herself alone. She gave a very audible sigh of relief and sagged back against the door, gazing round anxiously. The screen was folded back. There was no bath. There was not even a modest fire in the grate. The curtains stood open to the garden and the distant lake, letting in the golden evening light. It was a normal— and perfectly empty—bedchamber.

Yet she hesitated by the door, listening intently. She could see into part of the dressing room, but she could not be sure that it, too, was empty without going in. And what if he was there?

Act normally. Walk into the dressing room as if you had a right to be there. You have been sent to fetch a…a handkerchief. If he really is there, he cannot know for sure that you are lying. And you can take one and leave. Before he has time to do anything.

She straightened her back and walked quite slowly into the dressing room, looking calmly about her, as if to find where the handkerchieves were kept. There was the chest! And the huge clothes press, and the narrow servant's bed, and all the other paraphernalia of a gentleman's dressing room. But there was no one else in the room. He was gone.

'Thank God,' she whispered, unable to contain her relief.

It was but a brief moment of weakness. She had no time to wonder about the missing stranger. She must complete her search, and quickly. She returned to the bedchamber and looked about her for the most likely place to start. Yes! The small writing desk by the window. It was an odd piece of furniture for the host's bedchamber. After all, he did his estate work in the office on the ground floor, and he also had a desk in the library. If he wrote letters and documents here, in the privacy of his bedroom, they would be the sort of thing that no one else must see.

Yes. If there was proof, it would be in the Major's desk.

The desk, unlike Mr Lyndhurst-Flint's, was very tidy. There were no papers on the top. Just writing paper, pens and ink. Amy slid open the wide central drawer. It contained more writing paper, and wafers, and sealing wax, and other necessities, but nothing else. She closed it carefully, not making a sound. There were two small drawers on either side. She tried the topmost one on the right. It was locked! She cursed under her breath. Why should a man lock his desk when no one but his trusted valet was permitted to be alone in the room?

Amy refused to despair. She dare not break the lock. But perhaps the key was hidden somewhere about? She began to search frantically in the unlocked drawers.

'Lost your way *again*, Dent?'

Oh, no!

'For a high-class dresser, you have a singularly poor sense of direction, I must say.'

That deep voice sent a shiver through her body. He was there! Again! She had no idea where he had appeared from, but it did not matter. He was there. And he had caught her searching Major Lyndhurst's desk. What excuse could she possibly make? She pressed her clasped hands tightly against her body and stared down at the worn leather surface of the desk, willing her brain to think of something, to stop terrifying her with images of the ruin she was facing.

'It would be polite to turn round, you know, Dent, and to answer my question.'

Amy swallowed hard and started to turn, wondering what she might see this time. What if he—?

He was adequately—if not fully—clothed. Breeches and a loose-fitting shirt, open at the neck to reveal his upper chest. He was leaning nonchalantly against the dressing-room door as if his presence in the room were the most normal thing in the world. And those long fingers were absently stroking his still unshaven chin. With that growth of beard and his long dark hair, he looked infinitely dangerous.

He *was* dangerous!

She fixed her gaze on the floor between them. And said nothing.

For a long moment, he just stood there, motionless. Amy could hear only the pounding of her own blood in her ears.

At last, he spoke. 'Lost your tongue as well as your sense of direction, I see.' He straightened and began to move towards her. His feet made no sound on the worn carpet.

In that moment, Amy understood how a cornered mouse must feel, when the cat was bearing down on it. But this cat did not pounce immediately. He stopped in front of her. Waiting.

'Do you really have nothing to say?' he asked softly.

Amy looked up then. She swallowed hard, trying to bring some moisture into her parched throat. 'I…I was sent to fetch…' Her excuse petered out at the sight of his lifted brows. He knew perfectly well that she was lying. She pressed her lips tightly together. She was unable to hold his penetrating gaze.

'No, Dent, it's not a very good excuse. And we both know it.' He shook his head at her, rather in the manner of a fond relative, bemused by the antics of a naughty child. 'Tell me,' he said calmly, 'why are you doing this?' He reached out a hand to her.

Amy stepped back in alarm, but it was too late. With a quick flick of his long fingers, he had removed her all-concealing cap. 'You really should not hide such beautiful hair,' he said. Then, with thumb and forefinger of both hands, he delicately removed her heavy glass spectacles. 'And you should not hide those beautiful eyes, either.'

He turned his back on Amy and carefully laid her spectacles on the Major's desk. Very quietly, he said, 'You are playing a very dangerous game, Miss

Devereaux. What on earth possessed you to do such a thing?'

Amy found herself staring in horror at his back. He knew who she was! Somehow, he had recognised her, even though he was a stranger to her. She was sure to be ruined now. And it was all for nothing! She had not rescued Ned!

Marcus turned very slowly. It was important not to frighten her. One look at her stark white face told him he was too late. She was already terrified. Indeed, she looked to be on the point of collapse.

He picked up the chair from beside the desk and set it down at her back, pushing gently on her shoulder until she sat down. 'Forgive me, Miss Devereaux. I did not mean to upset you. But, truly, it is a mad start for a lady to come to a gentleman's house in the guise of a servant. With colouring as unusual as yours, you were bound to be recognised. And recognition spells ruin, as I am sure you know.'

Her hands were tightly clasped in her lap. Her knuckles were white. But when she raised her gaze to meet his, there was a spark of defiance in those violet-blue eyes. It was in her voice, too. 'I have taken the greatest of care, sir, to ensure that no one in this house would catch sight of my hair. If you had not removed my cap just now—'

'I recognised your hair at our last meeting, Miss Devereaux. And, on that occasion, if you recall, you were wearing your cap throughout. It just went…slightly awry.' He tried to prevent himself from smiling at the memory. Apart from those tell-tale wisps of hair, she had been more than adequately covered. He, on the other hand, had not.

'And how is it, pray, that you know who I am? I am not aware that we have ever been introduced.'

Marcus was glad to see that she had recovered much of her natural dignity. And some courage, besides. Miss Amy Devereaux was certainly no shrinking miss. 'That is easily explained,' he said, with a nonchalant shrug. 'I recall that you were pointed out to me some years ago at…some function or other. Colouring such as yours is not easily forgotten, even by one who has not been introduced. It was your first Season, I collect?'

She rose to her feet. Her back was ramrod-straight. 'If you saw me in London, sir, it was seven years ago, during my first—and only—Season. Do you expect me to be flattered that you have remembered my name?'

'No, ma'am. I expect you to be concerned. For if a man who set eyes on you only once can remember who you are, then other men will recognise you, too. You must leave the Chase before you are utterly ruined.'

'I cannot,' she replied immediately, with a small but decisive shake of her head.

'Why not?' snapped Marcus in exasperation.

She said nothing. She was refusing to look at him now.

Marcus took her firmly by the shoulders. 'I ought to shake you until your teeth rattle, madam. What on earth can be so important that you would risk your reputation for it?' A thought occurred. Instantly, he dropped his arms back to his sides. 'Oh, of course. I should have known. It is always the way with women. You are here because of a lover.'

Her open palm struck him full on the cheek before he had time to realise quite how much he had insulted her. Her face was alight with fury.

For a tense moment, they stared at each other, like

warring stags. Then Marcus raised both hands, palms uppermost, in a gesture of surrender. 'Miss Devereaux, I beg your pardon. That was an unforgivable thing to have said. And I fully deserved your chastisement.' He put a hand to his cheek, rubbing the throbbing skin. He smiled wryly down at her. She had a heavy hand, indeed. And she was beginning to look a little uncertain. His ready acceptance of her rebuke seemed to have thrown her off balance. Now was the time to press home his advantage.

'Miss Devereaux,' he said gently, 'it must be a matter of immense importance that has made you take so great a risk. Will you not confide in me? I may be able to help you.'

She looked at him in surprise. 'You? But I don't even know you.'

'No,' he said with a slow smile, 'but you are here at Lyndhurst Chase for a reason. And I know a great deal about what goes on here.'

'Do you?' she asked quickly. For a moment, she sounded eager. Then her voice dropped again. 'But I dare not trust you. Or anyone.'

Marcus reached for her hand. It was not as soft as a lady's hand should have been. It was the hand of someone who was used to much more manual work than any lady should be. 'Miss Devereaux, I give you my word as a gentleman that you may trust me. No matter what you may tell me, I promise you, on my honour, that I will not betray you.'

She did not remove her hand from his. Nor did she look at him directly. She seemed to be turning his words over in her mind. He could tell from the set of her shoulders that she remained undecided. And more than a little afraid. Marcus knew he must simply wait for her decision.

At last, with a deep sigh, she said, 'I do know that you saw my hair before. And I know, too, that you did not betray my identity then. If you had spoken of it to anyone, I should have been gone from this house long since. So, it seems that I *should* be able to trust you.' She shook her head a little. 'Indeed, it seems that I have no choice.'

Marcus tried to smile reassuringly at her. 'Miss Devereaux, you must understand that I have every reason to be suspicious of *you*. I did catch you searching Major Lyndhurst's desk, after all. Forgive me, but that is not *quite* the behaviour one expects of a lady.'

She coloured deliciously. Marcus suddenly realised how beautiful she had become, in spite of her appalling, shapeless clothes. All those years ago, she had been pretty enough, but young and unworldly. Now she was strikingly handsome, and a woman of character, to boot. He had thought her just another débutante on the catch for a rich husband. As, indeed, they all were. But to take a risk like this…? There might be more to Miss Amy Devereaux than met the eye. And what met the eye—to do the lady justice—was very attractive indeed. A veritable feast for the eyes of a man who had been cooped up for weeks without female company.

'I…' Her voice had sunk to the tiniest whisper. 'I came to Lyndhurst Chase to find my brother. I fear he has been kidnapped. Or worse. I came because I had to do something.'

If Marcus could have laid hands on Ned Devereaux at that moment, he would gleefully have strangled him. The lad was a selfish brat. And a loose-tongued gossip, into the bargain. He thought of no one but himself. Yet

this young woman—an older sister, taking the part of
Ned's dead mother, no doubt—was prepared to sacrifice
her reputation and her future to save such a ne'er-do-
well of a brother. Ned Devereaux did not deserve such
a sister.

In that moment, Marcus determined that Ned's sister
would not lose her reputation for such an unworthy
cause.

'Miss Devereaux,' Marcus said earnestly. 'Pray do not
be concerned. I know your brother. And I can assure
you that he is perfectly safe.'

'You know it?' she gasped. Her hands had flown to
her mouth.

'Yes, ma'am. I know it for a fact. I promise you that
he is safe. There is no need for you to go on with this
dangerous masquerade.'

'You know? I pray you, sir, tell me where he is. I
must go to him at once.'

'I cannot do that, Miss Devereaux. The information is
not mine to share. But I promise you, on my honour,
that Ned will come to no harm.'

Marcus could see in her face that she was trying to
believe him. Trying, but failing. She thought it was just
a story, to persuade her to give up her servant's role.
Her face had become a picture of misery, followed by
despair.

'Oh, my dear girl,' he said, touched immeasurably by
her pain. He took her in his arms and put a hand to her
hair, stroking gently as he would a frightened child.
Then he turned her face up to his, seeing the tears in her
shadowed eyes.

And then—he could not help himself—he kissed her.

It began as a kiss of comfort. And tenderness. To ease
her fears and remove the frown from her pale brow. But

soon it developed into something deeper. And when, a little hesitantly, Amy at last reached up to place her arms around his neck, Marcus had forgotten every notion of comfort. His whole body was driven to possess her luscious, tempting mouth.

It was like no kiss he had ever before experienced. Here was innocence and knowledge, purity and passion, all at once, spun together into a powerful whirlpool. He could feel himself being pulled down, and under. But he had not the slightest desire to resist.

Until his hand strayed to her breast and she groaned in response to his touch.

Marcus jerked away from her as if he had touched a living flame. What on earth was he doing? He was a fugitive, for heavens' sake!

If it were not for Anthony, Marcus would have been taken up long ago and thrown into gaol. Perhaps even hanged. It did not matter that Marcus was innocent of the attack on Frobisher. The whole world would believe him guilty. His own angry words would stand as his accuser.

With slightly shaking hands, Marcus put her from him and bent to retrieve her cap from the floor. When he straightened, he saw that she was still totally bemused by what had happened between them. Her violet eyes were wide and unseeing. Her lips were red and a little swollen. And still so very tempting.

He fought against the pounding desire to kiss her again. He must not. He was hiding from the law. It was thoroughly dishonourable to treat her so.

'Miss Devereaux.'

She did not react at all.

'Amy,' he said, more urgently now. 'Amy! You must go from here. Your brother is safe. You *must* believe me when I tell you that. But *you* are not. If you should be found here, in this guise, you would be ruined. You *must* leave here. Ned is not worth such a sacrifice.' He put a hand on her cheek. It was a gentle caress. Passion had been replaced by concern.

But she would not have it. She shook him off. 'Ned is my *brother*,' she said in a low, determined voice. 'Who are you—a man of the shadows—to tell me I must abandon him? Who are you—a man who takes advantage of a lone woman—to tell me what I must do?' She grabbed the cap and dragged it over her hair. But she was not so angry or so hasty that she failed to cover every last strand. Amy Devereaux was still being very careful.

Marcus knew that he had lost. With a despairing shrug, he reached out to the desk for her spectacles. Another part of her disguise, and a good one. They were so ugly that no one would try to see beyond them. They would not see those beautiful eyes, the colour of bluebells in the gathering dusk.

She took the spectacles and slid them into place with a nod. 'Thank you, sir.' She was back in control. 'And thank you for your assurances about my brother. You will understand that, with so little information, I am not prepared to give up my quest.' She turned and began to move towards the door. 'But I do thank you,' she added, in a low voice, 'for what little reassurance you have provided.'

'Amy—'

'Have no fear. I collect that you must have your own reasons for lying concealed here. I will not betray your presence in this house. You have my word on that.'

'And you have *my* word,' Marcus began, but the door had closed behind her retreating figure. He sighed. 'You have my word, Amy Devereaux,' he said to the empty room, 'that I shall not betray you.'

He stood for some time, gazing at the closed door. It had been the strangest encounter. He should have been in control. But somehow, his control had faltered. Faced with a strong, determined and totally idiotic woman, he had been outmanoeuvred.

Marcus sat down in Anthony's chair and began to stroke his chin. He must be starting to look like some mad hermit with this growth of beard. It had its uses, however. He had been able to fool Amy Devereaux into thinking that they had never been introduced.

Would she have recognised him if he had been clean-shaven? Probably not. Why should she? She had had admirers a-plenty during that single Season. There was no reason why she should have remembered those few dances with Marcus Sinclair. Indeed, Marcus himself was not at all sure why he remembered her so well. It could not have been merely her striking looks.

He recalled that she had been simple and innocent. And that she had shown a naïve enjoyment of her first Season. Unlike so many of the débutantes at the balls and routs, Amy Devereaux had not appeared to be on the catch for a rich husband. Marcus had assumed, at the time, that it was a clever act, that Miss Devereaux was no different from the rest of her kind. But, if that were so, she had been singularly unsuccessful. For she must now be in her middle twenties and she still had no husband. Instead, she had a feckless younger brother. Poor girl! Ned Devereaux was a heavy burden for any-one. Marcus would lay odds that Ned paid no attention at all to his sister's advice or even to her pleading. The boy seemed intent on gambling away his substance before he was more than a couple of years into his majority.

Marcus rose and crossed to the window, taking care that he remained sufficiently in the shadows that he could not be seen from the garden. He looked out. He could picture Ned Devereaux in his prison. Not only was the lad safe, he was also well away from the temptations he seemed unable to resist. If Amy Devereaux only knew the whole, she would surely be grateful that her brother was being preserved from further harm. And that she was, too. Marcus had been right to extract that promise from her. She would certainly be unmasked if she spoke to Anthony about discovering Marcus—

Anthony… Marcus ran his hand through his unkempt hair. Oh, God! Anthony! Marcus was deceiving his closest friend. He ought to tell him about Amy Devereaux. She was in Anthony's house under false pretences.

But Marcus had promised not to betray her. Besides, Anthony was in no mood to hear any plea from Marcus that the girl be treated with consideration. Indeed, Anthony was in no mood to hear anything at all from Marcus. They had not had a single exchange since that encounter over the miniature of Anthony's wife. Marcus slept on the narrow dressing-room pallet and Anthony slept in the huge marriage bed. He acted as if Marcus were invisible. Marcus had begun to apologise, more than once, but Anthony had simply stalked away.

Things could not continue in this vein. But, trapped as he was in the dressing room, Marcus had no opportunity to remedy matters. He must simply wait until Anthony had calmed down enough to discuss the situation calmly. It would be soon, Marcus fervently hoped. But, even then, Marcus would not be able to tell

Anthony about the presence of Amy Devereaux in his house.

She was risking everything for the sake of her feckless brother. Marcus could not be the one to betray her.

Chapter Four

Amy stood in front of the brown-spotted mirror, fingering her lips. It was not that her mouth looked different. Although it did. It was how it *felt*. Caressed. Desired. She had never been kissed before. Never like that. While he was kissing her, her insides had been melting, and glowing, like a river of liquid gold. Part of her was glowing still, in spite of everything.

She had wanted it to go on and on. She had slid her arms around his neck, skimming her fingers over the silken beard to the bare skin at the back of his neck, beneath his long hair. She had felt more alive in those fleeting moments than at any time since she had left the schoolroom.

She was a fool! She did not even know his name. She had been so bemused by her own reaction to him that she had not thought to ask. Not that he would have told her. Of course, he would not. He was determined to guard his secrets well.

And yet, he knew who she was. And he knew Ned, too. He had said that Ned was safe. He had said it over and over again. If only she could believe it—but she dared not do so. The man's words had proved, beyond any doubt, that someone here at the Chase had kid-napped Ned. Amy had been right. Her brother was being held somewhere. And the dark stranger was as likely to be the culprit as anyone else.

Dear God! Had she allowed herself to be kissed by Ned's abductor? Was it possible? She had no way of knowing. But there was every likelihood that Ned's dis-appearance and the presence of the bearded man were connected. He was clearly being hidden in the Major's bedchamber. He must have been concealed inside the huge clothes press when Amy checked the dressing room.

And she was certainly right about the Major's valet. Timms *must* be party to what was going on.

Amy frowned at her reflection, remembering. The stranger had said that her eyes were beautiful. And her hair. She groaned aloud. No matter *what* he had said, she was out of her mind to think about him! She must not go into the Major's bedchamber again. What she must do, right now, was to go below stairs and try to discover some clue to Ned's whereabouts.

She would start with Timms, if she could get him alone. And, failing the valet, she could always try to strike up a conversation with Eliza Ebdon, Lady Quinlan's maid.

Amy swallowed nervously at the thought. So far, she had always avoided the other abigail. It was too dan-gerous to become close to Ebdon, for a true professional would be the first to detect that Amy was a fraud. But—on the other hand—Eliza Ebdon was close to Timms. It was poignant, somehow, that two people well past the first flush of youth could look at each other with so much longing and shared understanding. Oh, they tried to con-ceal it, right enough, but Amy had seen the secret glances that passed between them. When Lady Margaret and Mr Lyndhurst-Flint's valet were summarily dismissed after that unsavoury episode on the back stairs, Ebdon had thrown Timms a look of absolute triumph. And he had responded with a flicker of a smile.

Ebdon had clearly known about Lady Margaret's predilections. What else did she know about what went on in this house? Might she even know where Ned was being held?

'Another glass of wine, Miss Dent?'

'No, I thank you. St Paul recommends only a little wine for the stomach's sake. I never take more than one glass. My compliments on the dessert, however. It was delicious.' Amy smiled myopically in the general direction of the cook.

The cook beamed back at her. 'The Major don't go in for fancy cooking, as a rule. But just occasionally, I like to try my hand at something different below stairs.' With a conspiratorial glance around the laden table, she added, 'Only for the senior servants, naturally.' The others smiled or nodded their agreement. Without a word, the butler unstoppered the decanter and refilled all but Amy's glass.

The little group in the housekeeper's sitting room certainly did not stint itself when it came to the Major's wine cellar. The butler, the housekeeper, the cook, the Major's valet and the two visiting lady's maids—they made a very select little company, Amy decided, grateful that the other valets were missing on this occasion. Amy would not have dared to sit here under the eye of the Earl of Mardon's valet. The man could ask awkward questions, for he knew that Amy had been employed for a few weeks only, while the Countess's regular abigail was nursing her sick mother. That was the story that Sarah and Amy had concocted together. But, on closer inspection, Amy's story would be shown to be thin and full of holes. She could not afford to be questioned by the Earl's valet. He was just one more servant she had to avoid.

Even in this small group, Amy knew she was risking much. She had already noticed a few searching glances from Eliza Ebdon. Lady Quinlan's abigail was no fool.

'How is Mr William managing without his valet, Mr Ufton? I know young Charles is willing enough, but I've always thought him a bit of a moonling. He was nowhere to be seen when we had to move Mr William to the second floor. Don't know how I'd have done it all in time without Miss Dent's help.' The housekeeper smiled across at Amy.

'I'll speak to Charles about it, Mrs Waller. You should have told me sooner. The lad does his best, but I agree he is slow. Can't understand why Mr William declined the Major's offer of your services, Mr Timms. For a gentleman so very particular about every last stitch of his rig, it does seem odd that he'd choose a green boy over a trained valet.'

Timms nodded thoughtfully. 'It's not for me to say, Mr Ufton. But then, I'm just an old army man, born and bred, not a knowing one like Grant.'

The housekeeper snorted. 'We're well rid of Grant. Couldn't keep his hands off the maids. It's bad enough that I've still got to keep the maids away from the wandering hands *above* stairs.'

The cook grinned. 'Come now, Mrs Waller, that's doing it too brown. Most of the gentlemen guests would never do such a thing. And young Mr Devereaux was only stealing a kiss or two. There weren't no harm in him. Not like Mr William, now. He—'

The butler glanced sideways at the visiting abigails and cleared his throat warningly. Chastened, the cook swallowed hard and said nothing more.

Amy hoped she was not blushing at this evidence of Ned's shameless behaviour. It was nothing new, after all. She was starting to rack her brains for some way of finding out more about Ned's time at the Chase, when the housekeeper broke the strained silence. 'Miss Lyndhurst was complaining about her bedchamber again today. Said that no lady should ever be housed in a yellow bedchamber. Ruinous for the complexion, she maintains.'

Eliza Ebdon gave a sharp laugh, which she tried to disguise as a cough. The butler nodded absently, before taking a large mouthful of wine.

'She wants to be moved to a different bedchamber,' the housekeeper continued. 'I heard her telling the Major so.'

Eliza Ebdon, recovered now, said, 'Since the Viscount has moved upstairs to join his wife, Miss Lyndhurst could have his old room, across the hall. It's large and comfortable. And it has the added advantage of not being yellow.'

The housekeeper shook her head. 'I'm afraid it won't do, Miss Ebdon. It has no dressing room. The Major offered it, too, but Miss Lyndhurst is adamant that she must have a dressing room for her companion. Won't hear of poor Miss Saunders being given a chamber of her own. And her a lady, too!'

Amy shook her head in a gesture of sympathy.

'Surely Miss Saunders could ask for her own room?'

the cook said. 'The Major would not refuse her, I'm sure.'

'That's as may be,' replied the housekeeper, 'but since Miss Saunders seems to go out of her way to avoid the Major, I fancy it is unlikely to happen. Why, last evening she did not even come down to dinner. Apparently she wanted to finish some sewing. Or that's what Miss Lyndhurst said. I had to send up a tray to the dressing room.'

Amy swallowed her frustration. Given half a chance, the housekeeper would continue to gossip all night. Amy must find a way of turning this conversation back to Ned. There must be something she could say—

There was a very discreet knock on the door. The housekeeper looked up in annoyance at the interruption.

Muttering a little under his breath, the butler replaced his almost empty glass and went to open the door, where he held a low-voiced conversation with someone outside. Amy strained to hear their words, but could not make them out. The butler had not opened the door more than a crack. No doubt he felt that the underling outside should not see what his betters were about.

When he resumed his seat, the butler was frowning. He looked round at the rest of the company, as if assessing them. 'We have a slight…er…difficulty. I shall say nothing of it to the lower servants. However, I must ask you, Mrs Waller, to ensure that all the female servants remain within the house.' He ignored the housekeeper's sharp intake of breath. 'It is not for me, of course, to order the comings and goings of our lady visitors, Miss Dent and Miss Ebdon. To you, ladies,' he said, with a slight bow of his head, 'I can give only advice.'

Eliza Ebdon glanced sideways at Timms. He gave her

a tiny nod of reassurance in return. It was yet another sign of their deep understanding, Amy was sure, yet no one but Amy seemed to notice.

'I have no desire to alarm you, ladies, but I must warn you that there appears to be a stranger lurking in the woods, towards the North Lodge. One of the keepers has seen him. Twice, now. The stranger may be harmless, of course, but…' He let the words die on his tongue. 'If you have occasion to walk in that direction, I would strongly counsel you not to do so alone.'

There was dead silence round the table while they all digested this unwelcome news. Amy's heart was racing. It couldn't be Ned, could it?

Timms glanced briefly towards Eliza Ebdon before leaning forward a little. 'Do we know what the man looks like, Mr Ufton?' Timms was always practical, it seemed.

'Not really. Medium height. Neither old nor young, apparently. Thinnish, the lad said.'

That did not sound very much like Ned, vague though the description was. Amy tried to mask her disappointment. 'Are you suggesting that we might be in danger from this man, Mr Ufton?' she asked crisply, putting just a touch of hauteur into her voice.

'Why, no, Miss Dent. No, indeed. At Lyndhurst Chase? Why, the very idea is outrageous. But…but I would ask you not to venture into the north woods alone. Just for a day or two. Until we have caught him.'

'I see. Very well then. Since I must.' If it were not Ned, could it yet have something to do with his disappearance? Might this unknown man be holding Ned, somewhere close by? Amy needed time to think it through, but the gossip and wine of the upper servants' room would be of no help at all.

With an apologetic smile, Amy rose to her feet and smoothed her skirts. 'Thank you for your hospitality, Mrs Waller, Mr Ufton. I hope you will excuse me if I retire now. I have much still to do this evening and it is getting late.' She clasped her hands together and tried to look self-satisfied. 'An hour's sleep before midnight is worth two after, as the proverb tells us.'

'Of course, Miss Dent. Of course. We appreciate your desire to have everything just so for her ladyship.'

'Well, goodnight then.' Amy made for the door. The butler hurried across to open it for her.

As he was closing it behind her, Amy was sure she heard the housekeeper whisper, 'Gone to read her Bible, no doubt. Thinks herself a cut above the rest of us. As if we were all heathens!'

Amy walked calmly through the servants' hall, pretending that she had heard nothing. It was gratifying to know that at least one part of her disguise was still working well.

The servants' candles waited on the little table by the door to the passageway. Amy bent to light one. Straightening again, she saw that her way was barred. It was Charles, the young footman who had taken on the role of valet to Mr Lyndhurst-Flint. Outlined in the doorway into the passageway, he loomed large and menacing. And there was no one about to help her.

Amy's heart began to race. Was this young man already following in his new master's footsteps? The way he was looking at her—

He put an arm out across Amy's path, forcing her to stop.

Amy drew herself up very straight and looked daggers at him. 'I will thank you to let me pass, Charles,' she said haughtily.

'I...I beg your pardon, Miss Dent,' the footman stammered, dropping his arm as if she had struck him.

Gracious! He was little more than a boy. He sounded just like Ned had used to do when he was younger and looking to Amy for advice.

'I've been searching for you, miss, these last fifteen minutes. I was sent to find you. Her ladyship needs you.'

'Her ladyship normally rings if she wants me,' Amy said flatly. The lad was well meaning, certainly, but there was something odd about this. Sarah would not send for Amy now. She knew precisely what Amy was doing below stairs. And how important it was.

'Ah, no, Miss Dent. Her ladyship ain't in her own chamber. She is on the first floor. I'm to tell you to go to her there.'

Had Sarah discovered something? 'Very well. I shall go at once.'

The young footman stepped back instantly. He almost bowed as Amy swept by him towards the backstairs.

Poor lad. He was big and strong, and he looked the part of a footman, but his understanding was not even moderate. The housekeeper had been right. Amy paused, one foot on the bottom tread, and turned back. 'Is the Countess in the ladies' sitting room?'

'Oh. No, miss. Beg pardon. I forgot. You are to go to her in the vacant bedchamber. The one as was the Viscount's, before he was wed.' He tried to smile. It wobbled a little. 'It's next to the master's bedchamber,' he added, trying to be helpful.

How very curious. With a quick nod to the footman, Amy hurried up the backstairs. Sarah must have found something in that room. But what on earth could it be? Surely Lord Quinlan could not have had any hand in Ned's disappearance? And, even if he were involved, he would not have left any evidence behind in an empty bedroom.

She ran up the flights of stairs as quickly as she dared, shielding her tiny flame from the draught.

Amy knocked on the door to the empty bedchamber. She must take care. Sarah might not be alone.

She waited. No answer.

There was no point in knocking again. Raising her candle a little, Amy opened the door and stepped inside.

The room was brightly lit. Two branches of candles stood upon the side tables. But Amy could see no one.

'My lady?' Amy heard the slight tremor in her own voice.

An arm slid between Amy's back and the half-open door. It closed with a snap. A moment later, a hand in the small of her back pushed her further into the room.

Amy whirled. William Lyndhurst-Flint! He was leaning against the door. One corner of his mouth was twisted into a very unpleasant leer.

'We have unfinished business, you and I,' he said curtly.

Amy retreated a pace, then forced herself to stop. 'I am summoned to my lady, sir. If I do not appear, I will be missed.'

He laughed harshly. 'Your mistress is below in the drawing room with all the other guests. She has no thought of you. I must say that you are very easily gulled, Dent. No challenge at all. Now…'

Amy took a deep breath. 'I warn you. I shall scream if you come one step nearer.'

'Go ahead,' he said with a wave of his hand. 'There is no one about to hear. Everyone is downstairs. Scream, by all means. It will add a little spice to the proceedings.

You owe me a deal of satisfaction after the episode with that stupid girl. It is time you were reminded of your place.' He straightened, and began to move towards her.

Amy was terrified. His eyes were gleaming with lust. And he was longing for revenge. She had saved that housemaid. Now he would have Amy instead. Somehow, fear sharpened her mind. There was only one door into this room. She must not retreat from it. She must fight here.

Without further thought, she stepped forward to meet her attacker and drove her lighted candle into his face. She was not quick enough. He fended it off. But Amy was already screaming at the top of her voice.

'A fighter, eh?' he muttered through gritted teeth. He made to grab her by the throat. 'I shall enjoy having you.'

Amy ducked under his outstretched hands and kicked out. Her heavy-soled boots made contact with his shin and he gasped in pain. She tried to make a dash for the door, but he was ahead of her. In spite of his injury.

'No, you don't, my fiery doxy. Payment first.' He grabbed her round the waist and threw her bodily against the wall. Amy was left with no breath to scream again. 'Now,' he said menacingly.

The door hit the wall with a deafening crash. Lyndhurst-Flint's jaw dropped. His eyes goggled. 'M...Ma—'

He was not permitted to finish the word. The bearded stranger reached him in two strides and felled him with a right to the jaw. 'You never learn, do you?' he snarled.

Lyndhurst-Flint touched a hand to his split lip. His fingers came away covered with blood. The sight of it seemed to enrage him even more. He scrambled to his feet and squared up to his opponent. 'So you are here, are you? Hiding out from the law. Like the coward you are!'

The dark man's indrawn breath hissed loudly between his teeth. Amy, too, gasped at such an insult. The sound was enough to distract the dark man from his opponent. For just a second too long. Lyndhurst-Flint hit him full in the stomach and bent him double.

Amy's hand went to her mouth.

The fight that ensued was short, and bloody. Although Lyndhurst-Flint had caught his opponent by surprise, he was no match for Amy's would-be rescuer. In a matter of minutes, Lyndhurst-Flint was sprawled on the floor once more, bleeding freely.

The dark man stood over him. 'By God, William, you won't try this on another woman!'

'And who will stop me? You? From your prison cell?'

The bearded man bent down and grabbed a handful of Lyndhurst-Flint's shirt. He started to pull the bleeding man to his feet.

'Sir!'

Timms, the valet, stood in the open doorway.

Lyndhurst-Flint tugged his shirt free and pushed himself up. With a scathing look at his opponent, he drew a fine handkerchief from his pocket and put it to his bleeding face. 'The family fugitive has appeared, Timms. Out of nowhere, it seems. You had best fetch the Major. He will wish to ensure that the law takes its course.'

Timms looked hard at the injured man. And then at his opponent. He spared barely a glance for Amy before turning on his heel and disappearing.

Marcus looked across at Amy Devereaux. She was deathly pale. But she was not about to faint, thank God! She was a fool to be alone with William, however.

William was infinitely dangerous to female servants. Did Anthony know that? Possibly not. More to the point, if Anthony questioned Amy now, her true identity might well be discovered.

He motioned her towards the door. 'Go,' he said sharply.

'But—'

'Go! I will deal with the Major. And this…apology for a gentleman.'

'We'll see about that,' William said. 'And as for her… Do you really think that Anthony will take the word of a mere servant against mine?'

'It is not the servant's word you have to fear, William,' Marcus said with venom. Amy was still standing against the wall. 'For God's sake, woman, do you never do as you are told? Go to your quarters! I will deal with this.'

Her eyes widened at the force of his words. But, at last, she nodded and scurried out.

Marcus allowed himself a deep breath once Amy was out of sight. She was safe enough. For the moment. Now he had only to deal with Anthony.

He had almost no time to prepare. Anthony was already striding along the corridor, with Timms at his heels.

Reaching the door, Anthony said, 'Wait outside, Timms. No one is to enter this room. Make sure no one knows we are here.'

Timms nodded.

Anthony shut the door and stood with his back to it. He was certainly furious, but he did not raise his voice. 'Well?' he said grimly, looking directly neither at Marcus nor at William.

Marcus chose to say nothing. The gulf between him and Anthony was clearly as wide as ever.

'Marcus has turned up here, of all places. You cannot harbour a fugitive, Anthony. He must stand his trial.'

'You would hand over your own cousin, William?' Anthony said softly.

'We must uphold the law, Anthony. You know that as well as I. If Marcus is innocent, no doubt the court will free him.'

'By God,' Marcus began, 'you—'

'You forget, Marcus,' William interrupted smoothly. 'I was there. I heard your threats. And your insults. Every last one of them.'

Anthony rocked back a fraction, as if he had been struck.

'I said many things that night. I admit they were…unwise. But they were only words. I did not attack Frobisher.'

'So you say,' sneered William. 'Anthony—'

'Enough of this,' snapped Anthony. 'I am not about to have my own cousin hauled off to gaol in the middle of the night. Whatever else he may be, Marcus is a gentleman. I will decide matters tomorrow.'

'But—'

'I have made up my mind, William. You will say nothing of this.'

William smoothed his hair and nodded politely. 'Of course. This is your house, and you are master here. I wished to say only… A suggestion, Anthony, nothing more. You might like to consider the potential harm to your reputation if Marcus, having once been apprehended, were to disappear again from under your roof.'

'I was not planning on leaving, as it happens. But William is right, Anthony. You cannot afford to be seen to be lenient with a dangerous fugitive such as I.' With narrowed eyes, Marcus fixed his gaze on Anthony and held out his wrists. 'Manacles would do the job, if you have any to hand.'

Anthony exploded. 'Damn you, Marcus!' He seized the handle and wrenched the door open. 'Timms! Escort Mr Sinclair to my dressing room and lock him in. He may cool his heels there while I decide what is to be done with him.' Anthony turned back and threw a look of loathing at William. 'I don't make such decisions in hot blood, William, even at your urging. I have a shooting party tomorrow, and I intend to enjoy it. The future of our…fugitive can be considered after that.'

Marcus laughed. He felt he had to show that Anthony's betrayal meant nothing. 'Why not take that smelly old setter with you? See if she can earn her keep.'

Anthony turned away. 'Oh, and Timms,' he said silkily, 'make sure that Mr Sinclair has the opportunity to speak to no one. Do you understand me? No one at all.'

Chapter Five

'Now, sir. You heard the Major's orders. This time, I'm afraid I shall have to lock you in.'

Marcus grinned. 'Don't look so long-faced, Timms. You know I could make a bolt for freedom if I wanted to.'

The valet looked a little uncomfortable. He was strong, and wiry, but he would be no match for Marcus's greater weight and skill in a hand-to-hand fight.

'There are enough black rumours about your master's reputation. I shall not allow anyone to say that Anthony Lyndhurst deliberately failed to hold a dangerous fugitive.'

'Aye, sir, I know that. Thank you. And the Major would know it, too, if he stopped to think—' Timms broke off, looking a little guilty, as if he had said too much. 'Got a lot on his mind just at present, the Major has,' he finished lamely.

'And so have I. You might bring me some supper, Timms, since I am to be incarcerated here.'

'Right you are, sir. And some hot water, too, if I may suggest? Now that you are known to be here, you have no excuse for looking like a wild man. Begging y'r pardon, sir.'

Marcus grinned again. 'That was another of the Major's orders, was it?'

'No, sir. This one is all mine.'

Marcus strolled into the dressing room. 'In that case, I shall not object. Bring on your hot water. And your barber's shears, too, if you will.'

Timms smiled grimly. 'It will be my pleasure, sir.' He went back into Anthony's bedchamber and closed the door. Marcus heard the key turn in the lock.

He stood for a moment, stroking his beard. He would miss it, somehow. However, Timms was right. If Marcus was to be dragged off to gaol on the morrow, he might as well look like a gentleman rather than an escaped felon.

He looked round his familiar prison. Timms had done nothing about the other door, leading into the corridor. Since Marcus's arrival, it had been kept locked, of course, but that was to protect Marcus, not to imprison him. The key was still on the inside.

Marcus pocketed it, wondering. Timms was too good a man to have forgotten about the second door. He clearly intended Marcus to take the key. It was not disloyalty on Timms's part, Marcus decided. Such a thing was unthinkable. But Timms knew Anthony as well as anyone. He certainly knew that, once Anthony's temper cooled—if it ever did—he would regret any hasty moves to hand Marcus over to the authorities. Timms had given Marcus a little leeway, that was all.

Marcus crossed to the window and stood, looking out. It was a beautiful, clear night. The filigree of stars against the blue depths reminded him of nights in the Peninsula, when he and Anthony had been fast friends, fighting side by side. They still were, surely? A friendship as strong as theirs could not be shattered by a single stupid incident over a woman's picture.

The knock was so soft that he almost missed it. It came again. On the door to the corridor. Someone was there. Someone who was trying to be discreet.

He strode quickly across the room and put his ear to the door. 'Who is there?' he said softly.

'Dent, sir. Lady Mardon's maid.'

Was there no end to the woman's risk-taking? The door was not in full view of the other rooms on this floor, but Timms could return at any moment. 'Amy,' he whispered urgently, 'you are out of your mind to come here. Have you not risked enough already?'

'I have risked no more than you, sir,' she replied calmly. 'In saving me, you put yourself in jeopardy. I know that now.'

'Nonsense!' Marcus lied instantly.

'I have some information,' she continued, ignoring his outburst. 'I don't know if it will help, but I saw a letter in...in Mr Lyndhurst-Flint's bedchamber. He was trying to borrow money against his expectation of becoming the Major's heir.'

Marcus drew in a sharp breath, between clenched teeth. Yes. William would do that. William was so desperate for money that he would do anything...almost anything. He was a gentleman, surely? He could not be responsible for—

'Sir?'

'Thank you, ma'am, for the information. But please go! You will be discovered if you remain here. I—'

'Miss Dent?'

It was Timms's voice. Marcus heard Amy's little gasp of shock.

'May I ask what you are doing here, Miss Dent?'

'I came to speak to the gentleman in there. To thank him.'

Timms cleared his throat, rather too loudly. 'Aye. Well… The Major knows nothing of that. You wouldn't want Mr Lyndhurst-Flint to complain of you to your mistress.'

'No, but—'

'I must ask you not to speak further with…the man in there, Miss Dent. The Major has given strict orders. You weren't there to hear, of course, so I can overlook it. Just this once.'

She didn't reply. Marcus fancied he heard her retreating footsteps, but he could not be certain.

He knew for sure when the door from the bedroom opened and Timms appeared. He was carrying hot water and towels. 'If ye're going to be carted off to gaol, Mr Marcus, you might as well look the part of the gentleman while you do it,' he said, echoing Marcus's own thoughts.

The sky had clouded over. What a pity. Perhaps it might rain on Anthony's shooting party. That old setter would come back filthy as well as smelly.

Marcus continued his pacing. He ought to be trying to sleep. Everyone else in the house was long abed, even Anthony in the bedchamber next door. But Marcus's growing suspicions about William would not let him rest. William had been at that gaming hell in London. William had heard Frobisher insult Anthony, and then Marcus's angry threats. Until their quarrel, Marcus had been a potential heir to Anthony's fortune. Marcus had no need of it. But William certainly did. What lengths would he go to, in order to remove a rival?

Oh, it was nonsense! William was Marcus's cousin. And John Mardon's brother, besides. The Lyndhursts were a family of gentlemen. Even William could not sink so low.

There was a tiny tap at the door to the corridor.

Who could be there at three o'clock in the morning? 'Sir? Sir!'

Good God! Amy Devereaux again! The woman had no thought at all for her own safety. Marcus felt in his waistcoat pocket for the key. He dare not leave her standing in the corridor. Not at this hour.

He had opened the door and pulled her inside before she had a chance to say a word. 'Shh!' he whispered urgently, relocking the door.

Her eyes widened. Then she nodded.

Marcus took the candleholder from her fingers and set it down. He cupped his hand against her cheek and whispered into her ear, 'Miss Devereaux, you are, without doubt, the most idiotic woman I have ever encountered. Do you never stop to think? Anthony Lyndhurst lies sleeping only yards from where we stand. And still you come knocking at my door?'

'I came to offer my help,' she replied in a tiny whisper. She looked him full in the face. Her brow was smooth, untroubled. She was quite determined on this.

And then he saw the flash of recognition in her eyes. Even her spectacles could not mask it.

Marcus clapped his hand over her mouth to cover her cry of shock. She must not be allowed to betray them.

She did not struggle against him. But her eyes left him in no doubt of her disgust at being manhandled in such a way. And by a man she knew!

Damn Timms and his valeting skills! He had turned Marcus back into something like the man Amy

Devereaux had met all those years ago. And it was clear that she was remembering.

Marcus put a finger to his lips and waited for her nod of agreement before freeing her mouth. She would not scream now. She must understand the dangers of her situation perfectly well.

'I came to offer my help,' she whispered again, 'to a nameless prisoner. But you are not nameless. You are Lieutenant Sinclair.'

Marcus grinned briefly. 'That was a long time ago, Miss Devereaux. It has been plain Mr Sinclair for many a year now.'

Amy nodded. She had heard about Lieutenant Sinclair's sudden departure from the army. He had been unwilling at first to bow to his widowed mother's pleading. But, as an only son, and the inheritor of a huge estate, he had had little choice in the end. He had resigned his commission and, barely into his majority, he had found himself one of the most eligible bachelors in London. She had seen at first hand how ruthlessly he had been hunted. She should have been one of the huntresses herself—the Devereaux estate had needed the money, even then—but instead she had felt sorry for him. Had it shown? Was that why he had remembered her?

'And even plain Mr Sinclair is not someone a lady should know.'

'Why not?'

'Because I am a fugitive, Miss Devereaux, sought by the law. You heard William say as much.'

'Yes,' Amy said slowly. But she was shaking her head as she spoke.

'And you have come to offer help to a fugitive?'

'I came to offer help to the man who rescued me. And I still wish to help you, Mr Sinclair.'

'You would help me to escape?'

'If that is your wish. Yes.'

A brief, rueful smile touched his mouth. 'I cannot do that. Not from the Major's custody. If he chooses to give me up to the law, well...so be it.'

'But what have you done?' Amy could no longer rein back her curiosity.

'I allowed too much wine to loosen my tongue, Miss Devereaux,' he said cryptically.

She threw him an arch look. 'If that were a felony, most of the gentlemen in England would be in gaol.'

'True.'

Amy said nothing. She waited.

'Oh, very well. It is not an edifying tale, however. There was an argument between myself and a man named Frobisher. He insulted my family. And I threatened to kill him. In front of witnesses. The following day, he was attacked and left for dead. He maintains that I was his assailant.'

'But you were not.'

'No, Miss Devereaux, I was not. I am not in the habit of striking from behind.'

'No. Of course not. But why should Mr Frobisher be so sure that it was you?'

'Ah, yes. I thought you were no fool, ma'am. You have put your finger upon it. I assumed, at first, that it was a simple mistake, that Frobisher was in his cups again, and confused. But it appears that it was no such thing. Whoever attacked Frobisher deliberately repeated my words. Frobisher was intended to believe I was his assailant.'

'But that is wicked! They could hang you.'

'Indeed.'

'You must escape.'

'No, Miss Devereaux, that is not possible. I will not.'

'But—' Amy broke off at the sight of the grim determination in his blue-grey eyes. Marcus Sinclair would rather be sent to gaol—perhaps to the scaffold—than betray Major Lyndhurst's trust. That was not the action of a dishonourable man. She touched his arm lightly with her fingertips. 'Mr Sinclair, if I may not help you to escape, allow me, at least, to help you to prove you are innocent of this despicable crime. Tell me what I must do.'

'There is nothing you can do.' He raised his hand and gently brushed his knuckles across her cheek.

Amy shivered.

'I hesitate to say this again, since you have ignored me on every previous occasion, but I do strongly urge you to give up this dangerous fraud of yours.'

Amy began to shake her head vehemently.

He stopped her forcibly by putting his hands to her face. 'You have courage, Amy, and determination. They are admirable, and unusual, qualities in a lady. But your judgement is sadly lacking. First, you indulge in this idiotic masquerade. And now you wish to help a fugitive from the law. You are clearly intent on ensuring your own downfall.'

Amy did not respond. She closed her eyes, so that she could focus on the warmth and gentleness of his touch on her skin. Such an innocent joining of their flesh. And yet she could feel it in the depths of her being. Her whole body was tingling. She wanted to melt into him.

She knew the whole now, and she knew who he was. It did not matter that he was a fugitive. She had not the least doubt of his innocence.

'Amy,' he said softly.

She did not open her eyes. He would try to make her promise to leave the Chase. And now, she was more than ever determined not to do so.

'Amy,' he said again.

She could feel his breath on her lips. He was so very close. He was going to kiss her. The warm glow that had filled her at his touch began to kindle into a tiny flame. She swayed towards him.

But he let her go and stepped back.

Amy's eyes flew open. Before she could help herself, she let out a little mew of disappointment.

His reaction was immediate. 'Pray, do not sigh, my dear Miss Devereaux. I am not worth it. You must have nothing more to do with me. If I were a free man, I could— Enough of that! I am not a free man. I pray you will take no risks on my behalf.'

Amy stared at him, refusing to give him the assurance he sought.

He gazed back at her. The temptation she represented was immense. Marcus wanted nothing more than to pull her against his aroused body and kiss her until she was mindless with passion. But she was an innocent. She would recoil from his ardour.

A thought struck him with the force of a douche of freezing water. He had been on the point of kissing her before, when she first came upon him here. And he had been completely naked. He had turned away, eventually, but she had shown no signs of surprise or fear. Perhaps Amy Devereaux made a habit of visiting gentlemen in their bedchambers? Perhaps she was not an innocent at all?

Marcus retreated a pace to put a safe distance between his still-heated body and temptation. Just the thought of kissing her and he was fully aroused. It was becoming plaguey uncomfortable.

'You saved me from Mr Lyndhurst-Flint. I am sure he was going to attack me.'

'Of course he was!' Marcus snapped, allowing his anger free rein, in an effort to divert his thoughts. 'You were a fool to go apart with him.'

Amy narrowed her eyes. 'You have a very poor opinion of me, sir. Of course I did not agree to be alone with him. He tricked me into that room. I believed I was going to meet Sarah.'

Marcus took a deep breath, swallowing a curse. 'It seems I owe you an apology, ma'am. Again.'

She looked up at him and gave a tiny nod.

'But I do not apologise for saying—again—that you should not be doing this. I own that I have some suspicions about how Frobisher came to accuse me. If I am right, I should be able to obtain proof easily enough.'

Amy's raised eyebrows were eloquent. She wanted him to know she did not believe a word of it.

'I thank you for your offer of help, Miss Devereaux, but I decline it. And now you must go.'

The determined set of her shoulders told him that she had no intention of doing what he asked. Ignoring every word he had said, she laid out her conclusion starkly. 'You think William Lyndhurst-Flint is to blame, do you not?'

By Jove, she was sharp!

'He is trying to trade on his expectations. We both know that. If you were to become the Major's heir, he would have no such expectations. If you become a convicted felon, however…' Gazing at him, wide-eyed, she let her words trail into nothing. When he did not immediately reply, she said, 'I see that I am right.'

'Amy—'

'And if there is proof to be had, it will be in Mr Lyndhurst-Flint's chamber. He will be out shooting all day. I shall have time to search his room much more thoroughly than I did on the last occasion.'

'No!' That single word was much too loud. Could Anthony have heard? He dropped his voice to a whisper once more. An urgent whisper. 'No, Amy! I beg you. It is much too dangerous.'

She cocked her head on one side and looked up at him with a tiny smile twisting the corner of her mouth. Then she dropped him an impudent curtsy. 'I will be able to tell you what I find. There will be no danger. Timms will be in the field with the Major.'

'Amy—'

'And now I must go. You have detained me much too long, sir.'

'Why, you—'

She grinned at him and put a finger to her lips. Marcus wanted to laugh, but he simply shook his head in disbelief. 'You are quite astonishing, Amy Devereaux. And if you remain here one moment longer, I will not be answerable for my actions.' He took a step towards her. To his surprise, she stood her ground, smiling up at him.

'Amy…' he said menacingly.

'Mmm?'

He must not do this. He forced himself to step around her and to unlock the door. 'Go, you unbiddable wench!' He reached out a hand to her. She placed her fingers in it and allowed him to pull her towards the door. He opened it and pushed her gently into the corridor.

But before he let her go completely, he raised her fingers to his lips and kissed them.

It was madness, indeed.

* * *

Marcus lent back against the door. He let out a long, heartfelt sigh. It was not Amy Devereaux who was out of her mind. It was Marcus himself.

He should have told her the truth about her brother. It would have meant betraying Anthony's role in the kidnapping but, given the huge risks Amy was taking to help Marcus, he should have given her the reassurance she was desperate for. She could be trusted with the knowledge of Ned's hiding place, surely?

Marcus's common sense spoke up over his feelings of guilt. If he told Amy where her brother was, she would be bound to go there, to see for herself. And if she found Ned, others could do so, too. Anthony had been wise to spirit the lad away. It would not be for much longer, in any case. Not if Anthony decided to hand Marcus over to the law.

Abstractedly, Marcus ran a hand through his hair, noticing how much shorter it now was. Timms had been determined to make him presentable. Blast the man!

Did Amy find him presentable?

That thought had formed itself without any prompting. What on earth did it mean?

Shaking his head in disbelief, Marcus strode back to the window and gazed out at the night sky. Some of the stars were visible still, bright and unchanging, always there, always the same. To be relied upon. As Amy Devereaux was to be relied upon.

It seemed she was quite determined to take Marcus's part against the world. And nothing he could say, or do, would stop her.

He had never before encountered a woman like Amy. Not in all his life. She even seemed to be totally different from the débutante he had met all those years before.

She had been very young then, of course, for it was just before her Season was cut short by her father's illness and death. She couldn't have been more than eighteen. Marcus had been little older. But, though only twenty-two, he had already learned to be very wary of single ladies. Single ladies coveted his fortune. He had had plenty of proof of that. Only Anthony's intervention had saved him from a disastrous marriage in Spain. And Marcus had had two other very narrow escapes after his return to London.

And yet he had danced with Amy Devereaux. More than once. Why? His memories of her were now a little vague—a pretty face, good humour, and a light step in the dance. Was that all there was?

He shook his head. There must have been something more.

There was. Of course there was. He had taken her on to a balcony. In a moment of madness, he had tried to kiss her. He remembered it now. He remembered the honeyed scent of her in his arms. Amy Devereaux had been so tempting that all his resolutions about single ladies had evaporated. But she had simply ducked away, with a merry laugh. Other young ladies would have slapped his face, or—worse—allowed his advances in hopes of ensnaring him. Amy had done neither.

Marcus could smile at the memory now. Even then, she had been a remarkable woman—if he had but seen it. He had been too young to sense her true worth.

He knew it now.

He gazed out at the brightest visible star and made a silent vow. If ever he should come through this terrible coil, he would seek out Amy Devereaux and find out the real truth about what she was. And what she had become.

Chapter Six

'And so I said I would search the room,' Amy finished, ignoring the slight prick of her conscience. Mr Sinclair had already betrayed himself. Half the household must have heard about that fight by now. Besides, Amy needed Sarah's help.

'I don't believe it,' Sarah said. 'Marcus would never have asked you to take such a risk. He didn't, did he?'

'Er…no. To tell you the truth, Sarah, he forbade me to do it. But I have no intention of obeying him. All the gentlemen will be out shooting and their personal servants will be with them. I can slip into Mr Lyndhurst-Flint's room when I am sure no one is about. It is next door to your bedchamber, after all. It will be easy.'

'It will be dangerous,' Sarah said flatly. 'But I can see that you are not to be dissuaded. So, obviously, I shall have to help you. Now, let me see… Yes, that will do, I think. Cassie suggested, just yesterday, that the ladies should have a picnic on the roof, so that we might watch the shooting. She even suggested we might use a telescope to see exactly what was going on. Great-aunt Harriet took Cassie to task for it, of course. ''Thoroughly improper behaviour for a lady. Viscountesses, my dear

Cassie, do not indulge in *larks*, as you so indelicately describe it.'' I was hard put not to laugh.'

Amy did laugh. Sarah's impersonation of Miss Lyndhurst was well-nigh perfect.

'But I fancy…yes, I think it is just what you need, Amy. The roof is normally out of bounds to servants, of course, but I can ensure that Cassie's maid accompanies us, so that she is kept well out of your way. I'll say we need someone to wait on us, hand round the luncheon, that sort of thing. You should have a clear run.'

'Sarah, you are brilliant.'

'Yes, I know,' said Sarah promptly, her eyes full of mischief. 'Once you have finished your search, come up to join us so that I know it is safe to return below. I will think of some excuse to justify your absence till then.'

'If there is no one else around,' Amy said thoughtfully, 'it *should* work. Provided only that you can persuade Miss Lyndhurst and her companion to take part in such an improper escapade.'

'I have no concerns about that. You forget, Amy dear, that I am the senior lady here and that I am, in effect, the hostess. Miss Lyndhurst may be thin as a rail, but she enjoys her food. I shall tell her that all the servants are required for the shooting party. The only food available for the ladies will be the cold luncheon laid out on the roof.' She grinned. 'Great-aunt Harriet will scold, but Great-aunt Harriet will not fail me, I assure you.'

Four ladies and an impromptu roof party seemed to require a houseful of furniture. Since all the male servants were occupied with the shoot, the two abigails spent more than half an hour carrying folding tables and chairs, cushions and work-baskets, and all sorts of other

apparently unnecessary things up the winding stairs to
the cupola and out on to the flat roof.

There was no doubt that the view was magnificent.
Amy stopped for a moment, her arms full of cushions,
to admire it. She could see the shooting party quite
clearly. The guns sounded just like children's pop-guns
from such a distance.

'The purpose of those cushions, my good woman, is
to provide comfort for your betters, not an excuse for
your day-dreaming!'

Amy whirled round. Miss Lyndhurst was making her
way slowly across the roof, with her companion in her
wake. The old lady had her ear trumpet in one hand and
a walking stick in the other. She was leaning heavily on
it, but Amy did not believe for a moment that she really
needed it. Miss Lyndhurst used her props as well as any
actress. If Amy went too close, the old lady would probably use it to poke her.

'Are you deaf?' Miss Lyndhurst brandished her ear
trumpet at Amy's motionless figure.

Amy curtsied and hurried to arrange the cushions on
the chairs for the ladies. She knew better than to say a
word. No mere servant would dare to cross swords with
this outrageous old lady.

'No, not like that!' Miss Lyndhurst pushed her cushion away. 'I may be getting on in years, but even I have
not yet shrunk to such a shape that I need a cushion
there! Sarah, this woman of yours is not at all the thing.'

Sarah and Lady Quinlan had just emerged on to the
roof and were blinking against the sunlight.

'Goodness, Aunt Harriet, what an admission,' Lady
Quinlan said with a grin.

'Nothing of the sort. It's Sarah who should be making

the admission. That her selection of servants leaves
much to be desired.'

'Oh, that.' Lady Quinlan waved a hand. 'Dent will be
gone in a few weeks. That's of no consequence. But *your*
admission, on the other hand... Now that *was* worth
hearing.'

'I *beg* your pardon, young lady?'

'Well, even though you are my great-great-aunt, I
never before heard you admit that you were getting on
in years. Are you feeling quite the thing today, Aunt
Harriet?'

'Great-great—! You are getting above yourself,
Cassie. Time was, you would never have spoken so. And
you are no better, Sarah Mardon. I can see perfectly well
that you have been encouraging Cassie in her outrageous
behaviour. Why, in my day—'

'Dent,' Sarah said sharply, 'you had better go down
to the kitchens to fetch our luncheon now. Take Ebdon
with you. Hurry along now.'

Amy curtsied and made for the cupola. Eliza Ebdon
followed without a word. The two abigails exchanged
glances. Miss Lyndhurst's voice carried all too clearly
across the rooftop. 'In my day, gels of your age knew
better than to insult their elders. Even gels who married
a title.'

The kitchens were buzzing with activity. Food was being
packed up, ready to be carried out to the shooting party.
By comparison, the ladies' luncheon was a very insignificant affair, with only a handful of mouths to
be fed.

'Careful with that hamper!' the butler called. 'If you
break those decanters, I'll have your hide, my lad.'

The two abigails flattened themselves against the wall

as the row of hampers and boxes filed past. It looked as though the house was feeding an army. The cook was bright red, shouting out warnings that none of the servants appeared to heed. The milling retainers seemed to have their own momentum.

At last, they were gone. The vast kitchen contained only the cook, the scullery maid and two abigails.

The cook collapsed on to her chair and began to fan her glowing face with her apron. 'Well, I never did,' she said to no one in particular. 'Never known such servants. Here am I, preparing the finest victuals for all these guests and no one takes a blind bit of notice of a word I say. Why, I—'

Amy coughed loudly.

'Oh, it's you, Miss Dent.' The cook turned in her chair, but did not rise. Amy was not sure the woman was capable of it.

'Lady Mardon sent us down to fetch the luncheon for the party on the roof,' Amy said calmly.

The cook waved a hand in the general direction of the pantry. 'It's all laid out, in there. Two trays. Mind you don't spill anything, if you please. That fruit bruises very easily. And there ain't no more to be had if you spoil it.'

Amy said nothing, but Eliza Ebdon was incensed. 'I should hope I know how to serve her ladyship's luncheon,' she snapped. 'And—'

Amy coughed again. The last thing she needed now was a first-class argument between Eliza Ebdon and the cook. 'We had best get on. The ladies will be waiting. And we have a great many stairs to climb.' She led the way into the pantry where they collected their trays. They did not seem too heavy at first but, by the time the two women had reached the spiral staircase leading up to the cupola, Amy's arms were aching. Being in service was very hard work.

She paused for a second at the bottom of the staircase to catch her breath. Then she started up. It was very narrow and it was difficult to manoeuvre the heavy tray round the spiral, but she emerged into the sunlight at last.

Miss Lyndhurst was still sitting in her chair, talking volubly. She now had an open parasol in her hand, instead of the cane. Her companion, Miss Saunders, was seated alongside. A book lay open in her lap. Sarah was standing over by the balustrade, a telescope to her eye, watching the shoot. Lady Quinlan was by her side, shading her eyes in an effort to see against the strong sunlight.

'At last! Thought you would never arrive,' Miss Lyndhurst scolded. 'Gossiping below stairs, no doubt.'

Amy knew better than to respond. But Ebdon bristled. She ignored Miss Lyndhurst and addressed herself to her mistress. 'I beg your ladyship's pardon for the delay,' she said evenly. 'We had to wait until the luncheon for the shooting party had been despatched. Shall we serve your luncheon now, m'lady?'

'Yes. Thank you, Eliza. You may lay it out—'

'Good gracious!' Sarah exclaimed.

Lady Quinlan turned back. 'What is it?'

'It's William. You know how particular he is about his dress. One speck of mud and he seems like to have an apoplexy. Well, it looks like… Yes, I'm sure. He is being accosted by the dirtiest little child you ever saw. I can't imagine why he allows such an urchin to come near him. Surely, he—? Oh!'

'What is it?' Lady Quinlan asked. 'Give me the telescope, Sarah. Let me see.'

'Oh, it's nothing. The child has gone now. No doubt he was asking for money.'

Miss Lyndhurst snorted. 'Wouldn't get anything out of William. He doesn't have two ha'pence to rub together.'

Sarah swung the telescope on to another part of the landscape. 'I think the shooting party is about to pause for luncheon. I suggest that we do the same.' She turned back to her companions and closed the telescope with a snap. 'I am sure we do not need two maids to serve only four ladies. If you are happy for Ebdon to remain, Cassie, I will send Dent back to her mending. I am afraid she takes rather longer over it than I should like.'

At Lady Quinlan's nod, Sarah said, 'I have no need of you here for the moment, Dent. Go to my chamber and finish mending the flounce on my gown. And do not forget the other chores I set you. I expect them all to be completed this afternoon.'

Amy curtsied. 'Yes, m'lady,' she said demurely.

'You may return here when you have finished. Ebdon will need your help to remove the chairs and tables.'

'Yes, m'lady.' Amy started for the cupola. Sarah was playing her part absolutely brilliantly. Even old Miss Lyndhurst suspected nothing.

Sarah was still speaking. 'Miss Saunders, you have such a beautiful voice. Might I prevail upon you to read to us, once we have finished our luncheon?'

Amy smiled to herself and clattered down the spiral staircase. Poor Miss Saunders was decidedly put upon. When she was not tasked with reading aloud to the ladies, she was being despatched to the dressing room to do Miss Lyndhurst's mending. What kind of life was that, for a well-born lady?

Amy knew the answer perfectly well. It was the kind

of life that befell a well-born spinster with no income and no other means of support. It was the kind of life that she herself might yet have to face.

Halfway through, and still nothing. Amy lifted down yet another expensive and immaculate coat. She began to search the pockets, one by one. She had been through every single drawer and all the other potential hiding places. After Mr Lyndhurst-Flint's clothing, there was nowhere else to search. What if she found nothing?

She tried not to think of that. Or of Marcus, locked in the Major's dressing room, at risk of being dragged off to gaol at any moment. There must be some evidence somewhere. She must find it!

She reached for another coat and began to search the pockets. Marcus Sinclair… How could she have failed to recognise him? He had not changed so very much. Oh, he was considerably older, but he was still the same man. How was it that she had not seen past his unkempt appearance? The beard had hidden the shape of his face, to be sure, but still… The truth was that she had been trying to avoid looking him in the face. Since the moment she had first walked in on him, she had been embarrassed beyond measure. She had been trying not to look at him at all.

Only one more coat.

She wanted so much to help him. She knew he was innocent of all these absurd charges. Why was she so sure? Everyone else seemed to believe him guilty, perhaps even the Major.

But Amy *was* sure. Marcus Sinclair was a man of honour. He would never carry out such an attack. Why, he had put his own life in jeopardy in order to protect Amy. Being protected was something Amy had never experienced before. In all her life, no one had tried to protect her. Amy had always been the one who protected others. First her widowed mother, and then her brother. It was a strange feeling to know that there was someone who was prepared to put Amy first. And to take such risks for her, besides. Marcus Sinclair was a very special man.

Amy slid her fingers into the last pocket of the last coat. It was empty. She had failed. She had promised to help Marcus, and she had failed.

She slipped back into Sarah's bedchamber and sat down heavily at the little writing table. Now what was she to do? She could not face the thought of telling Marcus of her failure. She had promised him proof, but she had found nothing at all. Soon, the Major and the shooting party would return to the house. Would the Major carry out his threat to deal with Marcus then? He might be taken off to gaol this very day. And it would be Amy's fault.

She dropped her head into her hands. But she refused to despair. She would not weep. There must be proof. Somewhere. She must have missed something.

What could it be? She had not found even the letter to Mr Lyndhurst-Flint's bankers. It had probably been despatched by now. Or perhaps he carried it on his person?

That was it! If there was anything to be found, William Lyndhurst-Flint would not have risked hiding it in his room. It would be on him. The pockets she needed to search were the pockets of the coat he was wearing.

Amy jumped to her feet. She would need to search Mr Lyndhurst-Flint's chamber again, while he was at dinner.

But what was she to tell Marcus? He would be furious

that she had risked herself thus far. He seemed so determined to defend her. Well, she would tell him the truth. Or part of it.

And she must do it now, before the shooting party returned. She rose, smoothing her skirts automatically. Then she walked smartly down the stairs to the floor below and tapped softly on the door to Marcus's prison.

'Who is it?'

'It is I, Dent,' she said. 'It is Amy,' she added, more softly. She heard the key turning in the lock. 'Do not open the door,' she said quickly. 'You never know who may come upon us.'

. She knew it would be easier to tell him her disappointing news if she did not have to look into his face. She waited until she heard the key turn once more. 'I have come to tell you… Forgive me, sir, I have failed you. I have searched, but I have found nothing.' She stopped, waiting for some kind of response. There was total silence behind the heavy door. 'But there is just one chance,' she went on, trying to sound more confident than she felt. 'If there is proof, he may have it on his person. I will search again as soon as he is gone down to dinner.'

'No!' Marcus's cry was a mixture of fury and exasperation. 'For God's sake, Amy, take no more risks!'

The anxiety in his voice made her heart turn over. He was truly concerned about what might happen to her. It was only a friendly concern, no doubt, but it made her feel…cherished. 'I will return as soon as I can, to tell you what I have found,' she said quietly.

'No, don't come here again. Not once the shooting party has returned. It is too dangerous.'

'How else am I to tell you—?' She stopped at the sound of Marcus's heavy sigh.

'You are incorrigible, Amy Devereaux. Where will I find you? Let me be the one to take the risks. I will come to you.'

'You cannot. The only way to my room is by the servants' stair. You would be seen.'

'Somewhere else, then,' he said sharply. 'I swear I will not speak to you if you come back here.'

'Well, I— Perhaps we could meet on the roof? The servants are not permitted to go up there. And there is no access from the servants' quarters to the staircase.' She heard a low laugh from the other side of the door.

'It sounds like an ideal spot for an assignation. Are you sure you dare to meet me in such a place?'

Amy was not in the mood for teasing. What was he about? His very life could be at stake. 'I will not fail you,' she said seriously. 'Wait for me on the roof. After the dinner hour. I will come to you as soon as I can.'

Miss Saunders was still reading to the ladies when Amy arrived back on the roof. She did read beautifully, in a low, melodious voice. Amy paused to listen, halfway up the stairs. No one would know she was there. Just for a moment, she wanted to forget all this interminable intrigue, to forget about her missing brother, to forget the dangers surrounding Marcus Sinclair. Listening to that lovely voice reading Shakespeare's sonnets, Amy could pretend that she was a lady again, and everything was normal.

But it was not normal.

The sound of men's voices drifted up to her. Someone was coming. Amy scuttled up the stairs on to the roof and hurried across to the Countess.

Sarah glanced in the direction of Miss Saunders. Lady Quinlan was listening. Miss Lyndhurst's eyes were closed and her head had fallen forward a little. Eliza Ebdon was standing apart, looking thoroughly bored. Sarah whispered, 'Look concerned, Amy. I want them to believe I am scolding you.'

Amy bowed her head meekly and laced her fingers together.

'Did you find anything?'

'No. Nothing at all. Perhaps there is nothing to find.'

'I think you may have been looking in the wrong place, Amy dear. That child I saw…that grubby little urchin. He gave William a paper. I am sure of it.'

Amy looked up in surprise, just as Miss Saunders began the next sonnet. *'Let me not to the marriage of true minds Admit impediments…'*

'Amy! Remember you are being scolded.' Sarah started to wag her finger. 'William kept looking round, to make sure no one was watching him. I am sure it is something important. Why else would he speak to a filthy child? He— Why, you are returned early, my lord!'

The Earl of Mardon and Major Lyndhurst were striding out on to the roof. Miss Lyndhurst sat up with a convulsive start and put her hands to her lace cap. Miss Saunders abruptly stopped reading and busied herself with putting her book into her bag, her cheap bonnet hiding her face from view.

Sarah crossed to meet her husband, who lifted her hand and gallantly kissed her fingers. She wrinkled her nose at him. 'Fie, my lord! But you are in no fit state to wait on ladies!'

The Earl laughed. 'Did I not warn you, Anthony? In your haste, you have given my wife cause to upbraid me.'

Lady Quinlan giggled. 'Do I take it that my husband is returned also?'

'Aye. But he said he would prefer to rid himself of the dirt of the chase before attending on the ladies. He will be in his bedchamber, I imagine.'

'I should think so, indeed,' snapped Miss Lyndhurst, looking daggers at the Major.

Lady Quinlan rose and strolled elegantly across to the cupola. 'It is really much too hot up here.' She folded her parasol. 'I think I shall go downstairs into the cool for a while. Pray excuse me.'

The Earl and his wife exchanged a knowing glance, but neither spoke.

Major Lyndhurst seemed to have noticed nothing. He walked across to the chair that Lady Quinlan had vacated and moved it a little closer to the companion. Sitting down, he said, 'Pray do not allow me to interrupt your reading, Miss Saunders. How does it continue? *"Love is not love Which alters when it alteration finds, Or bends with the remover to remove."* Admirable sentiments, are they not?'

Miss Saunders bent to her bag once more and began to rummage around in it. She had gone very pale. It seemed that she could not find her book.

The Major reached out a hand. 'May I help you, ma'am?' Although Miss Saunders was now clutching the bag tightly, he seemed to be about to remove it from her grasp when Miss Lyndhurst's cane struck him full across the knuckles.

'That's quite enough of that, Anthony Lyndhurst. No proper gentleman would ever pry into a lady's bag. I cannot think what has come over you.'

The Major tried to ignore her. 'Miss Saunders, may I invite you to—?'

Miss Lyndhurst got up from her chair in a remarkably sprightly fashion. 'Miss Saunders, please have the goodness to go below and lay out my evening gown. I have no need of you here for the present.'

Miss Saunders rose gracefully to her feet and gathered up her bag and her parasol. 'As you wish, ma'am.'

The Major offered her his arm. 'Let me help you downstairs with your bag, Miss Saunders.'

'Pray do not trouble yourself, Anthony,' Miss Lyndhurst said sharply. 'Miss Saunders is perfectly well able to descend two pairs of stairs without your assistance. I, on the other hand, would welcome the use of your arm for a turn around this rooftop of yours. I have been waiting all afternoon for a gentleman's company. Come. You may point out all the landmarks to me as we go.'

To Amy's surprise, the Major said not a word, though his neck had gone rather red. Perhaps he dared not speak, lest he insult the old lady. He simply bowed and offered his arm.

'Thank you, Anthony,' Miss Lyndhurst said with a bright smile. She waved her ear trumpet in the general direction of the lake. 'Interesting stretch of water, that. Do you take many trout?'

Marcus heard footsteps in the bedchamber and the sound of the key in the lock. He held his breath. Was this the moment?

The door swung open. 'I dare say you'll be wanting a bite to eat, Mr Marcus?'

Timms! 'Is it to be my last, Timms, before I'm consigned to bread and water?'

'I don't know about that, sir. The Major's not been…er…quite himself today. Drank a deal too much brandy last night. Must have had something on his mind, I suppose.' Timms looked sideways at Marcus. 'I can't imagine what it might have been.'

Marcus gave a bark of laughter. 'You are an old villain, Timms. Am I to conclude that the Major has a sore head today?'

'That's not for me to say, sir.'

'How was his shooting?'

'Ah…' Timms hesitated. 'Well, to be frank, Mr Marcus, the Major's eye was not in today. Not up to his usual standard.'

Marcus grinned. Poor Anthony. If he had been over-indulging in brandy, he probably had a terrible head. And that would account for his having slept through Amy's visit to the dressing room. If only Marcus had known. He could have saved them both a deal of anxiety.

'So, what happens now, Timms? My trial was postponed last evening. Does it continue tonight?'

'I don't know, Mr Marcus. Truly I don't. But the Major was planning to talk to his lordship about it. That I do know.'

'You mean Lord Mardon?'

'Aye, sir. Hasn't done so yet, I don't think. His lordship will take it mighty serious, us hiding a fugitive.'

Marcus tried to look grave. But that was not how he felt. John was an upright, level-headed man. He would make sure Anthony's temper did not rule him. With John involved, Marcus would get a fair hearing. Whatever might happen afterwards.

He squared his shoulders and raised his eyebrows at the valet. 'Can't imagine what happened to those promised victuals. Why, a man could die of starvation in this room!'

Chapter Seven

By the time Amy reached the foot of the spiral staircase, it was very late, much later than she had intended. She removed her spectacles and put them in her pocket. Carefully shielding her candle, she started up. Would Marcus be there? Would he have waited so long?

There was no one in the cupola. The circular benches were empty. He had not trusted her enough to wait.

She paused on the top step with her hand on the metal rail. She had to find him, to tell him.

'Amy!' His shadow filled the open door to the roof. Without another word, he reached for her hand and pulled her through into the warm night air, closing the door behind them. She saw that he had taken some of the long leather cushions from the benches in the cupola to serve as a seat. There was a clear impression of his body on them. He had been lying full length, waiting for her.

He blew out her flickering candle and put the candle-holder down. 'We have no need of feeble candles. Look above you. The sky is full of stars.'

Amy sank on to the makeshift seat and glanced up. The heavens looked enormous tonight, and so very clear.

There was much more light than she would have expected.

'I have it,' she whispered urgently.

'What do you mean?'

'I have the proof you need. Here.' She took the paper from her sleeve and pressed it into his hand.

He unfolded it. 'I cannot read a word by this light,' he said impatiently.

'You should have allowed me my candle, sir.'

'Amy, this is no time for exercising your wit on me. Tell me. What does it say? And where did you find it?'

'Some grubby child delivered it to Mr Lyndhurst-Flint during the shoot today. The note does not actually bear his name, but I found it in the inside pocket of his shooting jacket.' She ignored Marcus's furious intake of breath. 'There was no risk, I promise. It was the work of but a moment to steal it. It is a demand for money owed. For the attack on Frobisher. It says that, unless the money is paid, the writer will ensure that Mr Marcus Sinclair learns all the facts about the attack on Frobisher. It warns that Mr Marcus Sinclair is deadly both with the sword and with the pistol.'

'Ah.' He ran a hand through his hair. 'So that was why William was so desperate to borrow that money. He needed it to pay the man he had hired to carry out the attack on Frobisher. You are right, Amy. This note is clearly intended as a reminder of debts outstanding. The writer must be somewhere nearby, waiting his chance. If William does not pay up, his accomplice will betray him.'

'And this note gives us proof that your cousin is guilty of the attack.'

'Yes. No. Damnation! If William's name is not on the note, it gives us no proof at all against him.'

'But we do have proof. I found it in his pocket. I can tell the Major so.'

'Amy, you cannot.' He sat down beside her. He was very close now. 'William would surely deny it. Anthony could never take the word of a servant against the word of a member of the family.'

'But he would take the word of a lady, would he not?'

'You cannot tell him who you are. It would be folly.'

She frowned up into his eyes. 'Major Lyndhurst has to know the truth. If that is the only way, I shall do it.'

Marcus shook his head and let out a long sigh. 'Yes, I do believe you would. If I needed any more proof that you are not like other young ladies, my beautiful idiot, you have just provided it. You are one in a million, Amy Devereaux. And you will *not* betray yourself to Anthony. I insist on having your word on that. We will find another way.' He pushed the note into his pocket and cupped her face with both hands. 'Your word, Amy?'

'*Is* there another way?' she said in a small voice.

He smiled faintly. 'I will not be diverted, you know. There must be a way. And we will find it.' He smoothed his thumbs back and forth across her cheeks. 'I shall not let you go until I have your promise…even if I have to wait all night.' He raised his eyebrows, waiting for her answer.

'You are a tyrant, Marcus Sinclair.'

'No doubt. But, on this, I mean what I say. You will not ruin your reputation to save me. Promise me, Amy.'

'I—'

'Please, Amy.'

She could not deny him any more. Not when he asked in that voice. 'Very well. You have my word.'

He smiled with relief and dropped his hands.

Amy felt bereft. She tried to smile at him. 'Is it true?'

'Is what true?'

'Are you deadly?'

'Compared with William? Yes, I imagine I probably am. Unlike the rest of us, William never served in the army.'

'Will you call him out?'

Marcus rose and began to pace. He raked a hand through his hair. 'I don't know. He is my cousin. And John's brother. But—' Marcus turned back to Amy. Taking both her hands, he pulled her to her feet. 'Enough of that, my dear Miss Devereaux. If this note is as clear as you say, then at least it will prove to Anthony that I am no cowardly assailant.'

'That matters a very great deal to you, does it not?' she asked softly.

'Yes. Yes, it does. Anthony Lyndhurst is my closest friend. The thought that he no longer trusts me…'

'But why did he not believe you? You say he is your friend. It makes no sense.'

'We quarrelled.'

'Over this?'

'No,' Marcus said harshly. 'I do not wish to speak of it.'

Amy said nothing. She could feel the tension in Marcus's fingers. Without thinking, she began to rub her thumbs gently across his palms.

His deep groan found an echo in the pit of her stomach, as if they were connected by a taut, singing wire.

'Oh, God! Amy!' He pulled her roughly into his arms and began to kiss her hungrily.

She did not try to resist. She knew that she had been waiting her whole life for this moment. She loved this man. And he loved her. She had saved him. And now she was to have her reward. He was hers! There was no need to hold back any longer. She gave herself up to the moment.

The kiss went on and on.

Marcus was aching to possess this wonderful, impossible woman. She was truly one in a million. And the more he kissed her, teasing and tasting her lips and her tongue, the more he was certain that she was a true lady, and innocent. She had never been kissed like this before, but she was responding to him, following his lead with astonishing passion. If he wanted to possess her completely, she would not try to stop him. It was for him to stop. And he must.

He tore his mouth from hers. 'Amy, this is madness!'

'Why?'

Her response surprised him into a gasp of astonished laughter. 'Oh, Lord preserve me from unbiddable women! It is madness, my dearest girl, because you are a single lady, and I am a man, and because we are alone together, unchaperoned, in the middle of the night! How much worse could it be?'

With a satisfied smile, she wound her arms round his neck. 'Since I am ruined merely by being here, I think perhaps I should enjoy my ruin to the full.'

He groaned. Here was yet more proof of her innocence. She could not know what she was suggesting, or what she was doing to him. He could not hold out much longer. He must stop her. Now.

He took her arms from his neck, first one, and then the other. 'Amy, my dear girl, we must not do this. You are a lady. And I am still a fugitive.' At the sight of the sudden hurt in her eyes, he touched her face briefly with a fingertip. 'I want you very much and I— But I am not worthy of you. You must see that.'

It was as if he had struck her. She flung away from him, wrapping her arms around her upper body and hugging herself like an abandoned child. 'Who are you, sir, to decide who is, or is not, worthy? You demean yourself. And me. You say you are a fugitive. But we both know that is no longer so. The proof I have brought may not be enough to satisfy the magistrate of your cousin's guilt, but you may be sure that it will exonerate you.' She shook her head vehemently. She was lashing herself into even greater fury. 'Marcus Sinclair will fly free, as he has always done, to seduce the ladies and then abandon them. No doubt you enjoy the sight of women falling at your feet.'

'Amy—' He stretched out his hands and came towards her.

'Enough, sir. Keep your distance. I am a fool, I admit. I have shamed myself. No doubt Amy Devereaux's behaviour will soon be the talk of the London clubs. I wish you joy of it!' She dashed away a furious tear, before turning abruptly and bolting for the cupola.

There was pain in every line of her body.

Marcus moved swiftly to put himself between Amy and her escape route. He would not let her go like this— burning with shame and self-hatred. She had done nothing wrong. Her only fault had been to trust a fugitive with herself.

Faced with the barrier of his large body, she did not scream or faint. Instead, she glared at him. 'I will thank you to stand aside, sir. You have already humiliated me quite enough.'

'No, Amy. I will not let you leave until I make you understand. It is not that I— I am not the hard-hearted seducer you think me. If I were, would I have turned you down? I do have…feelings for you. I beg you will believe that. But I am in no position to do anything about them. I only wish I could.'

'Do you, indeed?' Her tone dripped sarcasm. She was trying to appear strong. But her whole body looked defeated.

What had he done to her?

'Amy, pray forgive me. It was not my intention to hurt you.'

'No, of course not,' she snapped. 'I have helped you to prove your innocence. And now you choose to spurn me. You have not even told me what you have done with Ned.'

Marcus seized her by the shoulders. 'Damn Ned! Your brother is perfectly safe. In the cellar of the North Lodge. By all accounts, he is enjoying his captivity, playing cards all day, and drinking himself under the table every night.'

Amy gasped and turned even paler.

'Amy, I am not spurning you. I am trying to save you from becoming entangled with a man whose reputation is in tatters. And who may yet end up in gaol.' He allowed his fingers to bite into her shoulders. 'That is not a price that I would ask you to pay.'

She raised her head and gazed at him. For a moment, Marcus fancied he saw tears in her eyes. He dismissed it. It must be a trick of the light.

'It is a price that I would pay,' she said simply. 'If you were to ask it of me.'

She stood there in front of him. Small, helpless, and unresisting. And yet she was as strong as steel. And as true!

Marcus could not fight it any more. He wrapped his arms round her and pulled her into the shelter of his body. 'Amy. Oh, Amy. I have tried to drive you away, but you will not go. Stubborn wench! You know what I feel for you. I am certain that you do. I have tried to resist, for both our sakes, but against you, I am totally lost.'

She looked up at him with a very wobbly smile. He was not mistaken about the tears. Not this time.

'You are an idiot, Marcus Sinclair.'

'And you, Amy Devereaux, are quite the most wonderful woman I have ever met. I am madly—hopelessly—in love with you. What on earth are we to do?'

'I have not the least idea.' She snuggled into his warmth, dislodging her cap. It drifted to the ground, unheeded. 'But you must become a free man again. Your innocence must be proved, beyond doubt. I am sure we can find a way of achieving that. Perhaps, if we work at it…' She put her arms round his neck once more. It felt exactly right. 'Perhaps if we work at it,' she said again, 'we shall find a solution.'

In that moment, Marcus made a decision. With the little they had, he could brazen it out. He must not accuse William, for that would risk alienating William's brother, John. Marcus needed John's support. With the powerful Earl of Mardon at his side, Marcus would be safe from arrest. Probably. There would be rumours, no doubt, about Marcus's black past, but he could ignore them. Anthony had survived worse, by withdrawing to Lyndhurst Chase. Marcus could do the same, if need be. Was that enough to offer Amy?

She was nestling in his arms as if she had always belonged there. She did belong there.

'I have the solution.'

'Marcus, that is wonderful. Tell me!'

'I shall have to marry you out of hand.'

'What has marriage got to say to anything? It will not

prove that you— Oh!' Even by starlight, Marcus could see that she was blushing. And her eyes were ablaze.

'Marriage will solve one—no, two—of my most pressing problems, my dear Miss Devereaux. First, it will require you to do as I say. You do recall, I hope, that part of the wedding vows is a promise by the bride to love, honour and *obey*?'

'Yes, but—'

'And, second, I cannot live without you, my dearest love. I want you by my side, Amy. Now. Always. I want to be able to make love to you slowly—very slowly— without fear of interruption. This…er…balmy interlude under the stars has a certain magic, I grant you, but it lacks…permanence. I need you to be mine.' He raised her hand to his lips and, still holding her gaze, dropped a kiss on her fingers. 'Will you?'

'Certainly not!'

'Amy!'

'I have no intention of receiving a proposal of marriage in a gown that resembles a sack and a cap that would be better used for straining curds.'

He grinned at her. She was fully herself again— strong, quick-witted, outrageous, and absolutely adorable. 'At the risk of interrupting your litany of complaint, ma'am, may I take this opportunity of reminding you that you are not actually wearing the offending item?' He pushed his fingers into the heavy mass of her hair and shook it out over her shoulders.

'Be serious, Marcus!' She tried to bat his hand away, but he held her firmly and dropped a kiss on the corner of her mouth.

'I am being serious,' he said. 'I was never more so. This is a proposal of marriage that I am making, you know.'

'And I am refusing it,' she said flatly.

Marcus began to nibble the lobe of her ear. 'Are you?' he said, rather indistinctly.

'Mmm.' She groaned a little. 'Yes. I am. For the present.'

'Ah. I see. And later?' With a single fluid movement, he picked her up in his arms. When he carried her back to the cushions and laid her down, she made no move to resist him.

He was looming over her, blotting out the stars. She looked up into his face. Even in the half-light, she knew his eyes were full of love and laughter. She was sure that her own must be the same. 'Later, sir, if you should chance to propose marriage to Miss Amy Devereaux, gentlewoman, instead of to Amelia Dent, common abigail, it is…just possible that the lady may entertain your suit.'

'And if I prefer to marry the uncommon abigail?'

Amy ignored him. 'It will all depend, of course, on— Oh, heavens! Marcus!' A shudder ran through her body.

'It will depend…?' he repeated wickedly, his lips still wreaking havoc against her skin. His busy fingers began to unfasten her gown.

Amy's voice seemed to have sunk by at least half an octave. 'It will depend on how well Mr Marcus Sinclair makes his case.'

'You mean…like this?' he murmured, trailing his lips down her throat to the pouting nipple he had just freed from her chemise.

Her only response was a deep moan of pleasure.

He suckled so gently at first that, for a second or two, only the answering ripples in Amy's belly confirmed that his mouth was still on her skin. But when the suckling grew stronger, Amy's whole body began to quiver in response. His long fingers were touching her, opening her body to him like a butterfly spreading its wings to the sunshine. He was her sun. Without his warmth, without his love, she would shrivel to a husk. She needed him. Now. Always.

When she touched her hands to his face, he looked up at her, kissing her still. His dark eyes gleamed.

'Marcus,' she whispered. She could hear the longing in her own voice. Could he hear it, too?

He sat up and began to shrug out of his coat and shirt, his intent gaze travelling over her body as if he were trying to memorise every inch of her skin. 'Ah, but you are beautiful, my darling abigail. So beautiful. And so very desirable.' He was suddenly very still. Distant. 'I want you so very much, Amy. But I must not do this. Not here. Not now.'

Amy allowed her swollen lips to curve slowly into a very knowing smile. She could see that every line of his powerful body was screaming with desire. Why could he not see those same signs in hers? They were meant to be together. They had both accepted that. And now was the allotted time for their joining.

She settled back more comfortably into the leather cushions, allowing that siren smile to broaden. When she saw the first response in his face, she lifted her bare arms invitingly. 'Marcus, I want us to be together. Now. Here, under the stars. Please, Marcus.' She saw his turmoil. And the moment when he yielded. The desire that had been so ruthlessly leashed now blazed in his eyes. He did not ask if she was sure.

He knew.

They tore off their remaining clothing, kissing, and touching, and tasting all the while. Their skin shone silver in the starlight as they gazed hungrily at each other, with wonder in their eyes. There was a long, long moment of utter stillness. Their love and longing sang between them.

Then they reached for each other, passion overcoming all else, as Amy drew Marcus down to her body, rejoicing in their joining. And together they soared to the stars.

Amy snuggled more comfortably into the crook of Marcus's arm.

'Are you cold, my love?'

'No.'

Ignoring her, Marcus pulled his coat more snugly over them both. They must part soon, but he was loath to let her go, even for a few hours.

Amy's hand started to wander over his body, under the enveloping coat. Marcus's nerves began to tingle. Especially as her hand moved lower. When she cupped him, he clapped a hand over her fingers. 'God! Amy!' he groaned. 'Do you have any idea what you are doing to me?' His flesh had begun to stir again. He would not have thought it possible. Not so soon. Amy Devereaux must be a witch.

She squeezed him gently. His response was unmistakable.

'Amy…!'

'When I touch you…there,' she began shyly, 'you… Does that mean—?'

'It is not simply when you touch me "there", as you so delicately put it, my love. You can have that effect just by being in the same room as me. I love you. And I desire you. A man's body is…not always under his control. Desire is an unpredictable mistress.'

'Oh.' Amy paused thoughtfully. Then she squeezed again. The reaction was even more marked than before.

She ran her finger up his hard length. 'Marcus, does this…er…evidence mean that you desire me? Now?'

He forcibly removed her hand and laid it on his chest, covering it with his own stronger one. However much he desired her, he would not make love to her again tonight. It had been her first time. Her body needed to recover. His own desires—no matter how urgent—would have to wait.

'The evidence you mention,' he began a little hoarsely, trying to ignore the demands of his body, 'is…um…not overwhelming.'

She had begun to rub her fingertips in tiny circles on his chest. 'I beg leave to differ, sir. I should have to be blind not to be overwhelmed by something so…er…' She laughed, deep in her throat, and tried to extract her hand.

'No, Amy. There is to be no more touching tonight. You may touch me as much as you wish after we are married.'

'Oh.' She sounded disappointed. But she did not continue to fight him. She relaxed even further into his arms, with a deep, contented sigh.

Marcus lay back and gazed up at the canopy of stars. He would have to find a way of recreating this idyll on his own estate. Making love under the stars, with Amy, was like a taste of paradise. He began to stroke her long hair. It looked ghostly in the starlight.

'Mmm. That feels wonderful.'

'By the way, my love…'

'Mmm?'

'I think I have found the solution.'

'Yes, you told me that before.' She sounded rather sleepy. 'You have decided that I am to marry you.'

'True, but that was not the solution I meant.'

She sat up so quickly that her hair was trapped in his fingers. She gave a tiny cry of pain.

'Amy!'

'Oh, don't mind that. A few missing hairs are of no consequence. Not if you have found a way to prove your innocence. Tell me, Marcus!'

'It will not prove William's guilt, but I fancy it will save me. I shall need your help.'

'Marcus! Tell me!'

'Impatient wench!' He trailed his fingers down her bare arm. 'Very well, my love. This is what I think we should do.'

Chapter Eight

Marcus felt as if he had been pacing the floor for hours by the time the door opened. Timms was standing there with a very knowing look on his face. Marcus assumed a puzzled frown. 'What now, Timms?' he snapped. 'Has your master finally decided what he plans to do with me? Or am I to pace this confounded dressing room for the rest of my days?'

Anthony appeared at his valet's shoulder. He was looking very serious indeed. 'Would you have the goodness to join me out here, Marcus?' he asked formally. 'There is something I need to discuss with you.'

'If I must,' Marcus said crossly, trying to hide his inward glee. Amy had done it. Of course she had!

'Marcus, there is a paper on my desk.' Anthony pointed. 'I think you should read it.'

Marcus nodded and crossed to pick it up.

'Timms. My compliments to Lord Mardon, and I should be grateful if he would join us here. Immediately.'

'Yes, sir.'

Marcus read the note through a second time. And a

third. Then he threw it back on to the desk. 'What is this supposed to be?' he said harshly.

'I should have thought that was obvious, Marcus. Though I can understand that you may be too angry to see it. You gave me your word that you had not attacked Frobisher. But I… Things were said that led me to begin to doubt you. There was no justification for my doing so. I can only beg your pardon.'

'I do not understand.' Marcus hoped he sounded suitably bewildered. 'Where did you get this note? I see that it bears no direction. And no signature, either.'

'Timms found it. Someone must have dropped it. It must have been directed to someone here at the Chase. We can pursue that later. The important thing now, Marcus, is that this note provides proof that you did not attack Frobisher.'

Marcus picked up the note and scanned it again. He waited.

'Whoever wrote that letter carried out the attack. That much is clear. And his principal has failed to pay him. There are a great many servants here at the Chase,' Anthony went on grimly, 'but I had thought that all of them were trustworthy. It is bad enough that I had to dismiss Lady Margaret and that disgusting valet of William's. But now this!'

Marcus shook his head, but said nothing. He would not be the first to suggest that the culprit could be a guest, rather than a servant. Anthony was grasping at straws. Understandably.

The outer door opened to admit John. Timms had carried out his errand in record time. The valet withdrew discreetly, closing the door behind him, just as John exclaimed, 'Marcus! So you really *are* here!'

'He has been here all the time,' Anthony said evenly.

'I could not tell you until today. You have always said that, as a member of the House of Lords, you have a responsibility to uphold the law. You were bound to say that I should have yielded Marcus up.'

'You are right.' John frowned. 'I do say so. Even though I have not the least doubt that Marcus is innocent of the charge against him. I know the magistrate who issued the warrant. He is a man of principle. He will not permit Marcus to be convicted without evidence.'

Anthony took the paper from Marcus and offered it to John. 'Until this moment, all the evidence was damning. But read that letter. It proves there was a conspiracy against Marcus.'

John quickly scanned the letter. 'Good God! This is infamous! *"If you fail to pay, I will inform Mr Marcus Sinclair that you hired me to attack Frobisher and lay the blame on him. Given Mr Marcus Sinclair's deadly reputation with sword or pistol, you may prefer to avoid that."* I can hardly believe my eyes. Who has written this?' He turned the paper over, looking for a name. 'I can see the importance of this, of course, Anthony, but I doubt it will be enough to convince the magistrate. There are no names here. Who is this would-be assassin? And what villain has promised to pay him to implicate Marcus?'

'One of the servants must be—'

John shook his head. 'No, Anthony. This is not the work of a servant. Nor could a servant afford to pay so great a sum.' He tapped the letter with a fingernail. 'This was done by someone who is your enemy, Marcus, someone who knew just how to ensure that you—and only you—would be accused of this crime. You must be able to tell us who it is.'

Marcus hesitated. He glanced towards Anthony for

support, but he, too, was silent. The grim set of his mouth suggested that he had identified the most likely culprit. John was frowning now. He looked truly worried.

'I cannot say, John. There were a great many people in the gaming hell that night. And we were all in our cups. It could have been any of them. Or perhaps it was someone who learned of it afterwards.' That sounded very lame, he knew. Especially as very few of those from the gaming hell were now guests at Lyndhurst Chase. But Marcus was determined not to name William. Not to his brother. Not without proof.

'Ned Devereaux was there, was he not, Marcus? He has done any number of outrageous things since he attained his majority. Might he be responsible for this?'

'I doubt—' Marcus began.

Anthony interrupted him. 'That is not possible, John. Ned Devereaux is a feckless young rascal, but he is thoughtless, not wicked. Besides, he…ah…' Anthony stopped, looking embarrassed.

'What Anthony is trying to say, John, is that young Devereaux is in no position to send notes to anyone, or to receive them. He is being hidden in the cellar of the North Lodge.'

'Good God!' John exclaimed again. He sat down abruptly in the nearest chair. 'This is not a hunting box. It is a madhouse!'

Marcus grinned at him. 'You understand now why Anthony could not tell you any of this. Believe me, Ned Devereaux has come to no harm. We had to lock him up to stop his gossiping tongue. He'd caught sight of me, unfortunately. Given half a chance, he was bound to tell the world. So we decided to…er…offer him an extended stay at the Chase. Don't look so concerned,

John. The lodge keeper, and that deaf old aunt of his, are looking after Ned. He and the lodge keeper have a shared passion for cards and wine. Timms tells me that young Devereaux has no desire to leave.'

'Young Devereaux is a wastrel!' John declared roundly. 'His sister has spent years bringing his estate into good heart, and he seems like to gamble it all away in a twelvemonth. Amy Devereaux is a fine woman. She deserves better than Ned.'

'Amy Devereaux?' Marcus repeated, sounding surprised. 'But surely she was married some years ago? To some rich old Cit, I heard. I thought, at the time, that it was a terrible waste.'

'And so it would have been,' John agreed, 'but it did not happen. Miss Devereaux is still single. She has put all her energies into saving her brother's inheritance. That is why she has not been in society for some years now. Why, even Sarah is hard put to persuade Miss Devereaux to make a visit of more than a day or two. The lady maintains that she dare not leave the estate for any longer.'

'With Ned Devereaux ready to plunder it, I am not in the least surprised,' Anthony put in tartly.

'She and Sarah are fast friends,' John continued. 'But I was not aware that you and Miss Devereaux were acquainted, Marcus.'

Marcus hoped he was looking suitably unsettled by John's enquiry. 'The lady did have a Season, John. Or part of one, at least. I met her then. We were—' He shook his head and turned away abruptly to gaze out of the window. 'I am much surprised to learn that she is still unwed,' he added in a stifled voice.

'As am I,' Anthony agreed. He sounded relieved that

the subject had moved away from the note and its un-named recipient.

'You will soon be able to judge for yourself whether Miss Devereaux is still in looks, Marcus. My wife tells me that her friend will be arriving at the Chase at any time. She would not leave the Devereaux estate for Sarah's sake, but she has learned that her precious brother has disappeared. She is coming here herself to look for him.'

Marcus threw up a hand and turned back to Anthony. 'In that case, we had better make sure that Ned Devereaux is released—and sober—before she arrives.'

Anthony laughed then.

John did not. 'That is not the issue,' he snapped. 'What are we going to do about Marcus?'

Anthony took a deep breath. 'Do you accept, John, as I do, that this letter provides proof of Marcus's inno-cence?'

John nodded.

'Good. Then, with your agreement, I shall announce to the assembled company that Marcus is here, that I have written proof that he was not responsible for the attack on Frobisher, and that the real culprit is being sought. If the culprit is here at the Chase, we may man-age to smoke him out.'

John nodded again. He looked more concerned than ever.

'You understand that you must not leave the Chase, Marcus? I shall warn the servants to hold their tongues, but as soon as you are known to be here, the gossip is bound to start. However, with luck, we will have iden-tified the true villain before the rumours of your where-abouts reach the magistrate in London. You must remain at the house, in plain sight, acting the part of an innocent and honourable gentleman who has been gravely wronged by these accusations. Remember that you are here at the Chase because I have insisted upon it. You were all for surrendering yourself to the magistrate, of course—'

Marcus gave a bark of laughter.

John was shaking his head in disbelief.

Anthony ignored them both. 'No doubt the magistrate will believe every word of it. Such defiance of the law is only to be expected—' Anthony's voice took on a note of real bitterness '—from a man who is known to have made away with his wife.'

Anthony finished his announcement to stunned silence. Everyone seemed to be staring at the floor, or the furniture. No one was daring to look directly at anyone else.

No one except Marcus. He had been hidden behind the heavy curtains in the corner of the room, from where he had been able to watch them all. Especially William. William had paled at the mention of Anthony's 'written evidence'. His eyes had flickered towards his brother. But John had been sitting with bent head, his mouth set in a grim, determined line. William had then leant nonchalantly against one of the huge fireplaces. He had even raised his eyebrows in feigned surprise as Anthony's gloomy recital continued. But there had been a bead of sweat on his upper lip.

'Marcus!' Anthony beckoned him forward.

Everyone turned. There was a babble of excited voices. Words of welcome, and congratulation, and astonishment.

Marcus smiled at them all.

'You may leave us now, Ufton,' Anthony said to the butler. 'You have my permission to share this information with the inside servants, though they are not to discuss it outside the Chase. Make absolutely sure they understand that Mr Marcus is innocent of all the charges against him. He has been wickedly maligned. And I intend to make it my business to find the culprit. Is that clear?'

'Yes, sir. Quite clear.' The butler bowed and silently withdrew.

William came forward, smiling too broadly. 'You've been dam…dashed lucky, Marcus, I must say.'

Marcus nodded, thankful that William had not offered to shake his hand. He was perversely pleased to see that William's split lip had not completely healed.

'Marcus! What the devil were you doing, hiding there? And where have you been all this time? Come over here at once. I wish to speak to you.'

'It will be my pleasure, Aunt Harriet,' Marcus lied.

'Now, what's all this about? Didn't understand a word of that nonsense Anthony was spouting. The man's clearly been losing his wits since the day he lost his wife.'

With a noise akin to a suppressed explosion, Anthony marched out of the room.

Great-aunt Harriet ignored him and turned to her companion. 'This is my scapegrace nephew, Marcus Sinclair. Marcus—my companion, Miss Saunders.'

Marcus bowed politely.

'Move to another seat, if you please, Miss Saunders. I wish to have a private conversation with Marcus.'

The companion rose immediately. Some of her embroidery silks fell to the floor in a scatter of colour.

'Allow me, ma'am,' Marcus said, stooping to help her retrieve them. Then he picked up her books as well and stood, looking round the room. 'Where would you wish to sit, Miss Saunders?'

Great-aunt Harriet pointed her ear trumpet towards a vacant chair. 'Stop fussing, Marcus, and come here. I said I wish to talk to you.'

'Presently, ma'am,' Marcus replied. He would help the companion to settle herself in her new place first. Great-aunt Harriet might treat the poor lady like a servant, but Marcus would not. He set the books and the silks on the little table next to her chair and helped her into it.

'Thank you, Mr Sinclair. You are very kind.' She smiled shyly up at him, with just a hint of a blush in her pale, flawless cheeks.

He gazed at her for a moment, narrow-eyed. Hers was indeed a very sweet face. 'It was my pleasure, Miss Saunders,' he said. And meant it.

The old lady patted the now-empty place on the sofa beside her. 'Sit here, Marcus, and tell me what the devil is going on.'

Since he had no choice, Marcus did as he was bid. He noticed that William had gone. All the others were drifting out of the room, too, probably going off into secluded corners to discuss Anthony's astonishing statement. And to wonder about Marcus's proclaimed innocence.

Sarah had remained sitting calmly in the window with her embroidery. John would have warned her, of course. Nothing Anthony had said would have come as a surprise to her. And she was in Amy's confidence, too. How much would Amy have told her about Marcus?

Sarah looked up just then and caught Marcus's eye. He could almost have sworn that she winked at him. He bowed his head and began to cough, covering his mouth to hide his laughter. Sarah had always had a wicked sense of humour.

'I don't know why you are sitting there looking so satisfied, Sarah Mardon. I warned you about that woman of yours. And I was right.' Great-aunt Harriet brandished her ear trumpet to reinforce her point. 'Was I not? Eh? Eh?'

'You were, Aunt Harriet,' Sarah said meekly. 'And next time I will take care to listen to your advice. Thank goodness my old abigail will be returning soon. I was quite deceived by Dent. If I had not caught her—'

'We seem to be remarkably well endowed with villains at the Chase,' Marcus interposed calmly. 'What precisely did this Dent woman do, Sarah?'

Sarah looked at him with narrowed eyes and pursed lips. 'I found her rifling through John's papers, Marcus. She had no excuse, of course. I dismissed her on the spot.'

'Quite right.' Marcus nodded sagely, avoiding Sarah's eye. 'Gone, has she?'

'Yes. She's long gone now. I doubt any of us will ever set eyes on her again.'

'Never mind that!' snapped Great-aunt Harriet. 'Marcus was about to tell us about this gaming hell of his. Well, Marcus?'

Taking a deep breath, Marcus launched into a suitably censored version of his quarrel with Frobisher and its aftermath.

'Miss Devereaux, Major.'

All the gentlemen rose immediately. Anthony moved forward to greet the new arrival. From his place by the window, Marcus gazed at the woman he loved. He had thought he was prepared, but not for this. She was breathtaking. He could feel a degree of warmth rising on his neck and realised he could well look like a love-sick boy instead of a grown man. It made him feel remarkably vulnerable, even though it was bound to be helpful to their cause.

Amy curtsied gracefully to Anthony. She had clearly taken considerable pains to ensure that nothing about her appearance would remind the guests of the missing abigail. Her glorious silver-blonde hair was piled high in a knot of curls. To draw attention to it, she had chosen a tiny little hat, with two long feathers, which was perched, rather drunkenly, on the side of her head. She was dressed in a travelling pelisse of deep blue velvet over a gown of a lighter shade. Everything about her was vivid and eye-catching, and the height of elegance. She gave Anthony a glowing and hopeful smile. 'Major Lyndhurst, I am come in search of my brother, Ned.' She frowned a little. 'I understand that he has not been seen since he left Lyndhurst Chase.'

Anthony nodded reassuringly. 'Do not be concerned, Miss Devereaux. Your brother is here. And he is perfectly well.'

'Oh, that is wonderful news. I have been so worried. Thank you, Major.' The frown had left her brow, to be replaced by a look of relief and enquiry. She began to scan the faces in the room, seeking her brother. 'Oh!' she gasped, when she came to Marcus. 'M…Ma…!' She put a gloved hand to her mouth and swallowed nervously. She looked suddenly very self-conscious. 'Why,' she said in a rather brittle voice, 'it is Mr Sinclair, is it not?' She dropped him a tiny curtsy. 'How do you do, sir?'

It was Marcus's turn now. He moved forward to bow over her outstretched hand. 'Miss Devereaux,' he said softly. Then, in an absurdly gallant gesture, he raised her fingers to his lips. 'May I say, ma'am, that you are looking even more beautiful than when I last saw you?'

Now, Amy really did blush.

'Flummery!' snorted Great-aunt Harriet from her accustomed place on the sofa. 'Young men today! Can't be doing with 'em!'

Marcus winced, but stood his ground. Amy had not failed him. And he would not fail her. 'This is your first visit to Lyndhurst Chase, I collect, ma'am? I should be delighted to offer you a tour of the gardens, if you are not too fatigued by your journey. There are some exceptionally fine vistas down by the lake.'

'Cut line, Marcus! The gel came here to find her brother, not to go wandering off with you.'

'Aunt Harriet is right on this occasion, Marcus,' Anthony said, a little testily. 'Miss Devereaux, I regret that your brother is not here to greet you. He did know that you were expected. No doubt he has been... detained. I will send to fetch him.' He crossed to pull the bell. 'May I offer you some refreshment while you wait for him?'

'Miss Devereaux might prefer to put off her travelling clothes first, Anthony,' Cassie put in. 'She is to have the room opposite mine, the one that was Lady Margaret's until you dismissed her.' She pretended to ignore Anthony's warning look. 'I am sure that your brother can be asked to wait a little, given all the anxiety he has caused you, Miss Devereaux.'

'I would welcome a chance to wash and change, certainly. It will take me but a moment. I do so long to see with my own eyes that my brother is safe and well.'

'He is very well, ma'am,' Marcus put in. 'I would go so far as to say he is in very rude health.'

Amy smothered a gasp and glanced to Cassie for support.

'Oh, ignore him, Miss Devereaux. He is incorrigible. Shall I show you the way to your chamber?'

'That is most kind of you, Miss...'

'Forgive me, I should have introduced myself. I am Cassie Quinlan. My husband is Viscount Quinlan. That gentleman over there.' She waved a hand in the direction of the Viscount, who bowed. 'We are lately married, you know,' Cassie added airily.

'My congratulations, Lady Quinlan,' Amy said.

Cassie took Amy's arm and steered her towards the door. 'Since you are such an old friend of Sarah's, I am sure we shall get on famously.' The door opened to admit the butler, come to answer Anthony's summons, but Cassie brushed past him, talking all the while. 'Tell me, Miss Devereaux, how is it that you come to know my cousin Marcus?'

Anthony shook his head at Cassie's departing back. 'Women!' he muttered. Then he turned back to Marcus. 'And as for you, Marcus! You must have windmills in your head to behave so! Make yourself useful for a change. Go and look for Miss Devereaux's brother. And don't come back without him!'

Marcus hurried out before his self-control deserted him completely.

Marcus was unable to get Amy alone until after dinner when the company reassembled in the drawing room. She had been prevailed upon to play and so he volunteered to turn her music.

'I have spoken to Ned,' Marcus whispered, under cover of turning her page. Amy began to strike the pianoforte keys rather more loudly than was required by the markings on her music. 'He says it's not a matter for him, but if you're determined to have me, he won't object.'

Amy's fingers stumbled. She glanced fondly across at Ned, who was lounging inelegantly in one of the wing chairs. He had drunk a great deal of wine at dinner. Luckily, it seemed to have made him sleepy, for, when fully awake, he was quite capable of complaining, all over again, that he was disgusted by all the 'lovey-dovey stuff' at the Chase. First, the Quinlans. And then, his own sister! It was as well that Ned was planning to leave on the morrow. And that he had been sworn to secrecy about Marcus's hiding place.

'*Are* you determined to have me?' Marcus murmured.

'Marcus, stop whispering in Miss Devereaux's ear! How is she supposed to concentrate on her music with you hovering over her?'

Amy coloured at Miss Lyndhurst's sharp words, but Marcus said nothing more. He waited until she had finished playing and then, taking her hand, he raised her from the stool. 'Miss Devereaux finds it a trifle warm in here. We are about to take a turn in the parterre. Perhaps you would like to join us, Aunt Harriet?'

The old lady responded with something between a laugh and a snort. 'I think not, Marcus. Sarah may go, if she chooses, though I see no reason why she should. We can all see the parterre perfectly well from here. If you must have company, take Anthony's deaf old dog. She seems to do nothing but sleep. And smell.'

The old setter under the tea table must have sensed something, for she lifted her muzzle and sniffed the air. Finding that her master had not moved, she went back to sleep.

Sarah, who had been in the act of rising, shot a quick

glance at Amy and resumed her seat. 'Aunt Harriet is quite right. Pray do not go beyond the parterre, Amy.'

Amy nodded and allowed Marcus to lead her through the open French doors and down the steps into the parterre. 'Marcus, how could you?' she gasped, as soon as they were out of earshot. 'What on earth will they all think?'.

'They will think, my love, that this is a whirlwind romance. As indeed it has been. And they will be delighted that I am to enter parson's mousetrap, I can assure you. Even Ned is pleased enough, I think.'

'No wonder. He thinks to touch you for money to pay his debts.'

Marcus pinched her fingers. 'And this, from the fond sister who has raced to Lyndhurst Chase to save her brother? Fie, Miss Devereaux! That is not the Christian charity I should have expected of you.' He tried to look down his nose at her.

'Amelia Dent was the one who advocated Christian charity, Mr Sinclair,' she replied primly. 'Amy Devereaux is merely a sister. And much put upon. By *all* the men in her life, I may add.'

Marcus's thumb began to trace a circle on Amy's bare palm, watching her face as her violet-blue gaze became increasingly unfocused.

She almost groaned. 'Marcus, do you know what you are doing to me?'

'Yes, my love, I do. To provoke such a reaction with just a touch… I cannot tell you how proud it makes me feel. I want you so very much. Will you permit me to announce our betrothal tonight?'

'There can be no betrothal, sir, without a proposal,' she said quickly. 'I should perhaps remind you that the lady on your arm is Amy Devereaux, gentlewoman. Not a mere servant.'

'Ah, yes. I had forgot.' He looked anxiously around.

'What is the matter, Marcus? What are you looking for?'

He waved a hand airily. 'I was hoping to find a patch of ground where I might kneel without getting too much dirt on my pantaloons.'

'But you cannot! Not in full view of—!'

'It is customary, you know, Miss Devereaux, to propose to a gentlewoman on bended knee.'

'No, Marcus! Not here!'

He stopped and turned her to face him, taking both her hands in his. He raised first one, then the other, to his lips. His erstwhile abigail now tasted of honey, and lavender. 'I want you to be my wife, Amy Devereaux. You have precisely five seconds to accept me, or I shall kneel in supplication at your feet, where all the world and his wife may see me. And pity me for a lovelorn swain. I am beginning to count now. One…'

'Marcus—'

'Two…'

'I do believe you would really do it.'

'Three…'

'Yes! Yes, you idiot! Of course, I accept you. You know that I love you to distraction.'

He smiled down into her eyes, marvelling at their misty depths. 'Thank you, my love. I may tell you that the feeling is entirely mutual. Though I fancy you already know that.' He raised her hand to his lips again, but this time he turned it over and placed a lingering kiss on her palm.

The sensation quivered through Amy's flesh so strongly that it was almost like a stab of pain. But no pain brought such warmth, or such a flood of desire. 'I think perhaps we should announce our betrothal this evening after all,' she said hoarsely. 'The sooner we are betrothed, the sooner we may be married. Shall we go in and tell them now?'

Marcus tucked her hand in his arm. 'In a moment, my love. I rather think there is a need for us both to…er…cool down a little first.'

'Marcus!' Amy was now bright scarlet.

He gave a low laugh and gestured towards the path through the parterre. 'Come, my love. Let me show you a little of Anthony's garden.'

Marcus drew Amy closer into his arm and enclosed her fingers in his own. 'Ladies and gentleman,' he began. His voice cracked. He cleared his throat and tried again. 'My dear friends, I have an announcement to make. Miss Amy Devereaux has made me the happiest man in the world. She has consented to become my wife.'

'Must be something in the water,' Great-aunt Harriet announced, in the sudden silence. 'Everyone appears to be rushing into wedlock in this house. Perhaps you should give up brandy and try water instead, Anthony?'

A babble of excited voices almost drowned her last words. Anthony simply turned away to pull the bell and order champagne.

Sarah was so delighted that she was almost jumping for joy. 'I told you so, John. Amy will never do what Marcus tells her. They are made for each other.'

'There are similarities with us, certainly,' John admitted with a rueful smile, reaching across to shake Marcus by the hand. 'Congratulations, Marcus. I wish you may both find as much happiness together as we have done.'

Sarah kissed Amy soundly. 'You, too, Marcus. Only I cannot reach unless you bend down.'

Marcus grinned and bent his head obediently.

'You will need to keep a tight rein on him, my dear,' Great-aunt Harriet boomed. 'He's been left to his own devices for much too long. Just like you, Anthony.'

Anthony's tight smile cracked.

The butler entered at that moment, carrying the champagne that Anthony had ordered.

'Thank you, Ufton.' He frowned. 'We do have one vacant bedchamber, do we not? Good. You may remove Mr Sinclair's things from my dressing room. Immediately. I am heartily tired of tripping over him.'

'At once, sir.' The butler deposited the tray of glasses on the table and withdrew.

Marcus and Amy exchanged hot glances. If their bedchambers were reasonably close, they might perhaps—

'I see that Ufton has brought lemonade for you, Cassie,' Quinlan said, smiling mischievously at his wife.

Cassie made a face.

'If you would prefer to have champagne, I shan't try to stop you, my love. We *are* celebrating, after all. And the last time you were foxed was…er…certainly something of a celebration. For both of us.'

Everyone laughed, except Cassie, who had gone rather red. 'No champagne for me, Anthony.' She was trying to sound nonchalant. 'You know how it upsets me.'

'No champagne for Miss Saunders either, Anthony. I declare she is looking quite unwell.'

Aunt Harriet was right. Marcus could see that the companion's pale face was quite flushed. Her hazel eyes were wide and feverish. She was twisting her fingers nervously together, looking now at Anthony, now at her employer.

'I suggest you take yourself off to bed, my dear,' Aunt Harriet said, sounding remarkably concerned, for once. 'You look as though you could do with a good night's sleep.'

Anthony nodded, though he was still frowning. 'Miss Lyndhurst is right, of course, ma'am. You must look after your health. You would do best to avail yourself of this opportunity to get as much sleep as possible. After all, one never knows what may occur to disturb it, does one?'

Miss Saunders was already on her way to the door. At Anthony's final words, her step faltered, but she did not turn.

'And now, perhaps you would open the champagne, Anthony?' Aunt Harriet's foot was tapping impatiently. 'We are all waiting to toast Marcus and his bride.'

With practised skill, Anthony opened the bottles and filled the glasses. But he took only a single mouthful of wine for the toast. 'Excuse me,' he said quickly. 'My dog… I must take her outside. Pray do not allow me to interrupt the celebrations.'

Surprised, Marcus glanced at Anthony's face and then looked round for the old setter bitch. She was still sound asleep under the table. Marcus opened his mouth to say as much and then thought better of it. Anthony was well able to make his own decisions.

Anthony thumped his heel on the floor. Disturbed by the vibration, the setter opened her clouded eyes and got to her feet rather grudgingly. Then she padded across the room and followed her master out.

Sarah caught her husband's eye and laughed.

'What maggot has got into Anthony's head now?' Cassie exclaimed.

'Really, Cassie! Such language!' Great-aunt Harriet

set down her ear trumpet in order to pick up the glass
that John had just refilled for her. 'I do declare that marriage has made the gel worse than ever.' She turned to
Peter Quinlan. 'May I suggest, sir, that you take her in
hand?'

Quinlan choked on his champagne.

Poor Quinlan. Marcus was beginning to feel quite
sorry for him. Had he any idea about the sort of family
he had married into? Marcus smiled down at Amy and
tucked her fingers more securely under his arm, pulling
her further against the warmth of his body. She looked
up at him with glowing, laughing eyes. There was no
need for words.

And there was no need for an audience.

Marcus decided that a diversion was called for. 'Since
we now have both a marriage and a betrothal to celebrate, I think we need to ensure that Anthony's little
firework party becomes the splendid affair that you suggested, Aunt Harriet. I am convinced that you will be
the one to persuade him, ma'am. He listens to you as to
no one else.'

Great-aunt Harriet fixed Marcus with a long, steady
glare. Then she broke into a deep chuckle. 'Be off with
you, you young dog. Take this lovely girl of yours out
into the gardens. I promise you that, just this once, no
one in the house will be watching.'

THE PRODIGAL BRIDE

Elizabeth Rolls

Available from Harlequin® Historical and
ELIZABETH ROLLS

Please address questions and book requests to:
Harlequin Reader Service
U.S.: 3010 Walden Ave., P.O. Box 1325, Buffalo, NY 14269
Canadian: P.O. Box 609, Fort Erie, Ont. L2A 5X3

Chapter One

Clinging to the shreds of his control, Anthony contrived not to bang the drawing-room door behind him. Curse the wench! Damn her to hell and back! Did she think to avoid him *ad infinitum*? The devil she would!

Fury scalded him as his gaze swept the hall, as if expecting her to materialise. A snort escaped him. Hah! She must know he'd be on her heels. Well, if she thought Great-aunt Harriet's chamber would prove a sanctuary this time, then she was sadly misinformed.

He caught Stella's puzzled, cloudy gaze and gently waving tail. Rudely awakened from her snooze beneath the tea table, she clearly expected something in the nature of a walk. Disgustedly, Anthony realised that he'd outwitted himself—now he'd have to take her to the stables for the night. Which gave his quarry plenty of time to go to earth.

He took her gently by the collar. 'Come along, lass.'

Half an hour later, standing in the darkness of the cupola, Anthony concluded that his quarry was not in the house. God only knew what the staff thought of his descent to the nether regions of the kitchen and cellars, but he was beyond caring. After all the brouhaha over Marcus's escapade, the staff were probably inured to shock. He hoped they were. They were in for another.

If she'd left the house...fear coursed through him as he stared out over the wooded park. It was a warm enough night, the sky clear and bright with stars, but still, there was that man thought to be lurking. A chill flooded him—he muttered a few choice words under his breath that would have given Great-aunt Harriet pause, and stormed down to his bedchamber. He'd have to change these shoes for boots or Timms would skin him alive.

Despite the darkness enveloping his bedchamber, Anthony crossed unerringly to the fireplace for a candle and the tinder box.

As light flared a quiet voice spoke. 'Are you looking for me?'

Anthony whipped around. There, by the huge bed, stood his quarry. The world stilled and contracted to a pair of defiant hazel eyes in a white face.

Every muscle tensed as he realised that she had walked straight into the lion's den. Eyes narrowed, he took in every detail—the thick, dark hair escaping its prim chignon, the wide eyes with their fringe of dark lashes, the delicate features and that soft, vulnerable mouth. The slight figure stiffened under his gaze. So familiar, yet...different. Older. A shadow in the eyes and a set about the mouth that had not been there four years ago.

'Sir—we...I must speak with you.' Her voice shook. *And well it might!*

An ominous silence spread through the room. Anthony was dimly aware that he stood at its centre, that she was waiting for his response. He didn't think it would be quite what she expected.

His fingers went to his cravat.

'Speaking,' he ground out, 'can wait.' His cravat hit the floor. 'Right now,' several buttons pinged off his waistcoat, 'at this moment—I have other plans.' The waistcoat itself landed in the general vicinity of the dressing table.

Eyes widening further with shock, she backed away, as he hauled his shirt off over his head.

'Anthony, no, please! Wait! I won't do this!'

'No?' He scarcely knew his own voice, his own hurt fury. 'Are you daring to refuse me?' He stalked her mercilessly as she retreated, his eyes locked on hers. 'I find you here. Here! In my bedchamber—and you think to deny me? Believe me, Madam *Wife*—you've ceded me any rights I choose to claim.'

He prowled closer. A large, powerful hand clamped about her wrist. Willing herself not to betray fear, Georgiana looked up into the face of her furious husband as he dragged her into his arms.

His mouth crashed down on hers. Possessive, demanding, his mouth ravished hers until her senses whirled, until she could barely think, let alone remember all the reasons she should refuse him. Her body melted against his, all the bitter regret and longing of the past four years welling up from deep within her in a wild outpouring. Her arms slid up around his neck as she clung for support, dizzy and breathless.

His grip loosened slightly as one hand slid between them. With a shock she felt swift fingers unbuttoning her bodice, felt her gown pulled from her shoulders to fall about her waist.

One large, warm hand closed over a breast and she

arched instinctively, accepting the caress, pleading for more as pleasure washed through her.

A rough sound broke from him as his fingers shifted to the neck of her chemise and jerked downwards. The worn linen ripped and his hand returned to her exposed breasts, his thumb stroking over her nipples, which burst into aching life.

He released her mouth and stared down at her, grey eyes stormy.

Her breath came in gasps, her lips swollen from his possession. A measure of sanity returned. This was madness. They had to talk…

'Anthony—'

He silenced her with his mouth at her breast, drawing it deep into the heat and wetness. A pleasure that was almost pain crashed through her and she cried out, her fingers locking on his scalp to press him closer.

Abruptly he released her and she staggered, only to find herself swept up into his arms. He strode back across the room and dropped her on the bed. Staring up at him, she could not doubt what he intended. And, God help her, she wanted it too. Her body sang and throbbed in longing for this man who had all but disowned her in public and then abandoned her.

He unbuttoned his breeches. 'It would seem, madam, that I can still drag a response from you. It remains to be seen what new tricks you have been taught since last you deigned to share *my* bed.'

His words made no sense. But the scorn and condemnation in his voice lacerated her.

'This ought to have been our marriage bed, Georgiana. Just once, I intend to have you on it, before I end this farce once and for all.'

She shuddered into stillness as his words sliced through her.

Just once…before I end this farce…

He meant to divorce her. The abyss she had feared yawned black at her feet, blinding her to all else. Doubtless she deserved his anger for her foolishness, but—

'Anthony, please, wait…'

His mouth silenced her as he came down over her, pushing her skirts to her waist and reaching between her thighs, to seek out and find the aching, molten softness. She trembled at his touch. It had been so long and it had never been like this, not this wild melding of fury and passion. He had been gentle with his virgin bride four years ago, but now he was all fierce demand. His fingers stroked, possessed, demanding her response. She gave it. Wildly. Desperately, knowing that this might be all she would ever have of him. And hoping that his passion was fuelled by some remnant of affection. Helpless, her body answered in liquid surrender. She wanted him. And he knew it.

With a growl of satisfaction he pushed her thighs wide and settled between. He braced himself over her and reached down between their bodies. Then she felt him, hot and hard, pressed against her.

'Mine!' he uttered. And thrust deep.

A momentary pain shot through her and she cried out in shock, her body jerking under his at the sensation of having him buried so deep within her after so long.

He froze, shuddering in restraint. She willed herself not to struggle, to lie still despite the unexpected pain.

'Georgie?' His voice sounded shaken. 'Oh, *Georgie*.'

His body lowered on to hers and he held her, a gentle

hand caressing her cheek. The unexpected tenderness shattered her control and she pushed at his shoulders.

'No! Let me go, damn you!'

'Georgie! No. Lie still—'

It was too late. Even as he tried to reassure her, the squirming of her soft breasts beneath him, the unintentional caress of her body, broke Anthony's control. All the pent-up hurt and guilt of the past four years, along with the savage frustration of the past few days, swept through him in a shattering release. He could only hold himself as still as possible while the storm raged.

At last it was over. Shaking and spent, he withdrew himself carefully from her body and rolled to the side. His lack of control sickened him. He had taken her, before she was anywhere near ready, practically forcing her, without bothering even to undress fully. He hadn't even removed his shoes.

'Are you…have you finished?'

The tightly controlled voice tore at him as did her very stillness. As though she dared not move.

'I didn't mean to hurt you.' He heard the restrained fury in his own voice and winced.

'I…it doesn't matter. May I go now?'

'The hell it doesn't matter!' he exploded, raising himself on one elbow. 'And, no! You may *not* go! You are my wife. You remain here.'

Instinctively he reached for her, meaning to comfort her, reassure her. She jack-knifed away from him in a flurry of skirts, clutching her ruined bodice. Shame roiled his guts as he drew back.

'You need not fear,' he said bitterly, hating himself for what he had done. 'I have no intention of dishonouring myself any further tonight.'

That stilled her. The hazel eyes met his gaze, bleak and shuttered.

'I will not be your wife for very much longer, Anthony. Even if I didn't learn any new tricks.'

He thought his jaw might crack under the strain of not roaring a denial.

'At the moment however, Georgiana, you remain my wife. And you will sleep here. In my bed.'

Georgie's heart faltered. The hard line of his mouth, the savage blaze in his eyes, told her that he meant it. If she tried to leave he would stop her. Physically. And she didn't dare let him touch her again. He hated her. His touch would sear her. She knew now exactly what he thought her.

'I…I…very well.'

What was she to sleep in? She had no nightgown in here. Her body burned in shame at the thought of disrobing in front of Anthony. Of feeling those grey eyes on her, assessing her. Dismissing her. As a whore.

'You can borrow one of my nightshirts.' His voice shocked her out of her daze.

'No!' Meeting his gaze, she flushed. 'Thank you. I'll…I'll just sleep in—' In the shift he'd nearly torn off her? 'In my gown.' She wasn't wearing stays. It wouldn't be too uncomfortable.

He was frowning again. 'As you wish.'

He turned away and she barely suppressed a gasp as he stood up and finished undressing. Shameless, to stare so as he walked naked to the dressing-room door. Yet she could not tear her eyes from that broad, muscled back, the narrow hips, so lithe, so… He disappeared into the dressing room and her breath returned in a rush.

Catching at her wits, she stripped off her stockings and garters, dropping them beside the bed. Better to be safely between the sheets before he returned. Frantic fingers rebuttoned her ruined gown.

Five minutes later he slid into the bed on the opposite side. She didn't dare to look to see if he wore a nightshirt.

'There is a cloth and ewer of water in the dressing room, if you…if you need it. If you wish to cleanse yourself…'

She felt her blush all the way to her breasts, felt a renewed awareness of her body, sticky and slightly tender from his possession.

'I…no. I'm fine. Th…thank you.' She hated the wobble in her voice. Hated herself for the vivid memory of the night he had finally come to her chamber in Brussels to complete her seduction and claim his bride. He had cleansed her himself that night, tenderly wiping away the traces of her virginity, easing her soreness. And then he had made love to her again. So gently, so completely that she thought she had never before been whole.

Now there was nothing to ease the soreness of her heart. The knowledge that she had behaved like a spoiled, frightened child and destroyed her marriage with her foolish flight. Her stupid dream that if he truly wanted her, he would come for her.

'Shall I snuff the candle, then?'

'Please,' she whispered.

The light wavered and was gone, plunging the room into welcome darkness. Turning on to her side, she wriggled a little closer to the edge of the bed, unwilling to intrude on his space. He had felt dishonoured in bedding her. The knowledge brought silent tears spilling over.

She had made this particular bed herself. If it was lumpy, she only had herself to blame.

* * *

He hadn't meant to hurt her.

He lay in the darkness, violently aware of Georgiana, finally asleep on the far side of the bed. If she tried to get any further away, she'd roll out on to the floor.

He didn't blame her. With horror and shame he reminded himself just how limited her marital experience had been. Knowing that she had cared for the heedless young idiot who jilted her, he had not insisted on claiming his seventeen-year-old bride on their wedding night. Instead he had applied himself to winning her trust, her affection, at the same time slowly, but surely, seducing her.

He had only permitted himself to bed her the night before the Duchess of Richmond's ball. Four years ago. His eyes closed in pain. She had been so damned innocent. She'd had no idea of what the marriage bed involved. Until he'd shown her. Step by gentle step. His restraint had been rewarded with a response that had seared him to his soul.

And now…

He swallowed. Now he had taken her with the assumption that she had enlarged her experience. He would give his soul to be able to take back what now lay between them. He had treated her as a whore and she had been no more experienced than when he left her bed on the morning after taking her virginity. Inevitably he had hurt her then, too, but at least he'd been gentle with her, had eased himself inside her trembling body tenderly, soothing her, reassuring her, until she softened enough to accept him fully.

Now…now he had hurt her. Carelessly. All the more so because it stemmed from his belief that she had betrayed him. In that at least he had been wrong.

Unfortunately he had said enough for Georgie to realise what he had thought of her.

Still—four years without a word! Not even a note to reassure him of her safety! And then the brazen little baggage thought to insinuate herself back into his life by taking a position with Aunt Harriet, damn her eyes. Where the hell had she been all that time, if she hadn't been under some man's protection?

He shut his eyes. All these questions would have to wait until the morning, when he was in better control of his temper. He dragged in a breath. God help him, but he hadn't lost his temper like that in four years. Not since that ghastly night at the Duchess of Richmond's ball on the eve of Waterloo when he had found her in her erstwhile betrothed's arms. Kissing him, no less!

And then she'd claimed to love *him*! Her fool of a husband, who wanted to believe it more than he had wanted his next breath. She'd begged him to trust her, to let her explain... He'd said things he shouldn't have said, lashing out in his pain. He remembered her white, frightened face as he raged at her, the despairing cry when he left her. And when he had returned, exhausted and bruised from battle, she had been gone, leaving everything he'd given her, bar her wedding ring and the Lyndhurst pearls.

Now she lay again in his bed. And he would have to decide what to do with her.

The downs rolled under his horse's pounding hoofs. On and on he galloped as if he intended to outrun the rising sun and the past. Above him skylarks soared unseen, their song pouring back to the spinning world to mingle with the silver light, the scent of gorse and painful memories tearing free of their shackles.

So many memories. Their first meeting at that picnic outside Brussels. Young Finch-Scott presenting him…

Georgie, this is Major Lyndhurst. Sir, this is Miss Milne, my…my betrothed!

He'd been lost the moment he looked into her face, seen the shy smile in the hazel eyes. Heard her sweet voice as she smiled and greeted him. He'd cursed the fate that had shown her to Finch-Scott first.

After that he had seen her often. Smiling on Justin Finch-Scott's arm as he introduced her to his fellow officers and the English community that had flocked to Brussels.

Within a week he'd heard the tale that Finch-Scott's mama, Lady Halifax, had appeared, scandalised at the rumour that her son had been *entrapped* by a scheming little camp follower. Then the whisper that the betrothal might not stand, that Lady Halifax had reason to believe that Miss Milne was no better than she should be…that Miss Milne's chaperon and guardian, Lady Carrington, considered the match most unequal…that Miss Georgiana Milne, with no connections and less fortune, should content herself with the position as a companion promised to her by her kind protectress.

He'd been furious with Finch-Scott when he'd heard that the betrothal was at an end. The young fool had stammered something about Miss Milne releasing him. Lord! With the prospect of that mother-in-law before her? Of course she had released him!

So when he'd seen her being cut at the start of a ball three days later, he'd stalked over, and announced that this was the dance she had promised him. Then he'd trodden on her slippered toes to stop the automatic denial on her lips. He'd swept her into the waltz and realised

that his search was over. He'd found his bride. Only she
was in love with someone else…

Yet still he'd courted her. And won her. Even knowing that she had cared for Finch-Scott, he had been prepared to take her. Hell, he'd been wild to take her, believing that she would learn to love him…if he gave her
time, didn't rush her. Didn't terrify her by revealing the
depth of desire and passion consuming him. How could
it not terrify her? It terrified *him*, for God's sake. So
much so that he'd presented the match to her as one of
convenience…

He pushed his horse harder, ignoring the pain in his
leg, trying to outrun the pain in his heart. It kept pace
effortlessly.

The Duchess's ball… William's embarrassed avoid-
ance of his eyes when, in all the confusion of the call
to arms, he asked if he'd seen Georgie. William's reluctant mutter that she was…*ah, talking, old chap…talking
to Finch-Scott…*

His own savage reaction.

Well, in the garden, old man…

And Georgie's tears, her frantic denials… *Anthony!
Listen! It wasn't like that! Please, let me explain…*

Why? Why had she fled like that if she had been innocent? Why had she not let him know that she was
safe? She and her mother had followed the drum for
years! Of all women, she had known what he faced. That
he might not return. She had said it herself. Yet she had
left… For all she had known he might have been dead
or injured! His leg twinged. Damn it, he might have
come by this blasted stiff leg at Waterloo, rather than
hunting last winter!

How the hell could he ever trust her again, even if

she *hadn't* spent part of the last four years warming someone else's bed?

Slowing his horse to a canter, he swung around in a wide circle to head for home. If he had the least modicum of sense he'd go back to the house right now, expose the little baggage and sue for divorce! Any man of sense and reasonable pride would agree with that course of action.

He rode towards the house, floating dreamily in its woods above the downs, savagely aware that he was *not* a man of sense…or pride, reasonable or otherwise. His fingers tightened on the reins and the horse flung up his head, sidling and snorting at the sudden pressure. Forcibly relaxing, Anthony faced the truth. Georgie was *his*! Whether he liked it or not. Like a fool, he still cared.

He met John in the park, riding in from the direction of Lynd.

'You're out early,' commented John.

Anthony raised his brows. 'Early is a relative thing, old chap. For me this is normal. You're the one who's taken to lazing between sheets until the breakfast gong sounds!'

John grinned. 'You shouldn't have such comfortable beds.'

Anthony smothered a wry laugh. He suspected that John's tendency to linger in bed had more to do with the delights of his Countess than comfort. For himself, bed had held no temptation to linger. Indeed, in four years of poor sleep, last night ranked as a record. He'd only dropped off shortly before dawn, to be awoken by the sound of the door closing behind his wife. From her restlessness all night, he doubted she'd fared any better than he.

John cast an odd sideways glance at him. 'It's none of my business, Anthony, but—'

He hesitated and Anthony waited, puzzled.

'About William—'

Stiffening, Anthony inclined his head. Most unlike John to plead William's cause…

'Look, Anthony, this is damnably hard for me to say—it's like stabbing him in the back—and I've no idea what you intend and I don't dashed well *want* to know! It's none of my business! But if you're seriously considering William as your heir, you should think again.' He glared at Anthony and charged on. 'And I don't want the Lyndhurst property either, so—'

Outraged, Anthony growled, 'I never thought you did, you gudgeon! It was just that—'

'I know,' said John. 'You wanted to make sure the property was safe. Well, I'll tell you to your head—William is not the right man.' He flushed. 'Listen. I know you always had a fellow feeling for William. Both younger sons and so on. No prospects to speak of, but only consider the difference between you! You went and joined the army, you did something with your life and, from all I ever heard, you lived within your patrimony.' He hauled in a deep breath. 'William has never done that. He has consistently avoided settling to anything. My father and I, both at different times, offered to buy him a commission or see him advanced in the church—'

Anthony could not repress a crack of laughter at that and John looked pained.

'Oh, very well! He'd make a shocking clergyman. But he ought to do something! He has no sense of responsibility and, to be blunt—he borrowed on his expectations as my heir for years.'

He pulled up his horse and said quietly, 'Anthony, whatever William may have told you, I've been making him a very generous allowance for the past few years since my marriage to Sarah, despite the fact that he is no longer my heir. In addition, I have paid his debts several times. I cannot do that forever and he has been told so. There are my own children to provide for.'

Anthony nodded. 'You think William is playing on my sympathies.'

John nodded. 'Yes. I know you were appalled when your brother died. That the last thing you wanted was to succeed to the property, but, believe me, Hartley was perfectly content that it should be so. He knew he could trust you. And there's another thing... That row between Marcus and Frobisher—what did William tell you?'

Anthony grimaced. 'Not much. He was very reluctant to say anything. I gathered that something had been said about my marriage.' His jaw tightened.

John looked at him narrowly. 'William gave you to think that Marcus had said something, didn't he?'

'Yes.'

John swore. 'You fool! Frobisher made the remark. And Marcus—who's even more of a fool than you are, if that's possible!—went berserk. Or so I'm told. For God's sake, Anthony! Did you really think that Marcus would have said anything about that business?'

Before Anthony could frame a reply, he went on, 'Listen—that's just William's style. He never lies outright, but lets you think...imagine...the worst. He twists things, like...' his face hardened '...like messages. He did that once with me. After I met Sarah. Garbled a message and I almost believed she was engaged in an affair with someone!'

Shock slammed into Anthony. '*What?*'

John's eyes were bleak. 'I know. Stupid of me. Sarah, of all women. It nearly destroyed us. But he can be so damned plausible—as though he hates to tell you. But afterwards, when I thought about it—he was desperate for money. If I married Sarah his expectations were gone. And he was drowning in the River Tick.' He gave a short laugh. 'To be frank, the only time I've ever known him to be beforehand with the world was straight after Waterloo. When he returned from Brussels I asked if he needed a tow and he actually refused!' His mouth twisted ruefully. 'First and *only* time he's ever refused an offer of money. Naturally I draw the line at accusations of plunder, but I can only assume that your fellow officers were too much taken up to have their minds on their cards!'

Slowly Anthony nodded. 'I see. Thanks, John. If it's any consolation, I doubt that I should have left the estate to William anyway.'

He waited. Would John say anything about William's possible involvement in the attack on Frobisher? He was certain Marcus had realised, but they hadn't had a chance to speak of it. He knew Marcus would be reluctant to voice his suspicions to John. But if it was the only way to establish Marcus's innocence then, by God, *he* would do it. He would not condemn his best friend and cousin to the sort of hell he had endured for the past four years. Gossip, innuendo. His jaw clenched. If he could come close to believing such rubbish about Marcus, what would society make of it?

John looked relieved. 'Yes, well. Hated saying all that. He's my brother, after all.' He glanced at Anthony, frowning. 'And now, having gone that far, I really am going beyond the line.'

'Oh?'

'Yes. Anthony—when are you going to find out what happened to your wife? If she's dead, you need to know it. If she's with some other fellow, then you need to know that, too, and divorce her. Then you are free to remarry, which would solve your problem. Make an interim will, by all means, but don't name William as your heir. Or me and mine! If I were you, I wouldn't tell anyone the contents of your will. Then find out what happened to Georgiana. It's time you stopped hiding up here like a hermit and got on with your life.'

Anthony took a very deep breath, on the brink of telling John the truth, when a dreadful thought occurred to him.

He felt dazed. William had tried to destroy John's trust in Sarah and his own trust in Marcus. Could he possibly have tried the same trick at the Duchess of Richmond's ball? But, damn it, he'd *seen* Georgie in Finch-Scott's arms, actually seen her stretch up on tiptoe to kiss him. There had been no possibility that he had taken that kiss against her will. She had given it freely.

'Anthony? Are you all right?'

He blinked. John was watching him with a worried frown.

'Sorry, John. You're right. As usual. It is time I did something about the business.'

John's brow cleared. 'Well, that's a relief. If there's anything I can do...' He left it hanging.

Feeling a complete hand, Anthony flushed. 'There is something—whatever my decision...er...whatever the outcome of my decision, you will support me, won't you? You and Sarah?'

From the look on John's face he might have been offered a mortal insult.

'I take it back,' he said grimly. 'Not even Marcus is

that big a codshead! Of course we'll support you! Not that I'll tell Sarah you asked. I might hesitate to draw your cork, but I doubt *she* would hesitate to slap your face! For God's sake, man! Get on with it and get your own heir.' A raffish twinkle came into his eye. 'Believe me—it's far more satisfying than making a will!'

Swallowing hard, Anthony refrained from answering. It was entirely possible that he had dealt with the problem last night. And with that possibility staring him in the face, his choices were limited. Limited to one.

Chapter Two

At Breakfast Georgie wondered when Anthony would return from his ride. He had not been seen at all and even Lady Quinlan had considered this most peculiar.

Mr Sinclair and Miss Devereaux appeared far too taken up with each other to concern themselves about an errant host. Their gazes kept meeting and the blush on Miss Devereaux's cheeks was far from delicate.

Somehow Georgie had managed to sneak back to her own bed without being seen by anyone. And since Miss Lyndhurst had said nothing, she could only assume that her night-long absence had gone undetected.

She pushed her breakfast around the plate with no real interest. It blurred before her eyes. All she could see was Anthony, asleep as she left his bed at dawn, the grim lines around his mouth at peace, his powerful body relaxed.

At least she had lain with him one last time.

She wished she had dared to caress his cheek before she left the bed, but she had not, drawing back her outstretched fingers at the last moment. Her eyes burned and she blinked.

'Eat, girl!' Miss Lyndhurst was glaring at her. 'Drat

it, child. Took me three years to get some flesh on those bones and bedamned if you aren't losing it all! Anthony's cook ain't *that* bad. Nothing that a watchful mistress wouldn't put to rights.'

Her cheeks burned as she stammered a disclaimer that her breakfast was lovely, she was merely woolgathering.

Miss Lyndhurst's bright black eyes narrowed. She snorted, but mercifully let it lie.

When Georgie dared look up from her plate, she discovered Mr Sinclair watching her as he had the previous evening, his blue-grey gaze piercing and an odd, secret smile playing about his mouth. She dropped her eyes to her plate. He couldn't know. He couldn't! None of Anthony's family had ever met her, apart from Mr William Lyndhurst-Flint. And *he* hadn't bothered so much as to glance at her. So why did Mr Sinclair keep staring at her?

If only Anthony would consent to ending their marriage quietly enough that Miss Lyndhurst never discovered what a viper she had been nursing. Otherwise she would be without a reference. Despite her waspish comments, Miss Lyndhurst had a considerable affection for her great-nephew. And she would be hurt by the deception practised on her. Georgie shivered slightly at the thought. She had caused enough hurt for one lifetime.

Breakfast over, Mr Sinclair announced that he and Miss Devereaux were going to take a walk.

Lady Mardon glanced up. 'Very well, Marcus. I shall be ready in fifteen minutes.'

Mr Sinclair gave her a withering look. 'Sarah—I said *Miss Devereaux* and I were going for a walk. Since when was *your* name Devereaux?'

Lady Mardon favoured him with the most quelling of

quelling looks. 'Marcus, just in case it had escaped your notice, I am Amy's chaperon here, and—'

Georgie could only describe Mr Sinclair's roar of laughter as unseemly and there was not a hair's breadth to choose between the shades of crimson adorning the cheeks of both Miss Devereaux and Lady Mardon.

He glanced fleetingly at Miss Devereaux and frowned as he turned back to Lady Mardon. 'Dearest goose, we are betrothed. Remember all that champagne? Miss Devereaux is perfectly safe with me and I'm sure you can count on Anthony and John to put a pistol to my head if I fail to meet my obligations. Why don't you chaperon Cassie instead?'

'We're married, Marcus, you great clod!' Lady Quinlan said. 'We can do what we like, when we like! Without your permission!'

Miss Lyndhurst gave a bark of laughter as Lord Quinlan choked on his sirloin.

'Waste of time, child,' she said to Lady Mardon. 'You may keep me company instead and tell me all about these boys you have given Mardon. Miss Saunders is going to take a rest.'

She bent a stern look on Georgie. 'Knew that truckle bed in the dressing room was no damn good. Bad for your neck. Have to find another bed for you. I'm sure Anthony will oblige.'

The blush on Georgie's face rivalled Miss Devereaux's.

Miss Lyndhurst charged on. 'You go and sit in the library. Nice, quiet spot if you've got a headache. No one will disturb you there. Off you go. Dare say Anthony won't be back for a while. Go on. Do as you're bid!'

Curled up in the big wingchair by the library window, Georgie dozed a little in the sun. She hadn't slept well, wildly aware of Anthony on the opposite side of the bed and her own hopeless longing to wriggle into his arms and be held. She had dreamt of him and kept half-waking, unsure of what was dream and what was memory. And now she drifted in the sunlight by the window, the print of her book dancing and blurring before her eyes.

He would return soon enough. To be told by his butler that most of the party was out about the grounds, but that Miss Saunders was in the library. He would know that she was waiting for him, would probably be only too glad to have the opportunity to be rid of her.

She awoke with a start and realised that he was there, in the other wingchair on the opposite side of the window, reading a newspaper with his old setter dozing at his feet, half on her back. One booted foot was absently rubbing Stella's exposed belly. If the boot slowed, an imperious paw put it in mind of its duty.

For a moment, she watched him. Knowing it might be for the last time, she absorbed every detail: strong, chiselled jaw, the slightly tousled auburn hair, the powerful form relaxed in the chair. And his unthinking gentleness with his dog.

Her husband. The man she loved—who was about to disown her.

He lowered the paper and regarded her over it. 'Good morning. You must have risen early.'

She sat up, conscious of untidy hair and a rumpled gown. 'I...I beg your pardon, sir. You should have woken me when you came in.'

His mouth tightened. 'You didn't sleep well last night. Are you all right?'

'I'm very well.' As well as she could be, anyway,
facing his cold grey eyes. Knowing that he despised her.

'It won't happen again.'

She flinched. 'You made that quite clear last night,
sir.' He had taken her for revenge and she had been fool
enough to hope for passion and forgiveness. Dear God—
and she'd thought she had grown up… Drawing a deep
breath, she said, 'There is something I must ask you, sir.
A…a favour.'

His face hardened even further. 'A favour. Madam,
you are scarcely in a position to be making demands!
Surely—'

'I'm not demanding,' she broke in. 'Simply asking.'
Clinging to self-control, she said, 'When you divorce
me—I don't know how these things are done, but would
it be possible for Miss Lyndhurst not to know who
"Miss Saunders" is? I…I will need a reference…and
she—I think she would be hurt to know the truth.' She
hurried on. 'Naturally you wish me to leave her employ,
but without a reference—' Her voice shivered to silence.
Without a reference and with a scandal like this attached
to her name, she would never gain another respectable
position. She might as well hang out a sign saying
'whore'. Which was, no doubt, how Anthony thought of
her.

'I see.' His voice was cold. Hard. 'It may come as a
surprise, madam, but I have no intention of acceding to
your request.'

She tasted fear. Could *Anthony* hate that much? 'Very
well.' Somehow she forced her legs to support her as
she stood and placed the book in the very centre of the
wine table beside her chair. It was oddly important to
make sure it was dead centre.

'Where are you going?' His voice cracked like a whip.

Holding herself together by sheer willpower, she said, 'To pack. You must wish me gone. If you will give me your solicitor's direction—'

'Dammit, Georgie! I just said I wouldn't divorce you! You're not going anywhere!'

The room whirled blackly.

'Georgie!'

Strong arms caught her, lowered her to the chair. Swift, shaking fingers undid the buttons at her throat, brushing lightly over her cheek. Her dream again—the one in which the past four years had never happened, in which he still cared for her...

The haze receded to reveal him leaning over her. 'Drink this.' A tumbler was pressed to her lips and something fiery tipped down her throat. Spluttering, she pushed the tumbler away.

'No. Please—'

'Drink it. You fainted. It's only brandy.'

His fingers closed around hers on the tumbler and she couldn't repress the tremor that rippled through her at his touch, the sensation of him surrounding her.

Abruptly he released her and stepped back.

Georgie wondered if she had misunderstood. Surely, surely he wanted to divorce her?

'Let us have this straight, madam. I will not divorce you.'

She sank back in the chair, dazed. His denial echoed through her. But, he thought she had cuckolded him—he'd made that plain enough last night.

It remains to be seen what new tricks you have been taught...

He had turned away to stare out of the window, his fists clenched at his sides. 'After last night...' there was a bleak pause '…after last night there is every chance you are carrying my heir. Divorce is out of the question.'

Pain splintered deep as other memories ripped free. *An heir…* If he knew? Would he still want her? If all he wanted was an heir…she would have to tell him.

'Then…then we could wait, until—'

'*No!*'

The old dog jolted up.

Anthony whirled, eyes blazing, his jaw a solid line of outrage. 'Dammit, Georgie! We won't wait! You are to remove your things from Aunt Harriet's dressing room today!'

That distracted her. 'Remove my things? But…but where am I to sleep? All the bedchambers are being used. You gave the last spare one to Mr Sinclair!' Even as she spoke, Anthony's stunned face gave her the answer.

Anthony couldn't quite believe that she'd actually asked. For a moment shock strangled him. Then, 'Hell's teeth, Georgie!' he exploded. 'You're my wife! You'll sleep where you slept last night! Where you belong—in *my* bed, of course!'

The shocked gasp from the doorway froze every drop of blood. Turning slowly, Anthony realised that this was one of *those* moments. The sort of moment when you wished the floor would hurry up and open, when you wished the world would crack open in fire and obliterate you.

Sarah stood on the threshold, her hand clapped to her mouth, with the rest of the house party crowding at her back. All of them: John, Marcus, Miss Devereaux, William, Aunt Harriet, Cassie and poor Quinlan, who must think he'd married into a family of Bedlamites.

Taking a very deep breath, Anthony braced himself

for explanations, even as Sarah gave vent to a delighted cry.

'Oh, Anthony! How simply—ooh!'

How John silenced her, Anthony couldn't quite see, but, judging by the squawk and the glare Sarah cast at her husband, he assumed she'd had her bottom pinched.

Smothering a grin, John said, 'Later, my love. Come along. There's something I forgot to show you in our bedchamber this morning.' He cast Anthony an amused glance. 'We'll, ah, leave you to the solving of your problem, old chap.' So saying, he steered his audibly giggling wife from the room.

What John might have forgotten to show Sarah during eight years of enthusiastic marriage, Anthony refused to contemplate. All he could do was face Marcus, whose eyebrows rose briefly as he propped himself against the door frame and grinned openly, with not the least sign of surprise. Damn Marcus! He'd seen the miniature, of course, but did he have to look so curst smug?

'But…but…' That was Miss Devereaux, whose extraordinary eyes suggested she had taken a blow to the head. Evidently Marcus had kept his mouth shut about his suspicions.

'Very discreet, our Anthony,' offered Marcus in soothing tones. 'Dare say he meant to tell us eventually. House parties are supposed to be, er, hotbeds of scandal. Have to keep the side up, you know.' He winked at Miss Devereaux and she blushed violently.

Anthony gritted his teeth. And forbore to ask just how Marcus and Miss Devereaux had been keeping the side up. There were things a host simply didn't want to know and there was something damned smoky about the pair of them anyway.

'Well…well…I mean to say…ah, Aunt Harriet, dare

say you'll need to lie down. Some hartshorn. Quite a shock and all that sort of thing...' William sounded as though *he* needed a restorative. He was staring at Aunt Harriet's erstwhile companion as though he couldn't quite believe his eyes and ears.

Great-aunt Harriet silenced William's tentative effort at tact with a glare and pushed his proffered arm away with her ear trumpet.

'You may presume to tell me what to do, William, when I'm in my winding sheet and not before. Cassie!' she rounded on her great-niece. 'Tell that maid of yours—Ebdon, isn't it—to remove *Mrs* Lyndhurst's belongings and take 'em to Anthony's bedchamber. I've not the least doubt that man of his will be only too happy to show her where everything goes!'

Cassie, miraculously lost for words, obeyed, with a last stunned glance at Georgie. Quinlan followed her with an incomprehensible mutter, and an all-too-comprehensible grin.

Aunt Harriet turned her guns on Anthony. 'As for you—God only knows what took you so long! I parade the chit under your nose for *days* before you come to your senses! Lord! I was beginning to wonder if I'd have to dose her with laudanum and have Timms and Ufton put her into your bed!'

Mentally reeling from this broadside, Anthony absorbed the fact that at least he was spared this particular explanation. The meddlesome old hag had known all along! Which meant... He swung around to find Georgie staring transfixed at Harriet.

'You...you *knew*! *That* was why you decided to come here! Why you insisted that I come!' Her voice echoed disbelief.

Shock hit Anthony. Then…Georgie hadn't planned it? Hadn't even wanted to come?

Harriet snorted. 'Knew? Good God, gel! Of course I knew. Your godmother was one of my oldest friends. She and I planned the whole!' She sniffed. 'Never thought it would take *this* long! Or that I'd have to practically drag you here! Four years! I ask you!' Her mouth tightened. 'Not that you weren't a good companion, though. Best I ever had. Now you get back where you belong and sort out this idiot great-nephew of mine.'

She turned on Anthony, eyes snapping, and poked him in the chest. 'And mind you keep her! I've interfered enough for one lifetime. As for the rest of you—out!' With a sweep of the ear trumpet that nearly clipped William's ear, she drove the others before her like chaff, stalked out after them and shut the door.

Battling to order her thoughts, Georgie faced her husband, her chin up, despite the flush of mortification burning her cheeks. After that, there was no way that she could quietly disappear with no one the wiser. 'You haven't given me very much choice, have you?' she said.

He flushed. 'Damn it, Georgie! I didn't know they were there. D'you think I *meant* it to happen?' He wiped his brow. 'Damn it to hell! I've never been so embarrassed in my life. Thank God it was only family!'

'What do we do now?' she whispered.

His mouth set hard. 'We put our marriage back together, that's what we do. I am sorry if you wish otherwise, Georgie, but I am not prepared to go through the scandal and expense of a divorce. Especially since I require an heir. You will forgive my plain speaking.'

Her throat ached with suppressed tears. He couldn't know the pain his words gave her. A marriage of convenience for an heir. To the man she loved. When he despised her and she had no idea if she could fulfil her duty... She had to tell him that. Tell him what she'd never told anyone— And watch him turn away.

'I...I see. Then...then you wish me to do my duty. You expect—'

'No!' The harshness of his voice shocked her. He took one step towards her, eyes blazing. She stood her ground. Damned if she'd back up!

He swung away and continued. 'After last night—I do not intend to press my attentions on you immediately. But you will share my bed.'

She swallowed the choking lump. He didn't even want her, then. She had thought nothing could shame her more than the unexpected revelation of her identity. Shame, she now learnt, had entirely unplumbed depths. Doubtless he didn't trust her enough to permit her a separate bedchamber. And when he could bring himself to touch her, he intended to do his duty and get an heir. Probably a spare or two as well.

What other reason could he have for wanting her back? Had he wanted anything else he would have come to find her four years ago. She had to tell him. Now.

She dragged in a breath like splintered glass and lifted her chin a little higher. The wrong words came out. 'As you wish, sir. And now perhaps you should conduct me to your housekeeper.'

The right words, the truth, remained where they had been for four years. Frozen. Locked away in her heart.

The housekeeper, the cook, the butler, the housemaids and the footmen—Georgie clung to what she hoped was a dignified façade as she was presented to the stunned servants. The only servant who didn't appear in the least surprised was Timms. But she had known from the first that he had recognised her.

Anthony's demeanour with the staff—calm, collected, as though errant brides popped out of the panelling as a matter of course—was enough to enrage a saint. Apparently he didn't even notice the surreptitious sideways glances.

The housekeeper, Mrs Waller, handed over her keys with thin-lipped civility. Uncertain, Georgie turned to Anthony. He shook his head very slightly.

Breathing a little easier, she said, 'No, Mrs Waller. You hold them. I shall ask for them when I require them. Another set can be made for me.'

'I'll leave you to it, then, madam,' said Anthony politely. 'Mrs Waller will show you everything.'

Stifling a protest, Georgie nodded. He had intended a marriage of convenience from the very first. He had been quite honest with her. But in Brussels the seventeen-year-old had still dreamed, reading more into his gentleness and tender lovemaking than she ought. And perhaps, had she not been such a fool, more might have been possible.

She should be grateful that she was not starving in the gutter.

Chapter Three

Mrs Waller did indeed show her everything. Including, quite unintentionally, just what the staff thought of this latest scandalous development. By the time she needed to change for dinner, Georgie was exhausted and all she wanted was a cup of tea in a quiet corner.

Mrs Waller received this request with a coldly respectful 'Certainly, ma'am. At once.'

Retreating to Anthony's bedchamber, Georgie found her single evening gown in the dressing room and changed as quickly as she could. If she hurried there would be time to sit quietly and sip her tea when it came. She had barely tied the last lacing when she heard the outer door open and Anthony's slightly halting stride. She wondered how he had hurt himself. She knew he hadn't been wounded at Waterloo.

He strode into the dressing room, already unbuttoning his shirt and pulled up short, staring at her.

She met his gaze, conscious of blushing at the glimpse of his powerful chest, warmth suffusing her as she remembered the rasp of it against her aching breasts. His weight holding her captive…her breath shortened. 'I'll leave you to change, sir.'

'Anthony,' he said.

'I beg your pardon?'

'Anthony,' he repeated. 'You're my wife. You use my name.' His mouth twisted. 'Georgie—don't make this any harder. We must try, both of us.'

If he wanted to try, did that mean he was ready to listen? Shivering, she remembered his fury that night, his public shredding of her character. What would happen if she brought it up? Wouldn't it be easier to just let it go? And live with a man who despised her, thought she would have betrayed him.

'Then, will you let me tell you what happened at the Duchess of Richmond's ball?'

His glance speared her. 'What happened? I thought that was a trifle obvious. You were kissing another man in the garden. I took exception. Perhaps we should leave it at that.'

He hauled his shirt off over his head and dropped it. Georgie's lungs seized and the breath she had taken got well and truly lost as she floundered for an answer.

'I wanted to say farewell, to see you,' she said at last. 'In case you were killed.'

His brows rose. 'You picked an odd way to do it, then.' He turned away.

I was so frightened. Her stomach lurched at the memory of how much she had wanted to hold him, in case she never saw him again. She willed herself to control. No good could come of telling Anthony that. He wanted a marriage of convenience, a conformable, well-behaved wife. He always had.

Not foolish, romantic Georgie Milne, who had made the mistake of falling in love with him and had misunderstood his skill and consideration in bed for something else. She pushed that memory away.

'I saw your cousin in the crowd and asked him to tell you I was looking for you. But then I saw Justin and he was desperate to speak with me. I *couldn't* let him go when he felt so badly about jilting me... It never occurred to me that you would think...that I...'

Her voice shivering into silence tore at Anthony, opening wounds he had thought healed. Now he knew otherwise—that they had barely closed.

Furious that she could still so effortlessly slip past his control, he snapped, 'Damn it! What else was I meant to think? When a man is informed that his bride is in the garden, bidding a fond farewell to her lover—why the hell did you do it, Georgie?'

'Bid Justin farewell? When the call to arms had gone out?'

He saw her face crumple, just before she turned away.

Her voice came, strained and tight. 'Because I wanted to wish him Godspeed, to tell him that I was happy, that I bore him no ill will. In...in case...in case he was killed...'

Anthony's gut roiled. Justin Finch-Scott *had* died at Waterloo. Died in agony with most of his stomach blown away by a French musket. He'd tried to ease the boy, but he'd died, screaming.

'You were kissing him!'

Her answer shattered him. 'Yes. I never thought how it must look to others.'

She turned back to him. 'I'm sorry, Anthony. I could not bear to see him go...with that between us. You see, he begged my forgiveness. Said he should be horsewhipped for giving in to his mother. He said that you were a better man anyway, that I had the best of the bargain. So, I—if he died—' She shuddered. 'Do you…do you think he suffered very much?'

Anthony swallowed. 'No,' he lied. 'It was swift. A clean death in battle. He knew nothing.' And God forbid Georgie should ever know anything about that screaming, smoking hell on earth.

I never thought how it must look to others… The inexperience of a very young girl. Something else flared in his mind. 'You said you saw my cousin. You mean, William?'

She stared. 'Yes. Mr Lyndhurst-Flint. I saw him in the crowd and asked him to find you. Tell you where I was.' Uncertainly she whispered, 'Did he not do so?'

'Yes,' said Anthony savagely, 'he did.' John's embarrassed warning came back to him. *Listen—that's just William's style. He never lies outright, but lets you think, imagine…the worst. He twists things, like…like messages…*

Shaken, he tried to recall exactly what William had said. Surely, if Georgie had made that request…but, no—William had been cagey. Had hesitated when asked if he'd seen Georgiana…as if he hadn't wanted to tell him. But he had, of course. Damn it all! It fitted the pattern. Exactly as John had warned him. Four years too late. Four years lost over a misunderstanding that could have been cleared up if she had not run away. Anger burnt inside him, but none the less…

'Then I owe you an apology for that night, madam.' For all the ache in his heart he kept his voice cool, detached. She had still left him. Without a word. But he held out his hand to her, palm up.

Briefly she hesitated, but then she came to him and laid her hand in his.

Relief jolted him as he closed his hand gently on the

slender fingers. For a moment he had thought she would not come, that he had frightened her too badly. But now her hand lay in his again. He drew her closer and slid his other hand under her chin. He intended only to stroke her cheek, but somehow his thumb found its way to the trembling corner of her mouth. His senses and restraint reeled. So soft, so damned sweet.

Aching, he bent his head slowly, giving her time to retreat. But she stayed. And his lips found hers. Softer, sweeter than he remembered, melting beneath his kiss. Desire hammered through him, the urge to sweep her into his arms and make love to her.

She left you. Over a misunderstanding. On the eve of battle. With no word for four years! What if she'd been pregnant? Would she have kept your child from you? How could he ever trust her again?

Besides which, he'd given his word not to press his attentions on her. He must have been insane. With a muttered curse he released her and stepped back, every muscle locked in restraint. 'I have rung for Timms. If you have finished, I suggest you should go downstairs now. Our guests will be gathering and I would like to take my bath.'

And if you don't leave now they won't see either of us until breakfast time, if then. He bit that back. Damned if he'd give her the power of knowing how desperately he wanted her. Better to wait until he was in control of himself, until he could bed her without all these curst emotions getting in the way.

Anger flared in her eyes. 'Is this not *my* bedchamber as well, sir? You have declined to furnish me with any other—'

'One last thing—what did you intend, had you been pregnant when you left me?' He turned away, adding,

'Did you ever think of that? That you might have had difficulty persuading me that the child was mine?'

'Yes.'

He waited, refusing to look at her. And waited, until he heard the soft footfalls as she left. And a cheerful voice in the bedchamber.

'Evening, mistress. Is the Major through there?'

Georgie's soft affirmation.

Then, 'Evening, sir. I've brought your shaving water. Would there be aught else, sir?'

He turned to face Timms, who continued with a grin. 'Nice to have the mistress back, sir. Looks a little peaky, though. Dare say she'll pluck up soon enough, though.'

'Timms?'

'Yessir?'

'Shut up and take that smirk off your face. And when you've put the water down and pulled off my boots, fetch that blasted trunk down from the attics.'

If anything, the grin broadened. 'Yessir!'

As his henchman departed, Anthony could only be thankful that at least he'd retained enough sense not to ask *which* blasted trunk.

To his immense surprise, the outer door opened a moment later. Wondering what the hell Timms wanted now, he stalked into the bedchamber, heedless of his nudity—to discover Mrs Waller carrying a laden tea tray.

Her jaw dropped, her eyes bulged and for a moment she appeared to struggle for breath, let alone words. But only for a moment. '*Master Anthony!* This is a respectable household, I'll have you know! What would your poor mother think?'

Anthony stood stunned, realising that sharing a bedchamber obviously had complications.

'What...what?' He gestured feebly at the tray.

'The *mistress* requested tea.' She swept on. 'And don't just *stand* there! Cover yourself! The very idea!' With which, she left the room, muttering direfully, 'Never seen the like! Not in all my born days!'

Given her outrage, Anthony doubted that could be construed as a compliment. Damn. Why hadn't Georgie said something about requesting tea? He swallowed. She had started to protest. But he'd overridden her and kicked her out. What an absolutely brilliant way to restart his marriage.

And what had she said *yes* to? That she had thought about what to do? Or that she had believed he would disavow a child?

By the time he came down everyone had gathered in the drawing room. He saw with relief that Georgie had a cup of tea. Plainly Mrs Waller had found her.

Aunt Harriet took umbrage at his late arrival. 'In *my* day, Anthony, both the hostess *and* the host were down before their guests! Georgiana was here. Where were you? Fiddling with your cravat, no doubt!'

Having made himself a promise while shaving that he would not rise to Harriet's bait, Anthony inclined his head and said, 'I beg your pardon, Aunt Harriet. How was your day?'

She snorted. 'In *my* day, there was provision made for a lady's entertainment! What happened to the archery targets your mother bought?'

Archery? Aunt Harriet? Anthony repressed a shudder at the thought and ignored Marcus's twitching mouth.

'What an excellent idea, Aunt,' purred Marcus.

'The targets are still here,' said Anthony. 'I'll have them set up.' With a courtly bow, he added, 'I shall look forward to seeing your skill, Aunt.'

He limped over to the console table that held the brandy decanter. Riding so far that morning had been a mistake. The muscles had stiffened.

'And what the devil's the matter with your leg? It wasn't like that last time I saw you, Christmas of fourteen,' barked Aunt Harriet. 'That wretched Bonaparte, I suppose! Waterloo?'

Georgie started, spilling her tea. 'But...no—Anthony wasn't hurt at Waterloo! Not so much as a scratch!' She sounded utterly sure. Then she turned to him, seemingly unaware of the others, her face white and whispered, 'Were you?'

He stared at her. 'No. Hunting accident last winter. I broke it badly and wrenched the knee. It's nothing to fuss about.' How in Hades could she be so certain?

Ufton's stately tones broke in on his thoughts. 'Dinner is served, madam.'

Anthony blinked. *Madam?* Then he realised— Lyndhurst Chase had a mistress now. A hostess. Shaken, he looked to Sarah, who smiled encouragement.

Drawing a deep breath, he said, 'John, perhaps you would escort my wife?'

Georgie had never imagined that Miss Lyndhurst's reference to her as the hostess might be literal. She found herself installed at the opposite end of the dining table to Anthony, in the chair that Lady Mardon had previously occupied, with Lord Mardon on her right and Viscount Quinlan to her left.

Determinedly, she pinned a smile in place and lifted her chin. Anthony should be given no cause to blush for her manners. Lord Mardon and Lord Quinlan were courtesy itself, chatting with easy informality, apparently quite unperturbed that the lowly companion had become their hostess.

She looked around the table. Her guests. It felt unreal. *She was Mrs Lyndhurst.* Again. Or was it for the first time? Or not at all? In requesting that she leave their— *his*—room, Anthony had confirmed her suspicion that the only reason she was to share his bed was that he didn't trust her anywhere else.

Her gaze met Lady Quinlan's. Tentatively, she smiled. Lady Quinlan had been very friendly to Miss Saunders, never seeming to remember the abyss between a Viscountess and a companion.

Lady Quinlan inclined her head and turned back to her conversation with Mr Lyndhurst-Flint.

Pain twisted a little deeper.

'Tell me, Mrs Lyndhurst, are you going to shine at this archery contest tomorrow?' asked Lord Quinlan.

She forced a smile. 'Oh, no! I've never touched a bow in my life. A pistol, yes. But not a bow.'

'A pistol?' Lord Quinlan looked startled.

She nodded. 'Mama and I followed the drum. So Papa insisted that we learnt how to use one.'

'Very wise.' His eyes twinkled. 'I dare say, if you can aim a pistol, that you have a good eye and will not find archery beyond you. May I help you to some of this excellent lamb?'

She smiled assent and gave thanks for the rule governing polite company that confined dinner-table chat to one's immediate neighbours.

Dinner itself was not such an ordeal. The drawing room, while the gentlemen lingered over their wine, was far, far worse.

While Miss Lyndhurst, for reasons best known to herself, subjected Lady Mardon and Miss Devereaux to a searching catechism, Georgie found herself obliged to chat to Lady Quinlan.

'I hope, Lady Quinlan, that you will not dislike the archery tomorrow? Pray, if there is something else you would care for, please tell me.'

Lady Quinlan inclined her head. 'Archery will be perfectly acceptable, cousin. Now that Aunt Harriet is bereft of her companion, we must find pursuits somewhat closer to the house.'

Georgie stiffened her spine. Lady Quinlan's chilliness shook her to the core, but she had expected no less. She had seen for herself Lady Quinlan's affection for Anthony, that she never lost an opportunity to tease him. Why should she welcome as Anthony's wife a woman who had treated him so shabbily?

'You need not think that I am suddenly loath to bear Miss Lyndhurst company, Lady Quinlan,' she said quietly. 'I have a considerable affection for her. If you prefer to ride, or go for a picnic, you need only say so.'

Lady Quinlan's eyes blazed, and she was about to speak—just as the door opened to admit the gentlemen.

'Just so,' said Lady Quinlan, as though she were gritting her teeth in restraint. She turned away to Lord Quinlan, her face softening, the bright brown eyes beaming.

With a pang of envy, Georgie saw the smile that passed between them, the heightened colour on Lady Quinlan's cheeks as her husband bent to murmur something in her ear. The tenderness in his face sent another shaft of pain through Georgie. Would Anthony ever look at her like that again?

Miss Lyndhurst, giving up on Lady Mardon and Miss Devereaux, demanded some music. Lady Mardon acquiesced, going to the pianoforte and embarking upon a Haydn sonatina, while her husband turned the pages.

Relieved, Georgie sank into a chair and let the music flow over her. She had no idea what to *do*, whether anyone expected her now to provide for their entertainment, or if it would be odiously *coming* if she suggested anything.

Fortunately, at the end of the sonatina, Lady Mardon said cheerfully, 'Your turn, Amy dear. And Marcus may sit by me! John can turn your pages this time. You'll find it much less distracting.'

Mr Sinclair, who had risen to his feet, sat back with a darkling look at Lady Mardon.

Miss Lyndhurst gave vent to a croak of laughter. 'You'll do, girl,' she said to Lady Mardon. 'John needed someone to keep him in line!'

Georgie relaxed again, closing her eyes.

'Tired, my dear?'

Georgie turned at the quiet voice and found that Anthony had drawn a chair up beside her. She shook her head, not meeting his eyes and aware that she had blushed.

He nodded. 'We won't sit up late, I assure you.'

Given the intent look in his eyes, Georgie was unable to work out if that amounted to a promise, or a threat.

The party broke up early, which, as far as Georgie was concerned, was a double-edged sword. The moment had arrived when she would have no excuse for not going to bed herself. With Anthony.

Miss Lyndhurst saved her. 'Humph. I'm for bed,' she announced. 'And having done myself out of a companion, I'll thank you, Georgiana, to come up and help me.'

Fixing Anthony with a beady glare, she said, 'I'll bid you a goodnight.'

He rose to his feet at once. 'Thank you, Aunt.' The odd note in his voice caught Georgie's attention. She stared at him, but he was lighting a candle for Miss Lyndhurst.

Upon reaching Miss Lyndhurst's bedchamber, Georgie busied herself finding the old lady's nightrail and readying her for bed, chattering inanely.

Miss Lyndhurst listened, answered occasionally and finally said, 'Enough, child. I admit Anthony's a dratted fool at times, but he's no Bluebeard or I never would have kicked you out of my dressing room! You two need privacy to make up your differences and, as far as I'm concerned, the best place for that is the bedchamber.'

The clawlike fingers closed on her wrist. 'Listen, my dear. He's a good man. Proud, arrogant, I'll grant you. And with more than his fair share of temper. But you can't hide for the rest of your life. Whatever happened in Brussels, you both need to put it behind you and go on. Don't try to tell me you've been happy without him. I'm not blind. And from all I've heard from the rest of 'em, he hasn't been happy either.' She hesitated and then said, 'Don't think too highly of men, myself, but Anthony, for all his faults, is one of the better ones. And you needn't tell him I said so! Now, off you go!'

Gulping, Georgie nodded. 'I…I know, Miss Lyndhurst. That's the worst of it. I was such a blasted little ninny! I…I mean—'

'That you were a blasted, little ninny,' agreed Miss Lyndhurst. 'We all make mistakes. Including Anthony. I've not the least doubt he was as much to blame as you.' She got into bed and settled herself back against the pillows. 'And you'd better start calling me Aunt Harriet. This Miss Lyndhurst business is wearing me down! Now, give me a kiss and run along!'

Shaken, Georgie obeyed, pressing a gentle kiss on each withered old cheek.

Gruffly, the old lady waved her away. 'Go on. Off with you. I'm tired. Tell Mrs Waller I'll want tea in the morning. Oh, one last thing. If there's anything, anything at all, that you ought to tell Anthony—tell him sooner, rather than later.'

Georgie stared, held by the compassionate old eyes. She *couldn't* know. She *couldn't*. She'd never even told her godmother the truth about that…

She hesitated outside Anthony's bedchamber, Aunt Harriet's words echoing…*he hasn't been happy either*…

The question remained—would she be able to make him happy? More to the point, did he even want her to make him happy? Or would he seek happiness outside their marriage? All he wanted of her was an heir…

With a shuddering breath, she entered. He was in bed, sitting up reading, and the breath strangled in her throat. Not at the sight of him reading, but at the sight of his bare chest. Drat the man! Didn't he *ever* wear any clothes? Unable to tear her gaze away, she stood, clutching the door handle.

He glanced up. 'Ah, there you are.'

She continued to stare.

'Er, were you planning to shut that door?'

She shut it with rather a bang as it slipped from her suddenly nerveless fingers. Still with her eyes on him, she began to circle the huge bed, the bed that she must share with him, towards the dressing room.

'There is a nightgown laid out for you here.'

Startled, she looked at the other side of the bed. Sure enough, a nightgown lay there, pristine white against the deep crimson counterpane. It looked familiar.

She came closer, staring. 'But…but that is mine…the one…' Her voice died in her throat. He had bought it in Brussels, sheer, flimsy, lace-trimmed lawn that hid nothing. He had brought it back to their lodgings and presented it with a wicked grin. And asked her to wear it for him that night. The night *before* the Duchess of Richmond's ball.

Heat swept her. Asking her to *not* wear it would have been more to the point. She hadn't worn it for very long after he came to her bed.

'You left it behind,' he said quietly. 'You will find the rest of your clothes in the dressing room. I had Timms bring the trunk down from the attic.'

Close to breaking, she grabbed the nightgown and retreated behind the screen. Her fingers fumbled with the lacings of her gown, as she struggled with the knowledge that Anthony had kept her belongings. Why? And why *this* nightgown? There had been others. Why this one?

The truth came with shattering clarity. Anthony had chosen it. Laid it out for her. Her stomach twisted into a knot of fear and longing as she remembered the tenderness of his loving, his gentleness, the blaze of desire that had consumed her utterly. The dawning knowledge that she loved him despite his intention that it should be a marriage of convenience.

Shivering, she slipped the gown over her head and tied the ribbons with trembling fingers. She had agreed to share his bed. She knew, without Aunt Harriet's reassurance, his sense of honour. He would force nothing on her. But if he asked…if he touched her… Her breasts ached at the very thought. There would be no need for

him to ask a second time. How long would she be able
to conceal what was in her heart? Bury the words he
would scorn? And how long before she would be able
to tear that other confession from its icy prison?

Slowly she removed the pins from her hair, releasing
it to fall down her back. Automatically she poured water
from the ewer into the basin and laved her face and
hands. She had no more excuses. She had to walk out
from behind the screen and join Anthony in their marriage bed. Lumps and all.

Chapter Four

Anthony tried not to look up too obviously as she appeared from behind the screen with her arms folded protectively over her breasts and her dark curls a riotous tumble. Damn! He must have been insane to put that particular nightgown out. His entire body hardened to aching need at the sight. Even with her arms crossed, his memory relentlessly supplied the hidden details.

Dainty, rounded breasts, their deep rose peaks a tempting shadow behind the gauzy fabric. He nearly groaned as he remembered the dress he had bought her in Brussels of that exact same shade. He forced his eyes back to her face, not daring to glance lower and see the other, darker shadow nestled below her belly. His memory supplied that detail mercilessly. Along with the silkiness and scent of her. The feel of her, soft and yielding beneath him. Every muscle locked against his instincts. His word had been given.

He noticed the hesitation as she approached the bed, the watchfulness in the hazel eyes. As though she approached a wolf. Hell, if she knew what he was thinking, she'd *know* she was approaching a wolf. In no clothing at all.

Surreptitiously, he watched as she pulled back the covers with shaking hands, her eyes suddenly shielded by the thick, dark lashes, and slid in. On the very edge. He should say something to reassure her after last night. Anything to take his mind off the need twisting his guts. Anything to stop her realising that his control was in ruins, smoking around the edges.

He said the first thing that came to mind. 'You *knew* I wasn't wounded at Waterloo. How?'

The lashes flickered up. 'The Duke. He'd come in to visit some of the wounded officers. I saw him in the street and when I asked, he said that you were perfectly safe. You'd been sent to him with a message after the battle. So…' Her voice trailed off and she looked away.

Grimly Anthony finished for her. 'So you left.'

She nodded, easing herself back against the pillows. He released a breath very slowly, trying not to notice how the dusky curls fanned over the linen as she wriggled down. Trying to close his mind to the memory of those soft tresses tangled in his fingers, the sweet scent of them spread over his chest in silken abandon.

Yet despite the aching need, something inside him eased. He *had* been sent to Wellington's headquarters the night after the battle. She could not have known that except from the Duke himself. Had she waited until she knew of his safety?

He crushed the thought. She had still gone. Without explanation. Abandoning him to four years of grief, doubt and slander. And what had happened to his mother's pearls? He thought he knew. She had taken very little and she certainly had not had enough money to reach England, let alone Devon, where, according to Aunt Harriet, her godmother had lived. No doubt the pearl necklace had found its way into the coffers of some pawnshop in Brussels.

He glanced over. She lay very still, on her side with her back to him. Better not to ask about the necklace or anything else tonight. At least she had not left Brussels without knowing that he was safe. One thing at a time. And she *was* back in his bed. If she didn't fall out.

Furious that he had given her cause to fear him, he said, 'There is no need to cling to the edge of the mattress. I've not the least desire to pounce on you tonight.'

Wordlessly she wriggled back towards him. About three inches. He swore mentally and left it. After last night, he could hardly blame her for being unwilling to share his bed.

In the morning he would speak to William—there had been no chance this evening. Not that he doubted Georgie. The whole thing fitted together too neatly. But he wanted William to know that the truth was out, without alarming him too much. Better to keep him at the Chase, under their eye, where he could do little harm. In the morning he'd tell Ufton to bring all outgoing mail to him.

Hours later he still lay there, staring at a page of his book. The same page he'd been trying to read for half an hour. His wife lay quietly. He envied her. Her breathing had relaxed into sleep an hour ago. Hell. His body ached. His head ached. Desire wrenched his guts. And something deeper. An emotion he had tried to bury, to forget, thinking it would never be needed again. Something that transfigured his desire, his need, into a burning brand.

Four years ago he had been close—so damned close!—to telling Georgie what a crass, unforgivable mistake he had made in contracting a marriage of convenience with her. When the call to arms had come, he had felt not just the usual fear of battle, the unspoken knowledge that he might not return, but a gut-wrenching terror that he might die without ever having told her that he loved her. That he would die with those words locked in his heart. Somehow that made death worse. Death with regrets. He'd never faced that before.

And then he'd found her in Finch-Scott's arms—kissing him. Any man would have been angry. But he'd said things. Things he bitterly regretted. Things he would have apologised for. Had she not run away, this mess could have been avoided.

Grimly he faced the truth: that he had very little—correction, he had *no* control over his emotions where Georgie was concerned. Finding her in someone else's arms had been bad enough. To then hear her sobbing that she loved *him*, had sent him over the edge.

How the hell could she possibly have loved him if she had left him?

Granted she had come back, but apparently only because Aunt Harriet had dragged her here. She had expected him to ignore her! And then to divorce her.

Swearing under his breath, he reached over and turned his lamp down. It flickered blue and went out. If he lay in the dark and shut his eyes, he might, just possibly, sleep. The lamp on *her* side of the bed still glowed.

Carefully he eased over beside her, reached across—and froze. She lay on her side, facing away from him, her eyelids reddened and swollen, her pale cheeks stained with tears. His gut twisted into a knot of pain. She had cried herself to sleep within three feet of him and he had not heard her. Feeling as though something inside him had ripped apart, he turned down the lamp.

Darkness enveloped them. Her quiet breathing surrounded him.

And the sight of her tearstained cheeks beat on his eyelids. With a groan he eased down beside her and felt her soft warmth. Gently he shifted her back against his chest, holding her there as he rested his cheek on her hair and breathed its sweetness.

She shifted slightly and he shuddered to stillness, fearing to disturb her. Then with a wriggle that nearly shattered his fragile control, she twisted in his arms, nestling against him, her damp cheek snuggled against his chest, one small hand over his heart. Holding it captive.

He took a very deep breath. Which was a serious mistake. The gentle scent of lavender wreathed through him. Lavender and Georgie. Herself. Innocence. His resolve shook as need blazed through him. Every muscle tightened in restraint as he reminded himself of all the reasons he could not take her. None of them convinced his aching flesh.

Tomorrow night he'd make damned sure he wore a nightshirt. He bit back a groan as she cuddled closer, soft breasts pressing against him through the flimsy lawn. God help him—tomorrow night, if he possessed the least iota of sense, he'd find another bed.

But, despite the physical discomfort, there was a measure of peace in having her in his arms. At least he knew that when he woke this time it would not have been a dream.

Dreams held Georgie safely. Gentle, steely arms cradled her against a broad chest. She clung to the familiar dream, breathing the musky, male odour of his body, sighing with pleasure at the warmth of his hand cupping one breast, a powerful thigh pushed between her own.

Her body ached softly. Soon, so soon she would awaken to the reality of a pillow damp with tears. Only this time it felt so real, the mat of hair on his chest tickling her nose...she had never felt that before.

Slowly the clouds of sleep lifted. She still lay in his arms, springy hair still tickled her nose. It wasn't a dream this time. The rest had been a dream, a nightmare of loss... She clung to the dawning reality as pale light filled the room. But memory followed. Bright and terrible.

Yes. She had returned to Anthony and he had not disowned her. But at what cost to himself? It seemed that he had only taken her back because he felt that he had no choice. Was he sacrificing himself, or her?

He awoke to feel her easing from his arms. Very slowly, scarcely breathing as she lifted from him. He lay resistless, forcing his arms to loosen, to let her go, when all he wanted was to roll her beneath him and kiss her until her lips and body softened. Until all her softness was his, pliant and yielding.

Aching, he let her go and listened to the faint sounds of her washing and dressing. Was she still in her chemise? Which gown was she wearing? If she chose the pink one, he was in for an appalling day. His imagination supplied every detail as the soft sounds continued and his body reacted with predictable violence. It was all he could do not to get out of bed and inform her that their truce was over.

He gritted his teeth. A physical need. Nothing more. He would not permit it to be anything more. Never again would he indulge himself with that particular idiocy.

The moment the door closed behind her, he flung back the covers and got up. Ruefully he realised that seeing him in the morning would not back up his claim that he had no desire to pounce on her. That had to rank as one of the biggest whiskers in history. Swearing, he donned a dressing gown.

Another night with her in his arms like that would wear his good intentions as thin as her nightgown. He pushed the thought away. This morning he had to catch William. He glanced at the clock. Plenty of time. William was not renowned for early rising.

Automatically he strolled to the window to assess the weather. In the clear morning light he could see the ducks on the lake and a small group of deer grazing by the shore. A lovely day. He'd have to think of something for them all to do, except, of course, that all Marcus wanted to do was sneak off to the gardens with Miss Devereaux and Cassie and Quinlan were as bad.

He started to turn from the window, but a flurry of movement drew him back. The deer had fled. As he watched, a figure came out of the woods and started around the edge of the lake towards the house. Stiffening, he narrowed his eyes. Could it be the man seen lurking? Surely not. From here the man's attire looked that of a gentleman. In fact… Disbelieving, he reached for the spyglass on his desk—the image came into focus and Anthony stared, shocked.

What in Hades was *William*, of all people, doing out before breakfast? Through the spyglass William looked worried, glancing around constantly…as though he feared being seen. Or, thought Anthony suddenly, as though he were looking for someone. Like the mysterious man who had sent that note to him? His mind began to work furiously. If William had been behind the attack on Frobisher, who would he have been most likely to employ for the task?

With a savage curse, Anthony knew he had the answer. The disgraced valet, Grant. If the situation hadn't been so serious he would have grinned. No wonder William was now being blackmailed, if that were the case— Grant would be determined to get his money.

Drumming his fingers on the window sill, he lowered the glass. If Grant was still about, someone must have seen him. If he drove out today and gave a precise description to a few people—offered a reward for quiet information as to Grant's whereabouts. Anthony clenched his fists. Grant could be persuaded to talk.

The door opened and Timms entered. 'Morning, Major. Saw the mistress and thought you'd be up.'

Anthony gave him a very careful look and replaced the spyglass. Timms moved around the room, picking up discarded clothes, seemingly oblivious to his master's very dangerous mood, while Anthony shaved and tried not to think about ways in which to seduce his very reluctant wife.

'I was wondering, sir, if you could see your way clear to giving me a morning or afternoon off in the next day or so?'

Anthony nearly dropped his razor. He couldn't remember the last time Timms had asked for time off. Beyond his usual half-day, of course.

'Well, of course you can. Take the whole day if you like. Today?'

Timms beamed. 'Thank you, sir.'

'A pleasure,' said Anthony drily.

'You'll…you'll be all right, sir?'

Anthony negotiated his chin carefully. 'I promise not to cut myself shaving, if that's what you mean.'

'No, sir. It ain't my place to say, but I've been with

you a long time, and well, things haven't been too good of late, have they?'

Anthony put down the razor and turned. 'What?'

Timms held his ground. 'Didn't do you no good, the missus disappearing the way she did and all. But now she's back, safe and sound. You'll do now. Get on with your life.'

'Have you been talking to Lord Mardon?' asked Anthony, suddenly suspicious.

'No, sir. Not but what it's easy to see he'd give you the same advice, as happy as he is with her ladyship. Does you good just to see 'em together, it does. Like Miss Cassie and her young lord.'

'And Mr Sinclair?' asked Anthony, fascinated. Lord! To think Timms was such a romantic!

'Aye, sir. And once you and the mistress sort out your differences, well, life's short, sir. You learnt that under old Hookey. Don't you waste no more of it. That's all.'

'Next you'll be setting up a match for Mr William,' muttered Anthony, rinsing his face.

'*That* waster!' exploded Timms.

Anthony splashed water on the floor as he jumped.

'You mark my words,' growled Timms, 'up to something shifty, *he* is. Came a-calling the day after you went off to battle.'

'Did he, indeed?' Why had William never mentioned *that* in the last four years?

'Oh, aye. The mistress was upset enough before he came, but afterwards! The poor lass could hardly stand, she was that shaken.'

'What the hell did he say to her?' Fury surged through Anthony.

Timms gave him a disgusted look. 'Sent me about my business double quick, he did. And his voice is that slippery soft, damned if I could hear aught through the keyhole. Just the mistress saying 'twas all a misunderstanding, but white as a sheet she was afterwards. Not too much I could say—she sent me out on an errand after he left.'

Anthony's brain spun as the whole pattern crashed into place. 'Timms?'

'Aye, Major?'

'Do you think this man that's been seen could possibly be Grant?'

Timms frowned. 'Could be. But why would he bother?'

Anthony bit his lip. Later he might have to tell Timms what he suspected, but not yet. 'Trying to get a reference?' he suggested.

A sceptical snort greeted this. 'If Mr William was a-going to give him one, he'd of done it by now. And it ain't as if Grant did anything that Mr William would likely refuse a reference over!'

Anthony forbore to comment on this scathing indictment of his cousin's morals. If his suspicions were correct, William's perfidy extended far beyond lifting Lady Margaret's skirts on the backstairs.

'Could ask a few quiet questions if you want, Major.'

Anthony nodded. 'You do that.'

Anthony was still reeling from Timms's advice and revelations when he found William just about to enter the breakfast parlour.

'William—have you a moment?' For the life of him, Anthony couldn't prevent a chill creeping into his voice. He fought down his rage. After his mistakes with Marcus and Georgie, he daren't accuse someone else, even without the risk William posed to Marcus.

His hand on the door handle, William turned and gestured gracefully. 'As many moments as you like. Something I can do for you?'

You've done enough already! Swallowing that, Anthony said, 'Perhaps the library, William. You'll understand that this must go no further…'

Make him feel that he is still trusted, that I don't really believe it… God knows I don't want to. He caught himself up. What did he want to believe? That Georgie was lying? He *didn't* believe that. She was a terrible liar. He remembered that once, before they were betrothed, she'd tried to convince him that she didn't care a rush about her broken betrothal to Finch-Scott, would be perfectly content to take a post as a governess or some such thing. She'd been unable to meet his eyes.

He remembered something else she had told him, on the eve of Waterloo, her eyes, bright with tears, meeting his savage gaze unflinchingly, the words he had longed to hear on her lips. He shoved the memory away. Perhaps she *had* believed it. A girlish fancy, born of their lovemaking the night before. Whatever, it hadn't lasted. Even if she hadn't consciously lied.

And now? The knowledge that she hadn't returned to him willingly, that she'd been tricked into coming, ground on him.

'Anthony? Anthony?'

Blinking, he realised that William was staring at him, waiting patiently by the library door.

Clearing his throat, he muttered, 'Sorry. Woolgathering. Did you enjoy your walk?'

William stared. 'W…walk? *Me?* At this hour? What…whatever gave you that idea?'

Swearing mentally at his slip, Anthony flicked a

glance at William's boots. And breathed a sigh of relief. 'Mud on your boots,' he said.

'Oh.' William gave a laugh. Rather shrill. 'I just stepped outside for a breath of air. Bit of a head this morning, don't you know?'

So he didn't want anyone to know about his stroll in the woods. Why not?

Forcing a grin, Anthony murmured, 'I trust that's not a comment on my cellar, cousin.'

'Lord, no!' averred William. 'Excellent cellar. Quite excellent. Just what I should like myself.'

Anthony raised his brows and William appeared to realise that his choice of phrase was infelicitous to say the least.

'Er, that is to say—well, it's excellent, quite excellent,' he finished rather lamely.

They went into the library and Anthony shut the door behind them.

Choosing his words, he said, 'I need you to cast your mind back—'

'Consider it cast, coz—'

'To the Duchess of Richmond's ball four years ago.'

Was it imagination, or had William's smile slipped a trifle?

'Oh. Well, as to that—confusing night, wasn't it? Lord! I wondered if I'd ever see you again! And—'

'When you saw Georgiana,' said Anthony, cutting across William's reminiscences, 'did she see you?'

William blinked. 'Ah, well. Dare say I saw her at the start of the evening. Said good evening and all that. I suppose she saw me then, if that's what you mean.'

'Later,' said Anthony ruthlessly. 'After the call to arms. When you saw her with Finch-Scott. Did she know that you'd seen her? Did she say anything?'

'Oh, er, did she say anything? Well, really, coz! Four years ago! How should I recall if she said anything in particular? Lord! Everyone was talking at the top of their lungs!' He slid his finger under his over-high collar and tugged.

Anthony held on to his anger. 'William—you implied that she and Finch-Scott had gone out to the garden in a havey-cavey sort of way.'

'Well—you found them. Wasn't she kissing him?' He shook his head. 'Don't know when I've been more shocked. Except of course when she ran off, coz. Felt for you. I really did. All that gossip afterwards.' He shook his head mournfully. 'It was too bad of her. Really too bad! Very generous of you to take her back, under the circumstances...'

Abruptly Anthony turned on his heel and walked over to the window. 'You called the next morning, I believe.'

'Called?'

'On my wife.'

'Oh, did I?' He appeared to consider. 'Yes, now that you mention it. Just wanted to reassure her. After all, the temper you were in that night! Really!'

'And you reassured her?' He could scarcely keep his hands at his side.

'Well, I tried, of course, but you know what females are. Mind you, I think she was more than a little miffed! Still, to run off like that, just because—'

Anthony cut him off. 'I see. I think that clarifies things. Thank you, William.'

'Oh, a pleasure. Glad to have cleared that up for you.'

Anthony gritted his teeth. 'You won't mention this to anyone, then?'

'Certainly not! Wouldn't dream of it! Er, if that's all,

I'll just toddle along to breakfast, old man. Are you coming?'

'In a moment.' When he regained his self-control, before he accused William outright and took him apart with his bare hands. An accusation could rip the family apart. What would it take for William to shop Marcus to the nearest magistrate? Better to let him think that he was in the clear on this, at least for the moment.

He shut his eyes as the door closed behind William. John had the right of it. He was a damn fool. William, knowing his temper, had trapped Georgie. Then he'd called the next day and no doubt encouraged her fears. Swearing, he paced around the room. He'd brought this on himself, never mind William's efforts. His blasted pride, blinding him to the truth. One thing was certain—if he wanted to save his marriage, it might be best if he never mentioned the pearls. After all, bar Timms, no one else knew they were gone.

His task now was to convince Georgie that the best way forward for them was a marriage of convenience. Without all these *in*convenient emotions creeping in. And in between he had to ensure that Marcus didn't get himself hanged.

Somehow he must find out if William was meeting Grant and if Grant was the man who had attacked Frobisher. He frowned. He'd gladly pay double the price Grant was demanding of William for information that would save Marcus's neck.

Chapter Five

Anthony walked into the breakfast parlour, shaken to the core. Instinctively, he looked for Georgie. His breath caught. Discreet, buttoned to the neck and wrist—she had chosen the pink morning gown he had bought her in Brussels. It was perfect on her, bringing out the delicate colour in her cheeks, reminding him mercilessly of the beauties it concealed.

His entire body hardened to instant, aching arousal. Fortunately, Aunt Harriet's comprehensive condemnation of Marcus's manners, morals and intelligence had everyone's attention. He helped himself to bacon and eggs and took the vacant seat next to Georgie, manoeuvring the chair as close to the table as possible. Anything to hide the fact that his breeches had suddenly ceased to fit.

Her tea cup rattled into its saucer.

He leaned over and murmured, 'Believe it or not, seducing you at the breakfast table is not an option.'

Unfortunately.

Aunt Harriet switched targets. 'Don't mumble, Anthony! If you have something of a private nature to say to your wife, it would be better said before you leave your bedchamber! Rubbishing generation!'

Pinning an unnatural smile in place, he said, 'Good morning, Aunt Harriet. Did you sleep well?'

She glared. 'Of course I slept well. Never do anything else. And don't change the subject. When do you mean to take Georgiana up to town to buy her some decent clothes? Not but what *this* is better than what she had when she came to me, but a few modish gowns wouldn't go astray.'

Beside him, Georgie stiffened. 'No. Really, there is not the least need and—'

Cassie cut in. 'Well, Anthony can hardly take her to town! After all—ouch!' She glared at Marcus, who glared right back.

Anthony breathed a sigh of relief. Better if that didn't come out over the breakfast cups. If at all. Could he ensure that Georgie never knew what had been said?

'Rubbish!' snapped Aunt Harriet. 'When I want your opinion, miss, I'll ask for it! No more than he ought to do.' She swung back to Georgie and continued, 'Should be showing you the family jewels as well! The pearls, for example.'

The clatter as William's knife hit his plate expressed Anthony's feelings perfectly. At times he wondered if Aunt Harriet had the least idea of what she was saying. This wasn't one of them. He sat, speechless, as John went purple and Marcus disappeared under the table, with an unconvincing gasp about his napkin.

The rest of the ladies all looked rather blank.

'The pearls,' she continued, quite unperturbed, 'would become her admirably.'

'They would,' said Anthony tightly. Trust Aunt Harriet to raise the subject in the worst possible way.

Well, Georgie was hardly going to take the subject up with him, so he'd just let it lie.

'Such lovely weather we are having, are we not, Miss Devereaux?' asked Peter Quinlan politely. 'Should you care to stroll with me in the park after breakfast?'

Miss Devereaux looked relieved, if surprised. 'That would—'

'Why don't you look after your own bride, Quinlan?' suggested Marcus, reappearing with his napkin.

'Well, naturally I would look after Cassie,' returned Quinlan, grinning. 'But you're doing such a sterling job of kicking her under the table, that I thought Miss Devereaux and I should leave you to it!'

'Marcus! You leave Peter alone,' ordered Cassie.

Anthony's shoulders shook at the sight of Cassie's indignant face.

'She's all yours, Quinlan,' said Marcus with aplomb. 'And you wouldn't believe the pleasure it gives us all to know it!'

'So glad to have been of service,' murmured the Viscount, with a wicked glance at his wife, who blushed scarlet.

Reminding himself that Cassie was no longer his concern and that he didn't need to know just why she was blushing or how Quinlan had been of service, Anthony concentrated on his eggs.

'Miss Devereaux and I thought we might go riding, Quinlan,' said Marcus. 'Perhaps you and Cassie would care to join us.' He raised a brow at Cassie. 'A chaperon is always useful.'

Cassie gave as good as she got. 'Really, Marcus? It's quite hard to imagine in what way you would find a chaperon useful.'

Anthony choked, avoiding John's eye. Or Sarah's.

Hell's teeth… If the goings-on at this house party ever got out—he shuddered to think of the scandal.

Hoping to change the subject, he turned to Aunt Harriet. 'What would you like to do this morning, Aunt? I could take you for a drive, if you would care for it.' She was bound to refuse, but he might as well get the credit for offering.

Spearing him with a glare, she said, 'If you think I'm getting up into a carriage behind any of your wild horses, you can think again! I have some letters to write. Take your wife instead!'

Beside him, Georgie appeared to have turned to stone, her tea cup frozen halfway to her lips. Forcibly reminding himself that strangling one's great-aunt, no matter the provocation, would make his house party even more scandalous, Anthony said, 'An excellent idea.' Or it would be if Georgie didn't look as though someone had offered to hand her into a tumbril.

Resolutely refusing to look at the pink gown, he said. 'You'll need something warmer. And a bonnet. Shall we say, in half an hour?'

With a pelisse over that gown he might, perhaps, stand a sporting chance of not driving straight over the edge of the escarpment.

'Did you expect her to salute?' asked Aunt Harriet blandly.

Belatedly, Anthony realised that he had issued not an invitation, but a command. Even Marcus was shaking his head. John simply looked pained.

Georgie's eyes lifted from her plate and he read her answer at once. Obedience. Conformity. Everything he had demanded of her. Suddenly he knew he didn't want it. Shaken, he thrust away the knowledge of what he *did*

want. He had been rude—rudeness had no place in a
marriage of convenience.

'I beg your pardon, Georgie. That was clumsy. Would
you care to drive with me?' The hazel eyes widened and
the soft lips parted in surprise. That stung. Was he such
a boor that a simple apology could shock her? Swiftly
passing his recent behaviour under review, he backed
right away from that question.

'You really wish me to come?'

William snorted. 'Wouldn't ask if he didn't!'

Silencing William with a glare, he answered her.
'Yes.' He forced himself to add, 'If it would please you.'

She smiled. The shy, beaming smile he remembered.
Uncertain, hesitant, as if it hadn't been used for a long
time, it trembled on her lips, lighting her eyes and opening the floodgates on everything better left buried and
forgotten.

Cassie's voice broke in. 'If that is settled, then I shall
ride this morning. Sarah, are you coming?'

Sarah smiled. 'No, dear. I shall bear Aunt Harriet
company. I wish to write to the boys.'

Anthony smiled at the faint tone of longing. 'Next
time, bring them,' he said. 'We'll find room. Timms will
help with them.'

Sarah beamed. 'Thank you, Anthony. I do miss them.
Even though their governess is such a wonder. They
would love it here.'

He nodded. 'Then I'll find a couple of ponies for
them.' It would be good to see a couple of boys romping
around as he and Marcus had done so long ago. As he
hoped to see his own children one day.

Cassie rose. 'I'll go up and change, then. And I had
better take off this ring.' She smiled at Quinlan. 'Much

safer for it than going out on one of Anthony's wild horses! Is it just the four of us?'

'I'll join you,' said John. 'William?' He glanced at his brother, who shrugged.

'Oh, I don't know. Think I might stay here for the morning,' muttered William. He looked, and sounded, thoroughly disgruntled.

Halfway to the door, Cassie glanced back. 'Are we still to have some archery, this afternoon, cousin?'

About to answer, Anthony realised that she was speaking to Georgie.

Georgie nodded. 'Of course, Lady Quinlan. Ufton assured me that the targets would be set out and that refreshments would be served under one of the trees in the park. I believe the gentlemen planned to shoot this afternoon?'

In response to her questioning glance, Anthony nodded.

Aunt Harriet sniffed. 'Good gel. Going on just as you should be. I'll look forward to that. Anthony! That dog of yours is lying on my feet. For God's sake take her away!'

Stunned, Anthony looked under the table. Sure enough, Stella was asleep with her nose on Aunt Harriet's feet. His lips twitched. By the look of it, Stella had been there for quite some time.

'I beg your pardon, Aunt,' he said. 'She must have thought they were my feet.'

Beside him, Georgie smothered a very strange noise. His heart lurched. How long was it since she had laughed?

Aunt Harriet glared at him. 'Dog's senile as well as smelly, blind and deaf!'

Anthony shrugged. 'That or she likes you, Aunt Harriet. Take your pick.' He waited, breathless.

This time Georgie burst out laughing openly. A glorious ripple of sound that flooded him with joy and set the whole world to dancing. He could feel his answering smile, spreading right through him as their eyes met.

Cassie's voice broke the moment. 'Aunt Harriet's right,' she muttered. 'It must be the water.'

Georgie remained silent as Anthony drove the curricle out of the stable yard. Unbidden, and unwanted, hope had come pouring back, in that moment when he had purposely made her laugh. And she could not forget the gentle look in his eyes when he had apologised. Nor the way he had held her last night. Just held her. Not waking her to demand that she fulfil her duty, but simply holding her. As if he wanted to.

The day seemed all the brighter as they drove through the park and out along the escarpment. And it made what she had to tell him much harder. It would be so easy not to tell him. So very easy. And then she would live with it for the rest of her life. Knowing that she had cheated him in the worst possible way.

The horses were fresh and she watched quietly as he settled them, driving them well up to their bits. She let her mind wander. A fragment of memory from breakfast, a question, teased her. She frowned.

'Is something bothering you, Georgie?'

She nodded. 'Yes. Why did Mr Sinclair kick Lady Quinlan? What was she about to say?'

As he had at breakfast, Anthony froze. 'I've no idea,' he said shortly.

'But—'

'Whatever it was, it is none of your concern!'

She could recognise a Keep Out sign when it hit her. Shivering slightly, she took a deep breath. Next subject. Something simple first. 'About the pearls, Anthony—'

'*I beg your pardon?*' He sounded as though he couldn't quite believe she would raise the subject. Perhaps he thought she was about to ask for them?

Hurriedly, she went on. 'I...I quite understand how you must feel, Anthony. And I—'

'Do you, Georgie? Do you?'

She bit her lip. Better to let him say it. The pearls had been his mother's wedding gift from his father. Anthony had given them to her the day before their wedding, asking her to wear them. And now he felt, quite understandably, that she had forfeited the right to wear them. Given what she had to confess, she could hardly disagree.

'It is not the monetary value,' he continued, 'although that was *considerable*, but the loss of something so dear to my mother. That I hoped would be passed down to my son's bride.'

Confusion hit her. 'I...I beg your pardon? What are you talking about?'

Anger flashed into his voice. 'What did you do with them, Georgie? Not that it matters now. They are gone beyond recall! But I should like to know.'

'Do with them?'

Something swirled at the edge of her understanding. Something she was sure she didn't want to see. No! She had done enough running away. This truth she would face squarely, no matter how much it hurt. 'What are you suggesting, Anthony?' She knew what he was suggesting. It cut to her very soul that he could think of her like this.

He swore. 'Dammit, Georgie! I accept that my behaviour at the ball was atrocious, that I upset you and frightened you, but couldn't you have found something else to sell to provide your passage back to England?'

For a moment she couldn't speak, could barely breathe for the pain of hearing him say it. Knowing to the last twist of the knife how he thought of her. Not only a whore, but a thief.

'Yes,' she choked, 'I did. My mother's wedding ring.'

For a moment Anthony didn't understand. Then... He pulled up the horses, set the brake and turned to look at her properly. Her face had blanched, all the delicate colour destroyed.

His gaze dropped to her hand. Her *right* hand, where she had always worn her mother's ring. Her small fist was clenched. And bare. If she had sold the pearls, there would have been no need to sell her mother's wedding ring...ergo, she hadn't taken the pearls. Then...*who*?

Hurt fury blazed at him from the hazel eyes. 'I'm surprised you didn't come after me just to recover the necklace!' she said bitterly.

Scorching anger obliterated the apology he'd been about to offer. 'Come after you?' he snarled. 'I'd no idea where to find you! I thought you were *dead*! Couldn't you at least have written to tell me you were safe?'

'But...I said! In my note...that I was going to my godmother in Devon. I gave her name and...direction...'

Note? What note?

'I thought when you didn't come, that you didn't want me, so of course I never wrote! You told me you should never have married me! What did you think I'd do when you didn't contact me?'

'You left a note?'

'Well, of *course* I left a note!'

He shook his head, words strangling in his throat. He

reached for her, needing to hold her, to banish the pain for both of them. Damn the necklace! What in Hades had happened to the note?

She jerked back. 'Don't touch me! You have made your feelings about me perfectly plain!'

'The hell I have!' he said furiously. The horses sidled, impatient in the breeze. With a muttered curse he untied the ribbons and released the brake. 'For God's sake! Listen to me—we have to sort this out! You say you left a note?'

She nodded, biting her lip.

He swore as he gave the horses the office. He had practically taken their lodgings apart searching for some clue to her whereabouts. There had been no note. And no pearl necklace. An appalling suspicion took root. 'Georgie—William called, didn't he?'

'Yes. The…the next morning. He was very much concerned about the gossip—'

'Gossip? What gossip?'

'About…about our quarrel—what you said…'

He'd been out of society for too long. He couldn't quite believe that there had been gossip. With Napoleon over the frontier and marching on Brussels, a battle looming that would decide the fate of all Europe… 'Wait a moment—you say *William* mentioned gossip?'

'And Lady Carrington. She called as well.'

Anthony bit off a savage curse. He might have known it. Lady Carrington, supposedly chaperoning Georgie, had been icily disapproving of the match, seeing it as most unequal. Especially when she had her own daughter to establish and had thought his visits to the house were to court Miss Carrington, not the penniless nobody she had taken in at her husband's insistence.

'What did she say?'

Georgie flushed and turned away.

'Tell me.'

'That I would be lucky if you didn't divorce me. That I had disgraced myself and your name. That—'

'Enough. Georgie—didn't you realise that she was being spiteful? That she was furious at our marriage? And—'

'It was no worse than what you said!'

'What *I* said?'

'That you would not tolerate being cuckolded, that you would decide what to do about our marriage when you returned. That…that you had been a fool to marry a designing little trollop! That if I had so little understanding of my *duty*, then I might as well take myself off and save you the trouble! That you would only tolerate my lovers *after* I had provided your heirs!'

Stunned, Anthony heard those words as they would have been heard by a seventeen-year-old bride of two weeks, in the most public of public places, on top of his stipulation that he wanted a marriage of convenience for an heir. That the question of love did not enter into their union.

God help him, she had believed his angry words. So she had left, assuming that he would not care, would be only too glad to be rid of her. With bitter certainty he knew she had taken nothing. She had sold her mother's wedding ring to get home. He wouldn't have blamed her if she'd sold her own.

'Georgie…' His voice died in his throat as he saw her face. Shuttered, leached of all colour and expression. As though she could no longer bear to feel anything. 'Georgie, I—' Too late. They were drawing into Lynd. The public street was no place for this particular discussion. He'd learnt that lesson at least.

Instead he pulled up outside the inn and yelled for someone to take the horses.

A lad came running out. 'Morning, Major!'

'Hold 'em!' snapped Anthony, softening the harsh command by flicking the boy a shilling. He leapt out of the curricle and strode into the inn.

Georgie watched him go, her mind whirling. He had never found the note. And someone had stolen the pearls. But who? Certainly not Timms. He was devoted to Anthony.

Did Anthony believe her? He had accepted her word about kissing Justin. He had even apologised. But this—all he had done was ask if Mr Lyndhurst-Flint had called... Her racing thoughts faltered, stumbled. No. It couldn't be true.

William Lyndhurst-Flint. They kept coming back to him. Somehow he had confused the message she had given him for Anthony. Could *he* have stolen the pearls? And destroyed her note? To create trouble? But why?

The reason for Anthony's house party crashed in upon her. He had intended to choose an heir. William Lyndhurst-Flint, with no fortune or expectations, had been a possible candidate. Had he always seen himself as Anthony's heir?

A familiar deep voice jerked her out of the nightmare.

'Thank you, Harry. Remember—do it quietly. And get word to me the minute you hear anything. Nothing else.' Anthony had emerged from the inn with a stout florid individual who could only be the innkeeper.

'Oh, aye, Major. Now let me get this straight. Middling tall. Thin. About forty? And brown hair. Wavy. Brown eyes.'

Anthony cast a very harassed glance at Georgie, and

said hurriedly, 'Yes, yes. That's all, man. I'll not keep you any longer.'

'Not at all, Major,' the innkeeper assured him. He glanced up at Georgie and touched his forelock. 'Morning, ma'am.'

She wilted under the blatant curiosity in his eyes, but murmured a greeting, wondering for whom Anthony was searching.

Anthony sighed. 'Ah, yes. My dear, permit me to present Harry Bamford. Harry—this is Mrs Lyndhurst. My wife.'

Bamford tripped over his own feet. Recovering, he spluttered some sort of apology and stared at her.

Georgie smiled politely. She would have to get used to this.

Anthony intervened. 'Yes, well. I won't keep your boy any longer, Harry. Thank you, Davy.' He tossed the boy another shilling.

The boy grinned. 'Thank'ee, sir.'

Anthony's smile flashed out as he ruffled the boy's hair. 'Have you been fishing recently, Davy?'

'No, sir. Me mam says as you might've of changed your mind.'

'Well, you'd better do some. Before you forget how. Tell your mother I haven't changed my mind. Come in the evening. The trout are jumping then.'

'Yessir!'

Anthony climbed back into the curricle and they drove out of the village.

'What was that about?' asked Georgie.

'Hmm? Oh. Davy likes to come and fish. His mother was my nanny.' He grinned reminiscently. 'You could say I've a fellow feeling for the lad.'

Georgie was silent, trying to reconcile the man who

offered to find ponies for his young cousins and gave permission for an urchin to fish in his stream, with the man who wanted an heir. Then she caught the careful glance he was giving her and realised his strategy had nearly worked.

'I meant—who is this man you asked about?'

Anthony's face hardened. 'Nothing that you need concern yourself about. A private matter.'

'I see.' She kept her voice steady with an effort. Any right she might have had to ask had been forfeited when she left him. Carefully, she said, 'You don't consider him dangerous, then?'

'*What?*'

'Surely, if I need not concern myself—' She glanced at him and saw that his face had gone absolutely white.

'You are to remain within the house and gardens unless you are with me,' he said harshly.

'But—'

'The house and gardens,' he repeated. 'I've no intention of losing you again.'

Another Keep Out sign. Very well, she'd have to find out some other way. And whether or not William Lyndhurst-Flint could possibly have stolen the pearls.

Chapter Six

'Oh, good shot, Amy!' Sarah, Countess of Mardon, clapped enthusiastically.

Aunt Harriet snorted. 'Humph! Any gel who could account for Marcus Sinclair, within five minutes of him laying eyes on her again, has to be expert with a bow and arrow. Never seen anything like it!'

She shot a furtive glance at Sarah. 'In fact, I'm fast coming to the conclusion that the men in this family are all more than capable of choosing the right female, without *my* advice! And even Cassie has come to her senses!'

Lady Quinlan laughed and set down her lemonade. 'Mmm. Lovely. Is there any more?'

Georgie looked at the jug. 'I think you've finished it,' she said smiling. 'I'll fetch some more.' She set off back to the house.

A moment later she heard Lady Quinlan's voice. 'Cousin! Wait please!' Lady Quinlan was hurrying after her.

'Is there something else?' asked Georgie.

Lady Quinlan nodded. 'Aunt Harriet would like a shawl.'

'Very well. I'll bring it.'

'I could fetch the shawl,' suggested Lady Quinlan.

Georgie looked at her sharply. There were things she needed to know. Things that Lady Quinlan might be able to tell her. 'Thank you, Lady Quinlan,' she said politely.

They strolled on, silence awkward between them.

Georgie didn't think what she was about to ask would improve matters. 'Lady Quinlan—do you know of a man answering the following description: medium height, thin, fortyish? With wavy brown hair and brown eyes?'

Lady Quinlan looked her surprise. 'Why would I…oh! That sounds like that horrible man of William's. Anthony dismissed him before you arrived.' She flushed. 'He was…er…behaving…er…inappropriately with my chaperon. She was dismissed as well.'

'Oh,' said Georgie. Then Anthony had merely been ensuring that an unsavoury character left the neighbourhood. She could well understand that he would want as few people as possible to know about the *inappropriate behaviour*. Lady Quinlan's crimson cheeks were enough to give her the general idea.

They were approaching the terrace.

'One other thing, Lady Quinlan.' She took a very deep breath. 'Why did Mr Sinclair kick you at breakfast?'

Lady Quinlan stopped dead, biting her lip.

'Lady Quinlan?'

'Did Anthony say anything about taking you to town?' she asked eventually.

'No,' said Georgie. 'But you said he couldn't. Why not? Not that I wish to go, but—'

'He isn't received in London,' said Lady Quinlan, a touch of bitterness in her voice.

Not received? Georgie tried without success to imagine why a well-born, wealthy and charming gentleman would not be received. 'But—'

'There was gossip. After Waterloo,' said Lady
Quinlan. 'People around here know it was all nonsense,
but London is different. People said that he ought to
have been cashiered.'

'But *why*? It doesn't make sense…'

'No?' asked Lady Quinlan gently. 'Tell me—would
you want to associate with a man you believed had murdered his wife and ensured that her lover died in battle?'

'No. *No.*' What should have been a scream of protest
came out as a broken whisper as the ground seemed to
shift beneath her.

'Yes,' said Lady Quinlan. 'That is why Marcus is in
danger of arrest. Because he defended Anthony's honour, and then the man he argued with was nearly murdered! So Marcus was accused. Forgive me if you do
not like to hear this, but I am very fond of Anthony!'

Blindly Georgie nodded. She took a couple of steps
and stopped, waiting for the world to steady.

'Cousin?'

The suddenly worried note in Lady Quinlan's voice
barely penetrated the daze of horror.

She had ruined his life. No wonder he wouldn't divorce her. After a scandal like this he couldn't afford it.
And indirectly she was responsible for Mr Sinclair's predicament. So much unhappiness. All because of her.

'Cassie!'

'Oh! It's Peter, back early from the shooting!'

Georgie looked around. Sure enough, Lord Quinlan
was striding towards them. Desperately, she clung to her
control. 'How lovely for you. Why don't you join him
and I will fetch the shawl and lemonade. And…and perhaps something stronger for his lordship.'

Lady Quinlan hesitated. 'If you are sure… Are you feeling quite the thing?'

Georgie summoned up a smile. 'Oh, yes. I won't be long.'

By the time she returned to the archery party with the lemonade and shawl, as well as ale for Lord Quinlan, she had managed to scrub away all traces of tears. To her relief, Lord Quinlan was regaling the other ladies with a highly coloured account of the day's bag, which included an old boot retrieved by one of Anthony's younger dogs.

'If you could but have seen his face!' chuckled Quinlan. 'And the dog looked so dashed pleased with himself!'

Georgie laughed with the rest of them, pretending that she didn't see the searching look Aunt Harriet directed at her. This time she must sort it out for herself.

She made the swiftest toilette that she could, remembering Anthony's request that she leave him in privacy the previous day. She was still pinning up her hair when Timms appeared, staggering under the weight of a large copper can for Anthony's bath.

'Evening, mistress,' he said cheerfully. 'The Major's just cleaning his gun. Be up soon, I dare say.'

Flushing, Georgie worked faster. She'd better hurry, then.

A knock on the door sent pins pattering across the floor.

'Come—who is it?' Her voice came out very huskily.

'Quinlan.' The door opened and Lord Quinlan strode in, frowning.

'Oh!' He blushed. 'I beg your pardon, Miss Saun…er, Mrs Lyndhurst. Thought it was Lyndhurst's voice. I'll take myself off. Thought he'd be up by now.'

Mutely she shook her head.

Lord Quinlan regarded her oddly. 'Mrs Lyndhurst, are you feeling quite the thing?'

'Yes,' she lied. 'I believe—that is, Timms tells me that Anthony is cleaning his gun.'

'Ah. I'll look in the gun room, then.'

Anthony locked the gun cupboard and put away the rags and oil. He could put it off no longer. He glanced out of the window at the deepening sky. Georgie would be dressed for dinner by now. He had to talk to her, beg her forgiveness for that morning.

The door opened and Quinlan walked in. 'Ah, there you are.'

Anthony looked up at him, frowning. 'Is something wrong?'

Quinlan's mouth tightened. 'I'm afraid so. You... er...might have noticed that ring Cassie has been wearing?'

Anthony nodded. 'Yes.'

'I gave it to her as a betrothal ring. My mother's, actually.' He grimaced and added, lightly enough, 'About the only thing my father *didn't* hock.'

Anthony winced. Despite the wry mockery, he knew damn well that what Quinlan had gone through with the Marquis was enough to sour anyone.

'Thing is, Lyndhurst, it's the only thing I had to give her, and, well, the blasted thing's gone.'

Every drop of blood congealed as all the ramifications of that streaked through Anthony's mind. 'Gone?' He clutched at the only straw in sight. 'You don't mean she's lost it?'

It didn't need Quinlan's categoric headshake to consign that forlorn hope to the flames. 'I don't think so,' he said. 'She took it off before we went riding this morning. Doesn't fit too well under gloves, of course. I saw her put it in her jewel case myself. She only looked for it just now.'

'Damn it all to hell,' said Anthony, conscious that his response was less than gracious. 'Sorry, old man. I'll call everyone together and then I suppose we'll have to quiz the servants.' He frowned. Hard to imagine any of them doing such a thing. They were all well paid and without exception they all adored Cassie.

'You're sure she put it in her jewel case? Not some other safe spot?'

Quinlan shook his head. 'Quite sure. Look, Lyndhurst, I can understand your reluctance to call in a magistrate, what with all the trouble Sinclair is in, but that ring—well, it was my mother's betrothal ring, and—'

'It's all right,' Anthony forced a rueful smile. 'You don't have to explain.' He knew exactly how Quinlan must feel. 'I can assure you Marcus will say the same. We must get to the bottom of this.' He swore. 'Look,' he went on, 'I'll go up and change for dinner. Could you tell Ufton that I want all the servants—*all* of them—together in the hall in half an hour?'

Quinlan nodded. 'Thank you, Lyndhurst.' His mouth quirked. 'Er…is half an hour enough for you?'

Despite his anger, Anthony chuckled. 'Not being a London dandy, like some I could mention, half an hour should be ample. And you may tell Cassie that if she finds that ring after all, I might just tan her backside for her!'

'Cousin Georgiana! Is something wrong? What on earth is going on?' asked Lady Mardon, coming into the drawing room just ahead of the Earl.

'N…no,' said Georgie. 'What do you mean?'

'The staff is in uproar,' explained Lady Mardon, sinking gracefully into a chair. 'Apparently Anthony has demanded that they all assemble in the hall in twenty minutes! Aunt Harriet is having a fit since the maid waiting on her is so upset, she broke a scent bottle all over the carpet!' She wrinkled her nose. 'It smells like a bordello in there.'

The Earl raised a languid brow. 'While I admit that the atmosphere in Harriet's room was a trifle overpowering, might one inquire precisely where your information about bordellos—*bordelli?*—was gained?'

'One *might*,' agreed Lady Mardon, 'but, if one were sensible, one wouldn't!'

The Earl gave a crack of laughter. '*Touché*. Remind me to enlarge your experience later on.'

Lady Mardon blushed and Georgie giggled. Obviously Lord Mardon wasn't nearly as starched up as he appeared.

The Earl turned and stared.

Georgie felt all the blood drain out of her face. Oh, God! She'd just laughed—*laughed!*—at an Earl. And at his Countess. Over the sort of exchange that she ought to have pretended not to understand. Would she never grow up?

'That's much better, my dear,' he said with a twinkle. 'If I were you, I'd be thanking every god in the pantheon that Aunt Harriet *did* kick you out of her dressing room. Believe me, you don't want to sleep in there tonight!'

'Who doesn't want to sleep where?' asked Anthony, stalking in. Georgie swallowed. He looked furious. What had she done now?

'Your wife,' said the Earl. 'Doesn't want to sleep in Aunt Harriet's dressing room. The maid broke a bottle of scent. Upset apparently at your decree that the staff should assemble in the hall.' He shrugged. 'From the sounds of it, they all expect to be dismissed on the spot.'

'John, don't be so unfeeling,' said Lady Mardon. 'Something must be wrong. Anthony?'

He flicked a glance at Georgie. An uncomfortable glance, she thought.

'We may as well wait until everyone is down,' he said quietly. 'No point in repeating it over and over.'

A chill condensed in Georgie's stomach. His eyes were like flint. Hard, uncompromising. And he avoided her gaze.

The rest of the party assembled, Harriet fuming over the accident to her scent bottle. Mr Lyndhurst-Flint was the last to stroll in. 'Devilish kick up,' he said. 'Why, I waited twenty minutes for my shaving water! Perhaps you might have a word to your staff, cousin.'

To Georgie's shock he turned to her.

'After all, they are your responsibility now.'

'Stubble it, William,' growled Mr Sinclair. 'There are more pressing worries than your shaving water.' He shot a glance at Anthony. 'What's all this about a missing ring?'

'Cassie's betrothal ring has been stolen,' Anthony stated baldly. He flicked a glance at Georgie. 'She left it behind when she went riding this morning and—'

'Oh, nonsense!' said Mr Lyndhurst-Flint with a scornful look at Lady Quinlan. 'I dare say you've misplaced it.'

Lady Quinlan fixed him with a furious glare. 'You may be careless with other people's property, William! I am not! I placed it in my jewel case and Eliza saw me—'

He snorted. 'There you are, then. It's obvious. Come to think of it, she was sneaking off in a very havey-cavey sort of way this morning with Anthony's man, what's his name—'

'*Timms,*' snarled Anthony. 'And I can think of far more likely contingencies than him having anything to do with it!'

'Eliza wouldn't do such a thing either!' Cassie said abruptly.

'Rot!' said Mr Lyndhurst-Flint. 'Servants. Really, Cassandra! This ridiculous taste of yours for low company is most unbecoming! Anyone would think—'

'That you were about to offer my wife an apology.' The edge in Quinlan's voice would have shamed a razor.

Icy horror flooded Georgie as Anthony's words echoed through her. ...*I can think of far more likely contingencies than him having anything to do with it.* Surely, surely he didn't think that *she* would have... She hung on to her self-control. He'd already shown how little he trusted her. If he thought she had taken the pearls, then—

'Good God, Quinlan! Must you take a fellow up so?' asked Mr Lyndhurst-Flint. 'It's plain enough. Ebdon saw her chance and—'

'Enough, William!' Anthony nearly exploded. 'I'll have no accusations against people not here to defend themselves. The staff should be gathered by now.'

Again his glance flickered to Georgie. She felt as if a knife had lodged deep inside. Gouging a fresh wound. One that might never heal.

Anthony drew a deep breath as he faced his staff.

'I regret to say that Miss Cassie's—rather, Lady Quinlan's betrothal ring has been stolen. It will be necessary to—' He broke off as an outraged babble erupted.

He didn't blame them. 'Necessary to question you all. We need to find out if anyone saw anything. Anyone who shouldn't have been in Lady Quinlan's chamber—'

'Rubbish,' said William. 'All we need to do is find out where Ebdon sneaked off to this morning.'

Ebdon's cry of frightened indignation was nearly lost as Anthony turned on William. 'That's enough!'

Timms stepped forward, his face set. 'Miss Ebdon was with me, and where we was—'

'Precisely,' said William smoothly. 'Two of you. Very convenient. I should think—'

'Not unless you can make a better fist of it than that, you shouldn't,' said Anthony, hanging on to his temper by a thread. 'I'll thank you to leave this to me, cousin. This is *my* home and *my* staff!'

'Well, what were the two of them doing so far from the house?' argued William. 'Really, coz—'

'Timms asked for the day off,' snapped Anthony. 'I granted it.'

'And Ebdon?' William's sneer was palpable.

Cassie stepped forward, shaking off Quinlan's hand. 'Eliza had the day off as well.'

William snorted. 'There you are. They had it all planned. For heaven's sake, Anthony! I dare say you need look no further for a solution to your missing pearls either. Timms was probably behind—'

Timms lunged at him. 'Why, you snivelling—'

'*Timms!*' Leaping forward, Anthony managed to grab Timms before he could reach William. 'For God's sake, man! Calm down. Let me handle this.'

Breathing hard, Timms met his eyes. 'Just as long as you do, Major. I won't put up with no one saying as how Liza stole Miss Cassie's ring! Quality!' He spat in

William's direction. 'That one's got all the quality of a bilge rat! And how the hell does *he*—?'

Anthony trod hard on his foot. He knew exactly what Timms wanted to know. How the hell had William known about a theft that *no one*, bar himself and Timms, had ever known about?

Timms swore and stepped back. 'I'd appreciate the favour of a word with you, sir,' he said. 'Privately.'

'The library,' said Anthony curtly. Best to get Timms out of here before he went for William.

Stalking into the library, he turned to see that not only Timms, but Cassie's maid had followed him, with Cassie right on her heels.

Icily he said, 'I believe Timms requested a *private*—'

Timms cut him off. 'I don't suppose there'd be the least chance of you leaving this to me, lass?'

Anthony felt his jaw sag.

Ebdon shook her head and went to him. With a resigned sigh Timms drew her to him, slipping his arm around her in a protective gesture.

Anthony's jaw collapsed further.

'I'll be giving notice, sir. Me and Eliza is getting leg-shackled. Spoke to the Rector this morning about the banns. That's where we went together.'

Cassie's gasp summed it all up.

Outraged, Anthony stared at Timms, who met his gaze calmly.

'I don't suppose,' he said, 'that it occurred to you to mention this to me this morning, did it? I'd have told you to take the gig! As for resigning—!' he snorted '—we'll work something out. The lodgekeeper said something about moving to the village the other day.

Apparently Mr Devereaux tried him pretty high. You can probably have the North Lodge.'

'You're stealing my maid!' said Cassie indignantly.

'Now, Miss Cassie,' began Ebdon gently. 'You don't need me now.'

Cassie laughed. 'Oh, Eliza! Don't be silly! I was only funning. I think this is lovely. And of course Major Lyndhurst and I don't think either of you had anything to do with my ring. Do we, Anthony?'

She turned to Anthony, a challenging glint in her eyes.

'Don't be a peagoose!' he told her. 'Of course I don't. Unless they pawned it at the Rectory!' He turned to Timms. 'Did you go anywhere else in the village?'

Timms nodded. 'The bakery. Mr Lyndhurst-Flint saw us. Dare say he thinks Martha Higgins is passing stolen jewels in her loaves these days! But what queers me is—' He stopped dead, his eyes on Anthony's face. 'Major—you don't think—?'

'Yes,' said Anthony. 'I do think. After four years I'm finally thinking—' Suddenly aware of Cassie's puzzled gaze, he stopped. 'Cassie—I beg your pardon, but could you and Ebdon leave us now? Ebdon, I know you would never have stolen so much as a pin from your mistress. I shall wish you happy. If Timms takes half the care of you, that he has of me—' He broke off and cleared his throat. 'Well, he's a damn good fellow. I'm only sorry that I've been partially responsible for keeping you apart so long. But, just now, I do need to talk to Timms.'

Cassie snorted. 'I dare say you know exactly what's going on and have no intention of telling the rest of us! Just as long as whoever stole that ring is caught. Poor Peter is terribly upset!'

Anthony nodded. 'I know. And I swear that it shall be found and returned to you. Trust me, Cassie.'

She held his gaze for a moment. 'Idiot! Of course I trust you. Very well. Come along, Eliza.'

As soon as the door shut behind them, Anthony turned to Timms. 'It all fits. He must have come back to the lodgings and taken the pearls after your mistress left. Apparently she left a note. Whoever stole the pearls also took the note. Apart from the thief, you're the only person other than myself who knows that the pearls are gone.'

'And you think he's taken the ring? Would this have something to do with that Grant?'

Feeling sick, Anthony explained.

Timms listened, disgust etched on his face. At last he said savagely, 'First the mistress and then Mr Marcus? His own family! Makes you fair sick! What are we going to do about it?'

'There's a spyglass in the desk in my bedchamber,' said Anthony shortly. 'My cousin has been taking an inordinate interest in the woods on that side of the house. I'm afraid, Timms, that you are going to become as sick of my bedchamber as Mr Sinclair.'

He cocked a brow at Timms, who grinned and said, 'I take you. Trust me, sir!'

'I do,' said Anthony quietly. At least he'd managed to get that right. 'If my cousin is in the woods, I want to know about it. If he's meeting Grant, it's more than likely that Grant's putting the screw on him. Without money, he may have taken the ring to buy Grant off.'

'Aye, Major.' He hesitated. 'Would it be all right for me to tell Liza about this? After His Nibs's suggestion that she might have prigged something from Miss Cassie—'

Anthony blanched. Tell a female?

Timms looked as though he were trying very hard not

to laugh. 'You'll get used to it, sir,' he said encouragingly.

Anthony felt his own lips twitch. 'Thank you,' he said. 'I think. Tell her if you are assured that she will tell no one else. Even Miss Cassie. That will be all, Timms. Please assure the staff that none of them is under any suspicion.'

'Aye, sir.'

'Ah, yes, well...' His throat felt beyond tight. 'Congratulations, Timms. And I expect to be a godfather!'

To Anthony's utter gratification Timms went absolutely puce.

Chapter Seven

By the end of dinner, Georgie had a perfectly genuine headache and her jaw also ached with the effort of smiling and pretending that nothing was wrong. To make matters worse, Anthony kept staring at her from his end of the table, frowning slightly every time their eyes met.

Aunt Harriet took one look at her when they retired to the drawing room and sent her to bed. 'Go along with you,' she said. 'We can look after ourselves.'

Lady Mardon backed her up. 'You look fagged to death, my dear. Don't worry about us. We will see you in the morning.'

Instead of going to bed, she went up to the cupola where she could face what she had done.

She sat, staring out at the dark woods. Above the stars blazed. What had happened to the note she had left? More importantly, what was she to do about her marriage? Anthony had been through four years of hell because of her foolishness. Four years of disgrace and slander. How could he even bear the sight of her?

Yet somehow she would have to face him. Apologise.

They had to build a life together. But how could they do that if he believed her capable of theft?

She sat for a long time, tired, but reluctant to return downstairs. Voices still floated up from the open drawing-room windows. Further away in the woods she heard the scream of a vixen. Closer at hand a dog barked.

When she went down she must tell Anthony the truth, that she couldn't fulfil his most important requirement for a wife. Pain shivered through her. She should have told him the moment he had said he would not divorce her. Now she had tied the knot that much tighter.

A footstep sounded and she swung around with a startled gasp.

'Good God! Who the devil—oh, Cousin Georgiana! I thought you had gone to bed.'

It was Mr Sinclair. He came towards her. 'How is your headache?' he asked, in kindly tones that tore at her.

'Much better,' she lied, hoping he wouldn't come close enough to see her reddened eyes.

'I'm very glad to hear it,' he said and strolled over to the parapet. 'A lovely night, is it not?'

'Y…yes.'

'We all came here for holidays as children. Anthony and I would sneak up here to sleep. Our fond mamas were not impressed when they found out.'

She could just imagine. 'And your fathers?'

He chuckled. 'Having sinned in the same way themselves, they knew all about it. Little did we know they took it in turns to keep an eye on us at first until they were confident we wouldn't fall off the roof.'

Despite her misery, Georgie found herself laughing a little. 'Just you and Anthony? Not Lord Mardon and his brother?'

Mr Sinclair snorted. 'No. John's a good bit older than we are, you know. And William! Well, he's only a couple of years older than Anthony, but he never took much notice of us younger ones. More interested in currying favour with Anthony's elder brother, The Heir.'

He stiffened, staring down into the park. 'Speak of the devil! What in Hades is he about?'

'Who?' asked Georgie.

'William.' He pointed. 'Look.'

Obediently Georgie looked. She saw a darker shadow moving in the park towards the woods.

'How can you be so sure that it's Mr Lyndhurst-Flint?' she asked. She could see it was a man, but how Mr Sinclair could tell… 'Oh!' The man below had bent down and was rubbing at his boots. 'Yes. It must be him. He's very…er…*particular* about his clothing, isn't he?'

'Damned man-milliner,' muttered Mr Sinclair. 'And I'll thank you not to tell Anthony I said that in front of you!'

'You don't like him, do you?'

'Anthony?'

She flushed. 'Mr Lyndhurst-Flint.'

'No,' he said shortly. 'And if you'll take my advice, Cousin—*you* shouldn't trust him any further than you can sp…throw him!' He frowned at her. 'Don't stay out too long, Cousin. It does become chilly up here, even on the warmest night. Goodnight.' He sketched a salute and was gone.

Anthony slipped into their bedchamber very quietly. It had not needed Aunt Harriet's assurance to convince him that Georgie had felt unwell. Even though they had been separated by the length of the dining table, her pallor had been obvious.

Aunt Harriet's advice had been, 'Leave her be. Sleep will be the best thing for her.' She had fixed Anthony with a beady eye and he nearly choked on the effort not to inform her that *he* hadn't been keeping Georgie from her sleep. At least, not in the way that she meant. He didn't doubt that it was his presence in the bed disturbing her.

Moonlight poured into the room, removing the need for a candle or lamp. He trod softly over to the bed to see if she were asleep. She wasn't there.

Panic churning in his gut, Anthony strode back out of the bedchamber and crashed into Marcus. Staggering back a pace, he swore.

Marcus blinked. 'Anthony, are you all right?'

'Georgie's gone!'

A positively delighted grin spread over Marcus's face. 'Oh. She's in the cupola. I just left her there.'

'In…in the *cupola*? What the devil is she doing there?' He stared suspiciously at Marcus. 'More to the point, what the devil were *you* doing there?'

Marcus raised his brows. '*Not* meeting your wife!'

'Dammit, Marcus! I never thought you were!'

'If you must have it,' continued Marcus in pained tones, 'I intended to meet Miss Devereaux up there, but your wife was there already. I didn't ask, but I would assume that she needed some fresh air since she had a headache earlier.'

'Oh.' He should probably pretend he hadn't heard that bit about Miss Devereaux.

'I think she'd been crying her eyes out,' added Marcus helpfully.

'Crying…oh, *God*!' Pain lashed him.

'Anything I can do, Anthony?'

He shook his head. All he wanted was to get to Georgie. 'No.' Then common sense cut in. 'No, wait. Yes, there is. Come into my room for a moment. Marcus.'

Without a word, Marcus followed him.

Anthony shut the door behind them and went to light a candle. He turned to find Marcus leaning against the door frame. 'I've been a damn fool,' he said bluntly. 'Over your mess and with her. But there's a link. William.'

'*What?*' Marcus's shoulders surged off the door frame.

Briefly Anthony told Marcus his suspicions. 'Don't you see?' he finished. 'Each time he has tried to safe-guard his own position by destroying my trust in some-one. And it's worked. Because he was dealing with a damn fool.' He said nothing about John's revelations, or the pearls.

Marcus swore. 'Damn him! I knew he had to be be-hind this business with Frobisher, but you! Hell, Anthony—he's stolen four years of your life. Every time *I* lay eyes on him I want to break his neck! How the devil can *you* stand the sight of him?'

'I can't,' said Anthony grimly. 'But if I kick him out, what odds would you give that he won't shop you to the nearest magistrate? And what of John? This will hit him hard.'

Marcus said a few things under his breath. 'Something else you should know,' he went on, 'William has de-veloped a yen for the beauties of nature.'

Anthony blinked.

'He was going into the woods just now. Your wife and I both saw him. At least, I thought it was him.

Anyway—it's his second trip today. Cassie mentioned that he'd taken a stroll this afternoon.'

'Third trip. He was there early this morning,' said Anthony, his brain whirling. 'And Timms says William was in Lynd today. Not his usual style at all.'

Marcus nodded. 'Mmm. Fishy. If we're lucky it's only an assignation with some wench, but there is the possibility that Grant is still in the area.'

'I know. I've put the word out quietly. You'd better be prepared to leave. Ufton is checking the mail, but if Grant, or someone else, posts a letter for him—we could have that magistrate down on us very quickly.' He swore as he saw the stubborn set to his cousin's jaw.

'I'll break William's neck first,' vowed Marcus. 'No, thank you. I'll stay and see this out.' He hesitated, and then said, 'One other thing, Anthony—'

Flushing, Anthony said, 'I know. I'm sorry. I was a fool to mistrust you. There's no excuse—'

'Oh, shut up, you idiot,' growled Marcus. 'I wanted to apologise for poking my nose into your drawers and finding that miniature. I had no business—'

'Oh, go to the devil,' said Anthony. 'And now, if you'll excuse me, I need to find my wife.'

She was still there. A small shadow, leaning on the balustrade staring over the dark woods.

'Georgie?' He kept his voice low, but relief made it harsh. He had somehow feared that she would be gone.

She turned. 'How you must hate me.' The tired whisper seared him.

'Hate you?' Swift strides took him to her, but she flinched and he forced his hands back to his sides, despite the aching need to hold her.

'I didn't understand, didn't know until your cousin told me—'

'Marcus?' What the devil had Marcus said to upset her?

'Not Mr Sinclair. Lady Quinlan.'

He knew now what was coming. Georgie's headache was explained. 'Damn Cassie,' he growled. 'If Quinlan hadn't taken her off my hands, I'd warm her backside. What rubbish did she tell you?'

'That people believe you murdered me. And Justin. That you made sure he died at Waterloo! That you were nearly cashiered for it!'

He froze at the horror in her voice. Oh, God. After the way he'd raged at her, after he'd informed Finch-Scott that his seconds would call—what did Georgie believe? 'And you? What do you think?'

'That I ruined your life! Oh, Anthony! If I'd known! How could they think such a thing? Didn't they *know* you?'

No. Of course she would never believe such a thing of him. Her faith humbled him.

He shook his head. 'No. They didn't. But the people who mattered knew. My neighbours. My family. And I wasn't nearly cashiered. Wellington sent a message to my colonel, demanding that the pressure to do so be resisted, and received a very dusty answer that the Guards could look after their own, thanks very much.'

'I'm sorry,' she whispered.

He came to her then, unable to bear any longer the pain in her voice. Ignoring her protest, he took her in his arms. 'No. Let me hold you.' His voice cracked. 'God, you don't know how much I've wanted to do this in the past four years. How much I've hated myself for what I said that night. My damnable temper! You were so young. It was my fault, not yours.'

He felt the sobs racking her slender body and pulled her closer, burying his face in her hair, absorbing the scent, the feel of her, drawing it deep. 'I told myself that if you ever returned to me, I'd do better...' He shuddered. 'And when you did come back, I hurt you again. Georgie, I've been such a fool. I was wrong to lose my temper that night, wrong to accuse you. Can you not forgive me?' He drew her closer, feeling the wrenching of grief as it poured from her. 'Will you let me be your husband again?'

She struggled free and gazed up at him, the despair in her face a physical blow. 'With all my heart,' she whispered. 'But I can be no wife to you, Anthony. I cannot give you what you want.'

'What I want?'

'A...a child.' Her voice broke and she turned away. 'I mean, an heir.'

Silence hung between them. He waited. Not understanding, but knowing somehow that he hung on a knife edge. That the wrong word now might lose her forever.

'You asked what I would have done if I had been carrying your child. Well, I was.' Her voice sounded remote, a distant echo of something that had happened to someone else. Something she could no longer bear to feel. 'I knew, whatever had happened between us, even if you no longer wanted me, I had to tell you about the child. So I wrote.'

She had written? 'But—'

'No.' The bleak voice cut him off. 'It was never posted. I had a miscarriage after I reached Aunt Mary, my godmother. The doctor who attended me said that losing the baby so early, it was likely that I would be unable to have children.'

'Oh, my God,' whispered Anthony. Grief and horror welled up inside him as he realised the pain, the fear and the bitter loneliness she had been through, believing that he had abandoned her. That all he wanted of her was an heir. No wonder she had not come back.

With hands that shook, he drew her back into his arms and rocked her, burying his face again in the fragrance of her hair. 'My poor darling,' he whispered. 'It's all right. I'm here now.'

A wave of peace flooded Georgie. At last. He knew. Whatever he decided later, he was holding her now, giving the comfort her bruised heart had needed. She clung tightly, never wanting to let go. And knowing that she must. But when she tried to pull away, he held on, his arms tightening, his hands trembling over her hair, her face. His tenderness surrounded her, warmth where there had been only the deadly chill of despair.

'Anthony, what if I can't give you a child?'

'It doesn't matter, Georgie. It's you I want. Just you. You're mine. I'll never let you go again.' His voice was hoarse, shaking.

'But—'

He silenced her with his mouth, with a kiss that said everything his breaking voice could not express. His longing, his need.

Urgency hammered in his blood. Fighting for control, he lifted his head and stared down at her dazed eyes, soft with passion. He wanted her more than his next breath. The night breathed around them, dark, seductive. If he took the cushions off the seats… No. He dragged in a deep breath, forcing himself to restraint. It didn't take genius to know why Marcus had been meeting Miss

Devereaux up here and the last thing he needed was any interruptions.

'Anthony?' The uncertainty in her voice tore at him. He had to tell her, show her, how much he needed her, loved her. But—

'Not here,' he whispered. And lifted her into his arms.

Georgie clung to him as he carried her downstairs, her thoughts chaotic. He *couldn't* want her, but— Kicking the bedchamber door shut behind him, he strode across the room and laid her gently on his bed. No. *Their* bed. Their marriage bed.

The windows had been left open and the soft night air stole in, wreathed in moonlight. He turned to her, his need blazing from him. 'Where is your wedding ring?'

Drawing a shaky breath, she said, 'In…my workbag. By your desk.'

A wry smile flashed. 'No wonder you didn't want me to look in there the other day.' He went to the bag and knelt down. A moment later he straightened and turned. The ring dangled on its chain from his fingers.

'I…I wore it under my clothes,' she said. Tears spilt over. 'It was all I had of you.'

His fingers shaking, he released the clasp and came to her, laying the ring on the bedside table as he joined her on the bed. 'Mine,' he whispered as his mouth came down on hers, cherishing and ravishing. A miracle of possession and giving. Gentle, caressing hands brushed her clothes away, leaving her defenceless, her skin quivering for his touch. And then he was naked too, pulling her against his hard, lean body, his mouth devouring her, burning kisses over her breasts while his hands stroked and explored.

She gave him back kiss for kiss, caress for caress,

caring nothing if he realised how much she loved him, if only he would hold her like this and make love to her. His mouth was a fire at her breasts, drawing her deep into the heat and wetness, suckling so that she arched and pressed him closer as pleasure laced her.

'Please…oh, please…' Her own voice, a ragged gasp, as she lifted against him, her body pleading. Yet still he held back, stroking, caressing, one powerful thigh clamped over hers, holding them together.

The silken shift of her body burnt him. Consumed him with the need to take her. To become part of her. Forever.

'God, Georgie,' he whispered. 'Do you have any idea what you're doing to me?'

'I want you,' she breathed.

His blood hammered. He'd hurt her the other night. This time he would be sure she was ready. More than ready. And he needed to show her that he loved her. That she was his. And that he was hers.

Gently he cupped the mound of curls, clenching his jaw for control as he felt her thighs part. Slowly he pressed further, feeling her trembling response as he found the honeyed slickness that bloomed for his tender caress.

Soft cries scorched his restraint until he shook with the need to take all she offered, give all she pleaded for. With a groan, he pushed her thighs wider and settled in the soft cradle. Her arms clung, drawing him down. His jaw clenched, he resisted the sweet temptation to take her there and then.

He reached for the wedding ring. 'Open your eyes, sweetheart.'

Slowly the dark lashes lifted. Her eyes were dazed,

dilated, bright with tears. He bent and brushed his lips over hers. 'Give me your hand, your left hand.'

A small, trembling hand was placed in his.

Braced over her, he slid the ring on to her finger and whispered, *'With this ring, I thee wed.'* Holding her gaze, he lifted her hand to his mouth and kissed the ring on her finger. Then, pressing against her soft, moist core, he said, *'With my body, I thee worship.'*

He took her mouth, fiercely, hotly, and pressed slowly inside, still restrained, feeling her close sweetly around him.

She gasped, her body tightening, raking him with fire.

He stilled immediately, fear streaking through him. 'Are you all right?' he whispered against her lips.

She could barely breathe. All she could do was lift against him, twisting, pleading for his possession.

'Georgie?'

'Please…don't stop!'

The breaking cry destroyed what was left of his control. With a groan he sank fully into her body and began to move, loving her tenderly, thoroughly until the world shattered around them and there was nothing left except the certainty of their love.

Later, much later in the darkness, Anthony lay with her in his arms, her breath sighing over his chest, and wondered if he'd get any more sleep in the next four years. He rather thought this sort of sleeplessness would sit a great deal better with him.

Her cheek shifted against him and he suppressed a groan as his body tightened.

'Anthony?'

'Sweetheart?' He traced the hollow of her spine with a teasing finger.

'I've been…thinking.'

Her sensuous wriggle had his blood hammering again. As did the curious fingertip circling his nipple.

'Thinking? Is that what you call it?' He let his hand curve and tighten over her bottom.

'Anthony!'

He chuckled. 'What were you thinking about, love?'

'That note. And the pearls. Why would anyone take the note? The pearls, yes, but—'

Fear stirred. 'Leave it, Georgie.'

'But—'

'*No.*' Black fear blossomed in a cold, spreading rush, strangling him. He had to get rid of William before Georgie worked it out. If William had ordered the attack on Frobisher, if he had plotted to have Marcus hanged, then what might he not have done had Georgie not left Brussels so precipitately? Why had he returned to their lodgings? Anthony's stomach chilled.

He'd had four years of hell *not* knowing. Had he narrowly missed a lifetime of grief actually *knowing*? Somehow they had to prove Marcus's innocence and get rid of William. If he thought Georgie knew enough to hang him…

'Anthony?'

Terror at the thought of what might have happened if she hadn't fled consumed him. With a groan, he rolled, silencing her with his kiss, feeling her wild response, her body softening in surrender as he settled her beneath him.

Georgie's body flamed as she felt his weight, tasted the need in his urgent kiss. Eagerly she obeyed the unspoken demand of his body, opening herself to his possessive touch. Delight took her as he caressed intimately, fire shimmering up from his teasing fingers.

Her breath broke as she felt his hunger, hard against her in passionate demand. She answered the only way she could, tilting towards him in pliant supplication.

He filled her, body, heart and soul until she overflowed, her love pouring from her in soft cries and searing pleasure. Until the world contracted to fiery need and she hung burning on the edge of desire. He took her spinning, tumbling, falling into flame, locked safely in his arms and heart.

Chapter Eight

Breakfast was an ordeal. She had absolutely no idea what it was that had the entire company avoiding her gaze and exchanging fleeting smirks and winks. Unless, of course, it was the fact that Anthony couldn't take his eyes off her and kept yawning behind his napkin.

She ate an enormous breakfast, shamelessly helping herself to everything in sight.

Great-aunt Harriet sniffed as she set down her tea cup. 'About time too,' she announced trenchantly.

'Time for what, Aunt Harriet?' asked Anthony, a wary look in his eyes.

'For Georgiana's appetite to return, of course,' she said, with a perfectly straight face. 'One can only assume it has something to do with the…er…water here.'

Mr Sinclair's napkin had apparently vanished under the table again, since he disappeared with a very odd noise.

Anthony, to Georgie's disbelief, actually blushed. 'Aunt Harriet?'

She raised her brows. 'Yes?'

He shook his head and came to his feet. Silence fell and he went to the old lady, bent over and kissed her soundly. 'Thank you. For being the most appallingly interfering, *nosy* old tabby of my acquaintance.'

Mr Sinclair reappeared with an unconvincingly straight face.

Aunt Harriet's black eyes glimmered with suspicious moisture, but she poked Anthony with her ear trumpet and said crossly, 'Get along with you! Save your kisses for your wife!' Notwithstanding, she lifted one hand and patted him on the cheek. 'You'll do. Now finish your breakfast and attend to your guests. Aren't the fireworks planned for tonight?'

He nodded. 'Yes. In fact, I need to talk to Ufton about that now. The staff are to watch from the lawn if they care to.' Glancing at Marcus, he said, 'Can you give me a moment, Marcus? I'd like your advice on this, too.'

Something about his voice caught Georgie's attention.

Mr Sinclair rose. 'A pleasure, Anthony.'

Lord Mardon broke in. 'Anthony, is it correct that this stranger has not yet been apprehended?'

To Georgie it looked as though Anthony's jaw petrified. 'That is correct, John.'

'Then it would be better if the ladies still did not venture beyond the gardens without an escort. A male escort.'

'Very much better,' said Anthony tightly. 'In fact, I'll make that an order. None of you—' his suddenly fierce gaze scorched Georgie '—should venture into the park or woodlands without one of us.' He hesitated. 'Indeed, Sarah should not go without John, Cassie without Quinlan, Miss Devereaux without Marcus. Or—' he looked at her straightly '—Georgie without me.'

Aunt Harriet glared at him. 'And what about me? Hey?'

His sudden grin softened the harsh lines of his face. 'Take your ear trumpet, Aunt!'

Anthony led Marcus out to the parterre and, in response to his cousin's raised eyebrows, said, 'I don't want to be overheard.'

'Obviously not,' said Marcus. 'But I should warn you—I don't know anything about fireworks.'

'I've set Timms to watching the woods for William from my bedchamber.'

Marcus frowned. 'Wouldn't the cupola be better?'

'Yes, but the servants aren't allowed up there. And, if one of the others goes up there, it would cause too much comment. That footman waiting on William, for example—'

'Point taken,' growled Marcus, his fists clenching.

Anthony blinked. Had he missed something? 'Marcus?'

With an obvious effort, Marcus controlled himself. 'Never mind. It's nothing to worry about. More to the point, have you considered what is likely to happen if William has shopped me? You could be seized for harbouring me.'

Anthony grinned. 'That *will* upset our dear cousin!'

'Oh?'

Too late Anthony realised where this was leading, and mentally kicked himself.

Very reluctantly he came clean. 'I told him before Waterloo that in the event of my death he would inherit twenty thousand. If my property is seized he'll get nothing.'

The air turned a little blue. 'You damned idiot!' continued Marcus. 'What about the rest? You might not be as rich as Cassie, but there's a good bit more than twenty thousand!'

Oh, hell! 'I left it in trust to Georgie and any child she might bear. Failing a child, Georgie has it in trust for her lifetime.' With a bit of luck Marcus might not ask about the next heir.

'And?'

So much for luck. 'Er…you. Followed by your heirs. And you're also her principal trustee. Along with John.'

Marcus gave him a level stare. 'Thanks. A lot.'

'Think nothing of it. The least I could do,' said Anthony.

Marcus swore again. Then, 'You've realised that he must have taken Cassie's ring? Probably hoping to buy Grant off.'

'Yes,' said Anthony.

'What was all that about the pearls?' asked Marcus.

Anthony explained.

Marcus stared. 'Anthony—if you don't break his neck, I will!'

'You had your turn the other night,' said Anthony. 'It's my turn now.' He stared out across the gardens to the woods. His childhood home had been little better than a prison these past four years. He might be able to forgive what William had done to him, but for what he had done to Georgie—the grief and loneliness, the despair… His jaw clenched involuntarily.

'I won't protect him,' he said shortly. 'If we can find proof, or force a confession, he'll either face a jury or leave the country. And I've sent to Newbury already for a lawyer to come and remake my will. But don't mention that. Not even Georgie knows.'

'The sooner the better,' growled Marcus. 'When are you going to tell John what we suspect?'

'This afternoon,' said Anthony. 'After our ride. He wants to try out that chestnut youngster I've been bringing on. Chances are William won't want to come. He'll probably take the opportunity to try and contact Grant. I told you, Timms saw William in Lynd. He may have sent a message to Grant from there, suggesting the woods as a meeting place. With Timms watching, we might have them. If Grant is fool enough to take the ring—'

'Too recognisable,' said Marcus instantly.

Anthony nodded. 'Exactly. If he were caught with it, nothing would save him from the noose. Too easy for William to shop *him*. I thought about searching William and his bedchamber, but—'

'Not a chance in hell,' interrupted Marcus. 'He won't make that mistake again!'

Anthony wondered if he looked as puzzled as he felt. He had a sneaking suspicion that Marcus had been up to a great deal more than he was letting on. 'Er…no. It won't be in the house, anyway. I've put a watch on Grant. A man fitting that description is staying in that hedge tavern on the back road to Oxford. It's easy enough to reach the Lyndhurst woods from there.'

Marcus grimaced. 'So we have to tell John. What about Quinlan?'

Painfully, Anthony said, 'In all honour, I have no choice but to tell him. He gave it to Cassie and it has been stolen in my house. I just wish I could spare John, that's all. The least I can do is tell him privately.'

Late in the afternoon Georgie slipped up to the cupola, wondering when Anthony and the other gentlemen would be back from their ride. Below her the gardens and woods stretched away, glowing in the golden light.

And far away on the downs she could see four small riders that must be Anthony, Mr Sinclair, Lord Mardon and Lord Quinlan. Mr Lyndhurst-Flint had cried off the ride. She frowned over that. She could have sworn that Anthony and Mr Sinclair exchanged a glance of satisfaction.

Everything had been so much easier today. The preparations for the fireworks party were all in hand. Servants had been hard at work all afternoon, bringing everything needful up here. She had seen to that earlier, in response to Lady Mardon's—no, *Sarah*'s gentle hint.

The Countess had checked her almost forcibly, refusing to be addressed formally any longer. *We are cousins. And Anthony is nearly as dear to me as John… We are all glad to see him happy again…*

Georgie sighed. Lady Quinlan might not be quite so happy. No, that was unfair. She was doubtless pleased that Anthony was happy, but understandably viewed the reason for his happiness with suspicion.

'Cousin?'

She looked up.

Lady Quinlan stood before her. 'Sarah said that I should find you up here. I have come to apologise. For my stupid meddling yesterday. Marcus and Anthony are furious with me. It was none of my business.'

'Well, they shouldn't be,' said Georgie quietly. 'You were right. Anthony would never have told me. And it is your business. You love Anthony too. Besides, I asked.'

Lady Quinlan flushed. 'You are very generous.' She came over and sat down beside Georgie. 'Do you know, I haven't seen Anthony so happy in years. It is as though a cloud has lifted.' She hesitated and then said, 'He didn't tell me very much, just that what happened be-

tween you was his own fault. Mostly. And that none of
the blame was yours.' A faint grin appeared. 'He said
that he'd been a *damn fool*, but that was no excuse for
other members of the family to perpetuate the failing!'

She grimaced. 'And then as if that wasn't enough,
Marcus came and tore strips off me! So, I'm sorry. And
I should like very much to be friends, if you have for-
given me. I did like "Miss Saunders", you know!'

As simple as that. Candid brown eyes smiled at her,
offering friendship.

Her heart lifting, Georgie said, 'There is nothing to
forgive, unless it will make you feel better. Tell me,
what are these fireworks parties like?'

Cassie giggled. 'Oh, famous! There hasn't been one
here since I was a child, but they used to have them
every summer. Only they have rather lapsed for one reason and another. First Anthony went to war and then his
mother died. It will be lovely to have them again.'

'Go on,' urged Georgie, enthralled.

Cassie obliged and half an hour sped by.

'Oh, look!' exclaimed Cassie. 'Isn't that Stella?'

Georgie leaned over the balustrade to look. 'Yes, it is.
Whatever is she doing out? I thought Anthony didn't
like her going out by herself?'

'He doesn't,' agreed Cassie. 'He worries that she'll
get lost in the woods or fall in the lake now that she's
so blind.'

'Well, she's heading straight for the woods!' said
Georgie, concerned. Leaning over the balustrade, she
cupped her hands to her mouth and called loudly.
'Stella!'

The old dog kept moving. Straight for the woods.

'It's no good calling,' said Cassie, sounding just as concerned. 'She's deaf, remember.'

Images came to Georgie. Stella, resting her grizzled muzzle on Anthony's knee, pushing her nose under his elbow for a pat, sleeping as close to his chair as she could get. And Anthony, slipping the old dog scraps of bacon at breakfast, his hands gentle on the grizzled head, tugging the silky ears.

'I'll fetch her back,' she said.

Cassie's head snapped around. 'But...that man! Anthony said that none of us should leave the garden!'

'Well, if I hurry, I won't have to go far. She's not moving very fast. Look.'

'What about the servants?' suggested Cassie. 'Or you could wait for Anthony to return.'

'The servants are all as busy as anything,' argued Georgie. 'And Anthony and the others won't be back for ages.' She indicated the tiny horses and riders out on the downs. 'Stella could be anywhere by then.'

'Then I'll come with you,' said Cassie.

'No. You stay up here and you can call down and tell me which way she goes. That will make it quicker.'

Cassie looked unconvinced. 'I don't like it. You shouldn't go alone.'

Stella was more than halfway to the woods. 'I *must* go!' said Georgie. 'He adores Stella. I won't be long. I promise.'

'Hurry, then,' said Cassie. 'I'll watch and tell you where she's heading.

Racing down the stairs, Georgie remembered Anthony's grim face as he forbade any of the ladies to leave the gardens. But this was Stella. He wouldn't want to lose Stella. Yet she hesitated.

Her pistol. The one she had carried in the Peninsula when she and her mother had followed the drum. She hadn't used it in years, but she knew exactly where it was and she was fairly sure that she could find a ball and charge in the gunroom.

Ten minutes later she ran out into the garden and looked up at the cupola. Cassie was hanging over the balustrade.

'I hoped you'd changed your mind!' she called down.

'No. Just fetching something! Which way?'

'She went into the woods about fifty yards to the left of the main ride,' called Cassie, pointing. 'There's a narrow path there that leads to the lake.'

'Thank you!' Georgie set off at a brisk walk. Five minutes brought her to the entrance to the path. She looked back. Cassie was still visible in the cupola. She waved. Cassie waved back. And pointed. Straight ahead.

Taking a deep breath, Georgie entered the woods. In a moment the house was out of sight as the path twisted away among the trees. She hadn't been into the woods before. They closed around her, but she shook off the feeling of unease. This was Lyndhurst Chase, Anthony's home. Her home. Nevertheless, the loaded pistol in her pocket reassured her.

Ten minutes later the woods thinned and water glimmered. The lake. She ran out of the trees and gasped. The dying sun gilded the water so that it fairly blazed with golden light. Best of all, there was Stella, sniffing happily in the reeds on the far side.

She opened her mouth to call. And shut it again. Stella was deaf as well as blind. Instead Georgie set off around the lake. By the time she came up with the old setter, Stella had found something to roll in and Georgie wrinkled her nose as she drew near. 'Stella!' she said loudly.

Startled, the dog looked around. In every direction but the right one.

Smothering a grin, Georgie walked up to her and spoke again. 'Come along, you smelly old darling. Before your master finds out where we are!'

This time Stella seemed to realise where the voice had come from and came stiffly towards her, nosing at her hands. Gently, Georgie looped the cravat she had taken from Anthony's drawer through Stella's collar and tugged. The old dog followed readily, if slowly. Belatedly, Georgie realised that the walk home would be a great deal slower than coming out. She looked back to see if the house were visible.

There it was, floating beyond the woods. And the tiny figure that must be Cassie. Georgie pointed to Stella and waved madly. Then she exaggeratedly mimed a very slow walk. The tiny figure waved back.

Encouraged, Georgie set off around the lake again. And immediately realised that she had made a serious mistake. In her rush to secure Stella, she had failed to mark which path had brought her out of the woods. Muttering some very unladylike remarks under her breath, she looked at the various tracks leading back into the woods. It was impossible to tell.

One appeared to lead straight back, but the track she had used had twisted around a great deal. And several other paths had intersected it. Under the trees it would be impossible to keep the house in sight. Well, the path had to come out somewhere. Perhaps on one of the main rides. At least she had found Stella. And if she stuck to the path, she couldn't go too far wrong.

Grimly Anthony watched as John swung away to stare out of the library window, his face drawn. Blast William, to hell and beyond. They had waited until returning from their ride to tell John privately. Quinlan had gone up to the cupola to find Cassie, but he would have to be told. As would the others.

He waited.

Finally, John turned to face him. 'I'm sorry, Anthony. Marcus. This is my—'

'The hell it's your fault!' exploded Anthony. 'You've done everything possible for him!'

John shook his head. 'I couldn't keep him from this,' he said bitterly.

'He made his own choices, John,' said Marcus quietly, from his stance near the chimneypiece. 'There was nothing you could do about that. The question remains— what to do now? As Anthony pointed out, there is no proof. Nothing that we could make stick.'

John sighed. 'Stubble it, Marcus. I know my own brother. Little though I like it, the whole thing rings true. Anthony may remember that I said the one time I'd known William to be beforehand with the world was after Waterloo. Which fits in with the theft of the pearls. There's no other way he could have known they were missing if even you and I never knew.'

The sad acceptance in his voice tore at Anthony. So much unhappiness because of William's inability to accept his responsibilities and make a life for himself.

Racing feet in the hall ended with the door bursting open. Cassie tumbled in, followed by Timms and Quinlan.

Timms began. 'Begging your pardon, Major—'

'Georgie's in the woods, looking for Stella,' gasped Cassie.

Anthony's stomach congealed to solid ice as fear hammered through every vein. 'Timms!' he snapped.

'Aye. Saw her I did. Mr William went in just before you all got back. I'd say he's heading for that little hut in the clearing the gamekeepers use. There's someone else there anyhow. Saw him go in a while back.'

Cassie went white. 'Anthony! I think Georgie missed her path back to the house! I saw her find Stella by the lake, but it didn't look as though she took the same path back. She'll go right past the hut!'

This definitely wasn't the path she had used on the way out. As far as she could tell it wasn't heading towards the house at all now. She hesitated. Perhaps she should go back to the lake and hope Cassie was still on the cupola. Anthony might be back by now.

A small hut was visible through the trees. She stopped. A familiar voice came to her ears. The words were indistinct, but she recognised it—William Lyndhurst-Flint's.

You shouldn't trust him… Mr Sinclair's warning echoed in her head.

Had William purposely garbled that message to Anthony? Stolen the pearls? Anthony hadn't wanted to discuss it at all. Did he suspect William of stealing Cassie's ring? Common sense told Georgie that she should leave. At once.

Yet…who was William talking to? Obviously someone who couldn't come to the house, which was suspicious in itself. She slipped closer and words emerged…

'Dammit, Grant! I've been trying to find you and give you this for the past day! The curst thing must be worth a fortune! More than what I promised you. Look at that sapphire. Take it!'

'I am looking,' came the other voice. 'For all I know it could be glass and foil! And if it isn't, it'd be right easy to identify, wouldn't it? How convenient for you! You could just *happen* to find out I'm still about. Suggest to a magistrate that I've got a grudge against her ladyship and prigged the bloody ring myself! Not flaming likely, *sir*. Your family'd leap at the chance to pin it on me!'

'Really, Grant!' blustered William. 'You insult me!'

'Insult *you*?' The other man sounded as though he might choke laughing. 'Insult you?' he gasped. 'Who told me to attack Frobisher and make it look as though Sinclair did it? Who just suggested that I should murder his cousin? Just so's you'd have the blunt to pay me off for attacking Frobisher! No, thanks. We'll keep your account current, my buck. Not but what I might consider the offer *after* you pay up for Frobisher.' The mocking laughter died from his voice. 'Major High-and-Mighty-Lyndhurst! Kicking me out for a bit of poop-noddy on the stairs with *Lady* Margaret. Hah! You pay up what you owe and we can talk about getting rid of Major Anthony Lyndhurst.'

The vindictive sneer froze Georgie's spine. William's response was lost to her. Shaking with horror, she tugged on the cravat. She had to get out of sight, find her way back to the house and warn Anthony.

Stella resisted, her ears pricked.

'Come on, Stella!' whispered Georgie, pulling harder. Then she saw the rabbit lolloping across the clearing. Stella snuffed the air. And barked. Her distinctive, wheezy bark.

William's voice fell silent. Then a vicious curse. And, 'That's Anthony's bitch! If she's here…'

There was no point running. They'd catch her in a flash. If she faced them, she had an advantage with the pistol. As long as they didn't have one. Nausea condensed, an icy lump in her stomach.

William's jaw dropped when he saw her. Then a very nasty smile curled his lips. 'Well, well, well. Anthony's bitch indeed! My gullible little cousin. And how much did you hear? Don't bother lying. It won't help.'

His scornful amusement lashed Georgie's temper. 'Enough!' she spat at him. '*You* stole Cassie's ring and then you tried to blame Timms and Ebdon!'

'Yes, well. It would have been a little hard to pin it on you this time,' he said casually.

She tasted fear at his calm admission of guilt. 'You won't get away with it,' she told him.

'Oh, I think so,' he said, edging towards her. 'You see, there's two of us. And you're only a female. I'm afraid this time Grant *will* have to help me. You've heard enough to hang us both. So—'

'Who the hell *is* this?' demanded Grant.

'Mrs Anthony Lyndhurst,' said William. 'Sadly the reports of her demise at the hands of my cousin were vastly exaggerated.'

Grant blinked. 'No doubt he'll pay up then to get her back. All safe and sound.'

'No,' snapped William. 'She's heard too much. We'll have to shut her mouth.'

The look in Grant's eyes chilled Georgie's blood. 'Pity,' he said. And came towards her.

Georgie pulled out her pistol and levelled it at a point between them.

'Stop there,' she told them, praying that they wouldn't call her on this. 'You can escape if you like, but if you come any closer, I'll shoot.'

'Shoot?' sneered Grant. 'I'll wager it isn't even

loaded!' He had stopped, his eyes wary. 'What female knows how to load a pistol?'

'This female,' she told him. 'And at this range I can put a ball wherever I choose.'

She set her jaw, biting her lip as she brought the pistol to bear. In this situation she would have to shoot to wound seriously, if not to kill. With two of them, she had no choice.

'Now!' snarled Grant. And rushed her.

She squeezed the trigger.

Chapter Nine

The sound of the pistol shot nearly stopped Anthony's heart. He could hear Stella now, barking hoarsely, and William yelling something. He burst into the clearing. Terror blanked his mind as he sprinted towards the hut, unable to see what was happening behind it.

Georgie! Oh, God! No!

Behind him he was vaguely aware of John, Marcus and Quinlan, yelling for him to wait. Ignoring them, he rounded the hut. And stopped dead.

Then he sprang, insane rage bubbling in every vein at the sight of Georgie struggling with William.

With a snarl, he seized William by the throat and flung him away from Georgie, speeding his fall with a savage right to the jaw.

Then he spun and caught Georgie before she could collapse. The sobs racking her shuddered through him. He held her tightly, whispering reassurance, unable to believe that she was alive and unharmed. That the pistol shot had not reached her.

Then he saw Grant, groaning on the leaf mould, darkness spreading inexorably over his chest. 'Darling, what happened?'

'Oh, Anthony—'

'Well may you ask, coz!' William had struggled to his feet. 'God knows how this is to be hushed up, but—'

'Hushed up?' snarled Marcus, coming up to them. 'If you think any of us will connive at hushing *this* up, you've windmills in your head!'

William smirked. 'Well, it would be no very pleasant thing for Anthony to see his wife stand her trial for murder and swing for it, after all!'

'What?'

Anthony felt Georgie shrink closer and shudder in his arms.

'She shot him,' said William. 'Accident, of course. I dare say she meant to kill me. I overheard her handing over Cassandra's ring. Now, where did it get to? Ah, here we are!'

Speechless with fury, Anthony watched as William bent down to pick up the jewel, dusted it off and handed it to Quinlan.

'I was trying to get it back from her when you came.' He shook his head. 'Sad. Very sad, Anthony. I knew you were unwise to trust her again. After the pearls...' He left it hanging.

In Anthony's arms Georgie froze—he could feel the fear leaching out of her. Anger surged through him that even now William could still threaten her. He looked down, words of reassurance ready. They strangled in his throat as he saw her face—the fear, the uncertainty in her eyes, the plea, unspoken on her trembling lips, for his faith, his trust.

Then, 'Anthony—I did shoot that...that man, but I swear, it wasn't like he said...they were...' Her voice died, as she stared up at him, despairing.

She thought he would believe William, as he had in Brussels. And it sounded so…so plausible, so reasonable. And he had refused to discuss the matter with her last night. Dear God, he hadn't even told her that he *knew* she hadn't taken the pearls.

It shook him to the very foundations of his being that he had left her in any doubt. His arms tightened, fiercely protective. Knowing that his betrayal had wounded her so deeply hurt him in ways he couldn't even name.

He looked at William. 'The pearls,' he said, in a queer, tight voice he hardly knew as his. 'It all comes back to the pearls, does it not? Perhaps you would like to explain, *coz*, how you knew them to be missing?'

Georgie's breath jerked in.

William paled. Then he blustered, 'Really, Anthony! Common knowledge. Not the sort of thing one likes to *bruit* about, but—'

'Not so common that *we* knew,' said Marcus coolly, standing shoulder to shoulder with him. 'Anthony never said a word to us. The first I knew of it was last night when you accused Timms.'

Frantically William looked to John.

Who shook his head. 'Not this time, William,' he said grimly and ranged himself with Anthony, reaching out to lay a hand on Georgie's shoulder.

'So if we didn't know, how did you find out?' repeated Marcus.

William's mouth opened and closed, but nothing came out.

'There's only one way you could have known, William,' said Anthony savagely. 'God knows why you went back to our lodgings in Brussels, but when you found Georgie gone, you searched the place. You read the note she left for me and then destroyed it and stole the pearls! You must have thought that one way or another it would be enough to destroy my marriage!'

And her. He left that unspoken.

Quinlan, who was kneeling by Grant, staunching the wound, looked up. 'This fellow is still alive. I think the ball might have missed the heart. Hard to tell, but the blood isn't pulsing, so... I've made a pad of my cravat, but if one of you has a spare shirt about you...'

Grant moaned again.

With a mutter, Marcus began shrugging out of his coat. In moments he and Quinlan had Grant bandaged.

Quinlan bent down again. 'Can you hear me? Can you tell us what happened?'

There was a slight nod.

Slipping an arm under his shoulders, Quinlan eased him up.

Grant opened his eyes and groaned at the sight of them. His voice came faint, but clear. 'He had that damn ring. Wanted...pay me off with it. For attacking Frobisher. Told me what to say...look like Sinclair did it.'

A howl burst from William. 'He's ly—'

It broke off, as Marcus turned and casually administered a punch to the midriff. Gasping and spluttering, William doubled over.

'Hold your tongue,' said Marcus.

Grant had shut his eyes again, sweat breaking out on his forehead. His face was grey. '*She* heard us,' he went on. 'Arguing. We'd have killed her, but she drew the pistol.'

Anthony made a low sound. His fingers, tangled in Georgie's tumbled curls, shook uncontrollably. He took a deep shuddering breath, reminding himself that she was safe, in his arms. She nestled closer, pressing into him.

Grant was still speaking. 'Tried to rush her, never thought she'd shoot. Might have done the trick... confused her...if *he* hadn't hung back.' He gasped and sagged in Quinlan's arms.

'So it was self-defence?' snapped Quinlan. 'If we wrote this down for you, would you sign it before witnesses?'

Anthony listened, breathless. Georgie was safe, no matter what, he'd protect her with his life, but—

The pain-ravaged eyes opened again. 'Will it ruin that *bastard*?'

'Yes,' said Quinlan.

'Then write it!' he gasped. 'Just keep me alive long enough to sign it.' He closed his eyes.

Quinlan checked the pulse in his throat. 'He should last long enough. Who knows, he might even live. We'll bring him up to the house, Lyndhurst. You see to your wife.'

With a sigh of relief, Anthony swung Georgie up into his arms.

'What now?' asked John tiredly, his face set.

'I'm taking her home,' said Anthony. 'There's a pallet in the hut. Bring Grant in on that.'

'It's a pack of lies!' protested William. 'You can't think—'

'Yes. We can,' said Anthony in tones of ice. 'You have a choice, William. Accept our judgement or risk a trial. Or you can make a run for it now.'

He turned his back, and began walking.

'Georgie. Oh, God. Georgie! You little idiot!'

Hoarse and shaking, his voice poured over her in a

torrent of love and relief as he walked. Steely strength held her cradled against his chest. She clung to him, dazed at the things he was saying, things she had never expected to hear. Words of love, of need. All she felt for him returned and redoubled.

He had believed her. Without the least hesitation. And he had known that she had not taken the pearls. She nestled against him, joy swirling through her. Vaguely she was aware when they reached the house.

'I can walk,' she said.

He ignored that, carrying her up the steps.

A frightened gasp greeted them in the hall.

Cassie stood there, her hand to her mouth. 'Anthony!' she whispered. 'Whatever happened? Is Georgie all right? There's a magistrate here! A Sir Charles Brandon. Looking for Marcus.'

He swore and she looked at him blankly. 'What does *that* mean?'

Ignoring that, he asked, 'Where is the fellow?'

'In the drawing room,' she said. 'Aunt Harriet has him cornered. Apparently she knows his mother. And his grandmother. She sent me out just now to warn you. At least I think that's what she meant, when she told me to hurry up and find ''Miss Saunders''!'

Anthony could almost feel sorry for the magistrate.

Cassie's gaze fell on Grant as he was carried in by Quinlan and Marcus. 'Why—that's Grant! *What is going on?*'

'Did you say Sir Charles Brandon, Cassie?' asked John, following them into the hall, his hand gripping William's elbow.

'Anthony—what will happen? I…I shot that man.'

His arms tightened. 'Don't think about it. You're safe. I swear it.'

'But—'

'You're safe,' he said. 'I lost you once. I'll never let it happen again.'

'Good God!'

Looking up, Anthony saw a middle-aged gentleman standing in the doorway to the drawing room, his jaw at half-mast.

He came forward. 'Mardon. Lyndhurst. I'm sorry for this, but I have no choice, you understand.'

Turning to Marcus, he said, 'I'm afraid you'll have to come with me, Sinclair. It's—'

'No!' said John, stepping forward. 'Sinclair isn't the man you want, Brandon. I'm afraid it is my brother here that you need to question. And his tool.' He indicated Grant, groaning on his pallet.

William protested. 'Damn it all, John! I saw Georgiana shoot this man! Are you going to—?'

A cry of terror broke from Georgie's throat.

The magistrate turned and stared at her.

Rage flooded Anthony. 'I'm afraid you may not speak to my wife at present, Brandon,' he said, 'She was—'

Gentle fingers were laid across his lips.

He stared down at her. She shook her head.

'No, Anthony. Set me down, please. I can speak to Sir Charles.'

He kissed her fingers. 'Sweetheart, it's not—'

'Yes, it is,' she whispered. 'Truly,' she went on, 'I will be all right. We must stay and help Lord Mardon.'

He bit his lip. She was right. He could not leave John to weather this alone. And if he kept Georgie away from Brandon, it could look as though they were frightened of what she might say.

'Very well,' he said curtly. Looking at Marcus, he said, 'Get Grant up to a bed and send for the doctor.'

* * *

'So how do we get him out of the country?' asked Quinlan as the door closed behind a grave Sir Charles. He had heard Georgie's story and Grant's confession. William was in the cellar under lock and key. Georgie was being taken upstairs by Aunt Harriet and Cassie to rest before dinner.

'We don't,' said John with savage finality. 'The only protection possible for Marcus and Georgiana was for this to come before a magistrate. Brandon has heard the truth and accepted it. I will not ruin the whole family's reputation for a brother who has betrayed us all!'

Anthony's heart ached for the bitter twist to John's mouth. Bad enough to know what a blackguard William had turned out, but to know that it would become public knowledge... His jaw hardened.

'I'm sorry, John,' said Marcus quietly. 'Had I not lost my temper with Frobisher that night—'

John's harsh laugh seared Anthony.

Marcus fell silent.

'No, Marcus. You were right. William made his own choices. He did his best to ruin Anthony's marriage and then you. And he would have killed Georgiana.' His face looked grey, gaunt. 'Excuse me. I should go up to Sarah. I shall see you at dinner.'

'John—if you would prefer not to come down,' said Anthony awkwardly, 'I'll ask for your dinner to be sent up.' This was the worst of William's treachery—John's shame and hurt.

'No thank you, Anthony. Not unless you prefer to have nothing further to do with a man whose brother has served you and yours so ill.'

Anthony went to him and gripped his shoulder. 'You

damn fool! After you supported me? Go and change before I lose the famous Lyndhurst temper with you!'

John smiled briefly. 'Don't let this spoil the fireworks tonight. We have much to celebrate after all. A betrothal. A marriage. Your happiness. And Marcus is completely cleared.' His mouth tightened. 'I would have been sorrier had it gone the other way.' He nodded to them and left.

'I repeat my question,' said Quinlan, as the door closed. 'How do we get Lyndhurst-Flint out of the country?'

Marcus and Anthony exchanged startled glances.

'What makes you think either of us is any more willing to stick our necks out for William than his brother?' asked Anthony mildly.

Quinlan raised a brow. 'I don't. But I think you'd do a great deal more to save Mardon the scandal. So...'

'Cassie married the right one, didn't she, Anthony?' said Marcus wryly.

'It would appear so,' said Anthony.

'Leave it to me, Anthony,' said Marcus.

'But—'

'Leave it. I owe you. More than I could ever repay. It goes against the grain, but I can't stand by and watch the damage this would cause John.'

Anthony nodded. Marcus had the right of it. This would ruin John if it became public.

'Very well,' he said. 'You'd better—'

'Leave it to me,' repeated Marcus. 'I'll give him some money. Enough to get him out of the country.'

'An allowance,' said Anthony, nearly choking on it. 'For as long as he stays out of the country. It ceases if he ever returns, or applies to John for money.'

Marcus's smile would have chilled an iceberg. 'Trust me,' he said. 'Our dear cousin will be under no illusions about the terms of our assistance.'

Anthony met his gaze and nodded. 'The entire staff,

including the grooms, has permission to watch the fireworks from the south lawn,' he said.

'Excellent,' said Marcus. 'Then—'

'I'll slip down to the stables and make sure he doesn't take the wrong horse,' said Quinlan calmly.

Despite the situation, Anthony exchanged a grin with Marcus. 'Yes. She definitely married the right man,' he said.

'So glad you approve, gentlemen,' said Quinlan drily. 'I know Cassie does!'

Sir Charles sidled up to Anthony as the gentlemen left the dining room to join the ladies.

'Shocking business, Lyndhurst. From what your great-aunt says, that scoundrel caused all *your* trouble as well! Your poor wife! Gallant little thing, coming down to dinner as she did!' He shook his head. 'Dreadful business! That confession of Grant's is absolutely damning, you know. It all hung together. Couldn't trip him up.' He flushed. 'Not but what I couldn't quite stomach the idea that *Sinclair* had attacked Frobisher! The thing is…' he passed a handkerchief over his face '…damned hard for John! But there's nothing *I* can do to spare him!'

'Naturally not, Brandon,' said Anthony gently. '*You* are bound to uphold the law. As is John himself, as a member of the House of Lords.'

'Quite,' said Brandon, an expression of something unaccountably like hope dawning on his face. 'As I said, Grant's confession will clear Sinclair…'

'I see,' said Anthony, flicking a glance at Marcus, who nodded imperceptibly. 'I think we understand each other, Brandon.'

Sir Charles sighed. 'I hope so, Lyndhurst. I certainly hope so! Now, these fireworks. Must say I'm looking forward to it. Miss Lyndhurst gives me to understand that your fireworks parties are quite famous!'

'Anthony, what are we doing here?'

Georgie had expected to watch the fireworks from the cupola with the rest of the party, but instead Anthony had led her out into the park. The balmy night blazed with stars and the full moon sailed overhead.

The arm Anthony had around her shoulders tightened slightly, drawing her closer under the spreading branches of an oak tree. It was darker beneath the tree and she looked up to find his face shadowed.

'We're going to enjoy the fireworks, of course.'

She could hear the laughter in his voice. And something else. Something leashed. Something that made her heart race and her skin tingle. 'But shouldn't we be with the others?'

He stopped and turned, smiling down at her in a way that stole every scrap of breath. Slowly he lowered his mouth to hers. Gentle, tender, the kiss deepened until her thoughts dissolved and her body melted against his and all she knew was the need consuming them.

Releasing her mouth at last, Anthony said, 'I don't think so, do you?'

Her mind thoroughly disconnected, it took her a moment to remember what she had asked. His mouth brushed over hers again, further scattering her thoughts.

To her utter amazement Georgie found that she was being drawn down on to a rug, spread beneath the tree. 'Anthon—'

His kiss silenced her again. It was, she realised, a very effective weapon.

When at last he raised his head, she had no further

thought of protest, but snuggled against him as he settled with his back against the tree.

'You can see enough from here,' he murmured against her hair.

Enough of what? The tree? And another thing... 'Anthony, what about the servants?'

'On the other side of the house,' he murmured reassuringly.

Her mind whirled, unable to think beyond the distraction of his fingers, which appeared to be...

'Anthony—you're unlacing my—' She gasped. Correction. He *had* unlaced her gown. Now he was sliding it off her shoulders and... Pleasure speared her as his lips slid gently down her throat and over her collarbone, tracing a fiery path to her breast. A startled cry escaped as he captured her nipple, taking it deep into his mouth.

'How—?' Her lungs seized. Somehow he had managed to remove her chemise as well as her gown. For several moments she could scarcely remember her own name, let alone what she had intended to ask. And somehow in those heated moments, Anthony disposed of not only all her clothes but his own as well.

The sound of a galloping horse penetrated the dizzying delight. 'Anthony! Listen. I think one of your horses is—'

He shook his head. 'No, sweetheart. I hope you can forgive me, but—that should be William.'

Wonder flooded her and she sat back to look at him. 'You're letting him go?' Despite that appalling betrayal, Anthony had protected his cousin.

He pulled her back against him. 'Yes. For what he did to you, I should have let him—'

'Me?'

He stared at her. 'Yes. You! When I finally realised what he had done, it was all I could do not to kill him. And this afternoon—he would have seen you taken for murder if he could! But Marcus had to be cleared first. And then, in the end—'

'Lord Mardon,' she whispered, understanding the depth of loyalty and honour that ruled him. To save his cousin shame and grief, he had forgone his own vengeance.

'John,' agreed Anthony. 'Can you understand, Georgie? And some of it was not all his fault, was it?'

She shook her head. If she had not been such a fool, such a muddleheaded little idiot…

'Can you forgive me, darling? If I had not been such a crassly jealous fool as to believe his lies—if I had trusted you—it could never have happened. Can you—?' He broke off. His hesitation, his uncertainty, hung between them in the velvet shadows.

She leaned forward, kissing him. 'I love you, Anthony,' she breathed against his lips.

High above the house, light and fire danced in a riotous explosion as the fireworks began. Anthony barely noticed the noise for the explosion of light and joy in his own heart. He stared at her, unable to speak for the emotion choking him.

'You love me?' he whispered at last. 'Even after what I did, the things I said—'

'*Love does not alter,*' she said softly. And something silver trickled down her cheek.

'*When it alteration finds, nor bends with the remover to remove,*' he finished. Pain laced his joy as he bent to kiss away the tear. 'Georgie—then you always loved me? Not Finch-Scott?'

He drew her to him.

She came, soft breasts pressing against him, igniting him.

'Always you,' she confessed. 'I liked Justin…he was kind… I thought that was enough, but then I met you…and loved you.'

'And I, you,' he whispered, hanging on to his control by a thread. 'From the moment I first saw you.'

'But—'

'Always,' he said, kissing her brow, her cheeks, nuzzling the curves of her ear and feeling her breathing shatter. 'But I was too damn scared to tell you. I told myself I didn't want to frighten *you* with what I felt, but *I* was the one who was frightened. So I told you that rubbish about a marriage of convenience.' He shuddered. 'And you still loved me.'

He lifted her over him, his need consuming him. She was soft, sweet, melting about him as he caressed her in tender intimacy.

'Anthony! Like…like this?'

He groaned, easing her down. 'Just like this, my darling.' He pulled her closer, capturing one tightly crowned breast with his lips, suckling gently as her body closed about him.

'Tell me what you want, sweetheart,' he whispered.

'You,' she breathed. 'Everything.'

Overhead the heavens exulted as the Lyndhurst Chase fireworks rioted and danced among the stars. Voices and laughter floated down, rejoicing, celebrating.

'Everything?' he murmured, his fingers teasing gently, until her voice broke on his name. 'Everything might take a very long time. A lifetime.' He kissed her deeply, tenderly. 'Two lifetimes,' he added.

'Two?'

His arms tight around her, he rolled, landing her beneath him. 'Mmm. Yours and mine. It means,' he said, against her lips, 'that I can take my time. And we might even prove that doctor wrong.'

Doctor? She had no idea what he was talking about. Her senses swam as he moved within her, deep and sure, driving away all doubt, all uncertainty as he loved her. Totally, unconditionally.

Later, as she drifted in the safety of his arms, she vaguely recalled the doctor. The night breathed around them in velvet shadows and glimmering starlight. Pressing a sleepy kiss against the broad chest pillowing her cheek, she dared to hope. On such a night...

'If that doctor *was* wrong, Georgie,' came a deep murmur, 'would you object to calling a child after Marcus?'

Was he reading her mind? 'What if it was a girl?' she asked provocatively.

A faint chuckle purred in her ear. 'In that case, my love, we'd just have to prove him wrong again. Wouldn't we?'

Major and Mrs Anthony Lyndhurst
request the pleasure
of your company
at Lyndhurst Chase
from 20th August 1820
to celebrate the
Christening of their son,
Marcus Anthony Lyndhurst.

---

*   *   *   *   *

AUTHOR NOTE
Warning! Spoilers ahead!

Thank you for accepting the invitation and joining us at Lyndhurst Chase. We hope that you have enjoyed the Regency house party of the Season!

A blank canvas is always challenging, but with three of us to create the setting, characters and plots for a house party bursting with romance and intrigue, we were raring to go.

We started with three very different basic ideas, which could have been a problem, but wasn't. Elizabeth's plot of the abandoned husband selecting an heir became the thread connecting all three stories. Once Joanna worked out the Lyndhurst family tree, and we knew who was who, we soon found a way to fit in the other two plots.

So how did three authors, two in England and one in Australia, do this? Enter modern technology. E-mails whizzed back and forth between the U.K. and Australia (over 300 during the course of the project!), characters evolved and Elizabeth Rolls decamped to New Zealand for a hiking holiday in the middle! She returned with blisters the size of Middle Earth on each heel and her final scene written.

Nicola found the ideal house that inspired our Lyndhurst Chase—Ashdown in Berkshire, complete with the cupola on the roof that is so important in the story. Joanna designed the inside of the house and Elizabeth furnished and decorated it for us.

Then there were the characters. Quite a few of them insisted on different names from the ones we had chosen and behaved in totally unexpected ways. Great-Aunt Harriet grew more outrageous by the day, determined to show her eighteenth-century origins. Initially called "Great-Aunt Harridan," she did eventually admit to a slightly gentler side. Although she doesn't appear in "The Fortune Hunter," Nicola nevertheless managed to herald her arrival in a suitably pithy letter. Joanna introduced the lady herself and Elizabeth brought her to her triumphant conclusion.

We all loved Stella, Anthony's black-and-tan setter, to bits. She started off merely old and smelly, but as the plots developed, she became deaf and, finally, almost blind.

Seeing our characters through the eyes of another author was amazing. For example, Elizabeth asked Nicola and Joanna how their characters would react to the dramatic unmasking in the final story. Armed with the replies, Elizabeth then wrote the scene. The crucial test was whether the characters felt right to the author who had created them. And on every occasion they did. We spent so much time talking and joking about the Lyndhursts while we got inside their heads that we got inside each other's heads, as well.

It was a wonderful project and we'd love to do more. Just one slight problem. Nicola and Elizabeth are pestering Joanna to write the prequel—John and Sarah's story—and Joanna is resisting, because she's not sure she can write a Lyndhurst story without a daily fix of e-mails from Nicola and Elizabeth. A pathetic excuse, since they are both only too happy to oblige!

With best wishes,

Nicola, Joanna and Elizabeth

Harlequin® Historical
Historical Romantic Adventure!

THE LADY'S HAZARD
Miranda Jarrett

As the chef of London's premier gambling club, Bethany Penny caters to the most elegant lords of the *ton,* but prefers to help the city's neediest residents. When a mysterious soldier appears in her soup line she suspects that beneath his cool demeanor and shabby coat he hides a wealth of secrets....

Major William Callaway returned from war a damaged but determined man. Keeping his true identity concealed, he is thrown together with the copper-haired beauty, Bethany. They must join forces to uncover a mystery that endangers them both.

On sale December 2005.

Harlequin® Historical
Historical Romantic Adventure!

THE OUTRAGEOUS DEBUTANTE
Anne O'Brien

Neither Theodora Wooton-Devereux nor
Lord Nicholas Faringdon is an enthusiastic
participant in the game of love. Until a chance
meeting sets their lives on a different course.
And soon the handsome gentleman, who has
captured the heart of the beautiful—though
somewhat unconventional—debutante, is
the talk of the town! But fate is not on their
side, it seems, when a shocking family scandal
rears its head and forbids that they be united.
Now Thea must end the relationship before it is
too late by playing the truly outrageous debutante!

The Faringdon Scandals

On sale December 2005.

If you enjoyed what you just read,
then we've got an offer you can't resist!

Take 2 bestselling
love stories FREE!

Plus get a FREE surprise gift!

Clip this page and mail it to Harlequin Reader Service®

IN U.S.A.	IN CANADA
3010 Walden Ave.	P.O. Box 609
P.O. Box 1867	Fort Erie, Ontario
Buffalo, N.Y. 14240-1867	L2A 5X3

YES! Please send me 2 free Harlequin Historicals® novels and my free surprise gift. After receiving them, if I don't wish to receive anymore, I can return the shipping statement marked cancel. If I don't cancel, I will receive 6 brand-new novels every month, before they're available in stores! In the U.S.A., bill me at the bargain price of $4.69 plus 25¢ shipping and handling per book and applicable sales tax, if any*. In Canada, bill me at the bargain price of $5.24 plus 25¢ shipping and handling per book and applicable taxes**. That's the complete price and a savings of over 10% off the cover prices—what a great deal! I understand that accepting the 2 free books and gift places me under no obligation ever to buy any books. I can always return a shipment and cancel at any time. Even if I never buy another book from Harlequin, the 2 free books and gift are mine to keep forever.

246 HDN DZ7Q
349 HDN DZ7R

Name	(PLEASE PRINT)	
Address	Apt.#	
City	State/Prov.	Zip/Postal Code

Not valid to current Harlequin Historicals® subscribers.

Want to try two free books from another series?
Call 1-800-873-8635 or visit www.morefreebooks.com.

* Terms and prices subject to change without notice. Sales tax applicable in N.Y.
** Canadian residents will be charged applicable provincial taxes and GST.
   All orders subject to approval. Offer limited to one per household.
   ® are registered trademarks owned and used by the trademark owner or its licensee.

HIST04R   ©2004 Harlequin Enterprises Limited

Harlequin® Historical
Historical Romantic Adventure!

OKLAHOMA SWEETHEART
Carolyn Davidson

The fact that Loris Peterson was carrying another
man's child should have been enough to make
Connor Webster despise her. But instead, he'd
made her his wife! Some said that she had betrayed
him. But Connor's fierce passion for Loris moved
him to rescue her from an uncaring family—and
protect her from a mysterious enemy....

On sale December 2005.

Silhouette Desire®

**Available this December
from Silhouette Desire**

NAME YOUR PRICE

by Barbara McCauley

(Silhouette Desire #1693)

The stunning conclusion of

DYNASTIES : THE ASHTONS

*A family built on lies...brought together
by dark, passionate secrets.*

Trace Ashton had never gotten over his lover's
betrayal. Had Becca Marshall really taken his
father's payoff money, or was it simply another
elaborate family lie? With Becca back in
Napa Valley, Trace was determined
to find out the truth...at any price!

*Available this December wherever
Silhouette books are sold.*